DEATH OF THE DAY

DEATH OF THE DAY

Tanith Lee

This edition published in 2015 by Telos Moonrise:
Criminal Pursuits
(An imprint of Telos Publishing)
5A Church Road, Shortlands, Bromley, Kent BR2 0HP, UK

ISBN: 978-1-84583-911-6

British Library Cataloguing in Publication Data. A catalogue
record for this book is available from the British Library.

CONTENTS

BOOK ONE

Brightness Falls From The Air

'Brightness falls from the air;
'Queens have died young and fair;
'Dust hath closed Helen's eyes.
'I am sick, I must die.'

Thomas Nashe ('In Time of Pestilence')

5.30 pm to 9.00 pm

1

It started with sudden violent death.

It started with a piece of the sun that seemed to break off and hit the windscreen.

That was how he phrased it to himself soon after. But then, he was a writer, wasn't he? He had a way with words.

Diesoptera. The Day-Wing butterfly, sometimes known as the Sun-Spot (symbol of the soul), had flown on its bright wings, with their central bold marking, from the Butterfly Garden of Esham Park. Not a great distance, by air.

How had it escaped? Perhaps, inadvertently, it had stowed away in an open bag, or in the fold of a skirt or loose summer sleeve. Cleverly: it had a wingspan of almost six inches.

The visitors were being herded out, the first of the earlier closing times being promptly adhered to, and taking some by surprise. It was September now, even if, as the visitors had been saying, it didn't look like it. 'In my young day,' self-mocking voices had clichéd over an Esham cream tea, 'the leaves were yellow and falling by now.' The seasons were changing, they said. Wasn't everything.

The butterfly, butter yellow as any long-ago leaf, clung somehow unnoticed all the way out of doors, to the lawns and the car-park.

Minds were turning back from the visit. Back to house and home, chores and duties, bills and mortgages. The homeward drive, or a delaying dinner in the town. If anyone saw a large butterfly lift into the deepening air, it caused no stir at all. So, the first ripple on the shore that brings the wave.

Over the massed green of the unseasonal park chestnuts, the sun was westering, a crushed blaze of gold.

The butterfly, paying no attention to the trees, the port-wine red rose-beds, even the wild meadows over the wall, flew on. Perhaps somewhere a flower tempted it, but only for a moment. A moment, of course, to a butterfly, is a long time.

Beyond the Park and the meadows were the descending woods. A horizon of fields, here and there with a distant toy of chugging harvester, proved no distraction.

The Day-Wing flew.

There was a road through the woods. Not busy, more a lane. It had no hum of noise, nor reek of fumes. The overgrown trees formed here a tunnel, closing the road in a river of shade that occasionally broke on shafts of the low fierce sun.

Out of the wood and into one of these shafts, the Day-Wing flew, large, rare, beautiful, the colour of topaz and blood, and danced in the dazzling, sinking ray.

Until death came roaring at sixty miles an hour.

Steven Grace had been thinking about the lunch he had had in London, with Piers Barker, and that maybe it had gone all right. Or not.

Barker was a pretentious twot, it was true, but he also had a lot of power, and plenty of money to spend if 'the Right Thing' came along. And the Right Thing might just be Steven Grace's proposed novel.

It had been, therefore, worth buying Barker the expensive lunch and all that pricey French wine, of which Steven himself had had only four and a half glasses – certainly not too much to drive on, since his head was, as usual, perfectly clear.

Jula, of course, had made difficulties about the lunch, but she always did about everything. And half the pleasure with Jula was in making her see sense and give in. Speculate to accumulate. That was all he was doing. In the end she'd even rung Barker to suggest the date. Afterwards she'd been nice about the guy, defended him to Steven when Steven reminded her what a pain Barker was. 'Oh, he's okay. He's kind, really. The money climate is bad for new books.'

'Unless,' amended Steven, bitterly, 'they happen to be by one of his dear little pets.'

'You don't mean me, surely?' said Jula. 'He hasn't taken anything of mine for two years.'

'That, dear, is because you can just about write.'

Jula shrugged, her tangly black hair, which long ago had been able to inflame him at one glance, shivering on her shoulders.

'Then he should be very happy with you,' she said.

After this there was the predictable row. But it didn't last long. Steven was becoming very tired of arguing. Even war games weren't much fun with Jula anymore. Their relationship was a corpse. Why try kicking any life into it?

Whatever, he'd got his way, and the lunch had been a bloody bore. Barker had rattled on about some book fair – abroad, naturally – and his obnoxious, over-indulged kids. Until, at last, the cautious-so-cautious acceptance of the book proposal, Barker holding the envelope in his manicured fingers as if it were faintly unclean –

Courting publishers, always, had cost Steven more than money. He remembered Jula saying, 'Choosers can't be beggars, Steven.' Well, it was all right for Jula.

Actually, he was going to have to call her on the mobile. He'd said he'd be back by 4.30, and he knew she knew not to believe him, he wouldn't get there much before 6.30, even if this road went where he assumed it must. Which wasn't his fault.

The icing on the post-lunch cake had been roadworks on the A21. They hadn't been there in the morning, as he drove north.

It was like a plot, a plot against Steven Grace, to wind him up as tight as some ancient bow-string. To add to the pandemonium, the temporary lights weren't working properly. Then, when he got off onto the Seatree Road, he had a clear stretch for about a mile, until there were roadworks again, new ones obviously, although they might just have been the same ones, cosmically spirited ahead and put down again in his path. Needless to say – what else? – the temporary lights weren't working here either.

Steven had lit a cigarette, but in the heat and dust and exhaust, it only made him thirsty for another glass of wine. Five and a half glasses weren't enough, with a Barker for company. Pity he'd drained the hip flask on the way into London. But he'd been cheerful then, being positive, taking the drink because it had suited his mood. The whisky in the flask had a rotten taste, though. The flask was going home, tainting what was in it. He'd complained about it before to Jula, but she had ignored the hint.

Trying to interest himself, Steven glanced about at the other exasperated drivers trapped in their cars. (None of which, he thought, was quite as smart as his own dark silver Porsche, even second-hand.) There *was* a brunette almost alongside, about forty, but not bad. He waited, amusing himself by willing her to turn and catch his eye. But she didn't, and he gradually revised his opinion of her. A big heavy creature with a fat throat. Bloody awful purple nails. God, some women.

He had to admit, it wasn't fair though, really. Men wore better than women as a general rule. His own lean blond good looks had only intensified over 35.

Finally the idiot lights let him past – the purple-clawed cow was away at once. He got almost ten miles that time.

Seeing the third tailback, approaching the new shambles of diggers and blinking lights, Steven Grace had chosen the nearest turn-off, not bothering where it went.

As he did so, he noted some drivers had left their cars and were shouting round the faulty lights. There had been something on the 8.00 am news about a similar incident last night. He had heard that while he was shaving for Piers. And something too about sunspot activity, which was apparently liable to affect mechanical devices, no doubt including diggers and traffic lights. Probably a load of crap.

Then again. Perhaps he should have paid more attention.

When he was incredibly late tonight, that was what Jula would think. Or that he was 'paying her out'.

Feckless, that was the word she had recently chosen for him. Long ago (three years? two?) she had only said, 'You live like a lily of the field.' She had liked it then, Steven having no care, taking no heed for the morrow. She had wanted to help him in this Christ-like endeavour. Said he was right, wished she was more like him.

There had been only one sign so far on this unknown road he had driven headlong into. It said *Esham Park*, and an arrow pointed away into the woods. He didn't concentrate. Esham Park was of no importance to Steven Grace.

It was after 6.00 when he tried to reach Jula on the mobile phone, and all he got was a crackling mush. He said to it, 'Come on,' but the telephone had no concern for him. It fried eggs merrily for itself, which the evening was hot enough to do anyway.

'Useless rubbish.'

Steven flung the phone on the seat. Then picked it up again, and held it. Calm down.

Jula had made him like this, he thought. A worrier. He never had been. And there was that scare over his blood-pressure last month – crazy – he was young and slim and fit. Take it easy though. That's right.

He watched the road. Though narrow, it was quite smooth, perhaps privately maintained rather better than the A21.

A nice silky drive in his pretty Porsche.

The light, softly, richly green through the tunnel of trees, was underwater-picturesque. The hotter spurts of naked sun burst past like an irregular strobe. He was going quite fast. Well, driving slowly got on his nerves. Though heavy and irritated, he felt better now, and his head was still crystal clear.

He had always been able to drive well over the so-called legal limit. Only a fool never worked it out that while some could be incapable with a spoonful of codeine cough-mixture inside them, there were others who stayed entirely able after a couple of bottles of Burgundy. To which six glasses was nothing. Okay, six and a half.

Maybe try that damn phone again.

He tried it.

Crackling mush, the spit of the frying pan, came up like a jeer.

It made him angry. Who wouldn't get angry? In fact the whole day was going to. Why lie to himself? It had been a sodding waste of time – sunspots, failures, Piers fucking Barker –

The trees broke on a glory of blinding gold. The sun shot full into his eyes. And out of the sun dashed two huge molten missiles – that exploded on the windscreen –

Oh God –

The wheel spinning under the one hand left on it – something – the mobile – spinning too – road, tree, sky, sun, the world rose upwards as if to cover and consume.

Terminus was a crunching bump and the knowledge of falling. Which seemed to be forever – into the abyss – and then something pulled hard across the chest as if to cut him in two –

The seat-belt. The seat-belt he had, for some reason, done up.

The near side of the Porsche toppled against him, and everything stopped.

Steven Grace was still alive. He sat for a long while, pushed uncomfortably sidelong in a tilted seat, the belt throttling him, thinking about this, amazed as a child on Christmas morning.

When he tried the door on the driver's side, it had jammed. When he got the passenger door undone, he hauled himself across, got out, and stood in the shallow ditch, breathing. He felt rather sick, and the belt seemed to have bruised his ribs, ringing his chest with a hot pain that slowly subsided.

He leaned on the car, and for a moment startled himself by sobbing.

It passed quickly. He pulled his jacket from the car seat, and his cigarettes; lit one. On the first drag it occurred to him he shouldn't perhaps be standing smoking by a damaged car. He couldn't smell petrol, but better be safe than sorry.

He climbed out of the ditch with an oddly fluid ease, almost laughing now.

Nothing had changed. The sun was a little lower. He could hear birds singing. And the car making anxious gruntings and poppings.

God, he'd been lucky.

Well, he deserved a bit of luck.

Something gleamed on the windscreen. The thing that had hit the glass, but not broken it as it had seemed to do. What was it? A bloody bird?

When he craned down to look, he felt dizzy. No, this wasn't any good. He needed a drink and to find a phone that worked.

He walked a few steps, and felt easier. The sun was slipping away beyond the trees in a series of bright blinks.

Sod the Porsche. Bloody useless second-hand rubbish. Leave it lie.

He did laugh then. Because all this would make a good story. It might even shut Jula up. And all those other bloody fools in the house. When he got home.

The woman stood at the window had death on her mind.

Beyond the garden, the fields were amber in the last of the sun, the woods very dark, with crests of gilt.

Gilt … guilt. A Shakespearean sort of pun.

This wasn't, however, remotely Shakespearean.

Her stomach turned inside her.

She could not remain at the window any longer.

The thing that was really ironic, she thought, was that if she had taken the right turning off the Seatree Road, she need never have hung about in that third misery of roadworks.

Was it true, what they said about women drivers, and women map-readers, and so on? No, of course not. Only, unfortunately, when it applied to women like herself.

Besides, all those accurate clever people – she had seen some of them in the last jam, running from their cars, howling round the erratic lights, red-faced with rage and panic. (Astonishing her too, a girl had been leaning from the window of her car, videoing the whole proceedings.)

Leigh Dover sat in the lay-by in the thickening light, quietly wishing she had a cigarette. But she had given up smoking seven years ago. Funny how you always missed it, smoking. Not constantly, in her own case, but at these random moments. Old films were the worst. She had only to see Bette Davis light up, for lips and fingers to itch for that long slender tube of fire and drug.

Leigh sighed. It didn't matter, the delays, missing the turn-off. After all, she wasn't expected anywhere. No-one was waiting. Her professionally shampooed hair and Purple Orchid nails were only for herself.

She spoke to the big-bottomed Morris that had seen better days.

'Sorry, old girl. Never mind. I think I've figured it out now.'

The car *wouldn't* mind. She liked a run.

Leigh Dover didn't care about imbuing her car with a personality, as she didn't care too much about making a mess of her route. She was still coming to terms with her weight problem, but she'd work something out. It was like her name, and how everyone always made a point of referring to her as Leaned Over. Or saying they knew her brother, Ben. So what?

Life was pretty silly. Nice though, being alive.

She started the car, and began to sing, as they turned off into the palely darkening woods, 'Just a song at twilight –'

Steven Grace had been walking for about ten minutes, he thought. He couldn't be sure, because his watch had stopped. One more casualty of the accident – although maybe not. It only said 6.15 …

He felt light-headed, almost exuberant. Not surprising,

maybe. In this state he missed perhaps pertinent details – such as a second narrow road, which presently ran off through the trees. But he took in other details that had no real bearing on his situation – a magpie chattering in a tree as the light went. The intense shadow that now filled the lane. And not another car. He *had* noted that. Not one, rushing to rescue him.

However, he almost walked right by the house.

There was a wall, a driveway, mattressed by tall evergreen hedges, and higher up, the house rising from a sheet of lawn. An ornamental, old-fashioned streetlamp caught one last feather of the sunset, burning as if a Victorian ghost had lighted it.

Twee, those lamps. Rich bloody twee. And the house was big, perhaps '30s built, with white upper parts that glimmered against the spreading dusk.

He thought, *Wait.* A house – it meant people and telephones. Perhaps sympathy, and a stiff drink.

And there was always Fate, too. Kismet. All this had happened to him, and possibly he had been meant to come here.

He had felt like that when he had met Jula in the theatre bar that night. He knew her from her book-jacket cover, seen by chance that very morning. Although he'd remembered her less from her photo, which wasn't that good, than from her name, which he thought was cretinously stupid. Cork. Jula Cork.

Steven retraced his steps, and walked between two open wrought-iron gates.

A blackbird dived across from hedge to hedge in front of him, making him jump. The countryside was alive with obstacles that night.

He passed the lamppost. There were terraces of begonias like dying rubies, and wallflowers giving off a last spicy scent. Jasmine cascaded phantasmal from an arch.

The house had a big wooden door with brass fitments. Above, the windows were mock-leaded, some with bulbs of coloured glass. Light was on in the lower storey, diffused across each window, subtle and dim. Like the afterglow of the lamp.

Steven pushed his hand through his well-cut hair. Probably

looked all right. Probably he looked wonderful. Face untouched, unspoiled threads. Pallor might elicit kindness, if a woman came to the door.

And who knew, she might be attractive, the woman, as well as rich. She might be intended by Fate to meet with Steven Grace.

No bell. He struck with the knocker. The sound went through the house and through his head. And, the door moved away from him. Like the gates, it was already open.

'As one door closes, another door closes,' Steven murmured. 'Only maybe not anymore.'

He let the door fold all the way back, and looked into the faintly-lighted, unknown hall, that might be something to him, in his future.

He wouldn't despise it. Though he'd want to change a few things.

A wide stair ran up, with an oak banister. The stair had a runner of white carpet, and the floor of this hall also had this carpet, which reminded him of the fur of a polar bear, or several polar bears. White for rich people, because they could afford to have it repeatedly and successfully cleaned.

But on a carved wooden chest stood a lamp with a rose-pink ruched shade. Which looked as if it properly belonged in some daft old whore's bedroom. Next to this was a large statue of a horse and rider, in some sort of smoky jade, Chinese Tang or Yang or Bang, whatever.

The walls and ceiling were (unbelievably) magnolia, with false beams – God. There were three shut doors, of finely grained wood. But, as he moved forward, to the left he could see now the hallway opened doorlessly on an immense living-room.

Steven gaped at it. It was money made flesh.

The high ceiling had been painted, exquisitely, like a summer sky, complete with cloudlets and swallows. Pillars rose to this sky, and to the gallery above, where a library of books, old rare books from the look of them, glinting with goldwork on leather, ran on oak bookcases above two-thirds of the room.

On the lower walls were swords, a painting he identified as certainly of the French Impressionist school, and which looked genuine, and a carpet of intricate red and blue, from some souk of the East.

There was a fireplace, marble and inlay. It was the very peak of elegance, and before it stood a bowl that looked like Tang-Yang-Bang jade, stuffed with the foulest of dried dyed grasses Steven had ever set his eyes on.

So far no-one had come to his knock. No-one had appeared on the stair, or out of the enormous room or any of the closed doors. No-one came now.

She must be a rich dope. But at least she was a clean rich dope. Like the perfumes of the flowers outside, this house smelled delicious of beeswax and potpourri. And it was spotless.

Not like Jula's place, ramshackle, untended, dusty and cobwebby, redolent always slightly of cigarette smoke and cats.

Steven, walking in the polar bear pelts, called up into the well of the house.

'Hallo? I'm sorry to trouble you –'

He wasn't. No. He was pleased to trouble them.

Just let them come down. Let *her* come down.

She needed him. If only to tell her about the beams and the pink lampshade and the godawful dried grasses. And that lumpy stone apple thing next to them.

But still no-one came.

There was, he realised, a strange noise in this house. He hadn't taken it in at first. A sort of thin rushing *scream*.

There was something much more interesting across the open-plan living room. This was a mahogany table stood under the gallery, on which poised two of the tallest, most cut-glass decanters he had ever seen. And, they were full.

Irresistible, to go over and look at them. So he went.

The white fur carpet, extending across the living-room, took, he thought, no mark from his passage. He walked like the undead on a carpet of snow.

The decanters held whisky and vodka. To be sure, he lifted

the stoppers, and drew in the wondrous smells.

It was an overpowering, vertiginous smell, alcohol. And this would be good alcohol. Then again, maybe not. Maybe these brands were the equivalent of the lampshade and the dried grasses.

There had been the hip flask, and then the double whisky he had had before meeting Piers Barker. And the two singles he had had just after parting from Piers Barker. Just to steady himself. Steven had needed them. He could do with one now. One or two. But there was nobody there to offer him a drink.

And yet, he might have been expected.

Dimmed globes with parchment shades lit the living-room. Outside, the world, the countryside that flung birds and golden missiles at him, was hardening into solid black.

The thin screaming rushing noise went on and on.

He didn't like it. It spooked him. Steven Grace didn't know why.

Oh come on. So what?

Suppose he went into the hall again, and up the stairs? Somehow this didn't seem feasible. Just a touch *too* intrusive.

What he should do was look for a phone.

He hadn't seen one, either in the hall or in here.

Steven began to move about the room, looking for the phone he hadn't seen.

It was so immaculate, here. Pristine was the word that sprang to mind. Experimentally he ran one finger along the marble ledge of the mantelpiece, and next over the roof of the heavy, golden clock, flanked by two uncouth figures in black onyx. No dust. Nothing. He glanced at the clock-face – practical. He grinned sourly. The clock had no hands. No time then, either.

And no telephone.

There were other downstairs rooms …

He was feeling a bit sick again. He needed something to steady him, stop this tight bruised pain around his ribs, the throbbing in his head.

And that bloody row that kept going on. What *was* it?

Steps led up to the book gallery. At their foot, on a side table, was a quantity of little boxes, made of mother-of-pearl, tortoiseshell and gold. He was fairly sure it was gold.

Steven Grace, the writer of twenty unfinished short stories and the proposal for a one hundred thousand-word novel, thought bizarrely of the *Mary Celeste*. For this house had just that quality – in reverse.

Where things had been left carelessly lying and abandoned unfinished, here everything had been made utterly tidy, and cleansed – as if for surgery. Indeed it was as if the house – as he had read that certain suiciders did with their own persons – had been prepared in perfection for death.

'Don't be a fool,' Steven said to himself aloud.

Surely the noise in the house was stronger? And there was too, now, a sort of knocking and thumping sound, all wrapped up in the first noise.

'Christ – is anyone *here*?' he shouted, rather like the traveller in that hackneyed old poem Jula liked.

And, as in the poem, no answer came.

One more bloody disappointment, then. The Fata Morgana of perpetual hope, perpetually deferred.

He clenched his fists, and just like the noise, the blood stamped in his temples.

Fuck her, then, this woman he might have met here.

The bitch hadn't even left him a telephone.

Once he was out on the road again, in the black, smelling the intensity of late summer dark, Steven Grace tried to pull himself together.

He had had a little assistance. You learned early on when to rely on yourself, trust your own instincts, put yourself first.

There was something weird in that house.

And it had been an ill-omened day.

When he turned to walk on up the lane that behaved like a road, into the cloud of the darkness, with burning throat and crashing head, lighting a cigarette, he somehow knew that all this was Jula's fault. She hated him. She had done him down.

Behind him, the soft film of the house lights faded. Ahead of him, in the tunnel of trees, there seemed to wait only unending night.

2

By day in summer, there were often cows still, in the hilly fields that ran up toward the house. Black and white they stood there, swishing tails and dropping dung, and torrents of cow-attracted flies flew into your face. By night, only the large silver blisters of the stars waited over the lane. All that remained of the cows was their odour.

Markessa wondered, as she always did at this point, why people thought (still thought, despite BSE) cows so wholesome.

Markessa considered that they stank, and had not been able to stomach milk since the age of 15. Which had done wonders for her figure.

At the top of the hill the track curved to the right, and the house appeared.

It was such a shame about this house. Markessa always thought that, too. If she had had this house, and Jula's money, my God, she could really have done something with the place. The basic structure was early 19th Century, or was it late 18th Century? – Markessa could never recall. But the house had a wonderful look, from a distance, the deep windows, the attic roof, the little front garden railed in by a low pale fence. Close to, you could hardly miss it was a dump.

Why didn't Jula ever get it seen to, at least the outside? If she was too stingy to pay, Jack would have done the work. Let's face it, Jack would have done anything for Jula. And she, chilly bitch, never let him, in case that meant she'd have to let him do something else.

Markessa Philbin smiled to herself. *Cold Comfort Farm*, that's what Steven had called them, the house and the woman collectively.

As the car drew into the bare, hedge-bordered space at the end of the track, Markessa saw a light go on suddenly in Jula's bedroom. And then Jula came across to the window and stood there, in silence, looking down. Slim, cool Jula, a silhouette with a too-big head shape from all that riot of black hair. But then Jula didn't care about her appearance any more than she cared about the poor old house.

Markessa got out of the car, slammed the door and waved gaily-in-the-old-fashioned-sense up at Jula. And Jula, of course, did nothing. Except suddenly turn away, and switch off the light.

'Charming.'

Below, back down the hill, the red sheen of Seatree. *A glow like Hell*, Steven always said. What Steven said was often so clever.

Markessa picked cautiously over to the gate in the fence, and slid it aside; it was only hanging there by half a hinge. Weeds and laurels fought with a stunted apple tree in the front 'garden'. Roots had come up through the path. No lights were on now. Markessa was very careful in her high-heeled ice blue pumps.

She looked, anyway, good enough to eat. She was certain of that. She had spent a lot of time making herself marvellous, teasing out the spikes of her freshly hennaed hair, applying faultless make-up, painting her long oval nails the sort of pastel colour Steven liked.

'Jula! Hallo, Jule!' sang Markessa, poking nail-warily at the doorbell.

She hoped Steven would come to the door, but then he might not be back. The Porsche wasn't parked in the barn, she could see that now, for the doors were standing open and the barn was empty.

He'd decided to go up to London, to speak to that awful man, Piers Something, about Steven's book. Jula had said Piers had offered two or three alternate days, but Steven had wanted to go today, the day of the dinner party. Jula had said that Steven would be late.

Jula was a bitch about Steven. But there you were. He admitted he couldn't be such a heel as to leave her. Maybe one day, he would realise he was just wasting himself, and that Jula was holding him back. She wouldn't even let him write, he said. Interrupting him, finding stupid things he had to do for her. It had to be Jula alone who wrote. Jula who ruled the roost.

She was such a fool. That wasn't the way to keep a man. Oh no. Even at 27, Markessa knew you didn't take that sort of risk.

And he *would* be late, of course. The traffic was appalling tonight; Markessa herself had met some of it. Apparently there were roadworks and diversions as far as the Seatree Road. London must have been murder.

Jula opened the door.

Behind her, a vague light stole from an adjacent room. The hall was otherwise in darkness. Glancing up, unsurprised, Markessa saw that the light bulb had not been replaced in the overhead fitment.

She did not mention this.

'Hallo, Jule. How *are* you?'

'I'm fine. How are you?'

'Oh, scrambling along. I had another customer today, asking when your next book will be out.'

'What did you tell them?'

'Oh, soon, soon. You know.'

'They must be getting suspicious,' said Jula, 'those two, or is it one person you keep telling me asks for my books.'

Markessa did not especially register this acid. They were negotiating the narrow side-corridor, in half light, and as usual one of the cats bolted out and nearly knocked Markessa off her three-inch heels.

'God, they're like wild animals, your cats.'

'They are.'

'Sorry?'

'Cats are wild animals. That's how they're classified.'

'Well, yours are.'

Behind them now, in the main hall, the phone made a twittering sound. Markessa cocked her head.

'It keeps doing that,' said Jula. 'There's no-one there. Something wrong with the line.'

They entered the kitchen. Markessa handed Jula the medium-expensive bottle of white wine she had brought. 'Better pop it in the fridge, Jule. Or it will be horrible.'

As Jula opened the large, rickety fridge-freezer, Markessa noted that no other wine was stood in it ready. Instead, Jula was now pouring out for her a glass of Mâcon Villages, and tipping into it cubes from an ice tray. Which was typical.

'Thanks. Cheers. It's good to see you, Jule.'

Markessa stared around. She could tell from the feel of the house, no-one else was there.

'I'm cooking for 8.00, now,' said Jula, passionlessly sipping her ice-cubed wine. 'Steven said 4.30, so maybe he'll be back by 8.00. I hope you aren't too hungry.'

Markessa made gestures of non-existent needs. They were realistic. She didn't like Jula's cooking, which was, Markessa thought, too rich, too complex, for someone who stood there in a slim-line knee-length black skirt, sleeveless form-fitting black T-shirt and sandals, with no make-up.

There was a waxing aroma of the meal wafting from the oven. Meats and sauces – definitely OTT for a close, hot September night.

The kitchen *looked* clean. It always did, oddly. Probably Jula must clean it (and the bathrooms and toilets) before she invited anyone. It was an old country kitchen, a cavern of a room, stripped decades ago of beams, but with a great orange brick fireplace, and deep windowsills where herbs luxuriantly grew in terracotta pots. Cracked dark blue plates piled with coppery onions, garlic and tomatoes, looked deceptively inviting. All a sham, obviously.

Jula was washing something up now in the huge brown stone sink.

A cat walked into the room. He was brindle-black, with a white underside, and a strange tawny flush under his chin, and on the back of his head. Jula had called him Nero, because she said he reminded her of an Emperor Penguin. Again typical. The other cat, the tabby, had the name of Lavender. You just knew, the minute you heard such names, what Jula might be like.

'Your cat's back.'

'Yes, he's come for his tablet.'

'*Sorry?*'

'I'm afraid he's on medication. Thyroid. Sometimes they get it when they're older.'

'Shame,' said Markessa without concern, squinting at the cat. She could see the pills now, too, stood on the apparently scrubbed table, among the sliced mushrooms, onions and celery, and open pots of mustard. Markessa thought of herself as inquisitive. She picked up the bottle.

'Neo-Mercazole,' she read, 'forty tablets.' She lifted out a leaflet from the accompanying box. 'They do info for *cats* now?'

'I don't know. These pills are the same ones that human beings take. Or so he said.'

'Human *beings*? *Cats*?'

'Yes, Markessa.'

'But that's rather – illogical, isn't it?'

'Oh, why?'

Markessa was reading the leaflet. 'If you become pregnant, consult your doctor –' she laughed. 'Trust your cats, Jule, to have to take people pills.'

Jula came, drying her hands on a cloth, and quietly took box and bottle. She looked down at the cat, which truly appeared to be waiting sensibly by the table leg for its medicine.

The bottle didn't seem as if it had forty tablets in it. Markessa tended to believe chemists would diddle you, if they could, out of a full prescription, like the time two of her 'flu antibiotics were missing. No doubt vets had also started to diddle their patients.

Jula, not counting the pills, took one out, and proceeded to crush it with a spoon into a saucer of some costly cat food, there on the scrubbed table Then she lifted the cat, kissed its head, and placed it also on the table, by the dish.

Lovely. Fur and fleas in the dinner. Aside from whatever it had picked up on its pads in the fields. Not the first time either.

And it had sat down, its cat bottom on the cutting surface. Markessa really would have a small portion of food that night. There was the eternal rumour of a stomach bug going around. She could plead that, if she wanted to be tactful.

'Any more wine, Jule?'

Jula … look at her. She had such advantages. That blue-black, silken hair, coiling, furling, to her shoulder-blades. Perfect skin. Dark eyes she had just deigned to accent that night with a little charcoal pencil. And her figure was sensational. Even her breasts, which seemed quite unsupported under the skimpy T-shirt. And she was 34. She made no secret of that. Her birth date had been on the jacket of all six of her novels.

So much, and not to know what to do with it. Pathetic really. Like not understanding Steven, who was so loyal and talented and handsome. And she'd lose him. She would. Markessa, like the cat, unconsciously licked her lips.

Again, Jula's eyes strayed to the clock ticking above the kitchen fireplace.

It was exactly her own age, 34, a big black clock that now, adapted, ran on a battery.

Steven had been very scornful of that. Why throw away all that money, when she could have bought a new clock that kept the right time?

Jula could remember her father and mother presenting her with the clock on her ninth birthday. Telling her she and it were the same age, and how it was bought the day she was born. And now it was hers.

They were, ethically, gypsies, her parents. Travellers. Moving always on. Fabulous, beautiful beings, like a prince and princess from a fairy-tale. She had never quite believed in them. Which ultimately had been wise.

The clock, which had recently become just a minute or so slow, despite the current battery, now told her it was 7.41.

Steven had announced he would be back by 4.30, which would have meant, ordinarily, 6.30. She knew he would have stayed drinking in the restaurant, using the Visa card to pay, until about 4.00. Although Piers would have escaped long before that.

Somewhere on the road, rather drunk but, like most habitual heavy drinkers, not showing it much, Steven would call her via the mobile he had asked her to buy him ten months ago. That had been because she had always nagged him on and on that he didn't phone her when he was going to be late, and this was due to so many public phones being vandalised, or in use by nagging women who would not get off the bloody line.

He *would* have called her; she had expected it. He always did now in these circumstances. Partly to gloat on his lateness, his carefree non-adherence to the meaningless promise of any early return. To start a row, if possible. In this case too, no doubt, to curse and condemn Piers Barker for something, everything, nothing.

When the anticipated and un-looked-forward-to call didn't come, Jula was at first only surprised.

He had wanted them to have this 'dinner party', had said he wanted it. Their – *her* – house was, he said, a mausoleum. For Christ's sake, he said, ask someone round. Her friend Markessa, that London wide-boy, Hastings. Anything else was better than one more night with Jula crouched scribbling.

This last year, she had got into the way of always doing what Steven wanted, where she possibly could.

But, as she had invited Markessa Philbin, who was not her friend, and more tentatively, Jack Hastings, who had a life of his own, Jula had grasped that Steven could make a point of being late for the dinner, now he had also fixed to go to London the same day.

Were there, even with Steven Grace, however, degrees of lateness? Yes, oddly, it was never much more than two hours. As if he had his own exclusive timetable, which he kept to. Besides, though he was scathing of Markessa, and Jack, he liked flirting with Markessa. He liked to do that with all women in public (Jula always excepted). And he liked to try to score points off Jack.

Steven would have wanted this lost third hour for a shower, to change, make himself alluring for Markessa and prosperous for Jack. Even if he meant to make an entrance, 7.30 would be the limit.

He liked food, too. He had a big appetite. He enjoyed – irony of ironies – Jula's cooking. It was his main grouse, he said, that she only ever did cook every blue moon.

No. *This* late didn't fit.

Jula showed very little of what she felt. She was accomplished at that. Inside herself – her stomach turning – No. Don't be premature. That's crazy.

There were roadworks of course. But then, one could still call from a traffic jam. That was the whole purpose of the mobile phone. You could call from anywhere. If you could call at all.

Markessa was getting restless. She stared round and round with her extraordinarily made-up eyes, as if expecting Steven to burst abruptly out of a cupboard.

Jula had been looking, too. From the window, mostly, off and on since about 6.15. She had even looked out when she heard Markessa's car, thinking this might be Steven – knowing it wasn't. Markessa's little vehicle didn't make the same sounds as the Porsche.

The phone twittered again. And then, irritatingly, kept on twittering.

'Don't you think you ought to –' said Markessa

'Didn't I say? There's never anyone there. It's a fault. Probably the heat.'

'But it might be Steven.'

It wouldn't be Steven. Jula believed it now. It *wouldn't* be. But then – but then …

She had gone to the phone quickly every time she heard it, after 6.00. Every time with her stomach churning. Running downstairs, lifting the receiver. And there was only a crackle, a chittering sound, rather like mice far down in the wires.

Markessa said, temptingly, 'It might even be your Jackie. It's late for him too, isn't it? Or did you ask him for 8.00?'

The phone twittered. Markessa, wriggling.

'You go,' said Jula, 'if you like.'

Markessa relinquished her third warmish glass of wine. She put on her school mistressy look, which didn't suit her, and which she probably thought displayed merely a very feminine and effective toughness. The look of that successful career woman who ran the plush bookshop in Seatree High Street.

'You're so happy-go-lucky, Jula.'

'Am I?' Jula seemed faintly wondering at this.

Markessa stalked out, clack-click, on her aquamarine heels.

Jula thought, *I mustn't think of it.* She must *not.* For all the most fundamental reasons –

In the hall, Markessa picked up the phone in the darkness, and unnervingly, two gleaming colourless pearls lit up at her from the floor. But it was only Lavender the tabby, sat by the cat-flap, with a stunned field-mouse clenched in her jaws, a present for Jula.

'Hallo,' said Markessa sternly to the mouse-voiced depth of the wires. The spirits of mice dead?

In the darkness Markessa scowled. She could now hear a sort of sudden hoarse breathing.

'Listen, you cretin, go and get a psychiatrist, why don't you, you fucking wanker.'

There was a silence. Into Markessa's earringed ear came a sculpted elderly female voice, actressy, educated and musical.

'I should like to …' A crackling. Then: 'This is Katherine –'

The cat leapt forward and up the stair, after all not trusting Jula to share the mouse with her, for Jula always took them away and obviously ate them herself. This ignorant cruelty Lavender constantly forgave her, but never quite forgot.

As the fur-covered, snake-like body, the helpless mouse-tail, reeled over Markessa's feet, she screamed and dropped the telephone receiver.

'Hallo,' said the voice of Katherine, patiently, dangling there, 'are you –?'

And then the phone died, silent. Not even mice, more dead than the mouse, as yet.

Perhaps as dead, Jula was hoping, hoping, at last, as Steven Grace.

3

Even by night, the seagulls sometimes flew their unholy choir above the land. Three or four miles in from the sea, easily as far as Seatree, and further.

Seeing the squadron go over in the dark, uncanny, cheeping, Leigh Dover smiled with pleasure. Savage, terrible birds, white as angels and strong as life. They opened their bowels on everything in the town. Hastings and St Leonards had several records of their Hitchcockian attacks on people and small dogs.

But she liked them. They were brave. Warrior birds. They aimed to survive.

She had had to stop off at a roadside tea-shop in the end, lost. Leigh had been driving up and down the lanes and by-ways, going in circles. In the café, the pot of tea had cleared her head, and she had sorted her directions out. (They had been closing, and still let her come in. They had even given her a free shortbread biscuit. There were a lot of nice people here, helpful, reasonable. She had missed that in London. But London drove virtues out, she supposed.)

Back on the Seatree Road, she took the proper turning at last. But it was dark now, and she was glad of her headlamps, drove slowly in case of oncoming traffic.

When she saw the wreck in the ditch, she caught her breath.

Leigh had pulled up on the opposite verge before she considered. Then she sat there, staring out at the spoilt car. Steady. Think it through.

She'd seen it before. Where? Somewhere on the A21 coming down. A luminous metallic Porsche. It had looked better then.

But the driver – she recalled him now, a blond man leering and glaring at her by turns, while she steadfastly ignored him.

There had been something threatening about him, very decidedly. In the rear-view mirror, he had been good-looking, with narrowed, depthless eyes. She didn't think she'd imagined the menace. But – well. She had been glad when the lights had stabilised and she could drive away. He had been gone after that.

It occurred to her now; he had taken the turning she had meant to, if she had read her map properly.

He must have, for here was his car, keeled sideways and down in a ditch like a silky stricken seal.

After an interval, Leigh took the torch from the glove compartment, undid her belt, opened her door, and got out.

She stood her side of the narrow road, shining the torchlight over onto the Porsche.

It looked bad, but not desperate. The near-side passenger door was open at the front, hanging there too wide, like a gate almost off its hinges.

Something burned strangely on the windscreen.

She took a deep breath and walked steadily over the road to see.

Oh, what was it? A splash of papery yellow fire – some huge insect, a moth or butterfly – smashed on the glass in a filth of liquid and matter. Poor thing.

Inside the car nothing was out of the ordinary, she thought. A mobile phone lay on the floor, probably put out of action by the impact, and so abandoned. (She didn't want to touch it to see.) The seat-belt lay over the seat, undone not broken, and holding nothing awful in its clasp.

No blood in the car, she was fairly sure of that. Only the blood of the dead butterfly on the windscreen.

She shone the torch down at the number-plate.

Leigh turned each way, slowly, shining the torch up now, along the lane, off into the trees and bushes. Nothing.

The scenario was straightforward, she thought. The driver had had the crash but had not been seriously hurt, saved by the belt. He'd got out, found the phone didn't work, rather sulkily and foolishly dumped it, and gone off along the road to find assistance.

If he was the one she had noticed on the A21, he had been a long time gone.

But then, maybe, as she had done, he had found a café, or even a pub, had a drink to calm himself. Probably help was on its way, an AA ambulance to rescue the car.

And yet. *Something.*

Well. It was just her, wasn't it? She had that feeling she would get – as if she had seen this before. And you haven't. You haven't.

There was nothing to be frightened of.

But the car *smelled* frightening. A kind of struck tinder smell – a struck match –

Leigh walked back to the Morris and got in. She secured her own seat-belt.

'Sorry, love,' she said to her car.

The Morris had witnessed the bringing low of another of its kind. Yes, yes, Leigh Dover is nuts.

She started the engine and drove very slowly along the road, looking, as she went, to either side.

In this way she observed the second minor road that ran in from the left. It had a weird name – the Ride Run. After that, quite quickly, the big, two storey, architectural house, all blazoned with lights, up on its slope of lawn and trees.

The opaque-eyed blond man would have gone to this house. Straight to it, Leigh thought. It was near enough, and he must have been, unless Superman, or insane, shaken by his ditching.

Again, Leigh drew over on the verge, and sat gazing up at the house of lights, a Christmas tree in the dark, wiping out the bluster of stars above.

She had solved her mystery. So drive on. Get to Seatree, and the hotel, and the things she wanted.

It seemed to her the demon of choice stood before her, offering in one hand a chalice of self-indulgence, and in the other the sword of responsibility. *Am I trembling? No? That's very good.*

The house was *bright.* It was a displaying house, as the

Porsche had been a displaying car. There was one of those unlit, dislocated lampposts in the garden, and a sensuous arch covered in white flowers.

The Morris hummed gently, car-purring, reassuring Leigh that whatever she did would be sensible and not mad.

The woman who opened the door was perhaps in her sixties, nicely and softly made-up, slight, a fragile grey-blonde. The sort of woman who could easily have been a youthful forces pin-up in 1945, and later nicknamed, no doubt, the English Marilyn Monroe.

In keeping with the fancy, she wore a sort of cocktail frock, in mulberry silk. Her bare arms were unusually firm and smooth, given her age and build, and on the left wrist was a bracelet of linked dark sapphires – real ones, Leigh would have said.

Incongruously, the slim nyloned legs ended in two overlarge fluffy bedroom slippers. The sort that represented animal heads at the front. These were rabbits.

Leigh gazed a moment into their twin pairs of hard and shining eyes. Then up again to meet the woman's blue ones.

Unlike the rabbits', hers looked tired. Really more grey than blue, as if eye-colour greyed like hair, with age.

But the woman smiled. She was – gracious, that was the word.

'Good evening,' she said. As with all of her but for the rabbit eyes, the voice was soft.

'I'm sorry to bother you,' said Leigh. She was glad to note she sounded in turn completely rational and self-possessed. 'I passed a car gone over in a ditch a couple of minutes ago.' She paused.

The woman stood, smiling at her, with just the mildest puzzled query in her eyes.

'Did he come here? Leigh said. 'The driver, I mean. To use your phone, perhaps. He had a mobile, but it was damaged.' She was saying too much, and maybe not what it was appropriate to say. She said it now: 'I was a little concerned in case he'd been hurt. Or I wouldn't have troubled you.'

The woman frowned, very *softly*. Simply still puzzling all this out.

'*He?*' she said.

Leigh felt herself flush, stupidly. As if she'd been caught out at something.

'Yes. It was a man. I saw him you see, earlier, driving down from London. The car – it's a silver Porsche. Quite eye-catching.'

'Oh …' murmured the woman.

That was all.

Behind her, the wide hall was blooming with rosy light. An oak stair, white carpeting, beams. A big room opened to the left.

They stood in silence, and from the big room a shadow came, crossing the beams of golden lamps.

A man seemed to *evolve* into the hall, and stood behind the English Marilyn Monroe. In his liver-spotted hand, catching the light, was a large cut-glass tumbler with what looked like a very large whisky in it.

He too smiled. Flawless stone-white teeth glittered from an iron-grey moustache. He – what would you say? – bent his *regard* on Leigh, directly into her face. He was in his late sixties, strong. Teeth and light blue eyes. He had an almost military authority. Wanted answers. As if – he suspected her at once.

'Yes?' he asked.

'Oh,' said Marilyn Monroe, half-turning, relieved, 'darling …'

'It's all right,' he said. 'You can talk to me,' he said to Leigh. His was a forceful voice but not loud. Self-controlled and used to addressing others.

Leigh said, flatly, 'I saw a car in a ditch just along the lane. I wondered if the driver had come here.'

'No,' he said. 'No-one's come here at all.' The smile got larger. The teeth were enormous. Leigh thought of Red Riding-Hood, the wolf. 'Only us chickens,' inappropriately frivolously said the man, and laughed. It was quite a hearty laugh, and the woman now laughed too, softly, shyly, obviously relaxing. The man said to Leigh, 'I'm being rude, aren't I, leaving you standing there. Come in, won't you, while we sort this out.'

Leigh felt a great reluctance. The wolf was luring her into Granny's cottage. A wolf not even placatingly in disguise. But

Leigh had got used to dealing with irrational qualms. She had had to. This was just one more hurdle. And hurdles were there to be jumped.

'Thank you,' she said, and stepped over the threshold, into the house of white carpets.

It was the carpets that caused the strange silence. As they walked, none of them made a sound over the thick, thick pile. Hence the slightly supernatural noiseless glide of the man into the hall.

In the harsh light of the vast two-storey room, English Marilyn's skin looked more papery, her eyes more lined. *He* was like the carved oak and mahogany all around. He wore a suit, formal as the woman, and one of those old school ties, navy and dull gold, with some crest.

Above them, a gallery of books, and then the sky, and swallows. The sky of day by night.

The man downed his drink.

English Marilyn went over to him and took his glass, smiling up at him her melting smile.

'I'll get you another, darling.'

She was limping. A foot or ankle injury – arthritis – even a corn … which explained the slippers, probably.

The man turned to Leigh and held out his hand, straight out, no nonsense.

'Alliat. George Alliat.'

Leigh shook his hand. To her braced surprise, he didn't wring her fingers to pulp. It was a boneless handshake, the sort they warned you against as a signal of lack of character. But George Alliat, surely, was *all* character.

Leigh gave her name. He made no crack. Polished manners, or indifference?

English Marilyn had limped back and proffered another colossal whisky. Her willowy body described a lovely curve as she did so. It reminded Leigh at once of the women in the old films she liked, Lauren Bacall offering Bogart a cigarette,

Jean Simmons waiting upon Laurence Olivier's Hamlet or Crassus. Feminine in a way that the times had ironed out.

Leigh envied Marilyn for a moment. The adoring look on her face was so evident. Not every woman disliked men.

Leigh blinked. The thought had crept up on her, *caught* her in its grip. It wasn't a thought that made her happy.

The man was speaking '... this is my wife.'

Leigh had missed the woman's name. Well that didn't matter. The names were Mr and Mrs Alliat. She wouldn't need any more. In a minute she could make her – be honest – escape.

'Have a drink,' said George Alliat.

'Oh, no thanks. I'm driving.'

Surely he knew that?

George Alliat smiled his teeth. 'One won't hurt you,' he decided

'No, really, thank you.'

'Vodka, I suppose. That's the ladies' drink. I don't keep gin. It's no use to anyone.'

He had just ignored her refusal. Or was he hard of hearing?

Mrs Alliat was already back again with the decanters, pouring vodka into another cut glass tumbler, a smaller one, more feminine one.

'She'll want some tonic in it,' said Alliat.

Leigh opened her mouth. Closed it.

She didn't have to drink the vodka, did she. Politeness only demanded a façade, not that one lose one's driver's licence. Which, if she had drunk the vodka, she might well have done, judging by the size of it.

Mrs Alliat limped up and put the glass gently into her hand.

'Thank you.'

Papery soft skin. Like the butterfly. Poor butterfly.

'Down from London?' asked Alliat.

He stood, in the midst of the room, upright. They all stood, even the woman with the sore foot.

'Yes.'

'People down here?'

'No.'

'Business then, eh? Career girl.'

'Pleasure, really. I used to live in Seatree years ago.'

Why had she told him? But it was difficult to avoid such direct questions without being just as rude as the questioner.

What an incredible painting on the wall. Trees and fields of blue flowers – like a Cezanne, yet not. And it looked original.

'You'll find it changed, Seatree. Where are you staying?'

'Oh, I haven't dec –'

'Let me guide you. The Fighting Man is the place. Or so I gather. And a two-hundred-year-old brandy in the cellar. But I expect that wouldn't interest you.'

Leigh, dismayed, heard herself answer, 'Yes. I am staying there. And I've had the brandy.'

'Really? I should be careful of that. Strong stuff.'

For my weak silly head.

Leigh said firmly, quietly. 'You've been very nice, but I'd better get going now.'

'But don't you want to,' the teeth, 'interrogate me, Miss Dover? Or do you like *Muzz*? Or Leigh?'

The painting, the dense leaning limbs of cypresses, other taller trees, the azure mists of flowers –

'I really was just concerned, Mr Alliat. But obviously the man didn't come here. And so –'

'Know it's a man, do you? How's that?'

'I saw him in the car earlier.'

'You'll make me think you followed him, Miss Dover.'

The eyes twinkled like broken bottles in arctic sunlight. 'Wanted him for something. Why does a lady ever want a gentleman? Hunting with blood-dipped nails.'

A weightless raft of inner masonry seemed to plummet through Leigh's body. Nausea billowed in her stomach. Her mind, relentless, pushed it away.

She set the brimming, untouched glass of vodka and tonic

on a table.

At once the woman came limping hurriedly, picked up the glass, inspected the table to make sure there had been no spillage on the wood.

'Thanks anyway,' said Leigh.

She walked straight out of the room, rather fast. She was shaking. She expected any second his voice, booming like an admiral's from the upper deck of male privilege. Or even the big spotted hand, unfirmly falling on her shoulder.

Somehow she didn't run.

In the hall, it was the woman who caught up to her, limping like a wounded beetle.

Having reached her, however, Mrs Alliat halted, speechless.

'Thank you,' Leigh said again. More coldly than she meant to.

'Please forgive George,' said the woman. 'He works so hard. He doesn't mean –'

'That's all right, Mrs Alliat. Really.'

At any moment might not George hove back into view? Let me get *out*!

'He drives up to the city every day. And when he's at home, he works here, in his office with the computer. Accountancy. The firm would be lost without him, but it's such a burden for him, too. He only has his holidays. He needs those so badly.' As she ceased to speak, the house lay utterly still in its autumn snowdrift.

The blond man hadn't come here. Either that or they – *George* – hadn't let him in.

And anyway, the blond man was nothing to Leigh, nothing at all.

'Don't be upset,' suddenly said this faded rose with anxious tired eyes. 'I'd hate it so if he upset you. He's such a wonderful man. He's all my life.'

Terror stirred in the depths of Leigh Dover. A primeval terror that had no sense to it at all.

'Mr Alliat is charming,' said Leigh, bright as a button on

an admiral's hat. 'But I really have to run now.'

And she opened the door, and as soon as she was out, she did. She *ran*.

In the dark, Seatree didn't look so altered, apart from two determined blue and white buses, and the tall ornate roofs of the shopping centre towering out of Rotheridge Road. The Fighting Man stood where it always had in the High Street, the hanging baskets cascading summer geraniums and ivy, as she remembered, the sign unchanged, a Saxon man, blond and berserk, swinging two-handed his battle axe.

It had been, the Fighting Man, the personal banner of Harold, the last English King, who had died on the Weald at Senlac, in 1066. Leigh had no doubt the King's banner had not resembled the pub sign remotely.

The lobby was modest, and still warm from the day. The heavy beams were real enough, going back three hundred years to the days when the hotel had been a coaching inn. A bar opened to one side, and the restaurant to the other, and in the great black fireplaces, that Leigh recalled ablaze in winter with logs, were china urns full of plastic hydrangeas. Oh well.

No-one was about at the desk. Presently Leigh dinged the bell. It made her feel like an irate dowager. And no-one came anyway.

Leigh glanced up at the clock. It was 8.25, apparently. Her shoulders sagged.

Suddenly a male child of about seven, with cropped hair and bluish smears on his face, dressed in jeans and a ripped T-shirt reading *RUINED*, belted out from the bar. An underage drinker, perhaps?

'Mum!' bellowed the child. None of those childish trebles, piping. '*Mummm!*'

A door opened along the corridor beyond the bar.

'What is it?' A London voice. A big female in a white suit, pinned by a gold sunflower at the bosom, crowned by wiry sunflower hair, came from the ladies', smelling sweet of Poison.

'Mum – it's a woman.'

'Mum' widened her eyes, mascaraed as if with robust black spider legs.

'*Dexter.* You don't say *woman.*'

And there you have it.

'I'm Honor. You must be Ms Dover. Your room's all ready. Do you want a hand with your bag? Where's the book? Look at this mess under here. Dexter, take your hands out of that plant! Sign here. Full breakfast? Dinner till 9.00. But the bar stays open for guests until 2.00. *Dexter!*'

Dexter hurtled up the red carpet before Leigh, as she carried her bag and the light holdall. After them trailed Honor's despairing cry.

'How long you staying?' demanded Dexter.

'Shouldn't you be somewhere else?' asked Leigh.

'Where?'

'Somewhere more interesting.'

'You come from London. We come from London '

'Did you?'

'I've got a cat.'

Leigh smiled, not meaning to.

'That's nice, what's it called?'

'Her. It's a her. She's called Oprah.'

'Oh. Is that for Oprah Winfrey?'

'Yeah.'

'You like Oprah Winfrey?'

'Yeah.'

They were in the corridor.

Leigh opened her door. Edged in. But Dexter only stood considering her, from the red carpet outside.

'See you later, Dexter.'

'Maybe,' said Dexter, suddenly male and offhand. He slouched away down the corridor, whistling. He was the image of an infant Marlon Brando.

The room was comfortable, not even very small. A four-poster had a coverlet embroidered with birds and flowers. The windows, before she drew the curtains to, looked onto the big garden at the back, to trees and a floodlit pool of lilies, large goldfish and carp. Only three or four people were sitting outside.

Over the hotel wall, a lagoon of fields swept in on the houses of Seatree, restful and serene in the darkness. The sort of view one craved, until the tractors and harvesters started up by day.

She ran a bath, made herself a cup of tea, switched on her portable CD player.

She lay in the cool water scented with seaweed extract and gardenia, listening to one of the new relaxation discs on replay. It was a rhythmic, cloudy melody. The tapering beat came and went.

Leigh drifted. It was all right. Stupid unimportant things happened, and meant nothing at all.

Half asleep, the water lambent on her creamy, heavy body, rimming her waist with silver, putting an opal in her navel. Budded nipples. Not a mark. She wasn't ugly. No. She was still herself.

The purple nails floated like closed poppy-heads. Opium. Just relax.

Through the pillars, the imaginary dream-girls were dancing to the melodic beat. In diaphanous gowns, waists cinched with silver. Water-light playing, and golden fish that swam like birds through the air.

But then a shadow slid around a pillar, a shark, a man – and seized one of the dancers, carried her away, shrieking, her arms out-flung. And no-one heard. The other girls danced on.

Honor carefully didn't frown.

'The local police? Is there any problem?'

'Oh no. There was a car gone off the road that I saw. I felt perhaps I ought to report it, but I forgot.'

'Well, they always say, don't they, let them know about anything suspicious. And with all these bombs and things. Do you know we had a bomb scare this summer? Yes, 2.00 in the morning. We were all out on the pavement. Not that it'll happen again.'

No evidence now of the little boy. Sat before the TV, watching videos of *The Oprah Winfrey Show*?

Leigh dialled the number Honor, mother of Dexter, had given her.

It rang a long while. She almost put down the phone.

Then a voice spoke, a policeman, courteous and bored.

She told him about the car in the ditch. Described it. Yes, she had noticed the number-plate. She gave it.

'About what time was this?'

She told him she thought it must have been about 7.30. Perhaps a little later. She was sorry she couldn't be exact.

Oh, and the ditch had been quite near a house, she said. A big house with an ornamental lamppost in the front garden.

He asked if he could have her name.

(She thought of giving it, Leaned Over, or Miss Held Over. No, she didn't think she would give her name.)

She put the phone down.

Leigh walked into the bar and asked for a brandy and soda. Not a two-hundred-year-old brandy, however.

She had seen the lane on the map and later, driving out of it into the road that would take her straight into Seatree High Street and the car-park of the Fighting Man, she had seen the name again, on a signpost wedged into a hawthorn hedge.

There were oaks, cedars, monkey-puzzle trees and some houses there in a loose group, wealthy large buildings, but not quite as impressive as the Alliat home.

Until she had told the policeman the name on the map and the sign-post, she hadn't spoken it aloud.

Now it kept sounding in her head.

With her own name, she was used to puns, rhyming similarities.

That must be why her agitated mind was doing this with the name of the Alliats' narrow, winding, ditch-sided road, Divers Lane.

Driver slain.

8.30 pm to Midnight

1

'Can you just give me a tiny kiddy portion? I've had that bloody tummy bug,' Markessa added winningly to Jack Hastings.

'Right?'

He gave her one of his looks. Thought he was something.

Markessa fluttered at him and glared back at her plate. Jula had taken her at her word and given her some tiny bits of meat and a scoopful of the vegetables and sauce. A pity really; it smelled appetising. But then Jula was dirty, and anyway, Markessa didn't want to lose her figure overnight.

No nervousness there from Jack Hastings. Jula was piling high the food before him. A self-employed decorator and self-styled designer, with a flamboyant line in new painting techniques and carpentry, he was eternally, she supposed, up and down ladders, sawing and hammering. Hastings had no need to worry about calories. It made you sick.

He had arrived well after 8.00. Markessa had never previously known him anything but punctual. He looked slightly dishevelled, too, somehow, and put out. He scowled black-browed at Markessa as she flung open the door.

'We didn't hear your van,' she accused him. She had hoped it was Steven.

'Right?' he said.

As he went in, Markessa had noticed his trousers were dusty, and there was a tear in his denim shirt.

His van had, with no warning, started playing up halfway between Hastings and here. (Gimmicky trademark, his name being the same as the town where he lived.) He'd nursed the van into Seatree, then walked up the hill. This he relayed to Jula flatly.

'I thought you had a job on here, in Seatree?' said Markessa. As always, she was rather antagonistic with Jack. 'You know, someone's flat, isn't it?'

'It's finished,' he said shortly.

But he was soon happy again, a bee round Jula's honey-pot.

Markessa was never sure why Steven put up with Jack Hastings. But then, Steven would probably be only too thrilled if Jula got something going there instead of clinging on where she wasn't wanted.

Hastings *was* good-looking. Very tall, six three or four, long dark hair tied back in a tail, long-legged, long-lipped, muscular, blue-eyed, with uneven, very white teeth. A sharp dresser too, in his own untidy way. But his *accent*. Markessa mentally grimaced. And he had no flare, none of Steven Grace's poise and charm. A wide-boy. A nobody. It went without saying, he'd be as interested in Jula's cash as in her skinny unkempt person.

Jula accepted the flowers Hastings handed her. They were astonishing blooms, silvery white and mauve, greenish bronze – but then he had subsidiary arrangements, to do with his work, at all the florists.

'They're wonderful, Jack,' said Jula, 'like ghosts.' And she put them, untrimmed, unarranged, into a tall black vase of filtered tap water. Where, Markessa had to admit, they formed their own perfect alignment.

Jula said they might as well eat.

'Isn't he here?' said Jack.

'No,' said Markessa sharply. 'Steven *isn't*. I'm quite concerned. He told her he'd be back by 4.30.'

'Wow, you don't say,' said Jack.

Markessa bridled. (She knew she did. It was what heroines did in the romances at her bookshop, the sort she read at the counter. She always maintained book-buyers liked to see the manager reading.)

'Yes, I know he's often late. And he was coming from

London, there was filthy traffic. But over *four hours?'*

'It's usually only two or three,' Jack Hastings agreed. He bit greedily on a raw carrot and drank the Guinness Jula had poured him – *that*, Markessa had noted, *had* been kept cold in the fridge.

However, Jula now went into the ancient stone pantry and returned with three plates of sliced avocado in a chilled mustard dressing.

The dining-room was small, but she had hoovered it. The mess and muck and muddle on the two sideboards and in the old creaky chairs were partly obscured by shadows. A glamorous apricot globe of a lamp hung low over the table, giving a ripe, rufous light.

Red candles burned in high sconces. A bowl of oranges glowed. Jack's flowers.

The wine was at room temperature, red. Markessa would still have preferred it cold, but there you were.

By some magic, the lamb-thing hadn't dried up. Jula knew culinary tricks, somehow. It *was* rather good. But all this garlic. Markessa would have to make her coffee with Listerine tomorrow.

Jack gazed at Jula. Talked to Jula.

There was no other woman in the room. (Probably not in England.) As for Steven, who would have made the conversation go with a sparkle, no-one mentioned him.

'That was fantastic. You're unbeatable. Any more, Jula?'

'Piggy,' said Jula.

Oh Christ, now she was getting flirtatious.

Jula heaped Hastings' plate once again.

Markessa could just picture his upbringing, some working-class council house, the slaving mum serving up grub in a trough.

And all those florid lying compliments. Steven didn't carry on like that. OTT.

Out in the kitchen, the black clock was ticking loudly, as it often did now, on the battery. It gave the time as 9.48, perhaps not correctly.

Upstairs too, they would intermittently hear the cats running and jumping.

Yet now Markessa said abruptly, 'There's – there's Steven's car.'

Jack Hastings saw Jula stop quite still, as if turned to stone. They all listened then, as if, he thought, for the crack of doom. But if he'd heard anything, and maybe he had, it had died away.

'Sometimes,' Jula said softly, 'they drive up the track at night into that field where the gate's off.' She added distantly, 'Lovers.'

Overhead, as if to mock Markessa's undisguised chagrin, there came another spasm of cat acrobatics.

'It brought in a mouse again,' Markessa said viciously, drinking the warm red wine.

'What?' said Jula.

Politeness was her middle name.

'Your cat.'

'Which one?'

'The tabby one – I was on the phone with that weirdo, or whoever it was.'

'Which weirdo? Oh, yes. You said there was an obscene call.'

'And from a *woman*,' said Markessa, genuinely shocked.

'Yeah, they really ought to leave that to the men,' said Hastings.

Jula laughed.

Markessa snapped, 'A field-mouse, too.'

'A mouse phoned you up?' asked Hastings, interested.

Markessa reddened. She unpleated her face. 'Jule's tabby cat brought in a mouse.'

'Was it alive?' said Jula.

'How do *I* know?'

'Little things,' said Jack. 'They move a bit, or breathe.'

Markessa gulped her wine and swallowed the wrong way. As she choked, Jack Hastings thumped her much too roughly on the back, and Jula, getting up, left the room.

Jula didn't drink much normally. But tonight she had had

two glasses of white wine, and half a glass of red. And it had –
not gone to her head – but got into her *brain*.

Be careful, Jula.

Yes, I will be careful. One appalling misjudgement had been
enough. She had to live with herself.

But the tension – *waiting*.

She was glad to get away from them, even from lovely Jack,
and come up here to look for the mouse Lavender had brought
in, and if possible rescue it.

How many mice had she rescued from her cats over the
years? Hundreds, maybe. In the Great Mouse Book of Shining
Deeds in a Catty World, her credit must be all right.

'Help me, O Great Mouse,' said Jula to the corridors of the
upper house. And giggled.

In the half-dark, beyond the lamp left burning outside the
lavatory, Nero bounded by like a bionic panther. The tablets
were suiting him. That was a relief. She would need to renew
the prescription fairly soon, as she had only 15 now to give him.

The shadows were friendly. They shouldn't be, not really –
but then that was long ago. Long ago.

She passed the master bedroom that had been her workroom
and library since first she took the house. The rows and piles of
books were like the bricks of her world. On the desk by the
window lay her notebook, a volume of Churchman's poems,
and two letters Jula had received from Churchman's
granddaughter.

She found Lavender crouching, beautiful as a flower, by the
wardrobe in the fifth bedroom. Lavender had assumed the pose
of tail-lashing annoyance rather than satiety. The mouse had got
away. Where was it? In the wardrobe, probably, judging by
Lavender's green-for-go eyes. Now came the tricky part.

Jula Cork had met Steven Grace one summer evening at the
National Theatre on the South Bank.

She had been waiting for Leonardo, who wasn't going to
arrive. It was the onset of his illness, but she hadn't known that

then, nor had he.

Leonardo was never late. And stood in the bar, with her small, old glass of wine, Jula began to have a strange dizzy feeling of – not hope. Surely not hope. Perhaps, hope.

The play was to begin at 7.30. She had wanted to see it for years, having read it in her teens. And Leonardo and she; the one thing they agreed on, often, was this, what people called the Arts.

He had played her the first Mahler she had ever heard, expecting her to take to it, as she had. And he had brought her fully to Dickens, and to Hardy, and to strangers such as Tolstoy. Not, however, to Churchman. Churchman, Leonardo had missed.

She had said over the phone, 'He's a contemporary of Tennyson. Not quite so highly thought of. Except, perhaps, by me.'

'I have reservations about Tennyson,' said Leonardo. 'Not always, of course.'

'This is incredible, Leon. It's a sort of parallel of *The Comedy of Errors.*'

'Hence the title?' Leonardo judged the notion as he spoke the words. '*The Perfect Tragedy.* I see. Well. I trust you, Jula. Let's go, I look forward to it, and to seeing you. That most of all.'

Sometimes Leonardo still made her want to cry. He sounded as if he really meant it. Looking forward to seeing her. *Trusting* her. Thinking her invaluable.

Although the play was probably unwise. He wouldn't have liked it. Yet – since apparently they must meet –

As she stood there in the bar, and it was first 6.30, when they had agreed on, and quarter to 7.00, and then 7.00, and Leonardo hadn't arrived, Jula swung unbalanced above the precipice brink, imagining a life where never again would she have to meet with him. And at last partly hopeful it was so.

In this condition, Steven Grace found her.

That summer, Steven went quite often to the National, not to visit the plays exactly, but the bars. A woman had told him he closely resembled one of the actors then performing at the theatre, and Steven, checking this out, had agreed with her.

Generally actors kept to the actors' bar behind the scenes, but now and then you might spot one in the public areas of the building.

Steven, half listening to a little of the live music, having a few drinks at this bar or that, would wait, inwardly amused, and a little unadmittedly excited, to see who would mistake him for his doppelganger. He thought it happened quite a lot actually. No-one ever approached him, but he saw the looks, as he casually sat, or leaned on something, smoking, absorbing the expensive booze.

The night he spotted Jula, Steven Grace knew exactly how he appeared, and superimposed on the image of the slender girl in her short green dress, her fantastic fleece of black hair, was his own image, what she in turn must see.

He was tanned. He had tanned easily on the terrace of the London house, basted with sunblock and Ambre Solaire. His hair had bleached almost white. He wore designer jeans, poured not shaken, the hand-stitched white £200 shirt with ebony buttons, Gucci slip-ons, steel-blue Swatch.

He was living with Felicia then, who never stinted. Later he would miss Felicia. She had been a shallow bitch, and too old for him, but she had known his value, never asked questions or argued. She had a bit of class.

Jula he had thought classier, that evening. And he'd seen the book-jacket too. A writer who had made it.

When he went to the bar and ordered another drink, he ran his eyes over her to be sure. Translucent skin. Hardly any make-up – she didn't need it. Unpainted healthy nails. On her left hand, the middle finger, a large polished emerald in gold. No wedding ring.

She was what? Twenty-five, twenty-seven? (When he found after all she was all of 31, he had felt cheated a little. Women should wear their ages on their bodies. How else did you know where you stood?)

Their eyes met. He thought she had been aware of him, and meant it to happen.

In fact, Jula did not see Steven, even looking right at him, for some moments. With her inner eye, she had been seeing other things.

'Can I get you a drink?' he said, straight out.

'No, thanks.'

He could tell it was a refusal of a drink, not of him.

'Go on. It's a hot night. No? What play are you here for?'

She said, in a still, alien way she had, like a foreign woman speaking English for the first time, '*A Perfect Tragedy.*'

'Oh right. Yes. Same as me.'

Her eyes seemed to have moved inside themselves. She was fascinating, curious.

'You know Churchman?'

Steven hazarded, 'No. Should I?'

'He wrote the play.'

'Well, yes. Of course. But do I *know* him?'

She smiled. She thought it was a joke.

He ordered another whisky, no ice, and persuaded Jula, who said she would have an orange juice.

She was like a little girl. Drinking her orange juice. Waiting for the play. One difficulty. Of course he had no ticket.

He said, 'Anyway, watch it for me, will you.'

She didn't say, as they did, *Sorry*? An apology for not following you. She said, 'I don't understand.'

'I lost my ticket. God knows how. *C'est la vie.*'

'But won't they –?'

'They might. But they make a real fuss. It doesn't matter.'

He thought she would say, never mind the show, she'd rather stay and talk to him. But instead Jula (they had by now exchanged names – and he knew anyway, didn't he, from the book-jacket seen in Waterstones that morning, with Felicia – even if he hadn't checked on the author's age), Jula said, 'Would you like to use this one? I was waiting for my uncle, but he hasn't turned up.'

She was waiting for her uncle, huh?

This too sounded like the title of a play. *Waiting for Unco –*

Steven was bored rigid by Churchman's bloody play. Guys

parading about in padded *cock-pieces*, and women in uplift corsets, all spouting Victorian treacle. *She* had sat entranced. Or she pretended.

He had some more whisky in the interval, and she had another orange juice.

When the grisly bore was finally done (three *hours*!), they went out and stood looking at the river.

She was starry-eyed at the play, or making believe.

'I hope you weren't bored,' she said, remotely.

'God, no. What a play. Theatre – I love it. It makes me want to get back to my typewriter.'

'You write,' she said, rather bleakly he thought.

She hadn't mentioned that she did. Secretive rather than show-off.

He sensibly left that and leapt the fence.

'Can I take you to dinner?' asked Steven Grace.

Her eyes were huge. Like the black Thames, they reflected all the lights of London.

She was beautiful. Fresh and young and successful.

'To thank you,' he said, 'for the ticket. I'll never forget that play, and I nearly didn't get to see it.' Then he looked down, modest, shy even. They liked that, sometimes. 'But I don't want to push you. Just say no.'

He didn't realise that although almost indifferent to him otherwise, she was full of hope, high and afraid and a little mad, together. And inebriated from the play, too, like champagne.

'Yes,' she said. 'I'd like to, Steven.'

Jula put Lavender out in the corridor, and shut the door of the fifth bedroom. She switched on the light. There were plenty of things she could use. She selected a cardboard box in the corner. They were small, but you had to allow room for the tail.

In the wardrobe, as she undid the door, was the faintest scrabbling. A tiny hole in the walnut showed where it had got in. How clever it was, the mouse. How brave. The moment Lavender in her horrible game had let it slip, it was away.

They said to you, *How can you love a cat when it does those things? Tortures mice to death. How can you like grey squirrels that steal birds' eggs? How can you stand magpies that steal baby squirrels?*

Jula had long ago stopped bothering to explain that it was the System that was bad, not the individual animal or bird. The *System.*

We all need to survive. Or most of us come with the built-in need to do so.

Life, the systems of life, make us into what, finally, we are.

During the play, she had been, now and then, vaguely aware of him. At those instants she wasn't sure if Steven Grace liked the play at all. But she didn't have the space to ponder. She was swept away, as she always was by music, drama, a book. It happened too when she wrote herself. She ceased to be, and became – what? Jula didn't know, or care. It was more than she could ever be, when she was only herself.

And in the theatre too, as in a concert hall, she, and all those who responded as she did, became an entity. One thing. She was a solitary creature. She liked to be alone. Was terrified, in a way, of the company of others. All the more so then did she value this occasional union of minds and hearts. If they existed, of souls.

While Steven was getting them more drinks, in the interval, she had rung Leonardo. There was no answer.

Jula hung in the silver void. She believed it had happened. She did. *Madness.* Had she known, he was in hospital in Blaymore. She would find out soon enough next day.

But she did not try to call again, that night.

On the other hand, Steven Grace called Felicia from the restaurant. He asked Jula to excuse him. The telephones were usefully situated outside the lavatories. Someone had had some sense.

'Fel? Sorry, baby. Peter's drunk too much and he's off his head. I'd better stay with him. Be back later. About 1.00 – if I can. You okay? Nice evening? Great. See you.'

Jula didn't eat or drink a lot. She was a delightfully cheap date. He was glad for Felicia, not having to make her spend too much.

Jula wanted to talk about the play. He let her. Even in this, she didn't go on. They sat in silence a lot. Their eyes kept meeting.

At midnight, the restaurant lowered the lights so only the candles burned. He took her hand, the one with the emerald. How smooth they felt, the hand, the stone.

'I hate to say goodnight to you, Jula. Where are you going to?'

'Not far. A hotel. I don't live in London now.'

'Have another brandy?'

'No, thank you.'

'I'll get us a cab.'

She said, 'We could walk.'

He didn't want to walk. He had seen plenty of London in the summer, walking, picking up women in the bars. Since he was 15.

'I'd like that. I'm old-fashioned, you see. I want to see you to your door.'

As they got up, she said to him, 'It isn't my door.'

'The hotel then. The hotel door.'

Outside, there was a cab. 'Forgetting', he hailed it. She didn't protest.

He was fairly sure, when he kissed her in the cab, that she would say to him, *Don't leave me here. Come up with me.*

But she didn't. Not Jula. She let him take her to the door and then, goodnight. He had to catch her hand again and say, 'I'll call you tomorrow. Will you be here?'

'Until 10.00,' she said.

And so he had to call her, at 9.30, he who normally woke at 11.00. He had a hangover, and thought she would be already gone.

All this he told her after. At first most tenderly. Humorously. Only later with venom and anger. 'What a fucking little hard-to-get. All you thought of was that rubbish of a play. Oh *yeah*. Not *me*. And the dinner and the cab. And, *Ooh, I'll be gone by 9.00 am*. You bitch.'

That was about the time he coined one of his names for her. Eyeless Jula. (Julia without the I.)

She'd never had a long-term relationship. A few sexual 'adventures'. She liked sex, had, reasonably early, taken to it quite quickly. For her, it had nothing to do with love. Love, indeed, put her off. When it seemed to her at last she had fallen in love with Steven, her libido lessened.

But the first time hadn't been like that. Even though Steven had insisted he wear a condom.

'I'm fine, Jula. I promise you. I just don't want you to have to worry.'

Nothing had been further from Jula's mind. She was a fiery innocent in that hour, kneeling naked before him, satin and heat, inflaming him with hair and six published books, her income and her house in the country.

She hadn't known, then, that Steven put on the condom to protect *himself* in case she might have HIV.

Lavender's mouse stared up with sequinned eyes. It wasn't hurt. Lavender, at her most 'playful', seldom seriously harmed until the ultimate bite.

Jula reached round the wardrobe, and scratched at its back, and the mouse scuttled forward into the box.

There were little holes ready-punched by a nail file in the lid. Jula pushed the lid down. The mouse rustled. She would keep it shut in her room for a while, let it get over the shock, then release it in the paved back yard. Like the others, it would run for the fields, while Lavender and Nero feasted on bits of lamb *julienne*.

The room was dark. Beyond the undrawn curtains, grave night lay on the countryside. A moon was rising, dense yellow, stained with low cloud.

Far down, the glare of a distant burning city, the lights of

Seatree.

A fox, bronze-coated in moonlight, trotted up the track between the hedges, lifting the icon of its face. It paid no attention to the unlit front of the house, skirted Markessa's car, vanished into the hedgerow.

The *was* a car in the lower field with the broken gate. A light had gone on for a moment under the trees there. Making their love, the lovers hadn't known what they had stirred up in Markessa's Steven-anticipating heart. Or in Jula's own.

I stand here, holding a mouse in a box, hoping that this time the grey magic has worked again.

Downstairs, the phone rang. Not a twitter. A full-throated alarm.

Jula lowered her head, resting her cheek on the box top, her hair rustling like the mouse inside.

No magic, then. It would be Steven.

Markessa ran into the hall. Night shapes fled from her pin-heeled shoes.

She grabbed up the phone.

'Hallo – hallo – Steven?'

In the dining room, Jack Hastings, about to pour himself a little more wine, heard Markessa say shrilly: 'No. Excuse me? *Sorry*? No. Yes. It is. No. *Oh* – oh my *God* – oh my *God!*'

2

The Ten O'Clock News was finishing on the big TV in the bar of the Fighting Man.

Detective Inspector Rawthorn stood watching it from the lobby, as he waited for Honor McCarthy to appear.

There had been some trouble on the Seatree Road, faulty traffic lights, which the news was pinpointing as a kind of revolution. (On the screen a crowd shouted. A short-haired young man in a suit waved his fists, an armlet or watch glinting. And now another man, his optical opposite, seized his arm –)

There had been breakdowns and failures all day, *incidents*, cars, lights, telephones. People out of control. Something to do with sunspots, apparently. It sounded like science fiction, *Quatermass*. Everything would soon break down completely, and then the aliens would arrive.

They'd probably beam straight up again, if they ran into Dexter.

'Who's dead?'

'Lots of people, Dexter.'

'What, here? You're barmy.'

'Shouldn't you be in bed?'

'Nah. *Who* died?'

'No-one, Dexter. Forget it.'

'I don't forget,' warned Dexter, and sauntered away into the restaurant, which was empty except for an interesting elderly woman, drinking tea. She might need rescuing.

Dexter wore pyjama bottoms at least, but that was as far as it had got. The T-shirt read: *Don't Wind Me Down*.

All the FM's regulars were in the bar. A haze of something, no longer much tobacco smoke, floated there; just alcoholic breath, maybe, bonhomie. Glasses clinked. A dark red atmosphere, blue-lit in flashes only by the television. The one-armed bandit had broken down, it seemed (Dexter said). The sunspots?

Honor was billowing to Earth from the hotel stairs.

'Can I help you?'

She always never knew him. He was used to that. She had lost her temper with the police over the bomb hoax. It was their fault, naturally. (The fact that, at the time, the whole South East was alert to potential terrorist activity, and suffering the malicious hoax calls that always seem to attend such events, had somehow passed Honor by.) Or perhaps she just didn't like policemen, uniformed or otherwise, disturbing her guests. Which was understandable.

'Someone gave us a call earlier.'

She switched suddenly to bright and helpful. 'Oh yes. That was Ms Dover. Where's the book? There we are. She drove in this evening. Saw a car gone off the road. Is that it?'

'Where would I find her?'

'Out in the garden. Didn't want a proper dinner. Nobody did tonight. Anyway, we stop serving at 9.00, properly.'

'Thank you.'

He started to go through the corridor as Honor McCarthy loudly called, 'Dexter! Dexter!' She must do that twenty times an hour.

The corridor, red carpet and photos of the Weald, and Battle Abbey, its ground once the scene of Senlac, ran straight through to the back.

Rawthorn stood on the steps and looked down into the garden.

Clipped leylandii hedges, two significant beeches, roses still in their full summer crinolines. A few gnomes herded out to graze. The pool below the terrace had pots of what looked like crimson cabbages. In the floodlight, which wasn't too unsubtle, the gold fins winked in the non-porphyry font.

Dexter's cat, black and very pretty, was sat to one side, staring down at the fish. Now and then she dipped in her paw and made a swishing motion, totally absorbed. No TV for this Oprah, just family entertainment.

The woman was seated on the terrace, alone at a fake wrought-iron table. A good choice; the night was coming, out here, into its full autumn coolness at last. She had before her a salad and half a bottle of white wine. She hadn't seen him, or if she had, didn't guess he had any business with her.

Odd, the number of people who still hadn't cottoned on that any time you dialled a number now, it could be traced back to you at once, unless you blocked this by first dialling the number-withheld code.

At the time the call had gone through, the desk sergeant hadn't been busy. And he was making the most of it, after a sunspotted day. So when the caller rang without giving her name, he simply dialled 1471, as anyone could, and traced her to the Fighting Man. This didn't, however, interest him very much until, having pushed the car's registration number through the computer, he had decided to ring the owner.

Unclaimed, ditched cars were usually stolen. This one wasn't. Or wasn't thought to be. And its owner, expected home apparently at 4.00 in the afternoon, had never got there.

Amazing really, the public. Some of them were on to the police if a husband, lover or child was forty minutes late. And others, like Steven Grace's partner and friends, didn't make anything of six hours. Which gave one to think.

Rawthorn descended the steps, and began to walk toward the woman at the table.

He sensed now that she was aware of him, and making out she wasn't. Even the cat had spared him a glance.

She was all right, this Leigh Dover. Heavy, *big*, they said now. He'd have said, voluptuous. Creamy skin, untanned. A black wing of hair.

'Ms Dover?'

She had to look up now, and she did. She was marvellous. Late thirties? A face someone should ache to paint, and maybe did. And that white column of a throat.

But her eyes were blank with – fright, it looked like. Pure, clear, gleaming funk.

He produced his ID. She stared at it. He thought she didn't properly see it, but even so knew and feared what it was.

'I'm sorry to interrupt your meal.'

She sat back. Then abruptly took her glass and drained it. Her hand shook.

'Do you mind if I sit down?'

Her voice surprised him. It was modulated. She had command of it. Husky, the sort of voice most men would like. An actress? But if so, couldn't act with her face. 'If you want to.'

'It's about the car, Ms Dover. The car you spotted in Divers Lane.'

She was bemused, couldn't work it out. How did he *know*? Yes, people forgot about the codes. He didn't tell her.

But he smiled at her.

'I could do with a bit of help,' he said. 'A bit more than you gave the sergeant when you rang.'

'I wouldn't have rung if I'd thought –'

We'd pursue you, he filled in mentally. *Hound you. Take up your valuable time as a free citizen.*

'We're very glad you did, Ms Dover. The driver is missing. We'd like to find him, if possible.'

'I don't know anything about him,' she said.

She poured herself another glass of the wine, and her hand shook so it slopped over.

He had the urge to take her hand and pour the wine for her.

Did she drink a lot? Had she been drinking when she was driving; had it been only something as predictable as that?

Before he came out, he had rung Knox from the station.

'You could leave it,' said Detective Chief Inspector Knox. 'See her tomorrow. It's nothing. One more car in a ditch. Men skiving off. Very likely just didn't fancy going home to the wife.'

'Yes, sir.'

'All right,' said Knox. 'Go. See if Father cares.'

'Yes, sir.'

The sergeant grinned. 'He wants to keep his feet up. Favourite TV his Mrs videoed – *NYPD Blue*.'

An old joke. Rawthorn nodded.

There was no reason to suppose this was anything much. Not even 24 hours had gone by to moot Steven Grace as a missing person. Knox was right, it could have waited.

But maybe not.

Not, going on this gorgeous woman's grey-green frightened eyes.

'Let me get this straight, Ms Dover. You didn't see the accident?'

'No.'

'I mean, you didn't see it?'

She stared at him.

'I said I didn't.'

'Let me try putting it this way. I'm more interested right now in what happened to the driver of the Porsche, than in any – well, let me say, aberration of your own. Unless of course you deliberately forced him off the road.'

He had tried for a reaction, and got it. The glass fell out of her hand. As it smashed on the terrace, the cat sprang away from the pool and raced around the side of the hotel.

'I don't know why I did that. I'm tired.'

'Yes. Obviously. You had a long drive from London.'

'How do you –'

'You wrote it in the hotel register, Ms Dover. Place of residence.'

'Yes. Yes I did.' She seemed to fall together and to change. Her eyes were lowered, then raised. She looked wary now more than afraid. 'I'll tell you the whole truth,' she said.

'I'm not a judge, Ms Dover.'

'Aren't you?'

'This is just routine.'

'I'm – nervous with policemen. That's probably very criminal.'

'Not at all, Ms Dover. You'd be surprised how many people are. Perfectly blameless, law-abiding persons.'

'It's supposed to be inner guilt, or something, isn't it?' she said. 'Yes, I've heard of that. I'm sorry. I'm trying not to mess you about.'

I'd love it, he thought, *if you did.*

He said, 'Take your time.'

She inhaled like someone with a cigarette, not plain tobacco either. And told him.

As Rawthorn listened, he saw it all in pictures. Most people did, he found. Chief Inspector Knox was one of the few who had ever told him that *he* saw in *words*. Even his memories.

But here, on the wide cinema screen of his mind, Rawthorn watched Steven Grace, a blond man he had never met, sitting slightly behind Leigh Dover in the traffic hold-up, and then the silver Porsche in the ditch, and Leigh Dover stood there, shining her torch. The dead butterfly. The mobile phone. Making sure that the man wasn't lying nearby in need of assistance. For such a nervy woman on her own, a valiant and altruistic act.

'But no-one was there,' he said.

'No. I thought I'd report it when I got to Seatree.' She hesitated, evidently made a decision, and said, 'When I drove on, very quickly I saw a large house just above the road. It was brightly lit up. Every room, it looked like. You couldn't not notice.'

He waited.

Then prompted, 'Yes?'

'Somehow I had an idea the driver might have gone to the house to ask for help – use the phone, if his own had been damaged.'

Rawthorn said, 'Or it could have been the driver's house, couldn't it?'

Her eyes came back to his face. Grey-green. You could swim in them.

'I didn't think of that at all.'

'But it could have been the obvious solution, couldn't it. Relaxing his concentration because he was near to home, then something going wrong, getting ditched. Then just getting out of the car and walking to the house. Either not bothering with the car until the morning, or else waiting for the rescue services in comfort, with all the lights on, so they wouldn't miss him.'

'That's logical. But I never thought of it at all. I'm not logical. I don't think I am. Perhaps quite stupid.'

'In fact it's too logical, because apparently this big lit house has nothing to do with the driver at all.'

'No,' she said, 'it doesn't.'

'Because you stopped at the house and inquired after him.'

She said, 'I feel you can read my mind. But it's only trained deduction, isn't it?'

'I can't read your mind, Ms Dover.'

She told him about the house, and its occupants, in quite a lot of detail. He had noted she hadn't said much about Grace, just his approximate age, blond hair, and the colour of the car. Maybe she had simply noticed the *car*. Liked Porsches. Despite her Morris, in the car-park of the Fighting Man. (If he told her that, she'd be startled again. He'd have to explain to her that he had glanced in on the car-park, and knew every car there but one. *Quod erat demonstrandum*.)

Leigh had finished. She sat, running her finger over the side of the almost empty bottle. The glass had gone, of course.

'You weren't keen on these people – the Alliats.'

'Does that matter?'

He shrugged.

She said, 'She was just that sort of old-fashioned woman who looks up to her husband, dotes on him, waits on him. The kind of lady who'd always have called him *Mr Alliat* a hundred years ago.'

'And not many modern women are going to like that.'

'I don't mind it that much, Inspector. My mother was rather like that with my father. And he was sweet. They were very happy.'

'You didn't think Alliat was worth it, though.'

'No. He was – disgusting.' She stopped. Said again, very low, 'Disgusting.'

Rawthorn considered he had got all of it from her now, all she would give or think he had a right to know. At this stage he couldn't push it any further. In a way, he was just prolonging the interview for obvious reasons. E R fancies L D, with a heart drawn round it.

He was going to say, *Well, thanks for your information, Ms Dover. I'll let you get back to your dinner. I'll tell them in the bar to bring you out another glass.* When she said, quickly and sharply, 'There was something there that was wrong.'

'You thought so?'

'I felt it. Something – almost uncanny. That sounds ridiculous. I don't mean to come across like the start of a ghost story, and that's what I'm sounding like. By uncanny I mean – *eerie*. That's worse, isn't it. I had a feeling.'

He wondered if she was waiting for him to say, *Ah, woman's intuition.* He didn't, obviously.

She said, 'All I can give you are the facts, as I saw them. The room was so *clean*. Too clean. It was like an operating theatre. Maybe she's just house-proud – she seemed to be – and fussy. The things in the room were odd. I mean they didn't match. What's called good taste, carved mahogany, folio edition books, and then the cheapest, dirtiest-looking dried fronds stuffed in a bowl – a *jade* bowl. And there was a painting that looked entirely out of place with any of it. It was an original, and whoever painted it had a very special eccentric genius. And I don't know who it was.'

'And you would know, would you, Ms Dover?'

'Almost certainly. I used to teach art. I've studied it. Seen it close to, quite often. Major examples in leading galleries, over here, in Paris, Amsterdam.'

She had gained confidence. Suddenly she was someone else. Or, perhaps, herself.

And then she caught herself, talking to him like this, giving opinions, telling him about Leigh Dover.

Her lovely face closed fast.

'I'm sorry,' she said.

You should be, he thought. *Clamming up like that. Disappointing me when I was just getting to know you.*

'Thank you, Ms Dover. You've been helpful. I won't take any more of your time.'

Surprising him, she took the bottle, which still had in it half a glass of wine, and swigged it from the top. He liked this. Under other circumstances he would have shown her an approving grin.

As he was standing up, Dexter came padding out through the garden door of the hotel.

Bizarrely, he was bearing – not a wine glass – but a glass bowl, and his one had something in it. Water, and what looked like a single large peeled carrot.

He walked carefully down the steps, and onto the terrace, skirting the broken glass matter-of-factly on bare hard feet.

He glanced at Leigh and Rawthorn, as he passed.

''S all right, 'snot hurt. She's always doing it.'

They watched him, the two adults with things to hide, the overt and wild child named Right, as he bore to the pool the goldfish, reclaimed from Oprah's mouth, and let it back gently into the floodlit water.

3

Also floodlit, on the tower of St Edith's, the clock read 11.13.

Rawthorn turned left from the High Street, and up through the gardened road of elegant Victorian terraces, which led, in due course, into Divers Lane.

It was late to be calling on witnesses. But then they might not be witnesses at all. Nothing might have happened to witness. And besides, he wasn't going to call.

Curious, actually. Normally, to reach the Seatree Road and the A21, he would take Harold Street, cut through the new estate into Saxon Vale, drive over the Brow, with the hospital and civic centre, and through Queen Aldyth's Park. A far longer route.

Yet he might still know the house in Divers Lane by sight. Such a big house, a rich man's house, and, she had said, isolated from the others nearer to the town.

Rich men liked their privacy. Many did, not always the rich, if they could get it.

Leigh Dover had been full of the ditched car, and the house with peculiar people. It had gushed from her, the story. And yet, on getting to the hotel, she hadn't called the police until 9.00.

That didn't mean much, really. She was tired. Hadn't forgotten, he honestly didn't think so, merely wanted some space herself first.

Privacy.

The lane was dark, no illumination, and an unadopted road, fairly well-kept. They liked it dark, then. No coarse Lucozade street lamps shining in at their windows, reminding them how built-up tiny England had become.

The first houses in the lane lay scattered around in large gardens. There were high walls, spikes, burglar alarms, security lights after all, some of which spurted on as the car nosed past.

Then a stretch of trees, with fields beyond, and the hills that humped over and down, eventually toward Battle, St Leonards, Hastings, and the sea.

He hadn't remembered any of this – and it came to him why not. Divers Lane, until recently, had been a private road. Out of bounds to the common trafficker.

When it appeared, the house, there could be no doubt. It was in what might be called a fanfare of lights.

'*Look at* me!' the house seemed to cry. '*Look on my works –*'

Rawthorn pulled over on the opposite verge, just as Leigh had done, where the trees gave back a little.

He sat there, as the house seemed to demand, *looking*.

The architecture was appealing but not classical. It was, in historical terms, a very young building.

The upper storey was faced with white, the lower was of brick, well-pointed, like a dolls' house. Leaded windows and some coloured glass. A wonderful garden, trailing flowers. Even here, he could smell the night-blooming jasmine through the open car window.

Into one of the downstairs windows of the house, a figure moved.

It was a woman's outline. Mrs Alliat?

As she stood there against the light, a silhouette, he caught the silver aureole around her hair. She held her shoulders, arms crossed over her body. She was looking out.

Could she see him? She didn't look as if she was dressed for bed, and might be concerned, noting an unknown car lurking across from the house. He should go over, reassure her.

Rawthorn got out of the car. As he did, she slipped back from the window, and suddenly all the lights were dimmed down to a honey dusk.

As he walked up the drive, Rawthorn heeded the garage. Only big enough, he would say, for one big car. The ground was dry. Tyre marks were not to be seen.

When he knocked, she came at once. Leigh had described her so expertly, colourfully, Rawthorn felt he knew Mrs Alliat already. Except, she was wearing a different dress. A long-sleeved black number. Although, below, the rabbit slippers had stayed faithful.

'Good evening,' she said.

He showed her his ID.

'Detective Inspector Rawthorn. Nothing to worry about, and I'm sorry to disturb you. I wonder if I could have a quick word. It's Mrs Alliat?'

'Yes.'

She didn't say, *How do you know?* Nor was she confrontational, as many women would be, even women in their sixties, summoned to the door by an unheralded police officer well after 11.00 pm.

She led him straight through (yes, limping) across the described white carpets, into the vast room with the gallery and the sky ceiling.

And then she stood there, bending gracefully before him, a slender willow before the potent storm of male power.

'May I offer you a drink, Inspector?'

'No, thank you.'

'A coffee, then. Or some tea?'

'No, thank you, Mrs Alliat. This shouldn't take long. Did you see me outside? When you came to the window?'

She shook her head. She smiled. 'I'm sorry, no I was … just dreaming.'

Her words were so inappropriate, dreaming, dreamy, and sorry she hadn't seen him, a man. A man should always be seen, unless a girl was girlishly dreaming.

She seemed relaxed, *malleable.* But she kept rubbing her arms, tenderly, as if she were cold on this night that still nursed its warmth indoors. Or nervous. As nervous as Leigh Dover had seemed to be?

'Is your husband about, Mrs Alliat?'

'George? No, no. He's resting. I'd rather we didn't …'

'You mean in bed?'

'Not really. Just on the couch in his study. He has to be away about 4.00 am tomorrow. To catch his plane.'

A terrible sadness swept through her face. Dramatic. More than sadness, a sort of despair.

'He's going somewhere, Mrs Alliat?'

She rallied. Gamely.

'Oh, yes. To South America. It's not for his work, it's a holiday. He works so hard, Inspector. He needs a break. He'll be gone three weeks.'

'But you're not going with him.'

The pain flickered again behind her skin, like white flame under smoky glass. 'No. No, George likes a little time alone. It – recharges him. And I'm happy here. Of course, I miss him terribly. I'm silly about that. But he does need to get away. I just put myself into my gardening, and remind myself how nice it will be, when he comes home. Something for me to look forward to.'

'In three weeks.'

'Sometimes he's away a little longer than that. He wants to extend his stay, and changes his ticket –' She checked. She said, 'Not this time. I don't think so. Just three weeks.'

Rawthorn considered. Should he get her to persuade Alliat off his couch? Had the holiday been booked a long time? Had Alliat decided to go recently? Tonight, say? South America was a fair distance.

She seemed now rather flustered and uneasy. But mostly there was that surging pain, coming and going. Alliat leaving her for three weeks, or more, hurt Mrs Alliat. But she was submissive, and docile. He came first. He needed his – privacy.

'He booked the holiday when, Mrs Alliat?'

Rawthorn thought he shouldn't be asking that, not yet. But she responded, unwary and naïve, or simply femininely assisting. 'A month ago, Inspector. I can't fetch the paperwork – that's what George always calls everything –' she laughed, softly and lovingly – 'paperwork. I'm sorry, but it's locked up in his desk and I don't want to disturb him –'

'No, Mrs Alliat, there's no need.' He gave her his wide,

disarming smile. 'That car that went into the ditch along the lane. I think someone called here?'

Mrs Alliat looked at him blankly. A total blank. 'I beg your pardon?'

'I'm afraid the driver seems to have vanished, Mrs Alliat.'

She looked puzzled now, as Leigh had described, and distressed by her own ignorance.

'I'm sorry – which driver? I don't understand.'

Rawthorn hadn't driven on, along the lane, to the spot where the car had come off the road. He had taken it for granted it was there. Unless by now the police or rescue had got to it. But there had been a lot of accidents that day. The services were stretched.

'I think a woman came to your house. A Miss Dover. She asked you if you'd seen the driver of the crashed car.'

Not pain now but wings seemed to fly up, behind Mrs Alliat's face of a faded yet still living Marilyn Monroe, a bit too old in her sixties.

'I'm so sorry. Of *course*, I remember now. Miss Dover. Oh, yes. George did like her so. Such a charming girl. He was very gallant to her, but he always is. George likes women. He says, I'm afraid, he prefers them to men.'

She rubbed her arms very fast now. Her face was vivacious.

'And you hadn't seen him, the driver?'

'The man in the car? Oh no. Did you say – he's disappeared?'

From vivacity to sympathy, and sorrow.

'It seems so.'

'How awful. And the car is up the lane?'

'Yes, Mrs Alliat.'

'Oh dear. I'm so sorry. Have you tried –' very diffidently – 'the hospitals?'

Rawthorn didn't bat an eyelid. He assured her they had.

Not only was there, now, not a hint of unease – let alone guilt – in her face, she seemed loosened. As if to be sad for the plight of another was an intriguing pleasure. An *enjoyment*. Like George's break in the sun.

'Anything could have happened!'

Markessa raised her trumpeting face and glared at them, Jack and Jula, then at the two cats on the table, eating garlicky lamb off Jula's plate.

'Sit down, Markessa,' said Jack. He was peeling an orange.

Jula settled the refilled coffee pot.

Markessa yowled: 'Don't give me orders! You're bloody mad, the pair of you. Don't you realise how late it is? Don't you realise the police said the car –'

'What do you think's happened then?' asked Hastings politely.

'What do I think?' she spat at him. 'I think he's left *her*, for a start. Who could blame him? I think that's what he's done. And I think he's under stress, really upset. Maybe he's had one of those lapses of memory you hear about – he doesn't know who he is –'

'Sounds like Steven,' agreed Jack Hastings. The cats came to investigate the gravy left on his plate, and veered away from the orange. 'Sorry,' said Hastings, moving the orange from their vicinity, and the plate closer to them.

'You!' screamed Markessa. 'And those filthy cats! Their *tongues* in the food – when they lick their own bottoms – and each other's! – it's *foul*!'

'Hasn't anyone ever licked your bottom, Markessa?' asked Jack, concerned and sympathetic.

Markessa let out a sort of steam-kettle shriek, and in the hall the phone rang loudly.

Jula tensed. But Markessa cried, 'Steven –' And sped from the room.

'Do you want me to get a cab and send her home?' Jack asked Jula. 'You've got enough to deal with.'

'How would you get her into a cab? I think she means to stay here.'

'Oh, I'd club her first, of course. I'd force myself.'

Out in the hall there was what sounded like a physical struggle going on, Markessa shouting, and something falling with a smash.

'You fucking pervert, get off the line. We *need* this phone line clear!'

Another crack as the receiver went down.

Markessa erupted back into the room.

'What broke?' Hastings inquired. 'The phone?'

Markessa ignored him. She shouted at Jula. 'That insane old woman again, that breather – can't we get her stopped –?'

'What was her number?' Jula asked without expression.

'Number? *I* don't know.'

Hastings got up and went out, and Jula sat facing Markessa across the table and the cats.

Markessa was very flushed and her make-up was very shiny. Whenever she shouted, spit flew out of her mouth past the remains of her lip-gloss. It happened again now.

'He loathed you, Jule. You know that? He did, I promise you. He told me what you did to him.'

'What did I do?'

Screw her, she looked *interested.*

'What *didn't* you? He would have left you. Now he has. You selfish, rotten cow.'

Hastings returned.

'It's the number of the FM in Seatree.'

'The *what?*' screeched Markessa.

'Fighting Man.'

'Yes, yes, I *know*, I *know* what it is. What are you talking about? What does it matter –?'

'It means the lady obscene caller is calling from the Fighting Man, and doesn't know enough to withhold the number.'

'Sod her. Sod it. *What about* Steven? *There* –' Markessa hissed – '*there* – I can hear him outside – listen – listen –'

Hastings saw Jula freeze again. And they waited again, in their weird stasis of before, that time that a car had made a sound down the lane, or Markessa had thought it had. Now, there was nothing.

Jula spoke, evenly. 'No, Markessa. There's a fox about, I saw it earlier. You probably heard the fox. And Steven wouldn't walk, would he? If he didn't have his car, he'd get a taxi.'

And Markessa began to cry. Streams of water exploded from her eyes, leaving her water-resistant mascara callous in its immaculacy.

'Oh, Markessa.' Jula stood up. She came over to Markessa and sat her in a chair. 'Jack, get her a brandy, please.'

I want Steven,' choked Markessa through her flood. 'Don't let him be gone. Please don't let him be gone. Oh God, please.'

Jula's face was stricken with compunction.

Jack Hastings glanced at it, and marvelled, yet again, at his exquisite Jula's capacity.

Knox had phoned in, and the duty sergeant presently handed the receiver across. 'The boss wants you.'

'Rawthorn, sir.'

'Hi, Ed.' Yes, he had been watching that videoed episode. 'I thought you'd still be about. What gives? Anything?'

'Not anything I can pin down, sir.'

'But he hasn't turned up?' asked Knox, more Englishly.

'No. I tried calling his partner, Ms Cork, but her phone's out of order. BT are checking it. Normally I'd have expected her to have called here by now.'

'I might pop by. Nothing doing indoors. Herself's in bed with her cocoa, or her daiquiri, whichever it is. Are you hanging about?'

'Yes, sir.'

'TV's on the blink,' said Knox. 'And the doorbell keeps going off by itself. Had to disconnect it. Anything else you want to confide?'

'The woman at the hotel, Ms Dover, mentioned a couple living just up from the scene of the accident. A big house. I went and took a look myself.'

'And?'

'The man wasn't around. Just the woman, well-spoken, sixties. The name's Alliat. She said she didn't see Steven Grace. Exactly what she told Leigh Dover earlier.'

Knox said, 'Knew her brother, Ben.' Then made the pip-

pipping noise he used when he wanted silence. Rawthorn remained silent.

'Alliat,' said Knox. 'I know *that* name. Why do I know that name? Something scummy. Something chummy? And those Alliats didn't meet Steven Grace.'

'Apparently not.'

'You're a bit doubtful?'

'A bit.'

'Whyzat?'

'It's something about the set-up.'

'Vague, Detective Inspector. You're such a responsibility. You need Father, don't you? Meanwhile, keep trying the partner, this Julia bint.'

'Yes, sir.'

'That's the spirit, my son.'

Not particularly cunning, as the countrysiders would tell you, the fox came first into the hollow down by the wall, where the monkey-puzzle trees grew high, their velvety claws losing a grip on the moon.

The food wasn't there yet. But something was. The fox disliked it, and ran away.

Ten minutes later, half an hour later than usual, because she'd been on the phone to her sister in America and lost track of time, Denise Hamilton came along the side path from her large red house.

Here the front garden sloped, through neat rockeries, to bold trees, the remains of an ancient wood, and so down to the wall above the road. From there, if you wanted, you could just see the lights of Seatree. But Denise liked to forget that, and pretend she was in the heart of the forest, where wolves still lurked by night.

She called the fox Wolfie. She had half a cold chicken for him that night.

When she struck something with her foot, something at once too soft and too hard, Denise looked down and dropped the chicken. It slid away into the bushes by the wall.

About twenty minutes later, when Mr Hamilton could leave her, he called the police.

Some people had foxes, others claimed to have fairies. The Hamiltons now had the dead body of Steven Grace at the bottom of their garden.

4

Inside five minutes, Leigh was deeply asleep. There were no dreams.

Waking, she felt at first drowsy and contented. And then a wave of adrenaline swept in on her, crashed against the beachhead of her mind. As if doused in cold sea water, she was rigid, shivering, tingling and panicked.

This happened very often. Familiarity didn't however make it more endearing. Or the remembrance of what might have caused it.

Serotonin in the brain, the new doctor had told her. Pre-menopausal symptoms, possibly. Would she like an examination and a blood test?

Leigh sat up. She knew where she was now. The hotel in Seatree. She switched on the bedside lamp.

Quarter past 11.00, the clock said. And she had lain down at ten past 11.00. Just five minutes of sleep, then. It had seemed like a century.

She knew from experience she had no chance now of sleeping again for at least a couple of hours.

The best thing was always to get up at once. Make mint tea from the teabags she had brought, read a book She could even plan her day tomorrow. Where she was going to go, what she would want to see, the places of her youth. Dad's grave, too, and her mother's next to it. (That wouldn't be so heart-breaking, not now, more ... consoling, oddly. The green garden of white stones, with the old Saxon church on the hill. The trees just touched with autumn.)

Above all, she mustn't lie there thinking.

When she had made the tea, Leigh drew back her curtains

slightly, and looked out.

The hotel had seemed very quiet. No-one was on the terrace, although the pool floodlight was still on. Then Dexter appeared, running barefoot in his T-shirt and pyjama trousers. From his hand trailed a length of string with something tied to it. Oprah the cat raced after him, batted the tied thing with her paws, snapping and trying to catch it. Round and round, round and round.

They made no noise at all.

What an unnerving little boy he was. Handsome, and somehow pathetic, as well as slightly sinister. Oh. Sinister Dexter.

Perhaps Honor had called him that very name in a sort of mediaeval urge to direct and protect him. The way children were called after the saints.

Leigh sat in the armchair, trying to be comfortable.

She had a feeling, if she had said all that to the Inspector, he would have been interested. Laughed at the figure that put sinister with Dexter. Or perhaps not. Inspector Rawthorn had been very correct. And alarmingly quick. But then *she* was rather slow on the uptake, wasn't she? First class at art, and its history, its means and makings, but hopeless out in the big, bad, real world, which the great painters had bent to their will.

Life's not the way it's painted, you know. Someone had said that.

She knew. Of course she did. She wasn't entirely crazy. But she'd been so lucky, got away with so much. Kind and caring parents, a good education, a talent for her own subject. Even her love affairs had been happy, exciting and, ending, never worse than sad. She'd stayed friendly, just as in the clichés, with almost all her lovers. Until there came that day.

Don't think.

All right. Think about Rawthorn, then. Why not?

She didn't like the police. Not anymore. It wasn't their fault, she knew that perfectly well. But even watching them acted in a TV drama now made her queasy. So much so that she would switch it off.

And Rawthorn was a policeman, the plain clothes kind. Indeed, his clothes had been very plain. In fact – what on earth had he been wearing? Something grey – light fawn – she couldn't remember. His hair was – between brown and light brown, perhaps. His eyes – his eyes had been very clear. What colour? God knew. And he wasn't particularly tall, a few inches taller than herself, she thought. Firmly but not stockily built.

So there he was, not tall, not short, not thin, not overweight. Medium colouring, as they said. Features that weren't unattractive, but weren't *arresting*. The kind of man you forgot the minute he was gone. Except, she hadn't.

He had the most extraordinary personality. Leigh Dover could look at this subjectively, since she would never want to capitalise on it sexually. But there would be plenty of women, she thought, who would want to very much.

Inspector Rawthorn had a type of electricity, the thing they called charisma, only it was more than that, and different. Because he could withhold it. *Disguise* it. And then, without warning, it was switched on, full power, like a glowing lamp. And he – came alive. He filled the canvas.

He'd done this with her. Which certainly meant he didn't know anything about her.

He'd done it, as a chameleon, lying ash-pale in ashes, shifts into full sunlight and changes into gold.

A waste, Detective Inspector. Sorry. A real waste on me. Although I have to admit, I'd give you a first class diploma for sheer ability.

When she'd dropped the glass though, what had that mind of his deduced? Well, don't think of that, either.

After she'd drunk the tea, Leigh got back into bed. She opened one of the books she had bought herself, essays on the pre-Raphaelites, and would have surprised herself, had she known it at the time, by falling asleep at once.

Only to be woken again, after a further 15 minutes, by Honor McCarthy's frantic, guest-careless, bellowing under the window.

'*Dexter!* Come down from that tree! It's not for climbing, it's for decoration. I've *told* you, Dexter. *Dexter*, I'll give you such a smack! *Dexter*, do you *hear* me?'

He was in the bathroom now, the main guest bathroom that was never used for guests. In this house, it was always possible to tell, once you knew. And she had lived in this house for almost two decades. With him. And before that, in London, in that quaint street near St James's Park. Also with him. With her husband, George, her darling, her life.

She had known he wasn't resting, catching some sleep before the early start for Gatwick. She couldn't argue with him as some women would. *But darling, you* must *sleep. You say you never can on the plane. And it will be so hot when you get there.*

That wasn't her way. Not with George. Her lovely, special, angel husband.

Tomorrow he would be gone. For three weeks. No longer, after all. Only three.

She rubbed her arms, slowly, rhythmically. She would make an appointment with Dr Terry. She had hoped she wouldn't have to, but now, she thought she probably would. There was no point in not facing facts. She would need something. To cope. And Dr Terry was so good with her. He never asked many questions. He always accepted what she said. He was quite old, older than George. She had heard Dr Terry drank. How could you condemn him? The things he must have to see and advise on, so much suffering and distress. He was always very kind to her. She was grateful.

George also drank, not too much – although he had an excellent head. But this too was all the stress of his work, and she must do her utmost to help him. The firm of accountants would be lost without him, done for. Even now, even now, when he had decided to retire, it could only be partial retirement. He would still have to go into London once a month, he had told her. But most of the time he would work here at the house, with the computer. You could do that now. It was so clever.

She, of course, didn't understand computers at all. But there was no need for her to. (Even the telephone made her anxious and she made mistakes with it. George kept it in his office upstairs. Although, during his absence, it would be in the upper hall, for emergencies.)

She would be lost without George, just like his firm.

'I'd be lost.'

When he had explained the new working arrangement, last week, he had opened a bottle of champagne. He had said to her, playfully, 'Will you be glad to see more of me?' And she had taken his hand, and kissed it, as supplicants kissed the rings of cardinals.

If he was home, she could look after him properly. He deserved only the best, the absolute best. Her dearest, her George.

Repeating these things, sometimes speaking them aloud, she walked up and down the white carpet of the two-storey room. She did not look at anything, not even the dried things in the vase. Not at the stone apple. Not at the painting on the wall, or the clock without hands.

She was trembling so much. She felt sick again. But she shouldn't have a drink. Drink didn't suit her, she couldn't hold it. He would ask her if she had. He was always so careful of her. Gallant.

Three weeks. Only three.

But tonight would be gone very fast –

It would, it would.

And Dr Terry would see her tomorrow, because he was elderly and kind, the old sort of family doctor who was seldom to be found anymore. How lucky she had been.

She would get through all this, she always had.

Day always returned, didn't it, after the long night.

Yet it was so much worse tonight.

Impossible to deny this. Because – of what – had – almost – happened. What might have happened. If –

'Hush,' she said to herself aloud. Of all her whispering chants, that one must never be vocalised.

And then she heard the ebbing of the bathroom sounds. She knew he would be standing at the head of the stairs. And then she heard his voice.

'I'd like a whisky. Is that allowed?'

'*Allowed*? Oh darling – you only have to – yes.' She called, 'I won't be a moment.'

She hobbled – the pain in her foot never seemed to ease, but it would, it would, she must simply ignore it, there were others far worse off, she knew – quickly to the drinks tray. The decanter. She took it up and held it in her hands. Tears filled her eyes. Three weeks. Oh God –

When she came into the hall with the full glass, and the decanter, George Alliat was standing at the stair top, looking down at her. His eyes were bright, and hot.

'Here it is, darling.'

'Bring it up, Miranda.'

She always knew at once, when he used her name like this. The tears in her eyes spilled over. She couldn't help that. But her face suffused with the radiance of utter self-abandoning love.

'Oh, my darling,' she said. 'Of course I will.'

And climbed, with some difficulty, but such great eagerness, a look of joy, the stair toward him.

11.30 pm to 1.30 am

1

In the kitchen, the black clock had stopped ticking. Markessa realised this first. She began to cry again, more weakly now. The first tears, like blood loss, had drained her. (Temporarily.)

'They stop for a death.'

'Can it, Markessa,' said Jack.

'They do. They *do.*'

'Yeah, in 1800s fantasy romances. Not here.'

Jula said nothing, only slid the box of Kleenex, what was left of it, across the table.

The cats were gone, off into the savage and sane night.

'Shall I call the cab people again, Jula?'

'I expect they'll be here soon.'

'I don't want to go by cab,' nasaled Markessa, childishly. All her make-up had been sobbed and rubbed off, but for most of the waterproof mascara. Hastings thought the cosmetics company could have made a top-selling advert out of Markessa. Cry a river, and hardly a smudge. 'Why can't I drive my own car?'

'You know why. You're pissed out of your skull.'

'*You* drive me, then,' gulped Markessa.

'I may have had too much as well.'

Markessa wept. 'Steven would've. He would. He never got drunk. Oh God, where is he? I'll never see him again.'

The doorbell sounded, a fierce drilling *tring*.

Markessa squealed and flung up her head as if in terror. 'I don't want to go!'

'Yes, you do,' said Jack Hastings, drawing her up from the chair. 'Come on.'

Jula's eyes, black as the night outside, met his. 'Would you –?'

'Okay. I said I would.' He spoke again to Markessa, more gently now. 'I'll look after you.'

Astonishing and disgusting him, Markessa dashed herself round into his arms. Her snuffling, hennaed form burrowed into his chest, the hot young-woman smell of her, tinged with deodorised sweat, perfume, female angst.

'It's all right. Here we go. Left foot, then right foot. That's brills-ville, girl.'

Jula rose, and followed them out. The perfect hostess. In the corridor, Jack said, 'I'll take her down and see she gets in. Then back here, okay?'

'Yes, of course. Thank you.'

'I'll let the cab go, maybe. Bringing the van just back up the hill should be all right. It's only in King's Street North.'

He had had the beer, two glasses of wine, but an entire pot of coffee. Markessa too was very sobering. He'd chance it, for once.

Jula said, 'I thought the van –?'

'Could have been the heat. Maybe it's cooled off. I'll give it a try.'

'Take care of her, Jack.'

He grimaced and bundled Markessa out into the front hall. She was right; normally she did drive herself back, and somewhat over the limit. Never in this state.

The driver from Arrow Cars, standing outside, his white Sierra waiting by the garden gate, looked at the passenger dubiously.

'She ain't gonna be sick, is she?'

Markessa screamed with grief. Insult to injury.

'She's just upset,' said Jack.

'I can see that, mate.'

Piteously Markessa bleated in erratic reverse, 'I want to go home! Take me home!'

'Have a heart,' said Jack to the driver. Who had one.

As they walked up the path, Markessa struggling faintly,

tottering and turning on her blue heels, the driver elaborated dolefully, 'Y'see, had this geezer in last week, brought up everything all over me new upholstery.' (And it had been a curry.) 'Firm's car, but I had to get it cleaned. Meant I was off the road, lost money.'

'It's a hard life,' said Jack, with genuine commiseration.

'Dead right.'

Jack opened the car door for Markessa. Before she would get in, once more she clung to him like a limpet. Jula stood, a slender smoke in the unlit doorway of her house. Barely to be seen, yet seeing. So Jack put his arm around Markessa, held her, and stroked the sweat-flattened spike-stalks of her hair. 'Ssh. Come on, Markessa. Markessa? You'll be fine.'

Finally she was in the car, and Jack shut the door. He would have preferred to sit with the driver, but chivalry demanded otherwise. He got in next to the snivelling Kleenexy drunk mass.

The driver slammed his own door.

'Shields Street was it, mate?'

'That's the one.'

They crept down the track so cautiously, it might have been the driver who was half-seas over. But Bill Mills knew his drunks. Keep it smooth and everyone might be all right.

He'd had it up to here, to be honest with you. Arrow had a lot of drivers off sick with this stomach bug. Bill had come on at 5.00 this morning, and wasn't due off tonight until 1.00. Already been verbally abused, he had, by two cocky ponces out of the White Bull wine bar on Horse Street. Apart from no tip. Then there had been the maniac earlier, just stood on the pavement under a lamp, looked quite normal, with well-cut fair hair and a suit on, and a flash watch. And then suddenly he lets fly a chunk of bad language and a slop of canned drink, for no reason, all over the car as it drives by. God Almighty.

But a notion was blossoming in Bill Mills' exhausted, harassed mind. It had to do with Shields Street and the free car-park by the Co-op, and the proven fact that his own house was only two minutes' walk from there. Plus the cab radio, which had been playing up all day.

Norm in the office had already spoken on the blower.

'You picked up that fare yet, Bill?'

'Yes. This radio's bad again. Can hardly hear you.'

'You're okay. Clear as a bell.'

'Eh?'

'I said –'

Bill didn't answer.

In the back, the girl wasn't doing anything too dodgy, just sniffling to herself. The chap looked all right, but you could never tell. The curry-ejector had been speaking happily of his holidays one second before.

Over in that field there, with a gap in the fence, under some trees, a car had parked. No lights. Kids, likely, driven in for a bit of the other.

Good luck to 'em. Get your fun while you could.

Thoughts elsewhere, neither Jack nor Markessa noticed the sable car pulled in close under the trees, where by day the black and white cows, smelling of grass and life, stood swishing their tails at the flies.

There was something else none of them had seen, not even Jula. Up in the lane, where hedges blocked off the track beyond Markessa's parked car, someone had been crouched in darkness. Eyes like gun-sights had watched. And *they* had not missed much at all.

Having cleared the table of its debris of plates, glasses, mugs and used Kleenex (cats' healthy backsides and tongues were dirty, Markessa's nose-blown tissues acceptable?), Jula left the kitchen.

She opened the door into the back yard, a term from the States that truly applied here. It was a yard, and at the back.

Over the years she had taken up slabs around the edges, by the high walls, and planted tenacious things in plots of sun or shadow. Golden hop, Russian vine, ivy and clematis. They fought together, sometimes one winning over the others. Then the winner would have to be cut back. The prize for success, a severe pruning.

At the zenith of summer, the walls were a pageant of black-green, green-gold, white froth and hyacinthine blue. By now only the variegated greenness was maintained in the tapestry. Soon it would be only the ivy.

Jula liked the seasons for what they were. Blake might have put it into words, but she thought he hadn't. Churchman had.

Spring kisses all awake,
Summer's ember swells,
Autumn blesses with last birth,
Winter braces iron with first death.

There were pots of geraniums still standing, scarlet Roman officers at their posts.

She sat on a bench by the kitchen.

Through the open door in the garden wall, she saw the unattended outer garden and orchard, once someone's pride, now overgrown and tumbling down the hill.

But here, one falling hill soon became another rising hill. A potent land, never far from erect.

The cats were out there, in the fields and copses. She wished one at least was here. To hold.

Lavender, the mouse-huntress, could be a tender mother even to humans, putting her paws around the neck, letting the pain go unremarked on. Nero would do tricks, clown about to take your mind off it.

She had needed them, with Steven in her life.

Of course, he didn't … hadn't liked the cats very much. Useless, he said. Parasites. Thieves.

Well, Steven should know.

He never hurt them, not as such. Only ignored them or toed them away, shouted swear words. Shut them out. Suggested fur hats.

They had learnt quickly. So had she. But by then, it had been too late.

She had thought she loved him, but how could she? She

had never been shown Steven, even when he was naked in her arms, to *know* him. And before Steven, there had been Leonardo.

But before Leonardo – yes, *there* was love. She had been happy then.

She grew up (what a strange phrase that was), in a two-room flat with kitchen, and shared bath and lavatory, in Eltham, South East London. That was, she *began* her growing up there, with her parents.

The flat was at the top of a peeling yellow house, which had white Georgian pillars at the door, and wide sash windows. There was no central heating, and even in her thirties, long after Leonardo and the perfect radiators, the hearths equipped with real logs, comfort to Jula meant a two-bar electric fire.

The story of her parents, which had become her story, was old-fashioned and ridiculous.

David Cork's father had been rich, a paper giant with a stationery empire. Leonard, the elder brother, made no demur at going into the family business, working solidly each week, deferring to the Old Man, and enjoying lunches and theatre trips and other perks. David baulked at it all.

When he got out, his father duly cut him off, in Victorian style, then relented and gave him a Victorian-style pittance to live on, which David took, as he always admitted. He augmented it with an ebb and flow of other 'unserious' jobs. He was an office clerk, waiter, male typist, pub pianist, part-time telephonist, sometime gigolo. Anything to pay a few bills. Nothing to stop him, as he had said, from *living*.

Feckless, so he described himself. A lily of the field. He had been proud of it, too.

When he met the beautiful Vivien Dunlass, this was more another point in common than something to stand in their way.

If Jula thought of her parents, she remembered them in an aurora borealis of lights. They had seemed to her magical. She had photographs of them still, and it was a fact, they looked like the film stars of that era, the '50s and then the '60s. Slim, graceful beings, dark-haired both of them. His eyes coal-black, and hers an incredible – the colour shots never caught it – peridot green. They should have been in pictures.

In a way they were. The Big Picture of life, the camera of Fate always rolling. Playing to that camera, and it loving them.

Jula had loved them. A love so powerful and – was the word *pure*? – so absolute that, only in her adult years could she recognise it as a love defined, in any context, as True.

And they loved her back. Almost – almost as much as they loved each other.

It had never occurred to her then. But there they had been, and then she had come, unplanned, unconsidered, except in the forethought of a diaphragm, which for some reason, this once, hadn't worked.

They'd told her that, in childhood. And that she was a bastard, since Vivien and David never bothered to marry. They only pretended to that state where it was necessary to avoid complications. They had impressed on her that she was a *love-child*.

They made her proud – though prudently never loud – about this, as they were proud of their 'fecklessness'.

But Jula had meant change for them. Previously they had moved many times a year, from room to room, from bivouac to hotel, in and out of London and its suburbs. For Jula's sake they took the flat in Eltham. David had already abandoned the most lucrative of his employments (prostitution). Now he took work that lasted months at a time. And Vivien, as soon as the child was old enough, gained a part-time job in an upmarket dress shop. From where she was able to bring home 'seconds' that looked, as David said, like a million dollars.

Sometimes, however, money came in a firework display. David had written one book, a collection of sketches and short stories. Printed, as a sort of patronising tax loss, by the publishing house in which Leonard had friends, the book received excellent reviews, and sold well.

Vivien, too, typed up fantasies she had told Jula, and once in print, they stayed so for years.

Usually in spring and autumn, cheques arrived,

unexpected – often quite valuable.

But there was so much to do, when not earning a little money to pay bills. No further books were written by Jula's parents. It was she who wrote.

They encouraged her. 'She's a genius,' said David. 'Yes, she is,' said Vivien.

Their occasional hysterical laughter at her work they did not disguise. Rather than offend or hurt, they managed to show her she had the gift of humour.

The flat's two rooms were allocated from the beginning, living-room and bedroom. When Jula was six, her parents had decamped with the double bed and set it up, disguised as a couch, in the living-room. Jula now had a room of her own, shared only with two important others, the Rabbit and the Bear.

Later, when she wrote about her first childhood, in carefully distanced and disguised terms, Jula still received the professional criticism that she had put on rose-coloured glasses. Leonardo, too, had been stern. Despite rigorous cutting and reshaping, the initial world of her life retained a gleam that others found 'cloying', or 'patently invented and unbelievable'. So many childhoods were unhappy, Jula acknowledged, that it was hard to countenance her own, that is, the childhood of the first Jula and her parents.

But she couldn't quite rid her work of those giggly bus-rides with Vivien, the walks in parks holding the strong and gentle hand of her father.

The flaws she tried to find – and found – or that were found for her by others, stayed intransigently insignificant.

For example, that the Cork-Dunlass flat was untidy. Books, papers, paints, records, shoes, lay all over it. While Vivien's clothes, her astonishing 'seconds', hung lopsidedly by hooks at the end of the hall, where the dusty stairs led down to Mrs White in the flat below, and the shared bathroom.

It was always turmoil. Perhaps not notably clean. The kitchen had crumbs, the cooker was wiped whenever, and once there were mice, which Vivien and Jula fed secretly (unsensibly?) by night. Needless to say, someone must have found the mice lower down the house, and someone else came and killed them all. That day Vivien and David took Jula to the pictures, and afterwards they stayed overnight in a hotel. (So providing evidence for deduction years after.) At the time, when Jula presently asked where the mice were, Vivien told her they had moved to the seaside. So her parents told lies. Pity those who can't.

Pets anyway were inadvisable in the flats – especially since the man who rented the basement and garden threw stones at all the local cats. For this reason too, that of complying with the taste of the neighbours, David had never bought a piano. They did play a gramophone, up to a nine o'clock watershed. However, Mrs White, met in the hall or on the stairs below, was always saying, 'Oh that was lovely, that music last night. Mind? It's a concert for me. And *he's* deaf, my Harry. He don't hear it.'

Some evenings, Vivien and David would go out, to X-certificate films Jula wouldn't be let in to, or to pubs, where in those days children were not allowed. Then they left Jula alone in the flat. She supposed it would be illegal now. But she never minded, amusing herself in endless ways. Once, on a night when she had been left, something black and terrible had seemed to bolt across the threadbare carpet of the living-room. Jula had duly gone down to Mrs White, as instructed to do if anything untoward should occur.

Mrs White valiantly searched with a broom.

'Was it a spider, lovey?'

'It looked too big for a spider. Anyway, I like spiders.'

'Do you love? Well, you're better'n I am. Maybe it was one of those mice.'

Jula said perhaps she'd just fallen asleep and dreamed it. She was very sorry, because if it was a mouse, then she wasn't afraid of that either, and Mrs White might be.

Vivien and David always returned from their outings exactly when they said they would, and never later than 11 o'clock.

They would come in, lightly tipsy, or simply energised, prepared to sit on Jula's bed and tell her the story of the forbidden film, perhaps demonstrating stabbings, vampires or exaggerated kisses.

In memory, her father's handsome Dracula, Vivien's green eyes and the scent of Emeraud, a perfume by then available only from France.

Uncle Leonard had given Vivien the perfume, on his visit. He had given David £200 in an envelope.

It was after this visit too that David had installed a phone in the living-room, but its use was rationed.

During those Eltham years, Jula had seen Uncle Leonard only twice. Though once David had gone to London to see him on his own, and come back very silent.

The night they went out with Uncle Leonard, when she was eight, Jula was quite excited, and her parents so beautiful they eclipsed even London, with its emphatic lights, studded again by blazing neons, some of which seemed to hang in the trees.

A huge white ship lay by the street of the restaurant, surreal, and the Thames was a sheet of hard obsidian streaked in fire.

As they ate their dinner, there was adult talk. (Only now did she see that her parents hardly ever spoke like adults.) What had been said? Adult Jula could guess. At the time, she had been aware mostly of everything else about her.

She recalled David saying, 'No, Leon. No. That's it.'

And Uncle Leonard, stiffly, 'You have a responsibility, David. I'm sorry, but you have. He's ill, you know. Has that penetrated? Out of decency –'

'And of course after what he said about Vivien?' asked David.

Vivien rose. 'Will you excuse me?' She held out her hand for Jula, who, unconcerned – what could anyone say about Vivien except praise? – slipped away with her to the ladies' room. Here they experimented with scent sprays and powder in bowls. It was the sort of place that seemed afterwards to have existed only in the then-and-now.

When they got back to the table, Uncle Leonard ordered liqueurs. The conversation had withered away to boring things. (David looked bored.)

Uncle Leonard was a mystery to Jula. He was not like David,

even though of the same build and colouring, and the same sort of looks. Yet where David was vivid and mercurial, Leonard was sour-jawed and dull.

(Jula could just recapture him when she was about five, during the visit, sat at the cramped table of the living-room in Eltham, nibbling crumpets, fussing for napkins, and unbelievably saying the tea wasn't hot enough, had Vivien waited for the kettle to boil?)

On the London train going home, Jula fell asleep.

In the morning, no-one mentioned Uncle Leonard at all, and they went to the park because it was a warm August, and Sunday.

In the afternoon they lay about in chairs, listening to Rachmaninov. They did that a lot. She could never play Rachmaninov now.

Bill Mills pulled up gingerly, at the kerb of Shields Street.

'All right? Three fifty. That's generous, mate. I won't say no. Been one of them days.'

Markessa opened her door violently, not noticing or caring about Bill Mills' wincing. She stood on the pavement, and then *slammed* the door. It was after midnight, and this part of town was sleeping, or had been.

'God, you got one there.'

'Luckily for me,' said Jack Hastings, 'she isn't mine.'

He got out. Markessa was stood waiting. She flung back her head and offered a wordless cry to the woken-up street.

'Shut it,' said Hastings. 'Some people have to work tomorrow.'

'My life is over,' declared Markessa. 'What do I care about their *work*.'

'Fine.'

He pushed her not too roughly toward the steps of her building, a tall, grubby semi now made flats.

Bill Mills curved the Sierra over to the car-park at the back of the Co-op. From there, he watched the man and the woman have some sort of altercation at the top of the steps, during which a key flashed and sang on the ground. Lord love us.

Bill switched off his lights. He turned the car mike right down, and just in time, because here was Norm again. 'Bill, can you hear me, Bill? I've got Reg down sick now with this gut-rot. Any chance you can do a bit extra tonight? Bill? Bill?'

He'd been waiting for that. He'd seen Reg in the office that evening, looking crook.

Now it would be, *Take a couple of hours off later, would you, Bill, and stay on, can you?* It wasn't legit, but there you were. Trying to earn a living.

Anyway, the radio was up the spout, wasn't it? If he took his break right now, that was too bad. He could say he'd felt funny too. Bollocks.

This was a mug's game. The driving was all right, but all these loonies about. There'd been a car, he thought, a smart one, following him as he came down from the countryside on the hill. But he was getting fanciful, through being overtired. He couldn't see it now, the car. Who'd it have been anyway? James Bond?

He needed a strong cup of tea and a cuddle with the old woman.

Bill Mills locked the Sierra and walked resolutely off across the car-park, heading home. He planned to be back by 1.30, since it was team spirit or the sack.

How could he know that when he returned, the Sierra would be gone without a trace?

'No, Markessa, I'm not going up with you.'

'Please, Jack. Jacky. Please. I'm so low.'

'There's the door. There's your key. You have to get up in the morning. Go and crash out. Take some aspirin.'

'They upset me,' she primly said.

'Some fucking paracetamol then, for Christ's sake.'

'You just want to run back to her. That snotty bitch. If you knew what Steven had said –' Hastings turned from her. He was down the steps. Markessa squealed, 'Jack – wait – don't leave me – I'm scared –' And he turned back. She had never seen him look *frightening* before. His face was pale in the sodium lights, carved from bones and a dangerous malevolent distaste. His blue eyes were black as Jula's. Blacker. He looked – murderous.

'Be scared of *me*, and get *inside.*'

Markessa turned and worked the key awkwardly in the lock. She slammed the door to shut him out. Ran up the stairs crying.

In the morning she would be embarrassed, worried at the things she had done, she vaguely thought. Possibly ill.

And she had to open the useless bookshop by 10.00 at the latest.

But the pain of loss caught her in a renewed spasm of anarchy.

Sod them all. Her life was in ruins.

The watcher watched. In the end, he had got out of his darkly gleaming car to do it. He took with him everything he might need. It wasn't part of a plan. Merely instinct, or supernatural guidance from the source he sometimes felt about him, in this uplifted state.

He drank the last of his Perrier. It tasted so beautiful. But cruel too, like this world.

From quite a precautionary way off, the watcher watched Jack Hastings cross the street and walk away, in the opposite direction.

That meant nothing. Less than the cabdriver.

Who could mean anything, tonight?

Only the woman. The red-haired woman in blue shoes.

The watcher put the Perrier can tenderly down in the gutter. Sweet can, lie soft.

Now there was no-one in sight.

He walked along the empty street, up to the house that was flats. Quietly. He had great abilities, there.

At the top of the steps, the watcher scanned the names above the bells. How lucky, or divinely inspired.

Two male names, one Asian name and then *her* name.

M Philbin.

He knew it was her – or *she* as they said in the US. (Better grammar often than the English. *Gotten*, for example. A mediaeval form of got. He could remember arguing that with Bash. Proving the point by reminding Bash that one did not say something was for*got,* but for*gotten*.)

They'd had a row, that man and this woman. Probably because she wouldn't let the man go up with her. It looked like it, watching from down the street, where the man couldn't see. She'd already been distressed.

But he'd heard the man call her by name, twice, when he was holding her close outside that house in the fields. Markessa. Markessa with an M.

The watcher pushed the bell beneath her name.

When Markessa heard the buzzer for her flat, she spoke into the intercom at once. It would be Jack. He'd realised what a bastard he'd been. He'd want to come up, and she'd let him. They'd have a drink; there was always cold wine in the fridge. Talk. He didn't want Jula. Who'd want Jula?

Jack was all right. He was sexy.

There had to be someone, now.

'Hallo?' She was coy, and cool.

'*Markessa.*'

She almost dropped the phone.

The voice, light and articulate, well-spoken – a blond voice – his voice? *His –*

'Steven,' she said. 'Oh thank God.' And pressed the button to open the lower door.

2

'Look who's here.'

Rawthorn looked, past Knox prancing in his skin. It was the pathologist, Smith.

He was like, Rawthorn thought, marvelling again at *how* like, an overgrown leprechaun. Thin, with a grinning brown monkey face. Not that a monkey would be at *all* like Smith. Funny that. The way no animals ever resembled those humans who could be, completely aptly, compared to them.

'Fine night, Chief,' said Smith.

Knox grinned boyishly. Rawthorn stayed blank. And they more or less forgot him.

Peering through the shadows, the lights, they all stared down at the body under the (apt again) monkey-puzzle trees. Was Smith going to be puzzled? Not for long, presumably.

But he would conduct this part as he always did.

'Now, Knox. What do you deduce?'

Detective Chief Inspector Knox scampered. Not literally. Just some sort of body language. He was a small, round man, with a thick head of grey wool, and the twinkling eyes of an optimist, who knew, if this was not the best of all possible worlds, for that very reason he'd get by quite nicely in it.

The body lay there, as they tended to.

A man, not normally classifiable as middle-aged, but past mid-thirties. Until now attractive to women, certainly, but no longer. The face looked puffy, and there were smears and crusts around the mouth. The lightweight summer suit was Versace, and the Swatch gleamed razor-bright on his wrist. He had £75 and a Visa card in the wallet they had found in the grass. No robbery, then. And no evident violence. He was stiffening up, but the night had been warm until about half past 9.00.

He had left his driver's licence a few feet away, with three pound coins, in a bush. Like the wallet, these seemed to have been shaken from him, most likely dislodged by movements of his own. On the ID he looked a lot better. But though death made him unphotogenic, he was still recognisable as Steven Grace.

Up the garden, among the rockeries and bird baths, Sterne, the SOCO, had positioned himself, with the photographer checking his camera, complaining it had been playing up.

'We-ell,' Knox cocked his head, 'it's not much on the theatrical side, but my first guess is a heart attack.'

'Ah hah,' said the leprechaun. 'And why's that?'

'He's got a look, I'd say. And he's coming into the right age range. Thirty-eight? Thirty-nine? It gets 'em young now; it's the way they live.'

'Go on.'

'Traces of vomiting, quite typical with heart. And then there's the general evidence. The give-aways.'

'Ah hah.'

Knox ticked off points on his pudgy fingers. 'He's not overweight, but that's all there is in his favour. There's the hip flask we found in the glove compartment of the car, smells of whisky, just as he does, and empty. Then the packet of twenty fags you can just see peeping from his pocket – in my day you didn't spoil a posh suit like that stuffing things in the pockets – not many left unsmoked by the way it's crushed. He may even have taken snuff.'

Smith in turn cocked his fluffy eyebrows.

'How's that?'

'Look there.'

They looked closer. Something shone on the ground, where it also had fallen from the pockets of Steven Grace, in his final galvanic struggle.

'Anything else?'

'That's quite a bit, I thought.'

'I'll tell you, Knox, I had an uncle, smoked seventy a day and drank a bottle of scotch. Lived to be 99. He only died because he broke his neck falling down the pub stairs, chasing after the barmaid.'

He and Knox laughed.

The laughter carried in the still, faintly-tree-rustling night. Rawthorn thought of the old superstition that you should keep silent when passing a monkey-puzzle tree. He was glad the Hamiltons had gone to stay with relatives in Battle.

Knox said, 'There's his little car accident, too. Enough to set anyone off.'

'It's not a bad diagnosis, Chief Inspector. You're getting very good. After my job, next.'

'No fear. I don't like knives.'

'Oh, we're too sophisticated for *knives*, now.'

'Not what I heard.'

'What about,' said Smith, 'the time of death?'

'Well he seems to be going rigid all right. The legs and feet less so? Beween 6.00 and 8.30, maybe. It's got cooler. May have slowed things down a bit. His watch stopped at 6.15. But with the crash and all, that doesn't help tremendously.'

'Still my star pupil,' Smith said, over Knox's big, round, furry head. Rawthorn nodded politely. 'But I'll tell you, laddy. I'm not with you one hundred percent. Not one hundred.'

Knox rubbed his chin, rubbing the words in hard. 'Yes. I've got an itchy feeling about this one. It's too neat. Too convenient somehow, for someone.'

'You have a suspect, I can see.'

'I don't know. But look at it this way, Smithy. The wife's no fan of mine, but if I was six hours late for a dinner party, she'd go up the wall. She'd try to *find* me. Be afraid that I was dead, because she'd want to kill me herself.'

'That's this Julie Cook, then.'

'Julia Cork,' said Knox.

Rawthorn added, idly, 'Jula.'

'Like the gold rings shop? Jeweller? Soppy name.'

'She's a writer,' said Rawthorn.

'Oh now look, he's been researching. Isn't he a good boy to

his old dad?'

'Seems so, Knox,' said Smith. 'Well, what do you want me to do?'

'It'd be a favour, I know,' said Knox. 'It's past your bed-time. But if you could open up the mortuary and do the doings for me. I'm not happy with this. Are you on?'

'If 'twas another, I would say him nay, Chief Inspector. But to tell you the truth, I don't want to go home.'

Knox said gently, making Rawthorn glance at him, as he always did in such moments, 'I know, Smithy. Chin up. Go and sharpen your knives.'

As Smith skipped away and the photographer moved down to set up for his shots, Knox said to Rawthorn, 'The old boy lost his wife last week. No, I don't mean he forgot her on the train. Cancer. He's got that big house out Crowhurst way, he hates it. The names he called her. Now he doesn't go home except to eat salmonella and oven chips and change his undies.'

'I'm sorry.'

'Yes, it's a stinker.'

They watched Smith dart lankily to his car and fold himself in.

'What about his team?' Rawthorn said. 'Are they going to turn out for him at this hour?'

'Count on it. Most of 'em. Times are hard and they'll like the extra money. You can sleep any time, can't you? Doesn't pay the mortgage. I'll send a couple of our boys down too, to work the lights and so on. Right, on with the motley. Who gets to go to the autopsy? DS Wren, for my money. Cast iron stomach. I'd sit in myself, but I think I'd rather have a chat with the Jewel as soon as she's identified the body. Or were you dying to watch Smith at work?'

'Wren's welcome to it, sir.'

'Thought so. What time is it? My watch isn't playing ball.'

'I make it 12.30.'

'Smith'll be on the off in an hour or less. He's tired of the living. As for our Jewel – what do you bet she isn't even in bed?'

3

Over the fields, something gave an eldritch chirruping. Almost undoubtedly an owl. It was cold now. Frost would soon be in the air.

Jula didn't move from the bench.

She sat back, her hands in her lap, her slim legs stretched out and ankles crossed. Like many slender people, it was easy for her to sit casually with charm. But she was unaware of this. Through the years, the endless compliments and envies had taken her by surprise. She had been loathed quite often as a 'chilly bitch' for her 'false modesty' and 'arrogance'. But behind the glass wall that separated her from the world, Jula was not particularly aware even of that. It meant nothing much.

The people she liked, and therefore noticed, never made dramatic demands of her. Steven had seemed like that. And with Steven, the glass wall had begun, centimetre by centimetre, to lower itself. When it was halfway, she had loved him already. But as he sprang forward like a bank robber to reach in, grab and destroy, the wall rushed automatically up again, stranding her behind it. Still in love, oh yes, for some while still that, but shut back in her crystal case.

Leonardo had started it, the idea of it. 'One must have pride in oneself. To thine own self be true, Jula. Who can hurt you then?'

You could, she thought. *You and Steven.* Even behind glass.

When she was a child, she had been – also a surprise to her, although in a different way – liked at school. Not popular exactly, because she wasn't a swarmer, happy only in a crowd. A solitary child, but attractive and mild-mannered, polite and intelligent, vocal yet untalkative. These facets brought her approval and sometimes momentary trust, never betrayed. Seldom rancour.

The boy who protected Jula from the jealous little girl pulling her hair, said next that he fancied Jula. He was seven and she was seven too. She was kind, receptive, but not encouraging. She told no-one else. If he wanted to walk along the street with her after school, to where David, and sometimes Vivien, waited on the corner, Jula let him. She let the boy kiss her chastely on the cheek. But really she was elsewhere, even then.

She didn't need other children. They interested her somewhat, as some of the lessons did, and the more talented teachers. But Jula believed only in the reality of her mother and father.

She wondered, years after, all grown up by then, and alone, if the intensity and perfect happiness of her relationship with her parents would in the end have ruined her for any other kind.

Would she have lived on with them, sharing days and partial nights? Going out now and then for brief sexual affairs, just as they had slipped off to the pub and the X films? Always returning to them, as they had always returned to her?

Would she have been clinging on to that triumvirate life until the day of their deaths? By then perhaps herself a shell, sixty years of age – for somehow she sensed they had been meant to live long, David and Vivien.

But that too was childish. It's the child who thinks its parents must never die.

It was about a year after the second meeting with Uncle Leonard that the solicitor's letter came. And, by the next post, the letter from Leonard himself.

Excitement. Jula joined in, not understanding.

Vivien said, 'We can get a piano now, Jula. And Jula, we can have a cat.'

Jula was in the seventh heaven.

So the house represented instantly this extra pleasure and delight.

It was explained to Jula that her grandfather, David's father and the father of Uncle Leonard, had decided to give Jula – Jula, not David – a house in the country toward the sea. It would become hers in name and deed on her twenty-first birthday. Until then, she might live in it, and so, incidentally, might Vivien and David.

'You're a lady of property,' said David.

There was money too. It was Jula's, but David might draw on it, for her.

He had been working in a tobacconist's and, since it made him, he said, smoke too much, had walked out last week. Vivien, on the contrary, would have to extricate herself from the dress shop, where they always panicked at the possible loss of her.

'When can we see the house?' Jula had asked.

Apparently they might go down to look from the start of next week. Next week, then.

Two days before the planned treat, Jula woke up with a cold.

Her colds never lasted, but it was a sharp, rainy late spring, and Vivien decided Jula shouldn't travel. It would be a long journey, up to Charing Cross, then down to St Leonards or Hastings. There was actually a station near the house, but you felt you *had* to see the sea first. Then, maybe after a fish and chip lunch, they would go back inland a few miles, by cab with driver, cabs being suddenly affordable.

Perhaps through willpower she would be over the cold in time.

That morning – it was a Wednesday – Vivien took her temperature. 'It's all right. But *you* don't seem quite right yet, do you?'

Jula shook her head, which felt sodden and heavy. She didn't.

David said, 'Well, we needn't go.'

They looked at her, Vivien and David.

Jula said, 'You go. You go and take photos, and come back and tell me.'

Why had she said it? So young, so attuned to them,

sacrificing her own first joy in the house that they should have it? What was hers was theirs.

After all, they could soon go there together.

They weren't sure. But then, the sun came out. It was an icy day but bright as a diamond. The sea would glitter and dance.

Vivien with her green, eye-matching necklace, the excellent oatmeal dress and coat. And David in his dark blue belted overcoat, that made him look more than ever like a film star.

Jula sat up in bed as her mother went down to Mrs White to make arrangements. Mrs White, as always, was amenable.

They worked out the times carefully, they showed Jula the train timetable. Vivien wrote down the sort of times that would elapse – from train to train, train to cab. At the house. A lunch, a drink, coming home.

'We'll be able to get this 8.00-something at Charing Cross,' said David. 'We'll give you a ring from the station coming back, if there's time – or if we miss the train. If we have to run for it then we can't. If you don't get a call, we'll be back by … what, Vivien?'

'About 9.00. No later than 9.30.'

'So if you don't hear from us, we'll be back not later than 9.30.'

They asked her (they the children, she the parent) if she could manage. Sat enthroned on her pillows, the Rabbit and the Bear to hand, books and transistor radio lying by, she laughed. Of course she could.

They kissed her. Vivien tucked her more firmly into the woolly cardigan. Half an hour later they were gone.

At 10.00, Mrs White brought Jula a cup of tea and two animal-shaped biscuits on a tray.

'All right, lovey? Do you want another bar on?'

'No, thank you, Mrs White. It's warm.'

'Well, they've got a good day for it. Smashing, at the seaside.'

At about ten to 11.00, the telephone rang in the living-room.

Jula leapt from the bed and ran to answer it.

It was Vivien who spoke first. 'We're at Charing Cross,

poppet. We're just going to have a coffee before the train. Are you all right?'

Jula said she was. David came on and said the London sky was lapis lazuli blue. 'Go straight back to bed and keep warm.'

'Yes, Daddy.'

In the background she could hear the grumble of trains.

'Goodbye, darling duck.'

Goodbye, goodbye … farewell, thou fair day –

The money ran out.

She hopped back over the cold landing to her cosy bed.

It was the last time she would ever hear their voices. Save in her head. The last time she would ever see them, except in a million dreams.

That was a happy, independent day.

Jula felt a lot better by the afternoon, after the sandwich and apple Mrs White had brought her at one o'clock. So Jula got up and made herself a cup of instant coffee in the kitchen. Then she went down and washed in the bathroom.

By 3.00, dressed, her hair in a pony-tail, she was sat on the living-room floor, drawing, with the electric fire on.

Her cold was almost gone. It was odd, ironic. She could have travelled with them.

But it didn't matter, did it?

She drew the house. In later years, Jula was startled to observe how accurate she had been, working merely on the estate agents' pictureless description. She'd even put apples in the orchard, like the fruit that had come with her lunch.

In the evening, about 5.00, Jula switched on the radio, and partly listened to uneventful news and current affairs programmes.

At 6.00, Mrs White appeared and asked if Jula, since she was up, would like to come down and have her tea with herself and Mr White.

Jula thanked her, and, lyingly, described the food Vivien had left ready in the fridge.

She didn't want to sit in with the Whites, who had a TV, as Vivien and David did not, and ate in front of it, as it blared and intruded, turned up to the range of Harry's deafness.

About 6.15, Jula had tomatoes on toast, as her mother made them, with a dash of mustard and sprinkle of Cheddar cheese. (She kneeled on a chair to reach the grill. Modern authorities would have been horrified.)

Probably they would eat all together soon, when her parents got back. There were often wild late suppers after their outings, macaroni cheese and frozen peas, or David's invented pudding with melted slabs of Cadbury's chocolate.

Where were David and Vivien now? She had thought of their whereabouts all day. By the sea? Still at the house? No, coming homeward now, on the rattling train. The landscape would go by, green and girt with trees. Sheep like fallen clouds, and brown-as-Marmite cows.

The sun was sinking by then. The evening was what David called a *wealthy* colour. Maroon and pink and a sort of mackerel gold.

Jula stood by the window of the living-room, watching behind the other houses and the high places of Eltham, the gilded lambency descending to the night. Day dying on the cinema screen of sky.

Stars broke out. Jula sat in her mother's chair. She put on the gramophone. She thought she would have time to listen to a pair of the Rachmaninov piano concertos, allowing a few minutes between them to avoid 'mental indigestion' (David).

And then she would wait for the second phone call from Charing Cross.

What had she played? The Second, almost certainly, and the Third.

In a trance, the child of nine. Safely adrift on a deluge of music.

Night came, and when she opened her eyes, the room was black. She'd slept? A street lamp picked out the edges of things, a silver lamp, for at that time not all the illumination of the streets was sodium.

Jula closed the curtains. She switched on the three side lights. The room looked friendly, but she would improve it.

Glancing at the new clock, she had been disappointed a little, because obviously there had been no time in the end for them to call before they caught the 8.00-something train. It was 8.30 now.

But it didn't matter. They would be home by 9.00. 9.30 at the latest. They had never let her down.

In the end, the room was as she wanted. She had put the bottle of sherry, bought last week, on a side table, with two green, washed and polished glasses. She had arranged biscuits on a tray. The cushions were plumped up, and the Rabbit and the Bear sat on the couch-bed, holding between them a carefully coloured paper, which read:

WELCOME HOME KING DAVID
AND QUEEN VIVIEN OF SEATRY.

She had spelled it wrongly, the place where the house was. Perhaps that was the great mistake.

At 9.00, she began to look out of the window. Cars came and went, and people were walking briskly up and down the road.

At 9.20, she left her vigil and went and filled the kettle, and put it on the gas on a low light.

She set the teapot and coffee jar ready, and lined up the bread, cheese and butter from the fridge. She felt she had been a bit dilatory about the butter, it would take ages before it was pliable enough to spread – it might take nearly until 10.00. At a quarter to 10.00, she rescued the boiling kettle. She went back to the window.

It was raining now, steel needles slanting through the white light. A few people ran under black umbrellas. A car or two swished past.

At 10.00, she went out and turned on the gas under the kettle again. She said, to the Rabbit and the Bear, 'They're late.'

Her voice, in the room she had known all her life, sounded too small, and too *young*, had she but known it.

At a quarter past 10.00, she remembered and again turned out the gas under the kettle, which had boiled almost dry.

The light in the kitchen was hard. Along the landing, Vivien's dresses hung, lopsided, here and there a button catching a strange light like a watching eye.

Downstairs there was the rough mumble of the Whites' TV, and lower yet, a rhythm-and-blues record playing mournfully. The house of flats was all alive and totally the same. And yet, it was not the same, the house. Not now.

Jula went into her bedroom, to see if somehow this would change things.

She had made the bed neatly, and drawn the curtains. Now she switched on the bedside lamp. No, the room was altered. There her paints put on a little table, the bookcase with her books – *Alice in Wonderland*, Hans Andersen's fairy-tales, *Cleopatra* ...

None of them was known to her. How could this be? All these years she had read them, and now they were these speechless strangers, lurking there, half out of the light.

Something else, too, was missing – on the mantelpiece of the blocked-in fireplace, the black clock, which Vivien and David had given her on her ninth birthday, with other presents, made no sound. It had stopped. She could never afterwards recall the time it said that night. And the next day, when someone moved it, the hands shifted. Loosely rolling, changing everything.

The living-room, as she re-entered it, was no room she knew. It had become very large. And cut in sectors by shadows. One could well believe now something black and unidentified had run across it, years before.

Beyond the window, the street was a street in an unknown city, depopulated, unrecognised.

At 11.12, Jula went down and knocked on Mrs White's door.

'My love – what is it?' exclaimed Mrs White.

Jula had been crying. She had wiped her face to hide it. She spoke levelly and clearly. 'My parents aren't back.'

'Oh, good gracious. But it's after 11.00. I was just getting his Ovaltine. When did they say they'd be home? It was 9.00, wasn't it? 9.00, Vivien said to me. But they'll have gone for a little drink, I expect.'

Jula knew this was not possible. In all the flighty measure of their lives, to this one thing they had stayed true. They were never later than they said. They had never let her down. 9.00 it should have been, 9.30 it could have been. Nothing else.

Jula stood staring at Mrs White's helplessness. In the past, going to the woman on a reflex of instruction, Jula had always found her adequate. But now they were both terrified. Neither could help the other.

'Anyway, it'll be some delay with the trains. But they'd have phoned … And there was nothing on the news. But don't worry, pet. Why don't you come in with me and Harry?'

Mrs White meant only comfort, but Jula saw before her the loud-papered room, bulging with foreign furniture and curios, its TV howling. Or, did she see before her this new alternative, all of life, foreign, and empty of love? She backed away.

'No – no, thank you, Mrs White. No, it's all right. I'll wait upstairs.'

'But you're all on your own, lovey. Come in and have some Ovaltine.'

A wave of perilous nausea swept through Jula. She shook her head, thanked Mrs White, and fled back up the stairs.

'If you change your mind, love,' called Mrs White.

'Thank you, thank you –' Jula cried, her voice ghostly, had she known it, as anything from a midnight tale.

And midnight came. It came alone.

And after midnight, Mrs White, unusually still vertical, knocked on the door.

'Jula, lovey. Let me in, Jula. Let me in.'

'It's all right, thank you. I'm all right.'

'But – are they back? I didn't hear nothing.'

'Not yet,' said Jula.

'What shall I do?' Mrs White asked piteously.

It was deaf Harry, somehow there and hearing, who replied. 'Let her alone for now, Mary! Come on downstairs.'

And so they left Jula alone, at the top of the house, in the deep of the night, and two unknown rooms, and an unknown kitchen, with the hanged dresses on their hooks, and the vast silence that surrounds all living things, and has only to be listened to.

About 2.00 am by the new clock shaped like a sun, Jula went stealthily to bed, clasping in her arms the Rabbit and the Bear, their banner forgotten.

There they lay, stiff as posts, three wounded in the midst of an invisible, personalised war.

She put out the light. She cried softly, not to attract attention.

The Rabbit and the Bear were soon very wet. And the room was icy, for she had, as always at bedtime, switched the fire off with the lamp.

Exhausted, she slept. Children do. They can. Before life, the *System*, takes it from them, that precious barbiturate.

The day was coming back when Jula woke, white on the edges of the room, as the street lamp had been in darkness.

Waking, she remembered. Or rather, she already knew. She had slept with the enemy of knowledge pressed close as her toys.

She got up, and padded through into the other unknown room. She understood that Vivien and David had not crept in by night, got into their bed, fallen asleep, all without a kiss. Without a whisper. Oh, she understood.

But still there was one last prayer in her left for that moment, opening the door and looking in.

Through the closed drapes, cheap and not thick, the dawn pushed its paleness. Nothing was there. No-one.

Jula kneeled on the carpet and wept with the Rabbit and the

Bear, until someone came at last; by this time she neither knew nor cared who it was.

After that point, in her memory, a cloud descended, as the curtains always closed after the Big Picture.

Vivien Dunlass and David Cork were never found. Police inquiries revealed that no-one had seen them, or recalled them at Charing Cross, or on the train for St Leonards and Hastings. They had never arrived at the agents' in Seatree to collect the keys of the house on the hill.

For a while the couple were spotted, together or separately, in Hastings, Brighton, Eastbourne, and on a plane to Orly airport.

None of these sightings led anywhere, and the objects of them, traced, bore little resemblance to Vivien and David.

A week after their disappearance, a handbag was discovered stuffed with some rubbish under the arches by Villiers Street. But there was nothing in it, and it was not an expensive or unique bag, only the sort of thing any smart, unwealthy, youngish woman might have owned. Offered a viewing by the police, Mrs White said it was *like* a bag Vivien had once possessed, and it might have been with her that day. But there was no certainty. There are always very few.

4

The Seatree night was not entirely silent as they drove toward the hills. Outside the White Bull, which kept open until 4.00 am, a group of local Beautiful People, rather older than one expected (as Beautiful People sometimes were), congregated on the pavement. Gilded limbs and eyes shimmering, frosted nails, Swatches, earrings. Behind them the bar's front windows, panes of glass held in place apparently only by matchstick-thin turquoise pillars. Sat in one, a vaguely smiling, unhappy-looking old man (like Old Age threatening some 17th Century tableau of Youth). As the car passed, he seemed to see and glance away.

'There's Terry.'

'Terry, sir?'

'The oldest doctor in East Sussex. My mum used to go to him, she says. Heart of pearl. I quote my mum, Rawthorn. She has a way with words, y'see.'

'Pearl, not gold.'

'Something precious formed about the torment of bits of grit. A doctor who hates pain and suffering.'

'That would be the general idea, wouldn't it?'

'Well, you see, my son. If you hate it so much it becomes unbearable, you try to shut it out.'

'But,' said Rawthorn, 'you said he was still practising.'

'And blind drunk, I hear, every night. He'll be in there till chuck out.'

Rawthorn turned the Ford Escort through the lesser streets, rambles of villas and small shops. Above, the hills in dark pelts rose against high skies and flecks of stars. As they had done for a million years or more.

When they slid up the gravelly lane between the fields and reached the house, no lights appeared to be on. A barn stood open-doored. It seemed to be serving as a garage, but the only car was parked further up, against a hedge.

Knox vigorously pushed open the gate in the fence.

'Blimey O'Malley O'Shaunessy.'

'Better prop it to the side, sir.'

'Come off in me hand,' said Knox. 'As they say. Wonder what *that'll* cost.'

He drilled the bell, holding his sausage finger firmly in place for quite a while.

'They must have gone to bed.'

'Then they must arise,' sang Knox. 'How many of them did you say were up here?'

'Grace's partner, Jula Cork, a man called Jack Hastings, and Ms Cork's friend, Markessa Philbin. Who, incidentally, answered the phone and gave us this information.'

'Jeweller, Cork, and Mark*essa* – what is this, Funny Names Night?'

The door opened.

The woman who stood there was, Rawthorn thought, officially one of the Beautiful People. That was, she was beautiful. She wore a black T-shirt and skirt and scuffed sandals, and her hair was a tangle of the night.

'You must be the police.'

He thought of Mrs Alliat. He didn't know why.

'If we must be, then we are,' amicably agreed Knox. He waved his ID as he always did, making it difficult for anyone to be sure of it, unless they executed a lunge and held it to see. 'Knox. And this is my sidekick, DI Rawthorn.' He was a con-man, Knox. And this woman, pale and composed, only gazed at him, and stood aside to let them in.

There wasn't a light in the hall. She led them through into a lit kitchen, where an appetising smell of food lingered, just settling to stale. The antique stone sink was full of dishes and matching brown water.

They went on into a small dining-room. Here a door stood open on the night. The smell in this room was fresh, flavoured by the geraniums and sleeping trees outside.

A cat sat on the doorstep, turning its head swiftly for one cursory stare.

'He's a fine-looking brute,' said Knox. 'Looks like a penguin with an orange flash.'

The young woman said, 'Yes. I call him Nero.'

'*Emperor* Penguin,' said Knox. He gave a laugh that circled like a friendly arm. Rawthorn tensed, and Knox said into the friendliness, 'And what do I call *you*, madam?'

'Cork,' she said. 'Jula Cork.'

Knox's face fudgily sank into gravity. His eyes bored into her.

Jula Cork did nothing, only waited.

'You'd probably like to sit down, Ms Cork.'

'Why?'

'You all watch too many detective programmes. You always know what's coming.'

'But I don't,' she said, still level. 'What is it?'

Knox said sternly, 'I'm afraid the news isn't good. It's bad. Bad news.'

'About Steven?'

'About Mr Grace. We seem to have found his body.'

'But you're not sure?'

Her response was swift. Hopeful?

Knox said, 'We would like you to assist us.'

'To identify the body,' she said.

'Yes, Ms Cork. And a couple of little things.'

'But it might not be him. Not Steven.'

'I understand you've lived with Mr Grace for three years?'

'Yes. We – I have.'

'Then I'm afraid I do have to ask you to do this.'

'Because you're not sure,' she said again.

That pedantic insistence.

Rawthorn had met women, and men, who flung themselves against you, imploring that the dead be not their own. This wasn't anything like that. She was cool as the night that genetics had made her eyes and hair from.

'Perhaps you need to get something, Ms Cork.'

'What?' she asked.

Knox shrugged. 'If you're ready as you are –' and suddenly – 'Do you need those tablets in the kitchen?'

'They're the cat's.'

Rawthorn said, 'Perhaps Ms Philbin could accompany you?'

'Markessa's gone home. Jack took her.'

'Gone home? Tired, was she?' said Knox.

'Upset, I think.'

'Oh, upset. Nothing like a friend in need, eh, Ms Cork?'

She said, 'I wouldn't know.'

'And Mr Hastings went with her?'

The cat in the doorway flicked its ears and turned again, and presently Rawthorn heard another vehicle crunching round outside on the track.

'Actually, I think that's Jack now,' said Jula Cork.

She walked back into the kitchen and, opening the fridge, took out two cans of premier league cat food, forking one each into a separate dish, before setting them on the floor. She filled a large bowl, labelled *Rabbit*, from a bottle of Evian, and placed it between them.

Knox watched. 'They live well, your cats. Two of them, is it?'

She didn't answer.

And someone opened the front door of the house, and walked without preamble into the kitchen.

So he had a key, this Jack Hastings.

Rawthorn looked at him, looked *up* at him, as many other men would have to. Tall and slim, a wolf's face, and long black hair tied in a tail.

For a moment, Rawthorn was at a loss.

Something ticked in his brain, the computer off on its search. *Where have I seen you? Where was it? And not very long ago.*

'Police?' asked Hastings.

'Police. Detective Chief Inspector Knox. *C'est moi.* I'm afraid I've had to give Ms Cork some shocking news.'

'*Christ,*' said Hastings. *His* face did alter, from mere wariness and dislike to a hard pallor. 'Jula –'

'They say they've found someone dead and it may be Steven. They want me to identify him.'

'At this time of the fucking night?'

He was shocked – or something more profound. He'd knocked about, Rawthorn could see it, and probably wouldn't normally shoot his mouth off in front of the Bill.

'It's nasty, isn't it, sir?' said Knox. 'The way of the world.'

After Jula had secured the back door – a key turned in a lock, nothing else – they went out onto the hill. No-one alluded to the gate lying broken by the fence.

A big, light blue van stood behind the car they had seen earlier. On the side, in arching black, was written GOTHIX.

'And that is your vehicle, sir?' asked Rawthorn.

'Yes.'

'Looks like a good one. Always use it, do you?'

'If I'm driving.'

He'd been drinking, almost certainly, but not a lot. In his own way, he was quite dangerous, Hastings. He had that aura.

And I've seen you, Rawthorn thought, as everyone got tidily and without fuss into the Ford Escort. *Not your van. But you. I've seen you today.*

The room was a sort of chapel. She hadn't expected that. He'd been right, hadn't he, the odd little man, this Chief Inspector Knox. It wasn't exactly that she had watched many detective dramas. Not even enough to understand about their ranks, these men. But she had anticipated a snowy hospital morgue, and a body drawn out on a tray. Like a frozen dinner from the freezer.

Mauve draperies hung down the wall. There were flowers – plastic, but meant well – in a vase.

The body was lying on an altar. That was what it looked like to Jula. Obviously it wasn't.

Also, Knox seemed to lead her forward – like a bride. Her father lending her to the altar, to her bridegroom. She stopped herself laughing the horrible laugh that rose up, raw and fluttering, in her throat.

Jula looked.

The face. Had she ever known it? No. She never had. The blond hair was damp-looking, greasy. The waxy skin, the mouth smiling slightly, as she had heard the mouths of the dead might, and there was even a name for the condition; it meant nothing at all.

One eye open a slit. A brownish hint of something there, like misted glass.

Stains round the mouth. What was that?

Steven was always so careful of his face, and teeth. Cleanness. Hygiene.

He didn't look clean now. Was death dirty?

'Ms Cork ...' softly.

'Oh, yes,' Jula said distinctly. 'This is Steven. Steven Grace. The man I lived with.'

Something in her vision. A top surface like transparent paper separating and floating up, and the underlying layer falling downward, into a flat non-dimensional nothing.

Knox skipped back. It was Rawthorn who caught her as she bonelessly dropped.

Like many slender, small-framed women, inert, Jula Cork was surprisingly heavy. But he only had to take her full weight for a second or so. Then she was regaining her feet. Punch drunk, but standing. He kept hold.

'It's – all right. Thank you. I can stand.'

Outside, when he had put her in a chair, the coroner's officer coming back with a glass of water, Knox standing there with his beady eyes merciless.

'Thank you. What nice water,' she bizarrely said.

'I'm sorry for your loss,' said Knox. Then, 'That must have been unpleasant. Identifying. In mediaeval times, everyone was afraid the corpse would bleed when they leaned over it. Even the innocent were afraid. You never know.'

'Why,' she said, 'bleed? Was he stabbed?'

Her eyes were still shut. But she seemed to be gathering herself in very well. Pulling herself, in the crass yet evocative expression, together. 'Not a mark on him,' said Knox, cheery.

Jula lifted her lids. There were hollows under her eyes. She sipped the water. She said, to the coroner's officer, 'You see, at my house, the water tastes of metal. Something wrong with the pipes, I think.' She looked at Knox then, straight at him. 'I didn't pass out from shock. Or distress.'

'No, Ms Cork?'

'No. It was from relief. I was so frightened it wouldn't be Steven. But it is. He's dead. I was praying he would be.'

'What do you think? Tell Father?'

'I don't think we can keep her here for long.'

'No? Not after that little outburst at the hospital?'

'It wasn't an outburst, was it, sir? It was just the truth. If she did it, would she hand us that on a plate?'

'Confession, my son. Confession. The needs of the soul sore--laden.'

'Then she'd have confessed. Properly.'

'And leave me with no work to do?'

Rawthorn shot Knox a look. Knox played on with his black biro, toppling it along the desk, making it run a race with a red biro.

'However,' said Knox, 'I'm not forgetting our other hobbies. Let's see. The Hamiltons who found the body were out shopping all afternoon and had a long dinner at the Pompadour restaurant, between here and Battle. The manager vouches for them roughly 7.00 to 9.05, and half a dozen shops will undoubtedly cover for them until 6.30. They *could* have nipped home in the odd half hour and bumped off Grace in the garden, but it seems fanciful. Otherwise there's your Miss Dover. And those Alliats that I keep trying to remember about – something fishy there. They bother me. And you say he's off somewhere abroad at 4.00 am? We'd better check him out before that. And I want a word with the upset Markessa Philbin. If only to find out how she got that name.'

'Yes, sir. And there's Hastings, too.'

'Him? He *is* too obvious, isn't he? Yes, I can see he likes her. There's his lack of finesse as well, when I get the impression he's usually a bit wary around us lot. But I don't reckon him somehow. Nah.'

'Let me help,' said Rawthorn.

Knox stopped the biro race. 'Go on.'

'I saw the end of tonight's *Ten O'Clock News*. The local stuff had some footage – it looked like a wobbly video – of a disturbance around six o'clock, on the Seatree Road.'

'Faulty lights on roadworks. The public won't stand for anything now. Hysterics. I often get the feeling,' said Knox comfortably, 'they're all mad now, all of 'em, out there.'

'The roadworks were just past the turn-off for Divers Lane, the turn-off Grace took between 6.00 and 8.30, going on the estimate of the time of death.'

'All right, so?'

'In the video of the crowd, I noticed two men. They were distinctly unalike, and one had grabbed hold of the other. It looked frankly odd – like some Communist poster of the '50s – Affluence struggling with Honest Toil – you know what I mean.'

'Hmm.'

'The only traffic I could see stuck there consisted of cars. I don't know which car or cars these two came from. One had a London haircut and a sharp suit, and the other had long dark hair casually tied back, and the same denim shirt he's still wearing. It was Hastings.'

5

Streamlined in their dark blue, the two warriors climbed the steps and rang a bell of the flats in Shields Street. By the kerb, the streamlined car. It was well after 1.00. No need to make a row. Not for this.

PC Tony Kenton and WPC Sharon Kenton. No relation, although perhaps soon to be, judging by the electric frisson that was in the air between them.

'*Yes*? Who's *there?*'

'It's the police, madam.'

'God, you took your time.'

Deadpan, the warriors looked at each other.

The buzzer went, and the door opened.

Ms Rajachatti was a sensationally lovely Indian woman of about 25, in a bad temper. She met them by her door on the second landing.

'For God's sake, why did I bother? I wasn't going to. That bitch upstairs. She's given me migraines! *Migraines*, do you understand me?'

'Yes, madam,' said Sharon Kenton, sweetly. 'My mother gets them.'

'Your mother – your mother – *I* get them. And I have to work all the hours God sends me, simply to hold on to this grotty flat in this stupid little street –'

They went into the grotty flat. It wasn't. Or she had made it not to be. It was *India* – although, oddly, a Westerner's idea of India, perhaps. Carpets on the walls, incense burners, a golden film of soft light. Ganesh, god of the physical world and its needs, in bronze. A scent of spices.

In a whirl of hair that, descending, hit the backs of her knees,

Ms Rajachatti flung out her arms, fingers, in the attitude of a temple dancer.

'I am sorry. So sorry. So *rude*. What must you think? Will you have masala tea? I made some – for my nerves.'

The smell of the tea was delicious, and Sharon at least was tempted, but they refused. A shame.

'You see,' said Ms Rajachatti, pouring herself the tea, and into a vessel like an azure eggshell, 'I work very hard. And she upstairs makes *noise* all the time. Banging about, loud music – I wouldn't mind if it was decent music, something classical, or someone who could sing. I have asked her, could she be a little quieter? At least after 10.00 pm. But no. She cannot. Won't.'

Sharon said, 'This is Ms Philbin? Have you tried –?'

'Reporting her to the council? *Oh*, yes. I have to make a list or keep a diary. I don't know. I haven't done it. I'm too tired to do it.' She drank the tea. 'Please sit. I am so sorry. It's so late and here you are.'

Her dressing-gown was a red silken sari-ish thing that Sharon would have killed to wear, and Tony would have killed to see her wear (they decided later) (but not who they would kill).

Ms Rajachatti sat, and regarded critically her own cinnamon feet with toenails of cinnabar.

'As a rule, the bitch is quiet after 12.00 midnight. She too must get up for her work, I imagine. Tonight this isn't the case.'

Like a Scheherazade, she detailed what had occurred. How she had been roused from sleep by shouts outside – the bitch – then made more wretched by the bitch galloping upstairs, making the sounds of a 'wounded buffalo'.

After this came a pause.

'I tried to return to sleep. But it wasn't to be. Someone else goes by my landing. Not very loud, I admit, But then – *then* –'

'*Then*?' queried Tony.

'There was a scream. A scream, like in a movie. And a crash. And then more screaming, and a man's voice, quite low – and next –'

'Next?'

'Nothing,' said Ms Rajachatti very seriously.

'You didn't go up to see?'

'I'm mad? *No.* Anyway, they go down presently.'

'They do, do they?'

'Yes, and out of the front door. Creeping now, so *quiet.*'

'You didn't,' said Sharon, 'by any chance look out of the window?'

Ms Rajachatti said, with an angry flash from her marvellous eyes, 'I have migraine by then. You say your mother has this too. Then you know, the vision goes. Instead all little zigzags and dazzles.'

'Yes,' said Sharon. 'My mother gets that. And then the rotten headache.'

'I have very good pills. Shall I recommend –?'

'That's very kind, Ms Rajachatti. But right now –'

'About what time did all this happen?' Tony interposed.

'After 12.00. 12.20, something like that. I did hear a car. But there are always cars here.'

'You waited a long time to call us.'

'I couldn't *see* the numbers on the phone –'

Ms Rajachatti appealed with eloquent hands to Sharon, who said, 'When my mother gets migraines, she can't make out much for about thirty minutes.'

'Thirty minutes to the dot!' declared Ms Rajachatti, bleakly triumphant.

'I think I'd put up with going blind for thirty minutes now and then,' said Sharon, 'to have eyes like hers.'

Tony said, 'You'd lose your job. And I like your eyes as they are.'

They climbed up the last flight.

They found the door of the upstairs flat with a broken lock. Someone had smashed it back against the wall, which had also chipped the plaster. This probably accounted for the crash that had been heard.

Inside, the flat was a parody of the appealing room below.

Comfortless was the word that sprang to Tony Kenton's mind. To Sharon, the decor was, she thought, an attempt at what was called Minimalist. But a Minimalist that had gone wrong.

White walls had two thin strips of abstract pictures. Resembling the described migraines. There were white blinds, and some black gauze looped over the curtain rail. Against one wall was a sofa covered in what Sharon thought looked like (hopefully fake) Dalmatian. Before it was a see-through coffee table no longer see-through, being covered by copies of *Cosmopolitan* and *House and Garden*, a gilt telephone shaped like a pineapple, nail scissors and a large roll of sellotape. A skeletal black bookcase, design-intended for three books and one object, sagged under a battalion of paperbacks.

'She likes bodice-rippers,' said Sharon.

'What?'

'Historical novels about swooning heroines and tough gentlemen on horseback.'

They looked around, glanced into a bedroom and a bathroom, and a tiny kitchen where, it seemed, nothing but toast and cereal had been eaten for years. Although the fridge had six eggs, some cottage cheese, a wilted lettuce, two bottles of white wine, and a carton of pre-ground coffee.

'Apart from the front door, no sign of a struggle,' said Tony.

'Yes,' said Sharon.

'What then?'

She bent and picked up, from under the coffee table, something that beamed like a Christmas decoration.

'What's –?'

'The heel of a woman's shoe, Tony. About three inches. Iridescent blue.

BOOK TWO

The Mask Of Night

'Thou know'st the mask of night is on my face,
'Else would a maiden blush bepaint my cheek,
'For that which thou hast heard me speak tonight.'

William Shakespeare

12.15 am to 3.40 am

1

As Leigh entered the dim bar of the Fighting Man, she saw that the only two living things there were: Oprah the cat, on the lap of an elderly woman with long, grey-white hair.

Leigh walked to the bar and silently stood as, she had been endlessly told, by non-Englishers, the English always did.

'I think our bar-lady's outside, looking for her son,' said the elderly woman.

'Oh … well I'll leave it,' said Leigh. She was fed-up, and sounded it.

'Can I offer you some of this, while you're waiting?'

On the woman's table was an almost full bottle of Pinot Grigio, stood in a vacuum bucket for coolness.

'Oh, well – well, why not,' said Leigh, thrown. 'Thank you.' She look a clean glass from behind the bar counter, and walked across. 'Leigh Dover. Hallo.'

'How do you do? My name is Katherine Churchman. And this exquisite being, I believe, is known as Oprah Winfrey.'

'Yes.'

'Can it be, I wonder, because she is black and so very pretty?'

'That would be my guess,' said Leigh.

'It doesn't seem quite politically correct, does it?' said Katherine Churchman, pouring the light, greenish wine almost to the brim of Leigh's glass. 'Or too much so, perhaps.'

Leigh drank the wine. 'This is perfect. I shouldn't really,

but I couldn't sleep. It's got to be a bit of a problem. And in a hotel –'

'I know. At home one can just wander round the house, find things to read, even switch on the television without fear of disturbing anyone else. So useful, all-night TV. Those classically bad horror films. And sometimes, of course, really excellent things tucked in about 4.00 am.'

Leigh found she had finished her wine.

Katherine Churchman leaned forward and filled the glass again.

'No – oh, well – you're very generous. *I'll* buy a bottle, and pay you back.'

The old woman's eyes sparkled. 'Much better than TV.'

How old was she? In her seventies, surely. The hair was glorious, halfway down her back, still thick and crinkly, soft as cashmere. Very lined skin, held firm on thin, sharp bones. Probably not one ounce of spare flesh. Paintable ancient hands, the left middle finger with a tigerish amber ring. She had silver earrings, too, dangling in the hair. And these grey owl's eyes full of life. And the actress voice.

Katherine Churchman had aged as Leigh herself would have wanted to, and knew now she almost certainly would not.

Honor McCarthy flounced back into the bar.

She took one look at Leigh and exclaimed, 'Oh Ms Dover, I woke you! I went and woke you up, didn't I? It's that Dexter. He's in the trees. He won't come down. Says he's looking at the marks on the moon.'

'But how wonderful,' said Katherine, 'to be so alert and imaginative. I thought he was, when we spoke earlier. That thing about the blue felt-tip on his face being woad.'

'It isn't wonderful, Miss Churchman, it isn't. Not tonight. He's got school in the morning.'

Katherine Churchman smiled, and ripples were gathered from her firm mouth of real teeth.

'But to develop the mind a little may be better than school, don't you think? All these tests and harryings. Education, you know, Mrs McCarthy, comes from the Latin, *educere*, which means *to lead out*. Both knowledge, and the pupil, are to be led forth, not crammed like shopping forced into a plastic carrier bag – which may then split. In all senses of the word.'

Leigh gulped her wine. Wow.

There was nothing overbearing about this woman. She could tell you things, using language like a familiar instrument, because they were there to be told. And she'd listen, too. You could *see* it. Or was that just the wine?

'Can I have another bottle of this, please?'

'Of course, Ms Dover. In fact you can have it on the house,' said Honor with a deciding flounce. 'To make up for me shouting under your window like that.'

She vanished through a door behind the bar.

'She did wake you, didn't she?' said Katherine softly.

'Well, yes. But I'd probably have woken up five minutes later anyway. Some pre-menopausal thing.'

Perhaps she shouldn't have said that. Katherine's generation were sometimes very shockable. Leigh's own mother, far younger, and so adorable and kind, had sent her at age ten to a book on the female cycle. Then again, Katherine's use of language itself seemed informed.

And, 'The menopause? Not always a pleasant time,' said Katherine. 'But it ends. And then – freedom.' Before she could stop herself, Leigh raised an eyebrow. 'I don't just mean sex without fear of pregnancy, Ms Dover,' said Katherine, unexceptionally. 'It's a coming of age for many of us, far more vital than 21 or 40.'

I know her name, Leigh thought suddenly.

And Katherine said, 'Like poor flustered Mrs McCarthy. She'll be a happier woman when she's past 55. And as for the appalling girl I had dealings with on the telephone earlier, I only hope she gets there.'

Leigh was relaxed. 'Really? Who was that?'

'One of the most stupidly rude women I have ever spoken to – no, been spoken to *by*. Rudeness, like everything, can be an art. Sometimes I've been terrifyingly insulted. But where there's wit, if not justification, one can almost enjoy it.'

'Can one?'

'Well, I can at this great age. But not, not that person this evening. And it was very frustrating. I couldn't get past her, and then the phone went wrong again. So I shall have to try tomorrow. It's been what they call one of those days. But in a way it *is* my fault.' She gave a laugh. It was throaty and deep, very different from her speaking voice.

Honor had come back into the bar. She undid a second bottle of wine and now stood it in ice.

'This should be quite cold already, if that's all right.'

She brought the bottle, tickled the cat behind the ear, and went hurrying off. Probably *she* wouldn't get to bed much before 3.00.

'You say the phone wasn't working. There's been sunspot activity. I heard it on the news. They seemed to think it had affected things, but it was clearing now. I suppose it's rather late for you to call back.

'No, that isn't the difficulty. The friend I wanted to see told me that she, like myself, goes to bed very late. Any time up to 2.00 am would be all right for telephoning. I say *friend*, I haven't met her yet. But one feels sometimes, doesn't one, that someone is a friend, from the very beginning.'

'Yes. It sounds nice. Why don't you try again?'

'I did, just before I came in here for my self-indulgence. I have a suspicion that the rude young woman banged down the receiver so hard last time that she broke it.'

'Do you have an address?'

'Oh yes. We've corresponded. And I should have written to her that I was coming down to the coast today. But it was a spur-of-the-moment thing. I was hoping very much we could meet, in person. But then the phone just rang, and then not even that, and the same thing when I got here. I'm afraid I've had a touch of the latest stomach bug, too, and it hit me rather hard this evening. And then – it was gone. Apparently the virus does that. But altogether, a muddle.'

There was nothing more than ruefulness in Katherine Churchman's face. Until she burst out laughing again. 'I think

I've solved the mystery, Ms Dover. Good lord. How absolutely *ridiculous.'*

Leigh found herself all sympathetic attention.

'You see,' said Katherine Churchman, 'I was out of breath when I called the number and finally got through. I'd just got upstairs, and my stomach was hurting. And the poor woman – how I've misjudged her – accused me of being a pervert – a heavy breather, obviously. It's only just dawned on me.'

'But it's – *You* of all –'

Leigh put down her glass and shook with laughter.

'Beyond price,' said Katherine. 'An anecdote my grandfather for one would have relished. He wrote so ethereally, but he was also delightfully coarse and quite daft among his friends and family.'

Still laughing, Leigh said, 'He's *the* Churchman, isn't he? The poet? A contemporary of Tennyson.'

'Oh yes. I'm so proud of him, still. I'm so glad people still read him. He lived to be a hundred and four. And he wrote his last poem on his deathbed. Only four lines.'

'I know it,' said Leigh. The wine laughter left her, and the tears of the vine filled her eyes. She spoke carefully and musically for Katherine:

'Spring kisses all awake.
'Summer's ember swells.
'Autumn blesses with last birth.
'Winter braces iron with first death.'

Norm was sharing a Mars bar with the dog, when the phone went.

'Arrow Cars.'

'Norm. It's Bill.'

'That's a bit of luck, Bill –'

'No, no it ain't. I've got this gut thing. Real bad, Norm. I can't move. Not in this state.'

'Jesus, Bill. I've only got one driver now, mate. And there's a run to –'

'Norm, it's no good. I'd be a bleeding danger. Not to mention the upholstery.'

'All right. All right. You sound pretty shaky. Give us a call as soon it you can. And if you feel any better in an hour or two –'

The phone went down.

'Well, Chubby,' said Norm to the black and tan Alsatian, 'I just wish you'd passed your test by now. I could really do with you tonight behind the wheel.'

Chubby looked concerned and willing, but then he always did if there was a chance of another Mars bar.

In the phone box off Shields Street, Bill Mills checked his watch on reflex. Just before 1.00 am.

He'd been too scared to spin it out at home any longer, and he'd come straight back after a sandwich, a cuppa, and a snog with the missus.

And his reward for honesty was this. The Sierra had vanished. The *firm's* Sierra, that he'd parked there less than an hour ago, at the back of the Co-op.

Bill hadn't known what to do. So he'd lied. He was thinking, if some joyrider had stolen the car, through his negligence, he'd have to have a hotter excuse than nipping home for some quick ones. He'd have to be stretched out near death to get away with this.

2

What's happening to me?

She didn't ask out loud.

Had more sense. Or too much terror.

The darkness, sometimes streaked with lights, rushed by.

Once, he saw a badger on the road, its striped mask lifted and eyes like drops of radium. He *slowed down* for that.

Then he was off again. Too fast. Perhaps a police car would stop him for speeding. But that wouldn't help. Because of the gun.

Every time she thought of the gun, that was, definitely, as opposed to the omnipresent *presence* of the gun, Markessa almost screamed.

But he didn't like her to scream. He'd made that clear.

She was helpless. She might as well be in chains. She wouldn't be able to get out and run, she couldn't use her hands.

He had told her to go into the toilet and pee, before they left. (*Not* toilet. Steven said you didn't say toilet. But everyone did, now. *This* one said khazi.) Because, he said, it would be a long drive, and he didn't want her to be uncomfortable. Not until the end, when he blew her brains out.

But she didn't believe that. She *lived* in this body, with all its little limits that let her down, low metabolic rate, dry hair, two capped teeth and many fillings – despite all that, she would forgive her body. She had to *keep* her body. No, he hadn't meant what he'd said.

After she had released the downstairs door, Markessa had run into the bathroom, and tried, in the few moments available, to repair her make-up. She had also cleaned her teeth, and sprayed on fresh deodorant.

She couldn't remember when she had felt so happy – so *alive*.

Steven had left Jula, dumped Jula. And now he had come to Markessa.

I'm in love with him, she thought, thrilled at her own naïvety in not being, until that moment, sure.

She had had sex with Steven only once.

Markessa had felt bad about it afterwards. Not *very* bad, but more awkward. Steven had told Markessa, and it was obvious anyway, that anything he and Jula had had between them was long over.

Besides, she'd never been Jula's close friend. They had met when Jula, the Local Author, came to sign copies of her latest book, *In Transit*, at the shop. Markessa had, that first time, felt a combination of impressed and affronted. The sort of books that Jula wrote were not of the type Markessa liked, too dreary and depressing, too *real*, as one critic had apparently (Steven) said. But Markessa nevertheless found herself saying to Jula that Jula must let Markessa take her to lunch sometime. And although Jula never actually petitioned for this, Markessa eventually made an excuse to go up to that awful house on the hill. Where she met Steven.

They hit it off at once. Well, he was fantastic. The kind of man, Markessa thought, she'd always wanted. A bit older, but in brilliant shape. A true creative, too, who'd only been stopped by Jula's awful dominance and selfishness.

But Jula was also insecure, and begged him not to leave her. She was afraid. And frankly, he'd worry about her if he did leave. Like all those bossy ones, she was weak. She had behaved foully to him, buggered his chances in publishing circles, made his life hell – but she was (it seemed) like a kid. Markessa (it seemed) around seven years younger, was the mature one. But there you were. He'd loved Jula once, he freely admitted it. You can't just throw those feelings away, even when they're dead.

For this reason, he asked Markessa to be discreet. Don't upset Jula, don't let her know. She'll have some sort of breakdown. She could get spiteful.

Markessa had been on the receiving end of spiteful pre-empted wives and female lovers before. She thought Steven's advice was sound, and stuck to it.

Their sexual liaison occurred when he turned up at her bookshop three quarters of an hour before closing time, and persuaded her to shut early. Then he went up to her flat with her, where they drank two bottles of wine from the fridge and ended by making loud love on the floor.

She wanted him to stay, but he had said he couldn't. He had to get back to Jula.

Markessa had expected, however, even though he hadn't even made the apocryphal promise to call, that Steven would come back for more.

He'd been complimentary, told her he loved her 'passion'. (Jula, of course, was cold, scared of sex.)

Markessa's impression was that Steven was an amazing lover. Or that he could be, if they had more time.

And she would have liked them to have that time. And thought he would want that too.

But nothing had happened, and when she had seen him in Seatree a week later, at the wine bar where she went sometimes for a salad, Steven had been in a hurry, had only stopped to drink the glass of wine she bought him, but told her she looked 'frighteningly pretty'. She had seen him next in Jula's house, at one of those strange dinner parties that Jula sometimes gave, and that Steven said he hated.

Steven was delightful to Markessa, as always. When he saw her out to her car, in the dark by the barn, he even kissed her, stroking her breasts.

'When can you – when will you come round?' she asked. 'Jule said you're sometimes away overnight – couldn't you –?'

'Oh, baby, have a heart. She's got me running in circles for about a month. Sometime, soon as I can. We'll make a night of it.'

'Oh yes, Steven. Please.'

'*If* you'll do the Dance of the Seven Veils for me,' he said.

'I'll do anything – everything for you,' Markessa vowed.

Reading the sort of novels she did, lines like this sometimes tumbled from her in unguarded moments.

This had happened as she stood drunk and desolate on the pavement tonight. *My life is over.*

So bloody Jack Hastings knew now, and so did Jula, come to that. Markessa had been in such a state she'd made it all fairly plain. Christ, she hoped Steven wouldn't be too angry – but then, he'd left Jula. He must have done. And here he was.

When she opened the door of the flat, someone was outside. The landing wasn't well lighted, but the overhead lamp blazed from Markessa's main room.

She was so certain it was Steven, that for a second, it was. Slim and straight, with a thick topping of white-blond hair, and wearing an expensive summer suit.

But then real life (too *real*) showed her, as if in a series of lightning flashes, that this man was not Steven Grace. Too young, even too slim, and – although she didn't realise – far too beautiful.

He had the face of a youthful Apollo carved in Grecian marble. The same sculpted lips and deep-lidded eyes. The eyes though were held very wide. Staring at her, gleaming and almost colourless – the eyes either of a petrified deer or a stalking leopard. Which? *Both*?

'So you're it,' he said.

And although he had just the sort of tailored accent Markessa approved of, a wave of alarm rushed through her.

'What do you want?'

'You, dearest. You.'

Three things happened. Four, really.

Markessa turned her foot, and as she did so one of the abused blue heels snapped right off, so she staggered, and her voice burst out in a violent scream. But even staggering and screaming, she tried to throw the door closed. And he caught the door and flung it back so it hit the wall with a crash and the whole house seemed to shake.

'No,' he said, and stepped forward.

He was inside the room.

Markessa shrieked, on and on. The novels hadn't taught her this, it was sheer instinct.

He spoke, now more loudly. 'Quiet, please. Do you want to wake the world?'

And out from some inside pocket he removed something and held it toward her. It looked like an undusted lizard. But her cries were swallowed down.

His voice grew soft again. 'I see you recognise my friend.'

Stupidly, stood there on one leg, Markessa shook her head.

'Oh, let me introduce you, then. Markessa, meet Walther PPK.'

'It's a gun,' she whispered.

He sighed. 'Are you always this bright?'

Once she saw the gun, Markessa tried to stop asking anything, or arguing.

She backed away, hobbling, and he said, 'Take your shoes off, or you'll have an accident.' So she kicked off the blue shoes, one lacking a heel, which had spun away. And he came and picked them up, and stared at them. 'Don't they hurt?' he asked, innocent as a child.

'No,' she muttered. Force of habit and a lie.

'Sit down,' he said. 'Sit on that black and white couch thing. Bash would *love* that. Your sofa. Probably serve dinner on it.'

She sat. She held her knees. She watched him carry her shoes through into the kitchen and presently open the correct cupboard, drop them straight in the concealed bin. She thought about trying to run for the door, but there wasn't time.

'You won't need shoes, you see,' he said.

He glanced round, looking at all the little room, which she had tried to make modern and effective. She could see he didn't like it.

What did psychiatrists say on the news? Be calm and neutral with maniacs. Get their confidence, try to make them trust you.

'Would you like a drink?' Markessa said primly.

'I don't,' he said. 'I don't drink. And I don't think you should have one either, Markessa beloved. But I think you should go and have a piss. It's going to be a long drive. I don't want you to be uncomfortable. Yes, go on. Leave the khazi door open. I might look, but I won't get excited, I promise.'

She obeyed him, and despite what he said, pulled the door to. She wanted to go badly. It was the shock.

As she sat there, helpless, she wondered if there was anything in the bathroom cabinet that might help her.

But when she came out, he said, 'Oh Markessa, you really are being silly. What have you got in that little pink fist? Let me guess – a nail file – scissors? Drop them on the table.'

She dropped them on the table: he had a gun.

He said, 'I hope you weren't going to stick those in my eye. I've got wonderful eyes, so I'm told. Maybe you just thought you'd trim your nails. Let's say that, shall we?'

Markessa was crying, loose, feeble drops of water.

'I'm startled,' he said, 'by you. You're not as I pictured at all.'

She hadn't meant to ask or argue, but she wailed, 'Why are you here? I don't know you, I don't –'

'But I know *you*. I know of you, Markessa.'

'Who –?'

'Too early for confidences. Just relax. We'll go for a drive. Now I've just seen the perfect thing.' And he walked over to the coffee table, where she had dropped the scissors, and picked up the roll of sellotape she had brought in from the shop that afternoon. She always took some stationery for private use, but only ever piece by piece. You never knew when you might need it.

He needed it now. He picked the sellotape up.

'Come here, Markessa.'

What bizarre sexual aberration was to be worked on her?

'That's far enough. Just hold out your hands. Together, please.'

He kept the gun in his right hand and, using only the left, stuck the open end of the tape across Markessa's hands, held prayer-fashion before her. He dragged the sellotape round and round her wrists, tearing out the little hairs she always meant to depilate.

When she was painfully and firmly handcuffed in this way, she stared at him, opened her mouth into a square, and sobbed soundlessly.

'I'm not going to hurt you,' he said. 'Ssh.'

She made herself be quiet.

He led her to the door, guiding her with his smooth left hand. He wore a ring of twisted gold on the second finger, and a Swatch, all gold coins. In the other hand, digging gently in her back, the gun.

No-one was about. Although she thought she had screamed very loudly, no-one had troubled.

They went down, and out onto the pavement, which struck cold now through her bare feet.

'I've got such a lovely car, Markessa,' he said. 'It's a Range Rover, black with a silver wash. Bash gave it to me. Bash, by the way, is what I live with. She has predictable tastes.'

He was looking up and down the empty road.

Markessa looked too.

Oh, make someone come. People – drunks – police in a car –

'You know, I think I prefer the look of that one, over there. If I can get the door open. I'm quite good at that.'

He took her elbow gallantly, and they walked across the road. Bits of grit and smashed glass ripped at her feet and she whimpered.

They entered the car-park. There was a white taxi there, with one of the cab signs up on its roof.

'Arrow,' said the young Apollo. 'Well, that must be for the Battle of Hastings, mustn't it? King Harold killed by an arrow in the eye. Only he wasn't.'

He leaned, still holding her, with the gun hand now, still looking at her, and did something left-handed to the driver's door. She couldn't see what, didn't know what was going on, felt she was losing her mind.

The door opened.

'There. Something even Bashy can't do. Get in.'

'Where –?' she said.

'Ssh.' He lifted the dusty lizard gun, and Markessa got into the front seat. 'Wriggle across.'

While she did this, she wondered again if she could get away. But she wouldn't get far, would she? Unless he couldn't shoot her? Surely he couldn't?

While she was trying to decide, he slid in beside her, and shut the door quietly.

He smelled bathed, and of Calvin Klein cologne. And of something else, rusty, tinderous, like a burnt firework.

The car started, and a little scratch of turned-down sound ebbed from the microphone attachment. Apollo leaned casually, and switched it off, as Markessa had often seen cab drivers do.

As they glided down the road, she watched the gun resting, perched in his hand on the wheel.

'I don't think we've woken a soul,' he said. 'They have to get up very early. But no fear of the morrow for us, Markessa.'

It was not until they left the town, and were out into the country lanes, cats eyes sparking on the road, stars above, trees and night around, that he confidently added, 'I'm going to blow out your brains before morning.'

3

Knox studied Jula Cork as she stirred her tea. Despite stirring it, she drank it black, without sugar, and the very thought of it turned his stomach. But *she* looked appetising enough. And clear as water, as his mother would say, 'That girl's got no side to her, Charlie. She's clear as water.' 'Yes, Mum. But you can put things in water now no-one can see.'

'You're being very cooperative, Ms Cork. I appreciate that. You've been through a lot. Tape doesn't worry you, does it?'

'No,' she said.

Knox said, 'It must have been a shock, Mr Grace dying like that. So young. What was he – 38 or so?'

'36, Chief Inspector. And I told you, I'm glad he's dead.'

'You're being a tease, Ms Cork, if I might say so. What are we going to make of it? You saying that?'

'It's the truth. I hated him.'

'But then you might have killed him, mightn't you, if it was bad as all that?'

'I didn't. But Jack said you'd say that.'

'Jack has had dealings with the Bill before, or I'm your uncle's monkey.'

She laughed. A great laugh, crystals, that sort of thing.

'I'm sorry. You see – my uncle really wouldn't want to own a monkey.'

Knox folded his arms. 'Mr Grace,' he said, 'how was his general health?'

She glanced at him. 'All right. Until a little while ago. And that was something with blood-pressure. His doctor told him it was stress. Or so Steven told me. The stress of living with me, of course. He had a prescription for some pills, and I suppose he took them.'

'And the doc will have said to ease off the alcohol, cut out the fags, and eat sensibly.'

'Yes, I'm sure he did.'

'And did Mr Grace take any notice?'

'Not that I saw.'

'What did you see, Ms Cork?'

She sipped the tea and put it down. 'When he was at the house, which he often wasn't, he drank and smoked the same as always.'

'Which was?'

'About half to three quarters of a bottle of whisky each day. Sometimes all of it. Wine at lunchtime and at dinner, if he ate in. Generally he went out. He smoked forty, fifty cigarettes a day.'

'My Aunt Ada!' said Knox. 'He should've lived to be 99. How did he fit all that in?'

She took him seriously. 'Steven said he couldn't sleep. The stress. He'd lie in bed and smoke.'

'Not very pleasant for you.'

'Actually I don't mind other people smoking. I like the smell 'Knox goggled at her. 'Besides, we don't – didn't sleep in the same room.'

He noted the slip of tenses, which might indicate purest innocence, and no doubt she knew that. He said, 'Sleeping tablets would be out of the question, with the drinking.'

'Yes, although I think he did get something. I think he took it now and then. Steven thought warnings about drinking and tablets were nonsense. He said the government dreamed them up to keep everyone in their place.'

'And that really works, doesn't it? What about grub?'

'I don't like cooking, Chief Inspector. But if I did or we were out, it always had to be meat, sauces, eggs – that's not a good idea, is it?'

'No. Unfortunately. I tell you, I'd give both my arms sometimes for a decent meal. Three courses of stodge, with chips in lard. All right. Drinks too much. Smokes. Eats the wrong stuff. Pops pills. What do you feel about the stress?'

'Yes.'

'You made his life a misery, Ms Cork?'

'He said I did. I think –' She hesitated, then said, 'I think Steven dreaded his own inadequacy. So he had to blame everyone but himself. It took a lot of his energy. He was always angry, het up. Pulling everyone to pieces. Getting back at them. He'd even steal things – stupid things – or valuable, sometimes. In the beginning, to sell, I imagine. But he never lost the habit.'

'What work did he do?'

'Nothing.'

'I understood he was some sort of writer.'

'No, Chief Inspector. That's me.'

'I've remembered. I've seen your books in the library.'

She said, flat and quick, 'Lots of people do, so they tell me. The thing is, if they take one out.'

'I'll make a point of it,' he said. 'I suppose it was a bit of a strain on Mr Grace, your success and his – er – failure?'

'I'm not really a great success. I had one very successful book. But I couldn't repeat it. My income was left in trust for me by my grandfather, together with the house where I live. I don't have any money worries, but if it was fame I was after, I'd be sunk.'

'Does that bother you?'

Her eyes, luminous, all black, pupil and iris as one.

'Not really.'

'Sounds evasive.'

'No. I love what I do. That's the most important part, for me. The fulfilment and the pain of writing. If I'm honest, I expect, too, the utter escape. To get into print is a bonus, not an essential. And I've explained about the money side. I'm very lucky.'

'Except in your partner.'

'Yes, except with Steven.'

'If it was so bad – you say he was unhappy with you and you hated him – why not break up? You didn't even have to file for divorce.'

'He wouldn't go. It was as simple as that.'

'Because of the advantages.'

'Of course. I fed him and clothed him. I bought him all his drink, his holidays, and anything else he wanted. I even managed to get him the car he told me he had to have. The Porsche. It was second-hand though. I'm comfortably off, but not rich – and Steven was very costly. My uncle … Someone in the business regularly buys these sort of cars and gets bored with them in a couple of months. Leonardo put him on to me. Steven was very pleased, but when he found out the car had had one careful owner for 64 days, he became sarcastic instead.'

'So he drove it down a ditch.'

'The strange thing is, that's almost what he *would* do. It fits his psychology seamlessly.'

'Drink up,' said Knox. 'Don't let your tea get cold.'

She glanced at him again. Away.

Jula Cork didn't respond like most people. Not in any way. Cool, fragile, childlike, impervious, oblique. She was absurdly, potentially unnervingly, frank. Almost, he thought, verging on the sociopathic.

Try this then.

'Right, he won't go. And he's taking most of your dosh, earned or otherwise. Couldn't you get someone else to kick him out for you?' Now she didn't look up. 'I can imagine,' said Knox, 'Mr Hastings might be glad to oblige you there.'

Jula said, slowly, 'It wasn't possible to kick Steven out.'

'And why was that?'

She turned and looked at the recording machine.

'Can I ask you to switch that off?'

DC Poecock raised his head. Knox exchanged grimaces with him.

'All right. Ms Cork's request is noted. Switch it off.'

When the new silence had settled itself, Jula spoke clearly and lightly.

'Steven was blackmailing me. If I turned him out or cut off any money, he was going to expose what I'd done. He swore to me he would and I believed him. I think he'd have enjoyed it very much, even though it meant he'd be left with nothing.'

DC Poecock began to speak. Knox shook his head.

'And the nature of the blackmail, Ms Cork?'

'Yes, I'll tell you, of course. That's why I want the tape off. I'm probably being trivial. But – I don't want anyone to play this back. If you like, I can write it down for you, sign it.'

'All right. First things first. Tell me.'

She told him.

They were still on, all of them, the lights.

Rawthorn got out of the car, and walked through the iron gates, and up the drive for the second time that night. It was like one of those books, he thought, where characters kept returning irksomely to the same spot.

But somehow the way the lights were always so manifestly alight here, put him in mind of Jula Cork's house, the front of which had been in darkness. Just as, when she opened the door, Jula had put him in mind of Mrs Alliat.

And why was that?

There were a lot of women in this case, but he didn't mind. He liked women. Especially, he must admit, the woman he had hunted down at the Fighting Man, Leigh Dover. Putting her name through the computer had brought some information, five minutes before he left the station, that had given him plenty to think about, on the drive through Seatree.

Meanwhile, the Alliats.

He couldn't see anyone, this time, but he rapped on the big wooden door. Only a Knox would risk all this at such an hour. Knox who had mooted Steven Grace had, anyway, died of a heart attack. Knox who was now having one of his 'chats' with Jula Cork, or Jack Hastings.

A little of Knox went a long way, Rawthorn had long ago decided. But he was a swamp from which rose, sometimes, shining cunning things.

And Open Sesame. The Alliat door was pulled wide. No chain, no caution, no apparent security of any kind.

She was wearing a dressing gown now, 1930s style, and, not

astonishingly, pink, with quilted revers. The rabbit slippers didn't look so incongruous with this ensemble. But on her face, which seemed rather heavily made-up, the incongruous was, dark and obvious as cloud across the sun.

'Oh, good evening.'

'I apologise, Mrs Alliat. I'm afraid there have been rather serious developments.'

The little soft frown he recalled so well, but she limped aside to let him in.

She said, 'Would you mind coming downstairs? I was in the kitchen at the back, making some tea.'

He'd meant to ask at once for the male Alliat to be summoned. But something, her face most likely, deflected this for the time being.

'Of course, Mrs Alliat.'

She led him along the white carpet. (Her limp seemed worse.) In the two-storey room to the left, no-one was. Only the light glinting on things. She went through a door to the right.

Rawthorn followed her down a small turning stair, without carpet, like a servant's stair in a mansion behind a baize door.

The kitchen however, when they reached it, was a black-tiled haven of modernity, with stripped wood cabinets painted in chalky white, and staring white units. To one end opened a breakfast-room-conservatory, with tall green plants that rose into the glass roof.

Beyond, the garden was also lit, theatrically, with spotlights among the trees. He could see banks of blue-green shrubs with flowers dotted through in coloured stars. A stone statue of a nymph held a basin overflowing with something purple. She at least would certainly have cost more than £1,000.

After the garden, the fields lay, like blankets cast over sleeping hills.

Something about this external view struck him. Gradually, looking at it, he became more aware of the distant portion of a stump of some enormous tree, perhaps an oak, which, before its felling, would have towered into the sky. It seemed to have left, bizarrely, an afterimage on the air.

Mrs Alliat was pouring from a teapot. The scent of herbs, faintly sweet and musky.

'It's chamomile, spearmint and rosebalm. Would you care for some?'

'Thank you, no, Mrs Alliat.'

She lifted her cup, but, drinking, pulled a little ragged face. Yes, it must hurt.

'That looks painful.'

'It's happened before now. A new packet of dustbin bags, and tearing the first one off. My hands aren't very strong.' She demonstrated, laughing at herself, although that too would hurt. 'You see, I lost my grip on the bag – my hand shot up and hit me in the face.'

Rawthorn had seen this happen, to a woman, when she was undoing a plastic bag of peppers. The same thing exactly. Although, where her hand had smacked her in the face there had been only the slightest mark. Definitely not a swollen black bruise like this one.

'It looks sore. Perhaps you should get your doctor to check it out.'

'Dr Terry. Yes, I'll probably see him tomorrow. He's the kindest man.' She sat down at the white, stripped table, putting a black placemat under the cup and saucer. 'He's used to me, I'm afraid. I'm one of those people who needs a season ticket to the surgery.'

Terry ... Oh, yes. The drunk seen in the White Bull. Heart of pearl.

Just then, the most – *minding-bending* was the term that came to Rawthorn – noise started up. It seemed to crack across the kitchen, and through his skull, juddering up at the same time through the terracotta-slabbed floor.

She took no apparent heed.

'What is *that*, Mrs Alliat?'

'What? Oh – you mean that awful sound. It's nothing. Something to do with the water pipes in the house. It requires a lot of re-plumbing, it seems, to put it right. Several workmen, excavating walls – so I'm afraid we just put up with it. It's a horrible sound, I know. I used to dread it. Now I hardly notice.'

She didn't notice *this*? A thin, rushing, stampeding *scream*.

She said, as if to reassure a child, 'It's George, using the guest bathroom. You can always tell, actually, which bathroom it is. The worst one is mine. I daren't use it at all during the night. I have to go along to the cloakroom. I suppose we ought to have something done. But,' she added, frisky, 'we're such hermits.'

Rawthorn said, 'I'd like to speak to Mr Alliat, in fact. To both of you.'

'That does sound serious. You said – developments. Is this about the driver of the car?'

'Yes.'

She looked worried. Not alarmed or even eager for another's bad news, as she had seemed to be last time. 'Haven't you found him?'

The unbearable noise of the pipes shuddered suddenly and was gone.

And there came instead the thump of George Alliat's footsteps, heavy and firm, on the kitchen stair.

Nor was he perplexed or astounded. He walked in, smiling broadly, holding out his liver-spotted hand.

'I saw your car across the lane. There have been quite a few of your fellows up and down tonight, haven't there?'

There was a well-known play or legend – what was it? Chinese, Japanese? – that showed how several people, viewing precisely the same event, saw quite different actions and different types of person involved in them.

Roshomon, that was it.

And – that, perhaps, was this.

Leigh Dover had described George Alliat. Physically at least, she had been more than reasonably accurate.

But the monstrous being that *inhabited* George Alliat was no longer there. Even the handshake was another one, firm and decisive. And his query as to Rawthorn's rank and name – his wife couldn't have told him, or hadn't remembered – was courteous and sensible.

Rawthorn thought perhaps none of this was so surprising.

The information the computer had delivered might have forearmed him.

'So, you didn't see Mr Grace. But didn't you notice the car in the ditch?'

'I knew nothing about it, Inspector Rawthorn, until the young woman mentioned it.'

'That would be Ms Dover.'

'Yes.'

'But surely you'd have passed the car, wouldn't you, Mr Alliat, coming in off the Seatree Road?'

George Alliat said, 'I've thought about that. I think I've solved the enigma.'

'Yes?'

'I gather from what's been said by yourself, and by Miss Dover earlier, that the accident happened just before the Ride Run, which *I* use to come into this lane. The turn-off from the Seatree Road appears about ten minutes before the Divers Lane turn-off, and I find the Run quicker, though the road's not much to write home about, worse than this.'

'The Ride Run?'

'Yes. The name itself goes back in history, I believe. Something to do with three riders who ran away from something down Hastings way. 1066 and all that.'

Rawthorn heard Mrs Alliat give a tiny gasp, as someone might before a sneeze. But she didn't sneeze.

He said, 'I believe I've been told about the other road. Yes, I see.'

'The Ride Run turn-off from the Seatree Road is virtually camouflaged at this time of year. No-one would think to use it unless they knew. That's why it's useful. I'd had enough of the traffic hold-ups this evening on the A21. I was very late home. After 7.00. Wasn't I?' he added.

Mrs Alliat said, 'Yes, darling. You were dreadfully late. I was worried.'

Rawthorn, looking at her casually, noted there was *something*. Not fear, or worry. Her eyes were large and fixed on shadows. More what Marvell had called magnanimous despair ...

'I understand you're driving to Gatwick in a few hours, Mr Alliat.'

'Yes, Inspector. Following the sun.'

'South America, wasn't it?'

'Yes.' He added, 'And there's an awful lot of coffee in Brazil.'

'Darling, I'm so *sorry*, your coffee – I lost track. Really, I'll do it now.'

Seeing a woman with a bruised face and damaged foot – and possibly something that hurt her elsewhere – leap up and somehow sprint across the kitchen, made Rawthorn feel rather sick.

What she did with the coffee endorsed this feeling. For she put eight heaped dessert spoons of the blackest ground powder into the cafetiere, and poured in enough hot water only for three cups.

'Will you have some coffee, Inspector?' asked Alliat. He looked amused, and as usual showed all the polished tombstone teeth.

'No, thank you, sir.'

'Rather strong, I expect. I like things to have a taste. On the trip though: I can't think why you'd need me for your investigation, but I can postpone it. I can cancel it if you like. I'm retiring, more or less. My time's my own. I don't mind staying on here, if that's what you want.'

Rawthorn was taken aback. This was the sort of tough-minded old-school-boy who, even dressed informally in polo shirt and sand-toned, cotton-twill trousers, tended to demand his rights.

It was the woman who reacted.

'But *no* – darling, you can't – oh he *mustn't*. Inspector. My husband needs this holiday so badly. It's out of the question.'

And she looked, there was no denying it, *frenzied*.

Alliat didn't even glance at her. Jovially, he toothed on at Rawthorn. 'My wife is very concerned for my wellbeing, you see. But take my word for it, I can cancel the trip.'

'I hope that won't be necessary, sir.'

The smell of coffee was oily as bitter chocolate melted on the air. Mrs Alliat, stood by the cafetiere, had gone pale under the extra make-up she had applied.

But the overhead light was very harsh.

She had said she would miss her husband. She had said she was 'silly' about that. As she had been 'silly' when she managed to punch herself on the jaw, her unstrong hand raising such a contusion it was a wonder it too wasn't marked.

'I think you've found this man's body, haven't you?' asked Alliat. 'Judging by all the police activity earlier.'

'We have reason to think we may have, yes.'

'You wouldn't be here now otherwise. What was it? *Foul play?*'

'I can t say at this stage, sir. But we have to check several avenues of enquiry.'

'Think *I* dun him in, eh?'

Rawthorn, neutral and polite, 'Why would I think that, sir?'

Alliat laughed.

His teeth were false. Hence the hedge of grey moustache to hide the toothless droop of his upper lip. But if he wanted to hide it, he shouldn't laugh with his mouth wide open. The plate was total.

Mrs Alliat had brought the coffee. She set it before her husband with a cup and saucer on a mat, all matching the black and gold cafetiere. There was also a matching jug of cream, and a bowl of dark Barbados sugar. Alliat scooped four heavy spoons of it into the coffee and lavished on the cream.

'You know,' said Alliat, 'I got that feeling from the girl – the one who came here. Leigh. Intelligent, but I had this notion she suspected me of something.'

'Oh darling,' fluttered Mrs Alliat, 'How absol –'

'But as I said,' Alliat overrode her, 'I can stay. This chap, whoever he was. You can't be too careful.'

'Well, said Rawthorn, 'women sometimes get these ideas.'

Alliat's eyes came up and met his like unsheathed steel. 'Do they?'

It had been worth a try. Since Alliat had let out that one little extra slip. *Leigh,* not Miss Dover. As if they had got on so well.

But he wasn't going to play.

Rawthorn rose. 'Thank you, sir. I'll leave you in peace.'

'That's all right, Inspector. Let me take you up.'

Alliat led the way from the kitchen, and up the stair.

As they emerged into the warm glacier of the hall, the older man turned suddenly, gazing across into his impressive two-storey room.

'There's something I'd like to show you, Inspector Rawthorn, if you have a moment.'

They walked across the carpet, and into the room. Alliat continued moving between the little tables, the brocade chairs, until he stood facing a wall with a painting on it. The painting Leigh had described.

'What do you think of this, Inspector? Or didn't you notice it?'

A test of culture now?

'It's a very fine picture, sir.'

'Fine, eh.'

'Ms Dover thought it exceptional.' And a mental apology to her for speaking her name again to this man.

'She did, did she?'

'But she couldn't place the artist, and neither can I.'

'An influence of Cézanne, perhaps,' said George Alliat. 'You can't escape your teachers. I don't mean necessarily that one was taught in person. But the masters you study, the ones you worship. Was it Catullus who said that if a man truly worshipped the gods with all his heart, he must eventually become like them?'

'It sounds more like Plato, sir, I'd say. And it might not be a comment on virtue, possibly.'

Alliat laughed again. 'Touché, Inspector. But tell me, where do you think I acquired this painting?'

Rather blatant, wasn't it? Like a kid. Then again, if he had –

'Abroad, sir? France?'

'Painted in France, do you mean? In the south. The south of any country, always interesting to me. *I* painted it, Inspector.'

'Did you, sir? It's impressive. Have you exhibited?'

'I was going to, one day. But then I thought better of it. A shock for you, I'd say, to find the old codger could once turn out something like this.'

Rawthorn waited.

Alliat turned and stared at him. Alliat's face was abruptly cold.

'I lost the knack,' he said. 'My talent. Gone.'

There was nothing to be said. If it was a lie, it was better left alone. If true, no words on Earth were suitable or worth a jot.

And now Alliat strode toward the whisky decanter. It had gone down, the whisky, considerably, since Rawthorn's previous visit.

'You won't have a drink? Didn't think you would. But I think I will.' His hand on the decanter, he added, 'Don't worry. Someone else is driving me to the airport.'

'Would that be your wife?'

'I don't think so. My efforts at teaching my wife to drive were to no avail.'

'I'll say goodnight, sir.'

Rawthorn turned and began to cross back toward the hall. As he did so, the light sprinkled itself all over the accoutrements of the room, particularly on some tiny boxes arranged on a table below the gallery stair.

He gave them only a fleeting glance. That was all it needed.

'By the way, sir, on the off chance. You leave for your flight when?'

'4.00 am, Inspector. Take-off 6.40. I like to give myself plenty of time.'

'Have a good journey, sir. Goodnight.'

Sometimes a lie had value.

Irritable, Knox, into the receiver: '*Yes*? Rawthorn? Why aren't you back?'

'I have to verify something, sir. I shouldn't be long. First, I thought you should hear this. I'm fairly sure Alliat is a wife-batterer.'

'Are you indeed? Well that's one for the album. Reasons?'

'Each time I've seen her, she's had a recent injury. This time a facial bruise. And she shows the classic victim response to Alliat, fawning on him, making too much of him. She covers up, but she did mention she'll be seeing her doctor. I've got a feeling darling George gave her a real going-over tonight.'

'Okay. You said first. What's for afters?'

'Steven Grace almost certainly was in that house.'

'*Was* he now. Are you going to let me in on why?'

Rawthorn let him in. Knox listened in silence.

'Alliat leaves at 4.00,' Rawthorn appended. 'For South America, of all places.'

'Could be telling porkies again. We'll check with Gatwick. And Rawthorn –'

'Yes, sir.'

'If you're going after her doctor, and it's who I think it is, keep your gloves on.'

As Leigh Dover had done in the presence of Rawthorn, Rawthorn now felt that sensation of having been read like an open book. By something shining and cunning, from a swamp.

In the fish-tank of the White Bull's window, Dr Terry watched Rawthorn approach. He seemed to know this messenger was for him. He didn't look away, only up into Rawthorn's face with bloodshot, watery eyes.

The preliminaries over, Rawthorn sat opposite.

It was after 2.00 by now, and only a few diehards were in the bar. While five tiddly girls with tie-dyed hair and biteable shoulders, were giggling themselves into insanity in a corner. The two barmen, not much older, rubbed glasses and sliced lemons with personal dislike.

Someone always had to work that others might play.

Or so Dr Terry just told Rawthorn.

'I need you to help me in reference to a Mrs Alliat.'

'Miranda Rosalind Alliat,' said Dr Terry.

'She's been with you for some time?'

'Years. As soon as they moved here. Nineteen or twenty years ago.'

'I gather you've seen quite a lot of her.'

'Now and then.'

'No, doctor. More than that.'

'Did she say so?'

Rawthorn watched Dr Terry fill his glass from a bottle of vodka, and top it up with very little green ginger wine. The White Bull had no scruples about serving other drinks than wine. As the cartoon over the bar demonstrated, with its drawing of a merry ghost and the words: *Spirits served here.*

'Mrs Alliat does tend to give herself a few minor injuries. She's one of those women who are accident-prone.'

Rawthorn felt his face redden. He said evenly, 'Careless, a bit scatty, that sort of thing?'

Terry looked at him again. The watery eyes were hard to decipher.

'No, I don't mean that. Some women find they become awkward, even clumsy, at certain times of the month, or during the menopause. Discoordinated.'

'Miranda Alliat is in the menopause?'

'No longer, Inspector. Now she's just rather unhappy. Her husband works in London, and he takes his holidays separately. That's always been the case, but she seems to find it harder to cope with now. I'm not a great fan of all the modern tranquillisers. Neither are the Alliats. She had a dependency on alcohol earlier in her life. She wants to be careful, and I respect that.'

He spoke of alcohol and drug dependency in a detached yet sympathetic way.

Rawthorn said, 'What sort of injuries have you treated her for?'

'Mostly minor things. Little burns, a cut hand, a nosebleed. I had to send her to hospital for an ankle X-ray once, when she fell down the stairs. Recently she broke a small bone in her little toe. But it's mending nicely. When she's upset, she misjudges. Psychologically, too, there's always the chance she may be trying to attract her husband's attention, make him more careful of her, more protective. The Unconscious, Inspector, can be a demon.'

'And there's another possibility,' said Rawthorn.

'Which is?'

'He's beating her up. Never anything too much, unless he makes a mistake. How did she say she broke her toe?'

Terry said, around the rim of his glass, 'She does a lot of gardening. She dropped something on it, a stone, I think.'

'Handy.'

'Footy,' said the doctor, deadpan.

'Dr Terry, I have to ask you if you might have – not ignored – but not analysed this situation thoroughly enough?'

The eyes swam. They had the blind look of someone shocked into indifference.

'And if I didn't, Inspector? If I only wondered? Over the years. Giving her the option of telling me another story?'

'You suspected? Why didn't you –?'

'She didn't want it. I can assure you of that. She wouldn't leave him. In this day and age, a woman can get help. She could even escape, couldn't she, on one of those occasions when he went away. But she never has.' He finished the glass, looked regretfully at the bottle, and then at the clock on the wall. 'No more for twenty minutes. That's my rule.'

Rawthorn pushed back his chair.

'She loves him,' said Dr Terry. 'It can happen, you know. Even after years of – of his beating her, if he does. She can still love him too much to go. In women of her generation – and of mine – it isn't so uncommon.'

As Rawthorn left the bar, the giggly tiddly September girls were singing 'Jingle Bells'. One had a large plaster on her left forearm. Maybe nothing. You couldn't tell.

But in the case of Miranda Rosalind Alliat, named for two Shakespearean heroines of charm and verve, Rawthorn would take a bet.

It angered Rawthorn, thinking of her 'putting up with it'. Staying. Not only a victim's slavishness and placation, but a genuine regard, conceivably even an *enjoyment.*

Steven Grace however had been young and strong and male, and, judging by what they were hearing, hated.

What would a bully like Alliat make of that?

Sometimes there was no-one to suspect of anything. The *Dramatis Personae* of your murder play all seemed blameless. Here there was getting to be a crowd of hopefuls. Hastings, with his proximity to Divers Lane. The hating Jula, possibly, if she was mad – and she could be. Even, although this one was disturbing Rawthorn, Leigh Dover. On top of all of it now, the person Rawthorn had to admit he would be pleased to see carry the can. George Alliat.

But even here, another mystery. If Grace had stolen, and been pursued and assaulted as a result, why then was the trophy not retrieved?

Because lying by Grace's body, under the monkey-puzzle trees, along with his wallet, had been that tiny snuffbox, gold and tortoiseshell, the sibling to all other little snuffboxes on the table in the two-storey room.

4

Near the end of the chat (the interview) Knox had said again to Jula Cork, 'But even so, you didn't kill him?'

Knox didn't play by the rules. It was almost a delight to come up against someone, even someone who might be a murderess, who never expected it of him.

She just gave him a glance. The sort that made you say, *If I were twenty years younger, and not stuck with the wife.* Although you knew then, you wouldn't. You wouldn't bloody risk it. Not with the Julas of this world.

(Had she fainted, or was it a ruse? Ed Rawthorn had caught her before Knox could be sure.)

'You know, Chief Inspector, I've written about murder.'

'Have you, indeed. I must make a point of looking out for that one.'

'I think I mentioned the title.' He raised his brows. 'If I've written about it, that means, of course, I've thought a lot about what it must be like to kill another human being. Writing is like acting in that. One puts oneself into the character's head. Into their *skin*. Or, I do. And so I know I couldn't kill anyone – at least not in cold blood.'

'And why's that?'

'Not fear. Not even fastidiousness. It's because of what comes after.'

'Discovery, Ms Cork?'

'No. *Not* being discovered. For example, *Crime and Punishment*.' She didn't ask him if he had heard of Dostoyevsky. He had. 'It's the *guilt*, Chief Inspector. I couldn't bear it. I'm too much of a coward.'

'I believe you said you prayed Steven Grace was dead.'

'If he was, then *I* hadn't been responsible … How often have you known prayer work? But even that, wishing him dead – I tried not to do it.'

When Knox had Hastings in, ten minutes after, it was a whole new ball game.

'Are you charging her with something?'

'No, sir.'

'Charging me?'

'No, sir.'

'Then when the fuck do we get out of this dump?'

Icy, calculated rage. The blue-black eyes blazing, and *watching* to see what was produced.

Nothing was produced except Knox's kindest smile.

'Take the weight off your feet, Mr Hastings. Would you like a drink?'

'I'd like to leave.'

'But we appreciate you *not* leaving, sir. Not just for a while.'

Hastings sprawled into a chair. Long, long legs spread out, face now a mask of cold nothingness.

'I must say, I'm intrigued by your name and address, sir,' Knox paddled happily on. 'Castlewest Road, Hastings. A quaint coincidence.'

'No.'

'Let me guess. You changed your name to match your new abode.'

'It was done through a solicitor, 11 years ago.'

'I see. And why was that?'

Jack Hastings left off trying to disrupt Knox's blandness. Instead he looked up at the cracked ceiling, evidently assessing its need of renovation.

'I wasn't keen on my father.'

'Ah.'

'So, of course I bumped the git off and put him down the waste disposal. Your police station could do with a real going over.'

'Yes, you're quite right, sir. It's lack of funds. We certainly couldn't afford your rates. Gothix, that's your firm, isn't it?'

'No secret. And I'm afraid I don't do gothic interview rooms.'

Knox beamed. 'Sure you wouldn't like a drink?'

'Okay. **A** Budweiser.'

'*Sorry*, sir, we're not licensed.'

Hastings brought down his eyes and glared. 'Then let's get this over with.'

In his own way, this one was fun, too.

Knox examined his notes.

'I understand from Ms Cork you were due to arrive at her *soiree* at about 7.30, your usual time, but you didn't get there until much later, because your van broke down.'

'That's what I said.'

'But later again, your van seems to have been all right.'

'Yeah. Sunspot activity, heard of it?'

'Mmm.' Knox looked sad. 'You see, you've become a film star, Mr Hastings.' Hastings sat, looking at him. 'TV, sir. A bit of a disturbance on the Seatree Road, around 6.00-ish, when the temporary traffic lights failed.' No reaction. 'Some woman videoed it. Apparently someone threatened her after a while, so she stopped filming. But what she got went out on Meridian's local news around 10.30. And *what* she got, sir, apart from some nasty wobbly reportage, was a shot of you, having a struggle with another geezer in a suit.'

The eyes froze. Not cold now, only adamantine.

'Yeah?'

'Oh, yes, sir. The section is nice and clear. They helpfully sent it straight up to us, and I've watched it. You look very effective, sir. About seven seconds before the film ends.'

'You're sure it was me, are you?'

'*Yes*, sir. I wish I could be as sure of the lottery numbers. My wife is always doing it. I dreamed them once, y'know. Won £10.'

'Congratulations.'

'Not enough to give me early retirement, though, so there we are.'

Hastings looked down at his well-shaped hands. They were strong hands, too. He was thin, but well-built, used to hard physical work. Could probably have taken Steven Grace to the cleaners and back again.

'You see, Mr Hastings, I'd really like to know what you were doing on that road so very near the time that Mr Grace must have been driving off it into that ditch.'

'Driving home from South London.'

'Yes, sir.'

'There was a chance of a job in Greenwich. Revamping a house. I went up to check it out.'

'And on the way home you got stuck in traffic, lost your temper and nipped out for a fight.'

'I got out to *stop* a fight.'

'The young man you grabbed hold of?'

'Yes. He was being a prat. I persuaded him to get back in his car.'

'Very public-spirited. And then what?'

'I drove on to Seatree.'

'In your van?' Hastings didn't say anything. Knox said, 'Were you in your van, Mr Hastings?'

'You know I wasn't, don't you?'

'I didn't see it in the video, no.'

'Then I wasn't.'

'What *were* you in, then?'

'A car, obviously.'

'You also own a car?'

'I don't own a car. It was the car of the guy I'd seen in Greenwich about the work.'

'How was that?'

'I'd gone up by train. Then wasted a lot of time. He drove me back.'

'A real Samaritan.'

'There were things to discuss.'

'About the job.'

'Partly.'

Knox put his fingertips carefully together, as if trying to superglue them in place.

'This man was a friend, then?'

'I know him.'

'Let me ask, by any chance, was this friend of yours the man you grabbed hold of, the one making a to-do at the lights?'

Hastings scowled. 'Yes.'

'Short-tempered chap?'

'Yes.'

'And you didn't notice Mr Grace or his car anywhere around?'

Hastings flamed into a rage again, like a struck match. 'He was the last bloody thing on my mind. No. I didn't see him.'

'So you had no arrangement to meet him, somewhere off the Seatree Road?'

'Why'd I want that? He was an arsehole.'

'Perhaps just for that very reason?'

Hastings blinked. 'What?'

Knox's spine prickled. He said, softly, 'I mean, Mr Hastings, that maybe you wanted to knock some sense into Steven Grace. Teach him some manners as far as Ms Cork was concerned. She's told me he had a hold on her. Maybe you were keen to break it.'

'I don't do people over,' said Jack Hastings. 'I do interior decoration. Now, I think, unless you want to charge me with something, or charge Ms Cork with something, in which case my solicitor is going to be woken up, unless all that, I suggest I get Jula and take her home.'

Knox rose, and Jack Hastings rose, towering over him with murder in his eyes, but whether past or to come was still unsure.

'You've been very helpful, Mr Hastings.'

'*Have* I? Christ.'

I appreciate your assistance, and Ms Cork's. We may need to speak you again.'

'Right.'

'Oh, by the way.'

At the door, Hastings turned. His face and fists were clenched. '*Yes?*'

'Your friend from Greenwich would be able to confirm all this? And that he went on to Seatree with you? I assume he did?'

'He might confirm it. I told you, he's a nutter.'

'That may be a nuisance, Mr Hastings. But could I just ask his name?'

'Dominic.'

'Dominic …?'

'I don't know his second name. I never asked. Maybe he hasn't got one.'

The door shut, with neither a bang nor a whimper, but with a vicious rasp.

A minute later the door was knocked on and flew open again. This time it was PC Kenton.

'Abandon hope all ye that enter here,' growled Knox. 'And it had better be good.'

'It is,' said Tony Kenton, 'but a bit late, too. Sorry, sir. I only just got in on all this. There's a girl, isn't there, friend of this Ms Cork's – Markessa Philbin?'

'Oh yes. Upset Markessa. So?'

'Well, she's gone missing, sir.'

Miranda stood before the long mirror. The light was muted in her bedroom, not at full pitch as George preferred it in the rest of the house. Even so, framed in the gilded coils of the mirror, she could see the bruising of her body quite distinctly.

Poor body. Poor, poor thing. She touched it carefully. She had been lovely once. But her breasts sagged now, and the awful little folded girdle of shadow got deeper every year, at the base of her stomach. Her thighs were quite firm though, as were her arms. She'd lied when she said her hands weren't strong. She *was* strong. Too strong. She'd lasted.

Her arms ached so, where he had seized her, and shaken her. She kept rubbing them absently, but it helped only for a moment. The facial bruise was nothing, and on her back it wasn't so bad. And she had stopped bleeding now, that was a relief. She hated it so when he made her bleed like that. As if she were a virgin.

Tomorrow, she'd be able to get something for all this, and then he would be gone – gone, her darling love – and she could try to find some peace –

If only peace were possible.

She heard him outside, even on the magic carpet, and snatched up her dressing gown.

Miranda was belted into it before George Alliat entered the room.

'Looking at yourself again? Preening.'

'Oh, just women's stuff, darling.'

His hand on the light switch turned it up to maximum radiance.

'I'm surprised you still want to look at yourself,' he said.

So she looked away. She went to her dressing-table and began fussing with some of the creams and lotions.

'But you always,' he said, 'surprise me, Miranda.'

He hardly ever spoke her name. Surely he didn't want to – not again – oh God not again? But if he must – he must have what he must have – her best beloved.

'Are you packed? Are you hungry, darling? Do you need anything?'

'More whisky, but I got it. I just wanted to look at you. You amazed me when that policeman was here, you really did. Your complete indifference. Some blighter's been killed just along the lane. So what?'

Terror.

'Oh – but – darling –'

'But you always were self-centred, Miranda. Nothing matters much, does it, unless it's inside that little rose-coloured world of yours.'

She was shivering, trying to smile, to seem adoring and glad.

Flattered by his attention.

'Don't give a damn, do you?' he said. 'Do you?'

'Darling, I –'

He was gone. The door shut. She was left alone under the brightness of the light, twisting in it, like a scorching moth.

5

The sky beyond the wall flowed with the night. It would be easy to fall asleep. But only for a moment. The bench was hard, meant for thought not slumber. Jula turned. Jack's profile might have been cut from the same slate.

'You're very angry.'

'That's the one.'

'Maybe don't be? They're just doing what policemen do.'

'It's not that great, Jula. You told that bastard quite a lot.'

'Is he a bastard? That's nice. He and I will have something in common.'

Sky, night. Behind them, the silent, broody house. Half sleep, forget your troubles. That owl, calling again. The moon was down – or hidden. Stars caught in trees, sequins on a vast black dress … *I love it here. Despite everything.*

'Jula.'

'… Yes?'

'You don't need me going on at you. Forget I said it.'

'I don't mind what you say. You're right, I expect. But I just can't be – what do they say? – careful. I don't want to watch every word.'

'Yeah, well. That Knox guy's a pain, but I don't think he's mental. Let's hope he's just clever enough to fall for you.'

'No-one ever does.'

'I bloody did.'

'Yes. But you're you.'

Steven had brought them together, that was the poignant irony. Steven and Steven's demands:

'All right. I've been put out into this room. But look at it. God almighty.'

'Would you like,' she said, 'to have it repainted –?'

'Repainted, re-everything. But I know better than to ask you, baby. All I'm worth is the box room and a second-hand Porsche.'

They hadn't slept together, in any sense, for months. He was seeing someone else, probably two someone elses at least. When he slept at the house, he lay down in one of the spare rooms that had a bed. He had burnt two holes, with cigarettes, in the blankets. And smashed the bedside lamp, knocking it over in the night.

Now Jula offered Steven the large back bedroom, with its view of the old garden and the fields. The room was about 18 feet by 15. The box room?

'I do grasp,' he said, 'you're too damned mean to do it up for me.'

'You want me to do it up.'

'Not *you*, for God's sake. I can picture the mess. Streaky walls. Cats hair in the paint. And don't say you're offering to whisk up some new curtains on a sewing machine? *You*, the arch undomesticated woman of the '90s.'

'I'll get someone in to do it,' she said, 'obviously.'

'Workmen. Bods. Ace. Just let me out.'

He left it to her, in this fashion. For some reason he always liked to have an excuse to be away. As if he couldn't say to her, *I'm screwing another woman, and spending your money on my card that taps into your account. And you won't do bugger all to stop me, because I know about your one major cock-up and now you're at my mercy, baby.*

No, it was always, *I'm seeing someone. Advertising. Theatre. There might be something in it for me. Which means* money. *What you like.* Comprendé?

At first, trying to be interested, she had asked who and what. (Trying also to believe him?)

'Stop fucking nagging. God, you're a bitch. You claw away my confidence. Third degree. Who? Who? Give me some space. You want to balls up everything I try, don't you?'

She had stopped asking.

Yes, Steven. Of course. Whatever.

Some space.

She knew from what he had flung at her that he wanted the room to be sparely contemporary – 'Even if the rest of the house stinks. Jesus, you're actually a miser, do you know that?'

'I know I have some money, Steven. But I'm afraid I'm not rich. Sometimes I do have to be – not too extravagant.'

'Earn some dosh, then. Get a book published.'

'That's not so simple now, as you're aware.'

'You write this airy-fairy rubbish and they've seen through you. That's the trouble.'

'You don't read my books,' she said. 'How can you know?' Sometimes she did answer back.

But he had only sneered, 'I did read one, though, didn't I? That was enough.'

He wouldn't discuss what he wanted done with the room. Christ, couldn't she get her head out of the clouds for five minutes and come up with something a normal woman would? Did he have to hold her hand for everything?

'I didn't think it was my hand you held,' she said. 'I thought it was my neck.'

Even though he wouldn't give her many clues, she had to solve the riddle of the room, however. She was well aware of that.

It was like arranging something for a child. A spoilt, manipulative, horrible child. A dangerous child one wished one had smothered in the cradle.

She had seen the flyer in the tea-shop window in Seatree.

Gothix wasn't a large outfit, but she thought she had heard of them and that they were effective and not extortionate. (It was a fact, she wasn't rich. Alone, she had been comfortable, of course. But she had just received the bill for Steven's latest Versace suit.)

She tried the number of Gothix and spoke to a man called Jack Hastings, who arranged to come out and look at the room.

When he arrived, the blue van pulling up neatly and on time in front of the fence, she'd been taken aback. Hastings looked familiar to her. She thought she probably had seen him, here, or down on the coast. He was quite distinctive, so tall, and the fall of strong masculine hair, like a black horsetail. His face. When serious, he was undeniably handsome. But, unusual in a structure of such strong bones, his face could also turn to rubber. When he grinned, it did so.

She liked him. Yet Jula was always cautious now, where she liked. People fooled her. It had happened quite often, the worst of course with Steven Grace.

Hastings looked at the room. He said it was two rooms knocked through, an interesting shape, altogether a good area. He'd like to do it, except the concept she'd outlined was a bit limiting, given the general style of the house.

'It isn't for me. And I'm afraid he won't change his mind.'

'Right.'

Jack told her later he'd normally have got out of it at that point, because what Jula had said her partner desired was going to bore Jack Hastings to tears. He'd have asked Barry or Surinder to strip the paper, and paint. And got one of his contacts, maybe Scandalabra, the lights and soft furnishings shop in Seatree, to fix the rest.

But he didn't. He decided he'd do most of it himself, even taking Jula to choose the necessary furniture and curtaining.

'I thought you'd see through it,' he said afterwards. 'If you'd known me better you would. It's not the kind of work I do.'

'I'd guessed that, but I thought you were being very kind. That you'd taken pity on me.'

'Yeah. That's the word. Pity.'

It was, she found, enjoyable. Going out early in the van, roaming about the furniture stores, antiques shops and auction rooms, and to the studios of Jack's mates, in one of which stood ten foot statues made of steel tubes, strange as beings from Mars, and beautiful. He didn't try to push her over her budget, but he knew where to find bargains.

She bought him lunch in Rye. Then he wouldn't let her pay. That didn't seem professional.

She knew she'd miss it, when the excursions ended.

But then, of course, he worked on the room.

He liked the cats. He would pick one up carefully and then hang it around his neck. He offered to paint them for her, Nero orange and Lavender – lavender. And bellowed with laughter when she took him for a moment seriously. He brought the cats presents, cat-nip mice and pilchards in tomato sauce.

As they drank tea and coffee in the kitchen, he would tell her he would like to work on the whole house. But she couldn't afford it, and he didn't press.

If it hadn't been for Steven, and the expense of Steven, she could have afforded it.

But they did discuss the kitchen. What could be done sometime. Jack offered to take her around some more, to look at things for the kitchen, not buying, just planning.

Steven wasn't at that time there in the day. That is, he was either away all day and all night, or still dead asleep when Jula went out in the van. By the day Jack started work in the house, Steven had gone off for a 'break'. All this was with one of the someone elses, Jula knew.

She began to hope that the someone else and Steven would decide they wanted to be together. He would almost certainly make demands on Jula for cash, but he wouldn't have to live there. At least, not unless he came back.

His comments on the room, when he inspected it now and then in the preliminary state – 'Hasn't the guy even started yet?' – were derogatory, grudging. Later, on a flying return visit one night, 'Some cheapskate covey of wide-boys. It's all right. I can live with it. That chair's not bad. No, that isn't bad at all. What happened? Lost your head and spent some money?'

'It was off a skip,' she unwisely said. 'It's been cleaned up, effected, and varnished.'

'Off a fucking *skip*. I might have known.'

Why had she told him?

Yes, she should long ago have learned to hold her tongue. Either she could be truthful, or she could be silent. Silence then. Silence.

In the end the room was done.

Of its type, it was elegant.

'It's like what that woman said to me,' Jack reflected, 'about some of the examples in my file. Not my taste, dear, but I can see it's all right.'

The best of the room was the dark blue ceiling. It had the effect of a swirling midnight sky. Jack had taken a chance with it.

'If he doesn't rate it, I'll paint over. No extra charge.'

Jack hadn't met Steven. Jula had said very little about Steven.

Strangely, strangely, Steven, coming back from his 'break' entirely a day early, took to the ceiling of dark sky.

'How'd he think of that?'

'It's what he does.'

'That's cool. I like that. I can lie and look up into that when I can't sleep. Yes. He's done a great job on the ceiling. Okay bloke, was he?'

'He seemed to be.'

'Yes. That's great. God, I'd have loved that as a kid.'

Coming home early was conceivably (as the flying return had been) an escape. The someone else must have got on his nerves. They always did in the end.

For a day or so, Steven was even rather reasonable.

He wanted Jula to take him out to dinner, to 'celebrate the room'. He said she ought to have one of her 'at home' dinners, and ask this Hastings bod round, if he was promising. Maybe he'd be able to do something with the rest of the house. Cut rate, if they charmed him. (Steven meant if Steven charmed him. But Steven could charm. He had charmed Jula. Even Leonardo.)

She put off the dinner invitation. She had told Jack she would meet him in Hastings, his eponymous town, later in the week. The title of the excuse for the meeting was *Jula's Kitchen*.

She knew it was an excuse.

Steven was away again that night. His fractiousness was already creeping, racing back. He was going to see some friend. Or another someone else. He'd be gone all night. He always told her, if in a sort of code. Because he was always later than he said he would be, and yet the time lapse was predictable. By the code, a given hour meant usually two hours after the one specified. All night was indicated by the words *I'll probably be quite late.'*

This reminded her of her parents, in some indefinable and perverse way. Always, it had reminded her.

Steven had reminded her of her father when she first met him. A lily of the field. Before he told her all the things he had done, the spiteful scams, the thievery, his life had brought back to her the life of David Cork. For David had wandered London at 15, and taken money from women for services rendered. And David had never held any regular employment. Vivien had been the 'breadwinner.'

But as Steven, never *known* to Jula, yet became for her *revealed*, her father, tender, wild and poetic, burnished with *joie de vivre*, faded away. It was her second loss of him. It hurt her very much.

Worse, in frightening sequence, Steven instead began to remind Jula of Leonardo.

She told Jack this, when they met that afternoon in Hastings. She told him in the first couple of hours, as if she couldn't any longer hold back.

Realistically she hadn't known what to expect. Yet none of it was a shock. Somehow she *had* known, and had known Jack. This was why he had looked familiar from the start. In some way she recognised him. Not only marriages are made in heaven.

A phone was ringing.

Apparently Markessa hadn't broken it.

'You were asleep.'

'No … maybe. I'll go and –'

'Come on. At this time of night? Leave it. It could be Markessa's heavy breather again.'

'I have an idea about that. You said the call came from the Fighting Man. There's a woman I've been corresponding with – Katherine Churchman –' Jula was already moving through the door – 'Just in case. She said something about coming down.'

She ran through the hall, not really in her body, drifting, and picked up the receiver.

'Ms Cork? *Sorry* to trouble you.'

'Chief Inspector.'

'I thought you might be up.'

A liar. A game-player. Dodgy, Jack had said.

'What did you want?'

'I forgot to ask you, Ms Cork. Aside from the high blood-pressure, did Mr Grace have any history of coronary problems in his family?'

'I don't know.'

'He never mentioned anything?'

'He ran away when he was very young. His mother mistreated him.'

'And the father?'

'I think his father was a bully, too. I don't know about his heart.'

'I see. Well, you've been very gracious, Ms Cork. Mr Hastings still with you? No, I don't need to speak to him. I hope you can get some sleep. Knit up the ravelled sleeve and so on.'

When she put down the phone, she was laughing softly.

Jack was in the hall.

'It was that skunk, Knox, wasn't it?'

'Playing – what do you call it?'

'Mind-fuck,' Jack Hastings said.

It had been a cold sunny March day with a ruffling wind. The sort of day it would have been, for Vivien and David, if they had reached the sea that afternoon years ago.

Jack and Jula walked along the promenade from St Leonards. The sea, surface-washed in blue, was struck about in troughs of smoky green. Light splashed on the faces of hotels. Clouds ran ragged, and gulls, white as if just released from a washing machine, strutted with dagger bills along the pebble beach.

After the walk, they had a drink, then sat on a public seat looking at the ocean.

They had been talking. Mostly Jula had. She said at first, once or twice, 'I'll stop now.' But he made her go on. No-one had listened to her in a thousand years. Hard to resist.

'I should hate that house. It took my parents away from me.' She had told him about that too, in the pub. Now he lifted her hands and warmed them in his own.

'Steven came out with something – I can hardly say it.'

'What did he say?'

'It was – oh, last year, I think. We'd had one of the rows with a capital R. He said I was a tragedy queen. He said the story about my parents – I'd made it up, so I could be little Miss Look-after-me. And then he said, if it *were* true, then they'd left me. Not vanished – just dumped me.'

'I'm getting a picture of Steven.'

'But – it couldn't be true, could it, Jack? He made it sound very plausible. They'd never meant to have a child. They lived a sort of uncommitted roving life, and then I came along and stopped them. But when the Old Man – David's father – took an interest, was going to provide for me – even left me a house for when I was 21 – Steven said my mother and father just made a run for it. He said, perhaps they didn't even plan to. Just got the inspiration on the way. And went.'

She was grateful that Jack didn't argue with this, find logical reasons why it could never be so. He understood the doubt was sown, forever. He said only, 'Odd things happen, Jula. People do go missing.'

'The awful thing is, I'm not sure if I'd rather that they were alive somewhere, happy – if it means they did that. All the years when I couldn't think about it, what might have been done to them –'

'Things happen,' he said again.

They went down and walked on the beach. Jula found it hard-going on the stones, but as the sun westered, the tide drew out, and the lower second secret beach of Hastings appeared, the wet sand a shining blue mirror of the sky.

They stood looking out to the horizon, the curve of the planet, and Jack said, 'You were very happy with your parents as a kid, weren't you?'

'Yes – yes – I was very happy.'

'Then they loved you. It isn't possible otherwise.'

'Yes.'

'God knows about the rest. But that's for sure.'

'Yes. Thank you, Jack.'

They began talking about things from childhood.

He told her how, at six, he had truly dyed his first dog's white front and tail with food-colouring. All the neighbours were out pointing.

'*What* colour?'

'Cochineal. Trouble was, the dog liked the taste. When my mum finally got it out, he wouldn't leave us alone, wanting more.'

Not once had they spoken of the kitchen.

They'd been going to have lunch, but not bothered. Then Jack suggested an early dinner.

'You must be starved,' she said, 'but – I don't really want to.'

'Not eat?'

'I don't really want to go in anywhere, somehow.'

They started to walk off the beach. At the top of the steps they gazed back. The sun was now in mist, a puddle of Oloroso gold spilling slowly down toward the far curve of the water, and the Marina drifted anchorless, like a phantom liner.

'The sky there's the colour of the ghost of a peach,' said Jula. She had trusted him, but then she tensed – she was used to Steven. But Jack only nodded.

'Yep. How about peaches for tea, and sausages?'

They went to Jack's flat up the West Hill by the last lift of the day.

Sat with him in the carriage, she saw the light fade below, and an ochre half darkness come, and then the light begin again on the other side as they reached the top. It reminded her of the passage of dawn to dusk to dawn. And of death. What was said of death. The dying of the light. The dark tunnel with a new and greater brilliance opening at its end.

She didn't speak about that. She had never been in the lift before.

Jack's flat was on the third floor of a vast and high-built house. From his window and the balcony before it, you could gaze sidelong at the ruined Conqueror castle, and right down to the toylike spread of Hastings at the sea's edge, under the cliff.

'It's wonderful.'

'Not in winter it isn't, when the gales get up. We're talking about storm shutters. When they had the hurricane in '87, all the windows in the house blew out. I didn't live here then. Shame; that year I could have done with the money fixing things.'

He told her he had changed his name to Hastings after a day visit. 'They say, if you ever come here, you always come back.'

It was a room with a feel of open air, sparsely filled by unusual furniture. The ceiling was a sky, classically realistic at its centre – milk-blue, fluted by cirrus – scattering in a whirlpool of ribboning blue cloud at the extremities.

'What's for tea, then?' she asked.

'Mulligatawny-owl soup, girl.' Jula giggled. 'That's what my mum used to say we'd got, when I asked her.'

Actually, the meal was rather more complex than their swift visit to the supermarket had suggested.

The pork sausages were cut long-ways and set to grill. Into a pan of sautéed onion and tomato Jack cast the tin of Heinz baked beans, stirring in black pepper, ginger, dried basil, chilli powder, English mustard and two chopped cloves of garlic. In the other pan, olive oil fried mushrooms and sliced green peppers.

Jack's narrow kitchen was scrubbed but muddled. You needed to *find* things.

Finally the contents of the two pans were mixed and added to the sausages on a mattress of lettuce. They ate the result in the main room, with Jacob's Cream Crackers and butter and glasses of iced tea.

During the cooking and eating of this meal, Jula knew exactly what she was being reminded of. The invented food was like the invented foods made by David and Vivien. The feasts of low budgets, childish playful minds.

'That was delicious.'

'Glad you liked it. You've eaten a lot, for you.'

'Yes, I have.'

The room was warm, and after dinner, they sat by the open balcony windows with a couple of brandies, and the peaches in a dish.

Pearl strings, Hastings' street lamps were on, and windows burned oblongs of colour down the hill.

Jack said, 'Jula, don't take this the wrong way, but Steven – he makes your life a bleeding misery, doesn't he?'

'Yes. He does.'

'Can't you shove him out?'

'No.'

'You're sorry for him? After the things he's done and said? Does and says. Come on.'

'I am sorry for him. But that wouldn't stop me. I was in love with him, but not now. I detest him. And he can't bear me either. But I'm useful, you see.'

'Then why do you stand it?'

She told him, choosing her words, going slowly. It was as if she must, just as she had told him all those other things. And yet she couldn't bring herself to say it all.

'Jack, I once did a very wrong thing. At least, it wasn't wrong in essence. I'd say I had to do it. But – it was also a terrible thing. Perhaps evil. If – I'm never found out, then – it will be all right. But if I were to be – I'd – I don't know how I'd cope with it.'

He said, after a long pause, 'You don't have to elaborate. But are you saying this shit Steven *has* found out?'

'He did. I wasn't very careful. Careless. I'm like that. It's – nothing I'm proud of, being such a fool.'

'He's blackmailing you?'

'Yes.'

Jack put down his plate of peach stones. He sighed. He looked at the ocean and the sky, which, sinking toward each other, were becoming the void.

'I'm not involved in anything tacky, Jula. But now and then I've met a few people. If you want, I can get hold of someone. I don't mean to kill him, Jula. I know you wouldn't stand for that. Just give him to think. Persuade him he'd do a lot better if he left you alone.'

Again then, silence.

Both of them looking far out to the edge of infinity, and the stars beginning, like imagined things.

'No, Jack. Thank you. No.'

'Okay.'

'Thank you, Jack.'

'I won't dress it up, and you don't need to. Just tell me, if you change your mind.'

Before she had left the house, she had put out cat-food and cold chicken in four bowls. She had known she might be away until late. It was a code, like Steven's.

Staying the night with Jack was as inevitable and ordinary as something that had happened already over and over.

A prologue of debating on cab fares, for the journey back, was followed by an examination of the pros and cons of remaining until tomorrow.

Then Jack made what he called a speech to her, explaining how things had come to be. During the speech he told her too of someone he had loved, years before, dead now, dead too young, not of any illness but of a mugging in a Bristol street.

Across the void, she and he looked at each other.

She wasn't astonished, even now, although she hadn't thought of this, hadn't anticipated what he had just said to her, and told her of. Minded none of it. Feared it not at all. There were too many laws in the world.

A quiet sweetness lapped her.

Across the void, contact is always possible, if only for a moment.

In the morning, waking up in Jack's bed, pillows piled high, toast and instant coffee, seagulls shrieking as they dive-bombed the town. Having studied several folders, they redesigned her kitchen at last, on an unlimited budget. Windows of stained glass in vegetable form, cabbage leaves, the hearts of garlic, segmented tangerines. Roman tiles and Etruscan glazes. Paint shades of pumpkin, crimson and burnt gold.

6

'How odd, isn't it, this thing about sleeping? It's late, so one goes to bed. Even to sleep, quite often. Only children really resist.'

'Rules, you see,' said Katherine Churchman. 'Life is supposed to run on time, like the trains. Naturally the trains don't, and neither does the human race.'

The first bottle of wine was empty. They were only toying with the second. Now and then Honor came in, asking if they were all right. She seemed worn out. She had said, 'I don't get upstairs much before 3.30. It'll be more tonight.'

'Won't you have a glass of this wine, Mrs McCarthy?' said Katherine. 'It's refreshing.'

'Well, I'd like to. Maybe later, if the offer's still open.'

Oprah the cat, eager to be helpful, ran after her.

Dexter had remained in his tree. Katherine and Leigh went to look. He lay stretched out high up, like a panther.

'I suppose there's no chance,' murmured Leigh, 'he'll fall asleep and roll out?'

'Nah won't,' advised Dexter.

'The sharp ears of youth,' Katherine said. 'And I don't think he will.'

Returned to the bar, neither of them showed any intention of going upstairs.

'I've meant to travel down to Seatree for years,' Katherine said. 'Ever since the claim was made for the bones. It seemed ethical to come, even if there had been a mistake, and that's more than possible. I'm obsessed by my grandfather, you see.'

'You mean he's buried *here*? I thought he was in Westminster Abbey.'

'Well, not quite that, but thank you for believing so. No, I don't mean my grandfather's bones – doesn't that sound Shakespearean? I mean the bones of the three knights. The housecarls, properly. King Harold's men who deserted the battlefield at Senlac.'

Leigh had once heard this story. Her father had told it to her about the same time he told her of the Sea Tree, which had, maybe, given the town its name. An oak so high that, although growing low in a valley, the sea was visible from its top. From where witches summoned storms.

The local myth of Harold's housecarls, his 'knights', became vivid for her more from a painting than from Churchman's poetry. She didn't admit this.

'Harold, the last English King. Killed by William the Conqueror and his Normans at Senlac. And although all the men of his immediate household were said to have died with him, three got away. Is that right?'

'One has to remember,' said Katherine, 'that Harold's men were Saxons. They had Viking blood. They fought in a battle-rage, berserker, swinging their axes until the Normans broke the shield wall and cut down every man with the King. In the poem, William's army was drunk on slaughter, and only jeered at the fleeing knights. But Churchman has it:

> 'Not for cowardice they fled,
> 'But to preserve
> 'One splinter of that hour,
> 'As carrying a taper from a sinking fire
> 'Men light the dark again.'

In the story, she said, they had dreamed of rallying the English, of summoning assistance from the blond lands across the sea. But these places were warred out, or had grown to like peace too well. And God, all men had seen, was on the side of William.

Somewhere in the hills above the battle ground, as sunset ended, they admitted to each other and themselves that there was no hope, and that they should have remained at Senlac, to perish with their King.

'And came we here at death of day,
'And soon the earth lay in the sun's black tomb
'That men call night.'

She waited a moment, considering.

'It could have been shame, too, couldn't it?' said Katherine. 'And guilt, and regret. Such emotions can make people do strange and sometimes terrible things.'

'Yes,' Leigh said. *Yes they can.*

'My grandfather's poem describes how they formed a circle, and raising their swords, hacked each other down. They wouldn't die the Straw Death of old men, or the maid's death of suicide. In the end it was battle valour they still wanted. Somehow they struck and struck until each one had given and received a death wound. When I read the poem,' said Katherine, 'I never doubt they managed it. Later, people stole up from a nearby Saxon village, and buried them in a wood. Buried them with honour, with their weapons by their sides.'

'My father told me that. He used to say we ought to look for the spot.'

'After the poem was printed and the legend was revived,' said Katherine, 'whole trainloads of Victorian gentlemen and ladies would come down to the countryside above Battle, digging about for the grave. It was mostly fields by then. The farmers got quite irate. One even wrote to Churchman, complaining. He wrote back, 'I am only responsible for the writing of my work, not for the actions of any insane persons who happen to read it.'

'Do you know the painting?' asked Leigh, casually.

'You mean by Rossetti's wife?'

'*Yes.* Lizzie Siddal. You know she married him. Not everyone knows. The painting is rather effective, but not rated, I'm afraid, because she wasn't Rossetti himself.'

'I do know it. Inaccurate clothing and accoutrements, but it doesn't matter. The atmosphere is so right. Two mailed men seated on their horses, the third standing, and the landscape all shadows, just that red smudge of dying sun far off.'

'She's said to have done that with her thumb. And she called it *Death of Day.*'

'Yes. That means more than sunset, of course. In pagan times – and there were plenty of pagan practices still current in England in 1066 – the day and the sun were both associated with a war-leader or king – any man who wielded great power over others. My grandfather had a theory too that Harold was a corn-king. That is, only in a spiritual sense. His death by cutting down would then be a sacrifice for the harvest, and the health of his country. Churchman argued that the sacrifice must always be of the best – like the white bull chosen for the same reason. And Harold was reportedly magnificent, gold-haired, and well above average height. But it's fanciful. The English people didn't want to lose Harold, and they suffered afterwards. The Normans were harsh masters.'

'You know there's a wine bar in Horse Street called the White Bull?'

Katherine nodded. 'And there's a pub between here and Battle known as the Barleycorn.'

'I take it from what you said,' Leigh ventured, 'that someone thinks they've found the bones of the three knights.'

'That's so. But it was years ago. In 1987, in fact, after the famous hurricane. A tree was blown down on someone's land, just off a place called Divers Lane. The grave came up with it.'

Leigh held her breath, not knowing why, and *knowing* why.

Katherine said, 'The grave-goods were all there, two-handed English axes, and swords, traces of clothing, goldwork. Even, of all sad things, a rose-head caught under a ribcage and somehow preserved. That was controversial. There may have been such roses in England then, brought from Byzantium. Or not. The only major hiccup at the time, or so I understand, was that there were too many.'

'Too many –?'

'Too many bones. *Four* knights, and not three. At first no-one quibbled. Then, with carbon-dating and so on – Three of the skeletons were very old, and had most of their teeth. The fourth was toothless, and had died in modern times.'

Leigh felt the hair shift on her scalp. Actually felt that. And a sort of sickness. Surely for no proper reason.

'How odd. When you say modern –?'

'I think they established, no earlier than the 1970s.'

7

Soon after letting the badger cross the road, they came to an all-night garage.

For a second, Markessa's heart staggered to its feet. But the garage was unmanned, only a couple of automatic pumps and a drinks machine.

'A drink,' said her abductor. 'I'm not going to offer you one, I'm afraid. For reasons outlined previously. Women, you know, are supposed to have bigger bladders than men. Which hardly explains why they are constantly piddling. Does it?'

'No,' she whispered.

He got out, shutting his door, and went over to the machine.

As it rattled and banged, Markessa tried to do something with her own door, and the sellotape rasped and turned into a tourniquet on her wrists. The door was locked, anyway.

In a few moments he was back, sliding into the driver's seat. He had the gun in his right hand, and an icy can of Perrier in his left hand, which he put on the dash. The green of the can looked violent to Markessa. It made her feel ill. It was coldly sweating, as she was.

'Now, let's go and find somewhere for me to drink it. Any recommendations? No, I think I'll decide.'

They were off down the narrow roads again, the night flung behind them.

Somewhere, a gravelled track ran up into a hilly pasture. He took this apparently at random. The white cab jounced and bucked.

'Going to mess up his suspension, I should think,' remarked the abductor, tolerantly.

Markessa had realised this was the cab in which Jack had

brought her back to town. But that was irrelevant. Then it struck her – while the man was at the drinks machine, she could have tried to switch the cab radio back on. Someone might have heard her. At her own idiocy she gave a strangled cry of appalled frustration, and he laughed, this man.

'You sound like a duck, dear.'

He pulled up at the top of the pasture. Trees stood there in a crowd, a windbreak, the foliage only one more aspect of the night.

'Look. A *view.*'

Dully, she looked. Some lights littered the dark below, not enough for the town. A group of houses with a lit street, maybe a pub – if she could reach them. But they seemed more than a mile away.

'Let's get out. Sit on the hill.'

He got out, and invited her, so she had to 'wriggle' across again.

The cindery track hurt her feet, and the grassy tussocks had plenty of knife-like stones concealed in them just for her.

'Oh, don't cry, Markessa, he said. 'You're such a disappointment to me.'

She blurted, 'Why am I? You don't know me.'

'I'm *getting* to know you, sweet thing.' He sang a line from the appropriate song, a song from *The King and I,* which Markessa hadn't heard since she had left her parents' house, nine years before. 'A golden oldie,' said the young man. (Younger than she was, she thought wildly. About 23, no more. Maybe younger than that.)

He helped her sit down on the chilled grass. She'd get cystitis; it had happened before. Was that going to count? Would she be alive to get cystitis?

But then, he hadn't murdered her yet. In a disgusting way, he was being chivalrous.

Now, however, he took a small packet, the sort that safety pins are sold in, from his pocket. Opening the can of Perrier, he poured powder from the packet into the water. Shook the can. Drank two or three mouthfuls

'Better,' he said. 'Oh, God. Yes.'

Markessa had taken the odd recreational drug. She had even managed to get some blow for Steven. But this – what was it – *heroin?* – scared her. This was serious. Quite at one with the kidnap and the Walther PPK.

'Are you very cold?'

'Yes.'

'That s a shame. This stuff stops all that. But none for you. We won't stay up here too long. But I thought I'd like to tell you, now.'

In the silence, she remembered the psychiatrists. Ask echoing questions. Gentle interest. A willingness to hear.

'To tell me?'

'About me. Because in an incredible way, we have a link, you and I.'

'A link?'

'First of all, my name. My name is Dominic.'

'Dominic?'

'And now, I think I'll tell you how I met Jack.'

'*Jack?*' Unavoidably, her voice had stopped being neutral.

'Markessa,' Dominic said patiently, 'don't keep repeating everything I say. It's unbelievably irritating.'

She was effectively gagged. She sat, shaking with cold and horror. Waiting.

'I met Jack in the restaurant. That's where Bashy works. Jack – I mean Jack Hastings, of course – used to take the train and go round a lot, leaving his flyers in what he calls pay-off areas. He does it less now, since his little business took off. But the Docklands is always worth a go. I quote. Canary Wharf, all that. And Greenwich.'

(A million miles above, Markessa heard a plane passing. A huge solid silver plane, packed with people eating or drowsing or praying they'd be safe. And here she was, a dot unseen below, less safe than they were in that safe, safe plane.)

Are you paying attention, Markessa?'

'Yes – yes, I am.'

'You must, you know. The day Jack came to the restaurant, I

could see at a glance that Bash liked him. Surprise, surprise. Her big bulbous black eyes lit up. She's the cook there, the – er – *chef*. And I have to say, Bashy *can* cook. The restaurant is in her repulsive thrall. What she wants, she gets. It's called the Iron Cherry, by the way.'

Markessa tried to say, *The Iron Cherry?* Without speaking.

'I have a suspicion they named it after Thatcher. I shall never know. Anyway, Bash was out of her kitchen, looking all shaggy and unshaven as usual. Did I say, she's about fifty. My word, what the years can do to a girl. Something you don't have to bother with now, my dearest.'

Markessa tried to say (unspeaking), *I want to have to bother. I want to be fifty, all my teeth capped, and hormonal, and with a little moustache that has to be waxed – I really do want that so much.*

'So Bash gets the manager and says, *See this young man? He's going to do up the bar area.* I have to explain here that the bar area had never been up to itch, let alone scratch. So Jack looks at it and says, *Yeah.* The way he does. And two days later he comes back all alone and does it. I have to tell you it was an innovation. Dark cherry red walls with black iron railings, the sort like spears, in front. And the ceiling a layered green leaf effect with hanging lamps – like cherries, in iron cages. So far over the top it was hidden by the height of the hill.'

Dominic licked the can, foreplay.

'The patrons of the Cherry went mad on it, and Bash says, *See how clever I've been.* But by then, by then –' He stopped and had another drink of drugged water.

Could she run away and down the hill toward the lights?

Her bare feet. Her toes would be broken, and she might fall and break her ankle or her leg. Or her neck.

And he had a gun. It sat there in his hand like a cute little pet.

'Speak to me, Markessa,' he said, affronting her by his illogicality. Even though, perhaps, that alone might save her.

'I don't know what – you *know* Jack.'

'My, you *are* so *quick.* Yes, I know Jack. And Jack – has mucked me about. That's the best way to say it. I think.

Mucked, or fucked. Yes?'

'You mean – you had a relationship with … *Bash* – and Jack –'

'Oh, worse than that. Jack led me down the demon road to darkness. Jack – dropped me into –' Dominic tilted back his head, and tears ran now, sparkling, almost bubbling, like the Perrier, over his face. 'Christ, Markessa. Oh Christ. Oh Christ.'

'But what can *I* do?' An error. She knew it as she said it. Too late to bite it back.

He turned and stared at her. He *did* have wonderful eyes. If only they were blind.

'You can do this. You can pay him back for me.'

'Pay him – how? What do you –?'

'When I kill you,' he said. '*Then*. Think I can't? You don't know, do you? Perhaps I've killed before. Today, even. It's supposed to get easier.'

He stood up.

Markessa managed to scramble to her feet.

'Please – please – I don't understand –'

'I've told you enough for now, you filthy whore. *Enough!*' He grabbed her arm. Fingers of iron like the railing and cages at the restaurant. 'Back to the car. I'm not ready yet. Have to get ready.'

He pulled her down the hill. Probably running down it the other way wouldn't have been any worse.

When they reached the cab, he pushed her and she fell against the side. So much for chivalry.

But he drank again, and his face smoothed out.

'I baptised this car earlier,' he said. 'It drove past and I threw some water over it. Not *this* sort of water, naturally. Not *special* water.'

She tried not to speak or to cry, and unspeaking, unweeping, to beg for her life.

He said, 'But, my dear girl, you're really *not* what he led me to believe.'

8

She hadn't wanted to speak about it. Not to Katherine. But something made her say, 'I drove through that way tonight. Divers Lane.'

And Katherine said, 'It's an odd name, isn't it? It's supposed to come from Dives, the rich man in the Bible – Dives' Lane. An old sheep path, I think, in mediaeval times.'

Somehow then Leigh felt herself begin to draw breath to say, *There was a car off the road –*

But before she could, Katherine added, reflectively, 'A coincidence. Everyone tells one that something is too much of a coincidence, that Dickens, for example, has too many coincidences. But life is riddled with them, don't you find?'

'Yes.' Leigh lapsed, grateful almost to let go of it.

'My grandfather said something about coincidences. He said that people themselves cause them to occur – a sort of collision of desires and fears, all adhering to each other. Caught in a web that was jointly spun … The life of thirty strangers, or more, might be meshed together, seemingly at random, even though years and times, even continents, divided them. Possibly we might say telepathy now. Or karma.'

Then she drew herself up. 'I must stop talking about him so much. I always do. I wrote a small biography of him – oh, a flimsy thing. But that was how I came to correspond with Jula Cork. She read it and wrote to me. She said she had been fascinated by his work, since her twenties. But not everyone wants an unleavened dose of Churchman. He'd have been the first to shut me up. He used to say I always had to have my own way and someone ought to rein me in – and no-one must. Which, of course, reined me in a little. He called me Katherine of

Arrogance.' She smiled. 'You see. Enough.'

'I don't mind.' And Leigh thought, *You must be a lot older than you look. You knew him when you were very aware, and he died when? 1918, I think. Is that how it works? Some of us die too young to balance those others who live into their eighties, nineties – crazy brain, be quiet.*

Honor appeared in the doorway. She was disarranged and blowsy, a worn-out sunflower, but carrying a tray of food and a teapot.

'Since you ladies are still up, I thought you might like a few of these. I always have something last thing, or I can't get off.'

There were cheddar cheese and tomato sandwiches, ham and horseradish, and some hot vegetable rolls.

She sat at the table with them, and Leigh wondered what would happen to the conversation now. Katherine simply poured an extra glass of wine.

'It's almost 3.00.'

'Yes. Thank God Shirley takes over the desk in a minute. But there's Dexter still to get in. That cat's had two more fish out of the pond, and I've put them back. I left the light on, you see. She loses interest in it, in the dark.'

But Dexter too had suddenly appeared in the bar.

'There you are! You've been a real pest, Dexter. You just know I won't smack you, and you take liberties. Do you want a sandwich?'

Her voice shaded so swiftly from agitation and rebuke to tenderness, that it was moving, Leigh thought.

Dexter approached the table, a somnambulist.

'Tired, Mum.'

'I'm not surprised.'

Without another word, he climbed up on her lap, laid his head on her white-suited breast, and slept.

'Look at this now.'

'He's a very handsome boy,' said Katherine.

'Yes. That's kind of you to say, but you're right. I don't know where it comes from. I wasn't so bad when I was younger, but his father – well. *Nothing* to write home about.' She stroked the child's hair, the felt-tip woad-smudged cheek. He was oblivious, gone far away. 'Usually I can get him upstairs to see his video, about 1.00. He always has to have a video before bed. He'll probably still want to, if he wakes up.'

'What does he watch?' Katherine seemed genuinely intrigued.

'Oprah Winfrey,' said Honor. She bit into a sandwich and closed her eyes.

'So he really does watch her show?'

'Number one fan. He's got every single minute they put out, on tape. He loves her. He certainly loves her more than me. But then … I had him rather late in life. Not planned. I thought it was indigestion. And then all those tests and messing you about, frightening you half to death. *It'll be brain-damaged*, all that. I was pleased when he was born, though. I've never wished I hadn't had him. Not even when I separated from his dad.'

'The best years are ahead,' said Katherine.

'Well I hope so. I think we've had the worst.'

She picked up the wine and drank it quickly, ate some more of the sandwich, then put it down. She looked at her sleeping child, her face a mixture of astonishment and thought.

Coincidences, confessions – the night was thick with them. What now?

'I probably shouldn't tell you,' said Honor McCarthy, on night's cue, 'but it's why he's a bit strange. Why I let him run wild. I don't like to curb him, or make him do things he doesn't want to.'

Leigh thought of the car in the ditch. She thought of Mrs Alliat in her rabbit slippers, and the ringing weirdness of that lighted house. She thought of the man who had come here tonight, asking questions, turning on the golden floodlight of his magnetism. She thought – of 19 months ago.

Almost she wanted to say, *Don't speak. Don't say any more.* Not because Honor's words could directly hurt her, but for all the other secrets, rising now like the fish in the pool, to a revealing light, and a crouching clawed shadow.

Rising up.

Honor said, 'I wasn't here then. We were in London. The Old Red Fox. I don't expect you know it. Dexter was only four and a half. He was off play-school with a cold that afternoon, and I had Oprah on the telly. Probably shouldn't have had him there, she deals with some adult stuff, but I didn't think he'd follow it. And he was asleep.'

Honor raised her sandwich, and put it down. Dexter, illustrative, slept. 'The programme was about these poor devils that'd been sexually abused in childhood. You felt you just had to watch. Riveting. Upsetting too. There was one man, sixty if he was a day. He broke down. Crying. And then I saw Dexter watching. I thought, *I'd better turn the telly off.* And then he said, in his little high voice, *That's what Uncle Wes does to me.* That was all. *That's what Uncle Wes does to me.*'

They sat very still. Katherine reached across and filled Honor's glass again.

'Thanks. I mustn't take all your wine.'

'Please.'

And Leigh said, 'We'd finished. It's too nice to waste.'

Honor said, 'I turned the telly sound down – he wouldn't let me turn the picture off. He sat looking at Oprah, and when I questioned him, he didn't tell me, you see, he told *her.* I cried about it for over a year. He'd trusted her to know, but not his mother. Well, he was right, I hadn't. Thank God it came out.'

'Were you able to –?'

'Yes. He was my boyfriend. Wesley. I liked him, his red hair and all that. And he had been so kind to Dexter. Taking him places, buying him things. Of course, he was bribing him – or just, just *buying* him.' She swallowed the wine like a triple whisky taken before combat. 'We got it sorted out. And the doctors were very good. I didn't want to prosecute, though. I know that's wrong. They told me I was wrong. But I wouldn't put Dexter through that. He'd been through enough. I put him first. Then we came here. He's been fine since.'

Leigh found herself fixedly staring. Made herself glance aside.

Honor said, 'Only I don't like to force him to do anything. And apparently that's wrong, too. I can only do my best, as I see it.'

'Mrs McCarthy,' said Katherine, 'you love your son. Of all the things you could do for him, that's the most valuable. No two people are alike, and no two children. He'll find his way, I'm sure.'

'Well, he has,' said Honor, lofty, offended, bewildered: 'He says he's going to marry her when he grows up.'

They looked.

'Oprah Winfrey,' said Honor. 'I explained she's rich and famous, not to mention a wee bit older than he is. But he says he doesn't care. I said she might be married already. He said he was sure she wasn't. I hope he grows out of it, because if he doesn't – I think she'll have to expect him coming courting. He's like a little bulldozer now. When he's 16 or so, I don't know.'

Somewhere outside a phone began to ring. Honor got up automatically, carrying the unstirring child in her arms. 'It'll be an American. Or an Australian. Some of them don't think. If it's still day over there, it must be here.'

They sat in silence when she was gone, drinking the strong leaf tea. She wasn't long, returning, still porting Dexter.

'Ms Dover – I'm really sorry. It's that policeman again, the plain clothes one. He says if you're about, he needs to speak to you. Bloody nerve. The Gestapo, that's what they're getting like. But I'd let the cat out of the bag. I'd said you were awake before I thought.'

It was like cold water draining down and down through her body, and as she got up, drained even of the coldness, she felt very empty.

'Don't worry. It can't be helped.'

'He's only outside, that's the thing. There's the doorbell now.'

Honor carrying Dexter, with no free hand, somehow let Rawthorn in. She looked exhausted, wilted, ten years older, as she did most late nights that he saw her, now. The child too appeared curiously aged by sleep.

'Again, I apologise for this visit, Mrs McCarthy.'

'So you should. I won't get anyone staying here at this rate. At least,' she added, defeatedly, 'it's not another bomb.'

Shirley was at the reception desk by now, a serious young woman with auburn hair. She sat reading by a telephone that wouldn't, normally, ring again until morning.

'Use the bar, why don't you,' said Honor. 'My other lady's gone up to bed. You were lucky we were all still around.'

And why had they been? He sensed female mysteries in the air. But Honor had put Dexter down now, and was gently coaxing him to wake up enough to get to bed.

'I dreamed about a tiger, Mum.'

'Never mind, dear.'

'No, he was brill.'

Murmuring, they wandered up the stairs, sleepwalkers speaking of dreams and visions.

Rawthorn crossed into the bar.

On a table were the remains of some sandwiches, and a cooling teapot, plus two empty bottles of Pinot Grigio. Quite a midnight feast. Good for them. He had left Knox opening, like a child on its birthday, a striped box of Mama's Pizza. He was lit up anyway, pleased with the mayhem of the night, bodies strewn, leads everywhere, girls gone missing or kidnapped.

'Yes, check your Mist-over-the-water. What makes you think she's not in bed?'

'She probably is. But I had a feeling she might have trouble sleeping.'

'Oh yes?'

'Just a hunch.'

'We still get them then, do we?'

'If not, it'll wait, won't it. She's hardly a prime suspect.'

Knox, hands pawing the striped box, eagle-eyed him.

'Do I detect you'd rather she wasn't?'

No use to argue.

'I'd much rather.'

'You've met her. What do *you* think? Apart from yummy.'

'She seems a model citizen.' He didn't want to tell Knox yet about the data that he'd received earlier, the little history of Leigh Dover – who might after all have nothing to do with any of this. Apart from being in the wrong place at the right time. 'Besides, we don't even know if we have a murder here, do we, sir?'

'Not yet. But Smithy's been a while, and that's generally a sign. I'm going to give him a bell if I don't hear in half an hour or so. Find out how the cutting up is going.' And opening the box lid, Knox had seized the smiling red and yellow pizza in both hands.

Leigh was sat against the far wall. The psychological language of that was unmistakable. But then, she had her reasons.

He walked across.

'I apologise for this, Ms Dover. I wouldn't have troubled you if I wasn't concerned that by tomorrow things might be worse, if we don't talk now.'

Her face was grave and pale. She had taken off her make-up, and as some older women do, looked very young without it.

'You know, don't you?'

'Know? Yes. If we're talking about the same thing. Are we?

'One year and almost seven months ago, in South East London.'

'Yes, Ms Dover. We are talking about the same thing.' Rawthorn sat down opposite her. She wasn't evasive now. She faced him, looking at him with her green eyes. 'This isn't official,' he said. 'I shouldn't really be here. I thought perhaps we could sort it out and then – well, it won't be a factor.'

'Or it might be. Have you found a body, Inspector?'

'Yes, Ms Dover.'

She said abruptly, 'Can you call me Leigh, please. This thing with my name drives me mad.'

Rawthorn grinned. It was too late, in several ways, to keep up the mask. She reacted to his grin with a startled half smile.

He said, 'Let me tell you *my* name. Rawthorn. Edward.

Usually shortened to Ed.' She watched him. He said, 'DI Ed Rawthorn'

'*Died.*'

She was on the verge of laughing. Remembered what he was, and why he was there, and shook her head, shaking amusement away.

She said, 'If you've found a body, than am I a suspect?'

'For various reasons, no-one is a suspect at the moment.'

'Natural causes?'

'It has to be established. But – very unlikely to be. I'm sorry.'

'And I saw him, and you think I may have had a reason to – to do something to him. As I had a reason to do something to a man last time.'

'It may look that way.'

'I didn't do anything, Inspector, then or now.'

'If I'm calling you Leigh, perhaps I should be Ed.'

Her eyes widened and burned. At least her guard was down. She was showing him her anger, and her furious shame.

'I don't *think* so, Inspector. Let me repeat, I didn't do a *thing*. It was done *to* me.'

He looked away from her deliberately. He said, 'I don't like to ask you, but I need you to tell me what happened.'

'Didn't I tell enough people? That night, days and days after. Men and women in blue, men and women in white. I've never had such a social whirl, and all so *intimate*.' She hadn't raised her voice but the heat seared from her. 'You patently got the information from *someone*.'

'A computer.'

'Oh, a computer. Yes, there's nothing secret anymore.'

'For the moment, it's only between us. You and me. And if I can, I'll keep it that way.'

'*You make me sick.*'

He looked up and met her eyes, like swords now. She was flaming white. He thought, slightly stunned, as if she had slapped his face without warning, that the hackneyed bad dialogue about women and anger and beauty could sometimes hit the nail squarely on the head.

'I undoubtedly do, and I don't blame you. But I still have to ask that you tell me, and tell me in some detail.'

'*What*? You want a porno show, do you?'

'Just the facts.'

'What can one say about the facts? Has the word a different meaning now? He took me to *tea*? He gave me a *wave*? I was *raped*. And worse than raped, because nowadays, as you're aware, I imagine, *Inspector*, rape can be a death sentence.'

'Yes.'

'And you want the facts.'

'Yes.'

'You fucking bloody shit.'

'Don't bottle it up. Just say what you mean.'

'*What*?'

Without moving an inch, she seemed to be rearing up inside her skin, *standing* up. Her hands raised to strike at him. Even as she sat immobile.

This rage. Murderers have been created from less.

He waited, unspeaking, meeting her power of anger with his own considerable will.

9

That night. Nineteen months ago.

Or was it nine hundred years?

It seemed to have happened far in the past. But also ... yesterday.

In dreams it happened always in the present moment, and yet, curiously, it was never quite the same. Usually, it wasn't even – him. Sometimes it was one of the doctors who was raping her, even once a woman doctor. Once it was her father. From that dream she had never, she felt, quite recovered. Her father had been wonderful, the utter antithesis of an abuser in any sense.

Those that counselled her, explained that this was only a symbol – a temporary fear of men, exemplified in the First Man, the one who had sired her. Man had raped her.

Mankind?

But what they said, although it made perfect sense, didn't seem to help.

She had spent so much time analysing herself, walking round and round her flat, talking to herself. 'Now *this* is why I think *this*.'

Her voice became hoarse and her throat sore, from all the talking she did to herself, all the kind and encouraging things she said.

'Okay, Leigh, if we get up now, I'll make you a cup of tea, a special one, with ginger and cinnamon in it. You like that. Just throw off the sheets. Come on. I know it's cold, love, but the central heating will soon warm up.'

'Right, Leigh. If you go into this park and walk right across, you can have that art hardback you want. I know it's

16 quid, and you've already bought six books, but you'll deserve it. If you cross the park. Lots of people about. And it's broad daylight. Come on, sweetheart.'

'Leigh. I've got you. I'm here. It's all right. Don't cry' (as she held herself in her own arms and wept her voice out).

She'd had it too easy.

Wrapped in cotton wool. Getting away with it. Until that night.

She had taught five days a week at the college, and on one Monday each month, she organised a slide show on a particular artist. That night, it was Klimt.

(Strange, she'd never dreamed of Klimt as the rapist. He had been crazy for women, his sexuality rampant and glorious in his painting. Perhaps some reasoning corner of the unreasoning id had grasped that genius and glory had no place in her rape.) The slide session ended at 7.30. Most of the students rushed out into the night, and one tried to detain her. It was always the same one. Orson Drury.

He was a lanky tall young man, 22 or 23, who spoke in the appalling accent of the verbally over-educated. What he was doing at the college was anyone's guess.

Orson always wanted to argue with her, both in class and after the slide-show lectures – she had persuaded him not to interrupt during the actual show.

'But Klimt is a total anachronism, isn't he? I mean, out of his time, a misfit.'

'Many of the greatest artists are, Orson.'

'But Leigh, Leigh – all that gold-leaf – I mean *de trop*, yes?'

'Oh. Would you call Duccio *de trop*?'

'Duccio's old hat.'

'I see.'

'I mean, you don't compare Klimt to God, do you. I mean the holy Picasso?' *Pick-arso* was what he actually said.

She tried to be fair with Orson Drury. So many, students and tutors both, laughed at him, wound him up. But conversely, he had a very nasty line in authoritarian male dominance, when thwarted by a peer. One of the girls had threatened to stab him, had actually picked up a palette knife to do it. He stole things from the others, too – paints, books, even once a cheap watch – no-one knew why, and no-one could catch him. But he was blatant, he even wore the watch. When confronted, he smiled. 'No, it's mine. Ghastly junk, but I'm skint, and I found it on the bus.'

'You've seen some of the paintings, Orson, albeit only on slides. Now you make up your own mind. No-one says you have to like every great painter. Just be aware that, even if you don't, they still may be quite talented.'

He opened his mouth. She felt she had had enough. 'For example,' she said, 'I can't stand Picasso, except for his early stuff. But I'd never disagree he was a genius.'

Orson followed her down the raw-lit March corridors. In glass-fronted rooms, the cleaners were at work.

Outside, a soft March wind was blowing, the just-budded trees dancing above the college lawns.

'Well, I think I could convert you to Pick-arso, Leigh.'

'I don't think so, Orson.'

'Why don't you come and have a coffee, and let me try?'

She would have stared at him if she'd had the patience.

All she said was, 'See you tomorrow, Orson,' and going through, let the swing doors swing shut in his face.

She had been wearing ivy green nail varnish that night. She recalled it vividly, and how the college's overhead lights shone on each green oval. She was slim then, and her black hair spilled down her back. She looked much like a student herself, if a rather older model. This wasn't a ploy. It had simply been her style.

She hadn't brought her car that day, it was in for its MOT – an it-car then, not a she.

There was the choice of a bus, or an expensive cab, which would charge around £5 to take her home. To think it out, she went into the college pub, and had half a lager.

She left about 8.15.

Spring suffused the air. You could smell it. Sap, and life returning. And the wind, though blustery, was soft and almost nourishing.

Leigh decided to get the bus, the quicker route, which meant crossing the park to reach the bus-stop. She liked the start of the walk. The park was more a stretch of open common, with a wide central roadway, down which the occasional car sailed to the main concourse. Street lamps there were, but far spaced, and between, over the height of tossing trees, the stars glittered moist and bright.

She had done this walk more times than she could number. If she didn't bring the car, it was what she would do. Other people also frequented the park. Even that night she had passed two couples, airing 1) dachshunds, and 2) wolfhounds.

Leigh was at the midpoint of the walk, where the odd little white War Memorial arose in a stretch of bare flowerbeds, when someone started calling her name.

She stopped and turned disbelievingly. But, as she feared, it was Orson Drury.

'Hi, Leigh. I saw you in the pub.'

'So?' She had begun to feel annoyed. He'd never come running after her before.

'Too much alcohol isn't very good for a woman,' prophesied Orson Drury.

'Really. Well I'll just have to cut it down to one bottle of gin a night.'

He gave his awful laugh, which sounded like a horse with adenoids. Then, 'I really think we ought to have a talk. You know, I like older women.'

'How lovely for you.'

'I know you're a lot older than I am, but age doesn't have to matter. You're not in such bad shape.'

'You think not?'

'Oh, you can take my word for it.'

'Listen. Orson –'

'Perhaps we could go for a meal? I'm afraid I'm rather skint. But then, I know the modern woman is prepared to pay her way –'

'Do you also know the modern woman isn't very interested in self-opinionated obnoxious little twits?' He gaped. Leigh, who had never spoken to pupil or student in such a way in her life, who had never had to, finished, 'I suggest, since you're so sure about everything, you go somewhere and offer thanks. Spelled with a W.'

She left him, still gaping. If he had had the unconscionable gall to come after her again, maybe everything would have been different.

The general rule said that if you had the last word, you could then forget the whole thing. It was the torture of *l'esprit de l'escalier* – only thinking of the put-down on the stairs going out – that drove you mad and kept the whole scene revolving in your head.

In this instance, though, Leigh found herself still fuming, and also unnerved.

He was a pillock, but should she have kept quiet? God knew what might have made him the way he was. His type were usually not seen in run-down art colleges in the suburbs. Perhaps just such wise-alecks as Leigh Dover had helped alter him, in the past, to the thing he now was.

She looked back once, but he was out of sight.

Soon after, and solely absorbed by this, she crossed diagonally over the park roadway, at a dark area between two lamps. And at this moment, a car, coming it had to be said too fast, seemed to burst at her out of nowhere.

She might have been knocked down. Instead, the car swerved, slewed up onto the grass verge, and came to a juddering halt. In another second, the door flew open, and a man sprang out.

'Bloody hell – are you all right?' He ran up to her.

'Are *you*?' said Leigh, jolted and feeling stupid. 'I'm so sorry. I wasn't concentrating. It was all my fault.'

'Well … it's dark here, and I was belting along a bit. Fault on both sides, I'd say. But are you really?'

'You didn't touch me. Is your car okay?'

'Hmm.' He peered back at it. 'There I'm not sure. It's not you. It's just a bit temperamental. Doesn't like the sort of treatment it just got from me.'

He was, as she explained later (over and over and over), probably in his very early forties, about six feet tall, well-built and fairly slim. His hair was dark, neither long nor short. He was clean-shaven, casually but not scruffily dressed in a dark pullover and grey cords. He had a diver's watch.

He was also quite good-looking. The sort of looks her mother would have called personable. There was the faintest trace of a regional accent, perhaps Yorkshire, but sometimes he sounded as if he came from further south. She was never totally sure on that aspect, and conceivably he had put the accent on.

They both walked back to his car. Leigh felt obliged to. She'd caused the accident.

It seemed tilted a little, and the door hung open, making it look more wrecked somehow than it could be. It hadn't hit a tree or anything.

He leaned inside and tried the engine, which made a spluttering sound and didn't catch. (Afterwards, she realised this was certainly a technique of his. Maybe all of it was, even to the almost-running-down of a potential subject.)

'Don't sound too good.'

'No. Oh, I am sorry.'

''S okay, just let me –' He was reaching about between the front seats for something. She couldn't see what until he brought it out and put it quietly against her neck.

Then she stood staring at him.

'I felt I didn't know it was a knife. And yet of course I knew. My blood turned to water. I *knew*. And yet, I said, "What's that?"'

'A very sharp blade,' he said, as if helpfully answering an ordinary question. 'Bowie knife, actually. A smasher. Keep still, or you'll get cut.'

'But why –?' (*Imbecilic.* How is it one is so reduced by shock and sudden fear? What happens to the brain?)

'Well, I thought I'd like to take you over there. We could

have a game.'

Her brain caught up. Or something did.

'No,' she said.

'I'm afraid so,' he said. He actually smiled, encouragingly. 'Just walk, not too fast or too slow. The knife won't slip if you're careful.'

'And if I won't?' How did she get it out?

'Well, I'll just slit your throat,' he said, as if remarking on some avoidable, but not too interesting, problem, rain perhaps, or the price of petrol.

Afterwards – she had two sensations. One was that it was over – and she had lived through it. The other was that nothing much had happened. They formed solidly in her mind, side by side, two unalike yet Siamese twins.

It hadn't taken long.

She walked with him and he ushered her in among the trees and bushes. She didn't struggle. Not for one moment, with that knife against her throat, did it occur to her she could.

Once she was, as instructed, lying on her back, she could see the trees racing against the night sky, and the stars flashing in their branches.

The visual memory of the trees and the sky and the stars was, afterwards, much more clear than that of the man – why call him a man? – the rapist.

He seemed narrowed and two dimensional, like a cut-out. Yet he was everywhere. His presence, that was, not his body. He scarcely touched her, except in one place.

'Undo your top,' he said. When she did so, he moved the knife a little, to assist. Then he slit open her bra at the front. Such a light flick of the blade she didn't feel it.

When he did this, she remembered, he nodded and chuckled. 'He seemed to think it was a bit of a laugh. That's the only way I can describe it. A joke we were sharing.'

He looked at her breasts. She supposed he did.

Beyond this point, had *she* looked at *him*?

No, she thought, she hadn't. It was like the dentist's, or a smear test. Somehow it was – *polite* – to look away.

He had told her to take off her own knickers.

He kept his knife against her neck as he did the rest.

Leigh wasn't a virgin. She had had several enjoyable, even transcendent sexual liaisons. But then, this wasn't sex … was it?

No, apparently it wasn't. It was violence. Abuse. Not sex at all.

It hurt. She had expected that, obviously, and – as in the old joke – braced herself.

Even so, it hadn't hurt her as much as it would have if she had been closed, younger or older, and he had been – what did they say? – well-endowed.

All over swiftly. Something so – what word was there for it? – no word that was any use – but this act, which defied even language – done in a minute or less. He made no sounds. His breathing, that was all.

Then he removed the knife, got up, and said, 'Bit parky. Shouldn't stay there too long like that, if I was you. You might catch cold.'

And – he was gone.

Lying there despite his comradely advice, she heard his car start by the road without a hitch.

Then she got up and tidied herself, and pulled her coat together.

Her legs weren't even shaking much. She didn't feel sick. Both these things had happened when he held the knife at her throat, but ended as he pulled himself from her.

He hadn't cut or killed her. She'd done what he said, and she hadn't been hurt. The soreness now was really no worse than she'd experienced before, after enthusiastic and prolonged love-making.

But this hadn't been love-making.

Hate-making?

Leigh felt very sensible, level-headed. She knew she should report the man at once. Not because she was upset, but in order that he shouldn't attack any other women, who might be.

He was so practiced, he had done it before, almost certainly.

As she walked out under the street lamps, she noticed a drop of something dark and wet on her sleeve. Had he nicked her after all? She examined herself, and found that she was untouched.

She realised then that, cack-handedly bumping about on her body, he must have cut *himself*.

She'd thought it funny. And coming out of the park, with the two feelings locked side by side in her head, there was almost an exhilaration. She had survived. It hadn't, wouldn't, mean a thing.

Leigh looked at the policeman. At the man. Edward Rawthorn.

He was frowning slightly.

He said, so softly she could almost not hear, 'They didn't catch him.'

'No. I expect that was my fault.'

Something came through his eyes, not the adamantine power that had held her there through these last twenty minutes. Something terrible. So he was cruel too. Well, he was a man.

'I hope,' he said, 'he fries in hell.'

'That doesn't sound very objective, Inspector Rawthorn.'

'No,' he said. 'It isn't. You can report me.'

'Do you want the rest?'

'Yes. I'm sorry, but I may need to know.'

'For those evenings alone?'

As soon as she had said it, she wished that she hadn't. Through all the turmoil of these two decades of minutes, she had felt him incredibly holding her, swimming with her for the land.

He didn't deserve what she had said.

Before she could mumble her apology, his hand came across the table and gripped hers.

He was electric. His flesh, so full of life –

'Don't throw us all in together, Leigh Dover.' And when he

spoke her full name, it no longer sounded like a joke. 'Not every man is like *that*. And you know it. It's only that bastard who made you forget.'

She said, 'You'll be aware of the procedures. I went through them. Looking back, they were considerate, the police. Even sensitive. Only one woman officer – I remember she put me on a kitchen chair – a *hard* chair. Then she said, "Is that uncomfy? It *usually* is, if a woman's been assaulted."'

'Christ. I hope you told someone about that.'

'They saw her do it. After she went out, I never had to deal with her again. Perhaps they hid her in a cupboard.'

'Let's hope so.'

'But – how can I explain? – it seemed almost trivial by the time I got there. And then, the more they asked me to go over my statement, the more they – did to me – I mean the doctors – the more *important* it became.'

'I understand. It can seem like that.'

'I felt that *they* were dramatising something that wasn't anything. I'd been raped. So what? All this fuss. And – I hurt worse from the examination. And – I kept thinking, *I could just have got on the bus and gone home. Had a bath and made some tea. Taken a couple of paracetamol. Gone to bed.*'

'You said you thought of other women. You were right, Leigh.'

'Was I? I told you – the two feelings. That I'd escaped something that didn't even have a word for it. And that it was hardly worth mentioning.'

The police, she said, seemed to make her go on and on telling them the same thing. As if to catch her out. She knew now that wasn't the case. They only had to be sure that *she* was sure of her facts.

But she wanted to go home. She *ached* to go away.

'And trying to identify him – the Identikit – they did everything I said, and – it didn't look like him to me. I'd say to change the nose a little. Or the eyes. And it would seem to be right – and then, it wasn't. He was like a *shape-shifter*.'

'Yes.'

'And – their *faces*, Ed. Those men. They were courteous and kind, and I'd think, *This one's brown eyes are like* his. *That one has his sort of jaw.*'

In the end, before she had got to go home, they had asked about the blood on her clothes. It wasn't hers. Was it the attacker's?

She said she thought it must be, and that he'd cut himself on his own knife, which was a real laugh, wasn't it?

Finally someone asked her if it was possible she herself had cut him in some way.

No, she hadn't.

But was she sure? She'd been fighting him off, trying to stop him –

She hadn't fought. She'd been too scared of the knife. Cowed. (And this too was surging in her now, worse than the rape, her *embarrassment* at her own victimhood.)

'That's usual, Leigh.'

'They told me. My counsellors. Women blame themselves for being assaulted in the first place. For "letting it happen". But I knew I had no choice. This was just – Oh God, it was another sort of ghastly *esprit de l'escalier*. It wasn't until I was on the mental stairs going out that I thought, *Why didn't I knee him in the balls? Why didn't I pretend to lose consciousness so he'd be off guard, and then push my fingers in his eye?* Surely I could have. I felt less a victim than a *dupe*. A *moron*.'

After they had asked about the rapist's blood, they had explained about the test for HIV and AIDS.

'And I hadn't thought of it, Ed. Is that *incredible*? I hadn't given it a single thought. All this was going to be over very soon. And I could go home. And get on with being me.'

She raised her eyes from the abyss she was staring at, and met his gaze. So steady, his eyes.

'It used to be a fate worse than death. Now it's a fate that *is* death.'

'They tested the blood,' Rawthorn said.

'And his – they tested his semen.'

'Yes.'

She drew her breath slowly, and he was again reminded of a smoker and the first drag.

Leigh said, 'It was apparently negative. But, as they carefully outlined, you can't be a hundred percent sure under such conditions. I wasn't a sterile container, as it were. If they got hold of him, and tested him in person – then I could be fairly certain. One way or the other. Since nothing had shown up, they said it was very unlikely he had passed the disease. But a chance.'

'So you took the test yourself.'

'Isn't it strange,' she said, 'the way we use these same words – tests, examinations – for skills and for health? As if, when you don't pass – if you have AIDS or cancer or multiple sclerosis – they you're a *failure*. You've been unintelligent, or not studied hard enough. Or – I suppose – had rotten teachers.'

'What happened?'

'I was negative. They expected that. Then I had another test after three months. Also negative. And after a year. Negative. And – the latest result was last month. Negative.'

As he had seen her draw in her smoker's drag of oxygen, she saw him now exhale. In wonder, she realised he had been holding his breath.

'But,' she said, 'it doesn't mean so much, does it? The filthy thing can be dormant at least for ten years.'

'Is that what –?'

'Oh no. My doctor was happy with me, as he put it. That is, my last doctor. Actually I have a new doctor now. And he doesn't know any of this. I started putting on weight and I went to the new doctor, because the first doctor said it might be my body telling me something. Weight *gain* isn't a symptom of AIDS.'

'It isn't.'

Their hands had separated. She had removed hers, when she spoke of illness. She'd felt foolish anyway. Sat in the dim light of the deserted bar, holding hands with a policeman around three in the morning. (Bacall and Bogart, circa 1940.)

'They didn't catch him, as I've told you. No-one knew him or had seen him. He'd gone pop into thin air. In the end I pulled out. I was so definite, they got suspicious – no, I thought they did. They kept asking again about the stains of his blood – oh, there'd been some on my skirt, too. But. They gave up, and so did I. I left my job. Nobody looked real. And the students – not just Drury – all of them. All so young and sure and cocky and *unblemished,* and I hated them and wanted them to be slapped awake and, Christ, I was turning into a monster, so I left. I stayed indoors for weeks. And then, just roaming around. Making myself do things. Go into a shop and buy a carton of milk. Walk along the high street after dark. Hurdles. I made myself jump.'

'That was why you stopped when you saw a car in the ditch.'

'Yes. The car was – very like his car. Not the make – I mean how it looked. Tilted, and the door open. I noted the number-plate this time. Never bothered with the rapist's car. Hadn't known I should.

'He probably changes the plate. Or the car.'

'Do you think so? I somehow feel he doesn't change a thing. That he just walks the Earth, always the same, unmasked, recognisable – and no-one sees. Yes, I know this is a common reaction.'

'That doesn't make it a stupid reaction.'

'There was some nature programme I saw. A herd of animals, deer, I think. A big cat hunting them. Not the sort of thing I normally watch, things preying on things. But the deer all ran. And then, when the cat – was it a cheetah? – brought one down – they stopped running, the other deer. They started to graze again not ten feet away. While the cheetah fed on the dead deer.'

'Survival,' Rawthorn said. 'A blind eye. We all have it. It comes built in.'

'The rather-you-than-me syndrome,' she said. 'Only it wasn't you, it *was* me.'

'I know.'

'You'd no doubt debate this, but I've coped with the rape.

Or, I am coping. I had some savings. I got a new second-hand car and bought some snazzy clothes, and I started painting my nails again. And I've come down to Seatree, where I grew up, to review my past. And I stop to help drivers in disabled cars.'

She rose. It was as though she had heard some inner bell, some summons. She rose and moved around the table, and went away a little distance.

'But the illness. The *chance* of the illness. I have ten, or 15 years to wait. I can't cope with that. I'm not coping with that at all.'

'Leigh it isn't –'

'If I'm realistic, that's my prison term. My punishment for being raped. My punishment for being *punished*.'

Rawthorn too got to his feet. But he didn't move toward her. Her anger was done, but the heat still hovered on her, about her, the ring of thorns or flame to keep intruders out.

'So,' she said, 'I'm celibate. I couldn't put another person through what I've had to go through, what I'm *going* through. I try to dislike men, and I manage to. And I've bloody *got* to. Because for me, now, no sex. Not till I'm in my sixties. *If* I get there. No sex. Worse, no making love.'

Rawthorn moved.

As he did so, he thought of the cheetah, and almost checked, but he didn't check.

He stopped three feet from her.

'You haven't got it, Leigh.'

'You don't know that.'

'I know we're all at risk. Do *you* know how easily it can be passed? HIV, AIDS? One in a million, but it can happen. Sweat on a handrail and a cut on your hand. A sneeze in a crowded room. Body fluids. You'd have to be unlucky, possibly as unlucky proportionately as the luck needed to win the whole roll-over in the lottery. But someone always can. And from a kiss, Leigh. Just apocryphal? It doesn't happen? You can't be sure.'

'I know that. I said, I don't have sex. And I don't kiss.'

They looked at each other.

'Leigh,' he said, 'my father had one most bizarre comment he used to make. He said, when he met my mother, "I looked at her, and I thought, *I could drink her bathwater."*'

Astonished, shocking herself, Leigh laughed.

'I could drink yours,' he said. 'It would do me good.'

He put his hands gently either side of her face, and from the contact the warm electric tingling charge flowed through her skin, her muscles, through the channels of her flesh, filling her body to the brim. Was this extraordinary touch also activated at will? His hands – felt like a healer's, or as she would have imagined a healer's hands to be. She stopped thinking. All at sea …

Rawthorn bent his head and kissed her.

Now they were once more in the ocean, not swimming, floating, buoyed up on the night sea journey. And the land far off.

Not pressing her, coaxing only a little, he felt her resistance unfold to allow him to come in. And fold back to keep him.

Who cared about reaching land? Let it wait.

3.15 am to 5.13 am

1

All cats look alike in the dark. But it wasn't dark, because he'd put on the light in the cab. And it wasn't a cat. And she didn't know why the useless phrase had come into her mind, but even so, she had a feeling it meant something. But then, she was probably, by now, going mad. She also wanted to urinate again.

Could she say?

He'd maybe just tell her she had to wait – until he killed her.

Like her constantly aggressive mother. 'You'll have to *wait*, Markessa. Till we get home.'

Under her lids, she glanced at him.

He was good-looking, but in a way she didn't like, which wasn't surprising, was it?

Outside was utter blackness, like the end of the world. She didn't know where they were. He had driven up some side road again, or onto some track, judging from the bumps. But there were no lights this time.

Was this it?

Was this –?

No. It couldn't be. He wouldn't do it.

Should she – should she try to get him to talk again?

'It's … dark.'

'My, yes, isn't it. Thank you for putting me straight. I'd been so puzzled. What ever is that black stuff out there? Tar? Liquorice? Choccy? But it's *darkness*. Where would I be without you?'

She gave a snuffling honk. She hadn't meant to. Tears and a

held-down frightened rage forced it up like a burp.

'Another of your animal impressions. What was it this time?'

'I need to go to the toilet, please.'

'The toilet. The lav. The bathroom. The ladies'. The loo. Bash says khazi. What does that tell us about Bash?'

'I really need to.'

He turned, holding up the gun, pointing it at her face.

'I'll get out, then you can get out. Squat by the car. Then get back in.'

'Thank you. I promise I won't run away.'

Humiliated and terrified, she heard herself.

'No, you won't. But we don't want a little puddle on the seat.'

They performed the manoeuvre.

She was so desperate she almost didn't care now if he looked. Like that time in Eastbourne, behind the parked lorry, her mother snarling, Markessa five years old and abashed, squatting as passers-by tutted. 'Disgusting, in this day and age.' Beyond a glance, however, he didn't look. Somehow the *gun* did.

She nearly fell twice, trying to deal with everything, her wrists locked.

Even outside, the night was total. Trees all around, long grasses, the smell of sheep pats. The sky high and hollowed with blue, and stars. But like the planes passing over, the stars weren't going to bother.

When they were back in, she started to cry again, she couldn't help it. She apologised.

'You're a waterworks,' he said. 'Like those revolting dolls that sob and wet themselves.'

'Why won't you let me go? Why have you done this? Please let me go. I won't tell anyone. Please – Dominic.'

' Oh, my name now. Well, *Markessa*, I thought I'd made it clear I'm paying him back, doing this. Our Jack.'

'How? *How?*'

'Because, dearest, you mean so much to him. The sun rises and sets etc.'

'Why would Jack care? I hardly know him –'

Dominic said harshly, 'You know him. He's obsessed by you.

Don't try to lie. He can't keep away from you. I've had nothing but you, you, you for months.'

'How can you have? I hardly ever see him –'

'All he talks about. *If* he talks about anything. You. No, actually. Not *talks*. Because he doesn't say much about you. I didn't even know your name until tonight. He never mentioned the colour of your hair – and such *red* hair, too – let's say he *thinks* about you. I can hear him *thinking*. See it. About *you*.'

Markessa had the most peculiar feeling, as if she were groping for an object in an unlit room. She didn't know what it was, but knew that it was there – and it was something she needed undeniably to find.

All cats are alike –

But Dominic was going on. Now he couldn't seem to stop. His musical and educated voice, his facility with words, would have impressed her at any other time. The hysteria behind it was all that she noticed now, and the gun nodding in his hand in time to it.

'*This woman*. That was how he phrased it. As if there were only one woman in the whole world. It amused me at first. I've come across that kind of thing in the past. A sort of insurance set-up. The untouchable and conveniently ungainable woman. Married to someone else, of course, or living with them. But there to be drooled over, so if any other woman starts to get heavy, there's this perfect unsullied unrealised relationship, all ready to drive the poor cow away.'

Silence. Markessa sat there, watching Dominic start to cry again. Unlike herself, not apologising.

She tried to speak very sweetly, soothingly.

'You feel so unhappy. Can I –?'

'Just shut your face.'

Rebuffed, scalded with panic, she did so.

'You want to know why I've got it in for precious Jack? Well, I'll tell you, Markessa. Because of him I've done something – I've caused something –' his voice, no longer musical, went up into a sort of thin, wavering scream – 'I've probably *murdered* someone – I didn't mean it – I didn't want to – I keep thinking maybe I haven't, that it isn't so bad – just insane lies – that he'll get over what I did – but then I remember his face – and running away – and – and Jack was the *reason* for it. *Jack*. And now he's dumped me with it. I've stopped being of use, so he's off without a care in the world. And I've got *this*. This boulder tied to my neck for the rest of my life. Oh God – oh, Bash –'

Markessa sat like shaky stone. She felt she ought to reach out and pat him, didn't dare.

He wept. He put his head on the wheel and sobbed. The gun was pressed into his own body. Fragments of language broke away from him. She put them together with care.

'I followed him tonight. After he threatened me and told me to piss off. He was so sure he'd scare me off. But I went up the hill after him. And he didn't notice, and I saw the house. The house where he'd said you were going to be. His fatal *woman*. That's all that mattered to him. Getting to the house where you were. You opened the door, didn't you? Yes, I remember you did. But I didn't think it could be you. He'd never described you, or said your name, but somehow – I hadn't imagined it would be anyone like you.'

Markessa listening, piecing the bits of words and sentences together, like alphabet bricks.

'Then I went down again, to the town. I was crazy. I went in some wine bar. Got some water. I thought, *There's nothing I can do.* But later I got the car and drove part of the way back up the hill in the dark and parked in a field, and walked the rest of the way again. I sat behind a hedge by the house. Just me and my beautiful Perrier with the beautiful dust in it. Nothing seemed too terrible then. Time changes. I had forever.'

Markessa, building up the bricks.

'In the end you came out. You were snivelling even then, but he put his arms round you, all tender and loving and protective. He said your name too. You both came down in this cab, and I got to the car and followed again, and your cab driver went at a snail's pace, which made it easy to catch up. Then you wouldn't let Jack go up to your flat with you, would you? Why's that? Not much good in bed, our Jack? Shit-hot, surely? Oh but then, with *you* – the *woman,* the *idée fixe* – I wouldn't really expect him to be much use. When he left I came over and rang your bell. And here we are.'

His tears stopped.

For a moment, he looked only smug. Clever. He sat up and drank from the Perrier can, on and on, until the can was empty, and then he crushed it, slowly, in his hand.

Markessa sat staring at her assembled wall of words.

'It's Jula.'

'Excuse me?'

'It's Jula you want.'

He had his original voice and tone back again. 'And Jula is what? Some sort of canned drink?'

Markessa said, 'The woman Jack is obsessed with is Jula Cork. She lives in that house. I was just – *there.* He brought me back home because I was upset. Then he went back to *her.* He didn't want *me.* He's never *liked* me.'

Dominic didn't react. He sat unspeaking and staring, as if idly out into the darkness that wasn't liquorice or chocolate, but night, tomb of the sun.

And somehow Markessa resisted the urge to jabber on at him her same news of Jula, again and again.

Finally, mildly, Dominic spoke.

'What does Jula Cork look like?'

Markessa's instinct, honed by about three hours of misery and terror, didn't play her false. She put criticism aside and spoke the truth.

'A bit shorter than me, very, very slim. Masses of blue-black hair and huge dark eyes. Cool as a cucumber. And she's beautiful. She writes books.'

Dominic breathed in and out, slowly and deeply.

'Yes,' he said. 'I recognise that. That's what I would have thought. Something like that.'

Viciously, Markessa added, 'And she's got money, too.'

Dominic began (fluidly and relaxedly) to laugh. In the middle of this, he turned and dropped the gun, the Walther PPK, into Markessa's lap.

Markessa jumped as if a snake had landed there. Then her hands closed over it.

'Don't try to shoot me,' he said, cast up on the shore of his mirth. 'It's not loaded. Bashy just kept it to freak out burglars. And I stole it, in case – but I don't expect that will matter much.'

'You've done all this to me – and it isn't *real!*'

'Unloaded, I said. It's real. Unlike you. You're not real at all, just a snotty little phantom I picked up by mistake. Dominic has done everything wrong. Well, well.'

'And you've had me like this – all these *hours* – all this – this fucking beastly *rubbish* – and it wasn't – and I wasn't even the one –' Markessa flung up her sellotaped hands and clubbed Dominic in the head with them. 'You stinking bastard!'

He toppled, laughing again, and fell against the door. Then, as laughter ended, turned matter-of-factly to open it. He swung out, and moved away, leaving the door wide open.

'Get out, Markessa.'

She swarmed over the seat and erupted onto the stony, gritty track, not feeling it for the moment.

He watched her, leaning on the cab, as she boiled there in the dark.

'*Undo my hands.*'

'No. You're too dangerous. You can stay as you are. Get lost.'

She began to shriek at him, and then his face altered again, and even through her relief and maddened anger, she could see some other thing, some fearsome thing – There *was* death in his face, despite the unloaded gun. And he'd spoken of death. Dominic had said he thought he'd murdered someone. And if he had killed once, he could kill twice.

Markessa's instinct (honed) turned her, and she stumbled away.

The vague light of the cab's interior quickly faded. Soon she was alone among hedges and high brambles, the trees like columns holding up the seemingly moonless sky.

She was cold. And every step was like the step of a mediaeval penitent, treading barefoot on burning dagger-tips.

But she was alive.

2

'Great timing,' said Knox. 'You should be on the boards, you should. I've called Smithy, and one of his chaps said he's going to call me back. They had a bit of a problem with the mortuary. Hospital attendant, apparently, not keen to open up in the middle of the night. Held everyone up till they persuaded him. Beats me. Still, Smith's been cracking on and got some ideas, I gather.'

'Can I have a word, sir?'

'Sounds ominous.'

'It could be.'

Knox waved Rawthorn into a chair. The desk between them was now littered with paper, pastel coloured documents, pens, and augmented by plastic coffee cups, a station canteen cup and saucer, and the pizza box, vacant.

'You may want to take me off this case, sir. If it is one. I'm emotionally involved.'

Knox scrutinised him. But you could rarely tell anything from Rawthorn, jammy beggar, unless he let you. If he was worried, upset, embarrassed – who would know?

'With your Mist-over-the-water, right?'

'With Leigh Dover, yes, sir.'

'I must take a gander at this paragon.'

'I hope you won't have to.'

'Would you say I *will* have to? Do you think she's done anything dodgy?'

'I don't. For what it's worth.'

'But are you saying this before or after you got or get your leg over, Eddy, my son?'

And not a flicker. Not a whisper.

'Neither I nor she is going to move as fast as that. And so, before,' said Rawthorn calmly.

Knox bared his teeth. He looked like a hard fat terrier panting at play.

'You don't ruffle, do you, son? No, you're not going to lose your head. For my money, which is about 50p at the moment, seeing the wife took the last ten quid out of the pig to gamble with – you'll do. If your Leigh Dover is implicated, we may have to change that.'

'I understand.'

Knox's phone gave its jangling trill.

'And now. Any bets?'

Knox took up the receiver.

'Hail, Smithus. What ya got?'

'The time of death I'm placing now,' said Smith's dislocated clever voice, 'as probably no later than 7.30 pm. Almost definitely no earlier than 6.30.'

'Right. Good.'

'But I shall want to do a little more there, possibly. Certain factors will have warmed him up, and also the temperature dropped noticeably this evening.'

'Right, right.'

'Eager as a hound, Chief Inspector?'

'Eager-er.'

'You said, I recall, you had a feeling for a heart attack.'

Knox's face slumped.

'Oh – don't tell me that was what it was?' There was a tantalising pause, and Knox's visible disappointment began to perk up. 'It wasn't?'

'I *have* noted some thickening of the coronary arteries. His lungs, by the way, were healthy, though they looked like two unswept chimneys.'

'*But –*'

'Want to guess again?'

Knox thought, screwing his lips together, frowning, almost cross-eyed.

'What about bruising, say a doing-over by a couple of strong young heroes, who avoided the face?'

'Ah. No, I'm afraid not. There is some bruising, but it tallies, I'd say, with the seat-belt doing its job and keeping him in one piece, when the car went off the road. And with dying where he did, among all those tree roots.'

'Ho. Right. I'm stumped then, for the moment.'

'Shall I go through Mr Grace's last meal?'

'Do that.'

'It was impressive. Salmon, probably farmed, blue steak, potatoes and asparagus, and some strangely prepared peas.'

'Delicious.'

'There was a cheese-board, too. Camembert and a nice wedge of Stilton.'

'A health-conscious chap, as we suspected.'

'He had also drunk quite an impressive amount of whisky, and certainly well over a bottle of red wine.'

'French or Californian?'

'Do you need to know?'

'Only joshing, Smith. Beats me, not how he went off the road into that ditch, but how he could *see* the bloody Porsche to get into it in the first place.'

'Judging by his liver, he was a practised heavy drinker. He wouldn't feel it as much as you or I would.'

'Yes. The last time I felt like that *was* the last time.'

'There was something else, however, that Mr Grace had ingested. Partly but not entirely ejected.'

'Don't tell me. A double pastry fruit pie with sugar coating and a double helping of double cream.'

'No. A mixture of Mogadon and white spirit.'

Knox, excited, came to his feet as if for a goal. 'What? What – ? Smithy, are you saying –?'

'Whatever his heart was doing, Chief Inspector, someone tried to poison him. Ironically, and I need to do some more tests before I can substantiate that irony, Steven Grace was killed. I have no doubt of that. Unless he had a bent for suicide by a very unpleasant and perverse means, you can assume he was the successful victim of intended murder.'

Knox turned to Rawthorn, glowing with his triumph. It had taken Rawthorn some while to grasp that Knox was not, at these moments, a ghoul. It was a longing for the chase. To hunt down wrong and snap its neck in his shovel-shaped jaws.

'I want them both back in. Jula Cork and Hastings. Give them their rights. Let them contact their solicitors. That'll take them a while at this time of night, getting the legal crowd out of their jim-jams. Maybe the odd word will fall. There's this thing with Markessa Philbin, too. No-one's traced her, we don't even know the make of the car she's in. But I think Hastings is also at the back of this one, somewhere. Maybe she found something out she shouldn't.'

'And George Alliat, sir?'

'Alliat?'

'I see how you're looking at it, sir. Grace had sleeping pills prescribed and Jula could have got hold of them. Then Jack Hastings will use white spirit in his decorating work. But George Alliat boasts *he* was a painter – and he still could be. He'd use the stuff too.'

'Ye-es. And he's violent. Possibly potty. I don't know. Hastings has a thing for Jula, who hates Steven Grace, who in turn is blackmailing her. But Alliat. Where's *his* motive?'

'The snuffbox? He wouldn't like a thief.'

'The snuffbox which he didn't retrieve.'

'He was interrupted.'

'That would have to be in the Hamiltons' garden then. The Hamiltons weren't there, though. You remember they were shopping and dining at the Pompadour. They're vouched for till nine o'clock They walked right past the body on the other path coming home. They could have missed Alliat … But anyway he'd be long gone by then. Anyone else who disturbed Alliat over a dead body would have reported it. Would they? I suppose there could be a reason why not.'

'Alliat makes me uneasy, sir.'

'You? Uneasy? He must be trouble then. But you're right. He does me, too. Alliat – *Alliat* – put it through the computer, Edward. I know the name. I *know* it.'

'I have, sir. Nothing came back.'

'And in the meantime he leaves for Gatwick at 4.00.'

Knox strode for the door of his office. 'We'll put a police car outside. An obvious one. Let him see it. Though there have been cars up and down all night since we found Grace's body.'

'And when Alliat sets off?'

They can follow him. Follow him and let him see them following. Let's give them a mobile phone, too. Keep them in direct touch. And I'll get on to security at Gatwick. You said the plane doesn't take off until 6.20 –'

'6.40.'

'Time enough,' said Knox. 'It could even be delayed. Not unheard of. Happy now with your old dad?'

3

The phone box at the end of Saxon Vale, lit in the comparative dark, showed up its occupant like a fly in white amber.

'Bash – Bashy – come to the phone. Please come and answer it. Pick it up, Bash. Please Bash, *please* Bash – please.'

Talking to the ringing receiver.

'Bashy – please – Oh God, Bash – what I said – I know – *please*, Bash, don't let it be true – *please*, Bash. Pick up the phone.'

Face of the young Apollo, maker of music and arrows. White in the white amber in the black middle of the night.

'Bashy – please – *please* –'

Even on nights when Steven had been away, and Jack had stayed in the house, they had never slept together in her bed. It was wide enough for two; she had always, in adult life, preferred a double bed. But somehow, to share it hadn't been appropriate. Steven could, after all, have come back unexpectedly, like some fictional husband, and found them together. And what would he have made of that?

But Steven was dead now.

And still it was Jack alone, stretched out and sleeping here, only his shoes off, not under the covers, his head on the pillow.

Lavender lay on the other pillow, as deeply slumbering as the man. And Jack, asleep, had his forehead pressed against Lavender's side.

Nero was in the armchair by the window, on his back, white belly uppermost. Jula alone would not sleep any more tonight She had tried, lying down by Jack, listening as his breathing altered and his long body loosened. His face had a curious purity in sleep, wiped of all personality and every experience.

She didn't think she would look this way. Jack had said that, sleeping, she seemed like a child. But children frowned in their sleep, rolled their eyes under the lids, spoke words in unknown languages. This then, her repose.

After she had got up, she went down and washed up. Then made tea but didn't want it or drink it.

The night outside was cold now, swimming strongly toward morning. Nothing moved or called in the land beyond the house. Seen from the upper front windows, the conflagration of Seatree's street lighting burned on.

Jula had moved from her bedroom to her workroom. She went to her work chair, and sat down, in the dark. She had always been safe, here.

She shouldn't have spoken to the policeman, Knox. She shouldn't have said as much as she had. Jack was right. But the faint, though momentary, had confused her. She knew now she had given herself into the role of suspect, and – far worse – pulled Jack into the net with her.

The scenario was so inevitable.

They were lovers and wished to be rid of the hated blackmailing partner who refused to leave.

How much more would have to be admitted, in order to free them from this shadow? And could any admission do more harm than good?

'But we're not lovers, Chief Inspector.'

'But you sleep together, Ms Cork.'

'Yes, we sleep together sometimes, in the literal sense. We go to sleep in the same bed, and even in each other's arms. But we are not lovers.'

He'd sneer, 'And pigs might fly. Flappity snort.'

Then everything else must be said.

She rested her head on her hand. (How heavy the head was, full of its brain, which, so often, refused to be of any use. The 'passenger in the turret', she had called the brain in her first novel, *Under a Cloud*. The body its vehicle, carrying it wherever it wished to go, obedient slave to its every whim, at its mercy in life or death.)

She remembered the night in Jack Hastings' flat, that first time, after the walk on the beach and the sausages and peaches. After they had decided she would stay.

Had she been anticipating love-making, a sexual affair? No? If ever that had crossed her mind, surely the image was fleeting. Somehow she *had* known, known so certainly, that even inside herself she had never had to give the knowledge voice.

'Jula, I can only say this straight out. I'm crazy on you. I fell for you the moment I got a look at you. I think you know that. So what I have to say now may be a big let-down. You may just walk out. I won't blame you. It'll make me sick, but I'll get over it, and no bad feelings. I'm tough as old boots. Okay?'

She had sat, looking up at him, wondering, but not perturbed or afraid. And when he told her, no crash of shock or disillusion, no frustrated jealous urge, no clumsy need to say some unsuitable insulting nonsense: *What a waste*! Or, *Just my luck*. It was irrelevant. She had always been aware at least of what was extraneous to their coherence. While the love – the love she recognised, as she had recognised Jack himself.

'People don't believe me when I say this. It's not that I put on an act. I'm not covering up or in a closet. I'm just the way I am. I'm homosexual, Jula.'

'Gay,' she said, reflexively.

'Do I strike you as gay? It's a nice idea, that word, but not for a moody bastard like me. Homosexual. I can relate to that.'

When she smiled, he said, 'Shall I open the door, or will you just walk straight through the woodwork?'

'Can't I just brush my teeth and go to bed, as you said I could?'

But they spent some time talking before individually they used the bathroom, and together got into the bed.

Jack told her brief things. That he saw someone now, not often, a man, someone he was thinking seriously of finishing with. And of the earlier relationship, the man two years his junior, who had died in a mugging. 'I think we'd have lasted. But you never know. Since then I'm choosy. You have to be nowadays. Don't worry, by the way, I'm the carefullest safe-sex practitioner you've ever met. And I get myself checked. You don't have to be afraid of being around me.'

In the bed they lay curled into each other, unaroused yet sensually at grace, soothed and consoled, hand on hand. It was familiar, somehow. 'You do believe I love you?' he said.

'I know. I couldn't be here otherwise, could I?'

'I'd do anything to keep you safe.'

'I know that too.'

'You're a marvel, girl,' he said. 'You know *that*?' He said, 'I was on pins. You might have run out yelling. I wouldn't have blamed you. But Christ. Yet – I thought you wouldn't. Do you believe it's possible to be in love like this, total love. But without sex?'

'Yes, Jack.'

Sex she had had, and not thought less of it because it was not accompanied by love. Sex *with* love, for Jula, who had found it only with Steven Grace, had become a volatile commodity.

But non-sexual, utter love she still remembered. It was what she had had with Vivien and David, long, long, long ago.

When the knocking came on the front door, Jack, who had been unconscious, was there ahead of her, and more awake than she was.

They stood at bay in the lower house.

'Steven's sleeping pills? I don't think they were, as such.'

'Could you fetch them anyway, please, Ms Cork. The WPC will go with you. No, Mr Hastings, we don't need a search warrant. We're not searching.'

And presently, 'And these?'

'Blood-pressure, Inderal – he took one a day. When he thought of it.'

And again: 'And *these*?'

'Those are the cat's.'

'Neo-Mercazole. That's for thyroid, isn't it?'

'Yes. Humans and cats take the same pills, apparently.'

'It says forty. Has it had all these?'

'The vet gave me twenty, all he had at the time, in this bottle. And I've given the cat one for five days.'

Outside, official, a police car, red, white and blue.

'You can call your solicitor from the station, Mr Hastings.'

Jula said, 'My solicitor's in London. I don't think I can reach him so early.'

'Don't worry,' said Jack Hastings, wolf-faced in the cruel lights of the car, 'mine is ready to go 24 hours.'

'Used to dealing with villains, is he?' asked the enemy in blue.

Hastings said nothing, and in the event, the two numbers he rang gave no answer, beyond a faulty recorded message.

In Divers Lane, which had been Dives' Lane, the sheep-owner's sheep-walk to riches about 1403, Sharon Kenton and Tony Kenton, Mr-and-Mrs-Kenton-to-be, sat in the car.

Opposite, a carnival of lights, the Alliat house.

'What a wonderful house, Tony.'

'Bit flash.'

'No, but – Oh, can't you imagine it. Living there.'

'No. All I've known are basement flats and semis.'

'Me too. Well, not basements, though.'

'They glanced at each other. Every assignment was a date, and they knew it, and pushed it sternly from view.

Side by side in this car, so easy to slide into each other's arms. They thought they would rather have died.

'Call in,' he said.

'Why?'

'Say nothing's happened.'

'But I already did.'

'That was ten minutes ago. What time is it?'

'Quarter to four, or nearly. This watch is messing about.'

The rate of the heart can affect a watch, as well as sunspots. They knew this, and kept their own counsel.

Markessa had walked ten thousand miles, over dagger-tips and hot coals.

Above, she froze, coatless in her summer dress, on the first autumn night that had turned toward winter. But her feet were laved in fire.

The track had led down to a road or lane. It was badly made up, and not much better. When she clambered into the meadows on one side, flints tore at her like fangs, and once she caught her foot in a knot of grass and fell headlong.

She tried to get her hands out of the sellotape. It was amazingly difficult. The more she strained and pulled, the more tightly it bit into her. And the stickiness – somehow it made her cringe. (She had thought of trying – in turn – to bite through the tape – but the idea of it snagging on one of her dental caps, dislodging it – deterred her.)

She had stopped crying. Her mouth hung open.

Here in England, which as everyone knew was built up to the ruination of its greenbelts, she was as uprooted as any stray abandoned in the desert waste.

When she saw the house, she couldn't believe it. Then she tried to run, and fell again, cutting her knee open on a stone.

It was an ugly house, futuristic in the 1960s (a future that had been bypassed), with a lot of glass.

At first she thought it was deserted. But as she staggered to it across rough lawns and startling horrible little flights of steps, a security light blazed up, blinding her, and then another and another.

By the time she reached the house deck, and found a wide glass door, Markessa was trembling and once more sobbing. But she could collapse now. Someone would take care of her.

Well behaved, a visitor, she rang the bell.

Markessa heard it, through the thick glass. A peel of chimes that sounded like a copy of some church on Easter morning.

The noise was so incongruous among the sighing trees, the light-slashed emptiness of the night, that she hung there stunned, for what seemed half an hour. Before she tried again.

Still no-one answered.

Were they gone? Away somewhere, some remote haven in France or Bermuda – flown like swallows for the winter.

Markessa lifted her head to all the blank upper tiers of glass.

She cried in a wavering howl. And when, still, God and the world paid no attention, she threw herself on the doorbell, carillon chime on chime, screaming and screeching, unable to stop.

Through her own tumult, she heard a window thrown wide.

'Oh thank God – help me! Help me!'

'Listen,' said a male voice far above her as the angels. 'Stop that, or I'll let the dogs out.'

Markessa stared. There was no light. Only a shade, leaning forward a little, the cultured voice quite cool and almost friendly.

'No – you don't understand – I've been attacked –'

'I do understand. We get plenty of your kind. Drug abusers. So-called gypsies. Just fade away. I have two Alsatians here. Also a shotgun.'

He moved and she heard a dog growling. The face of the dog poked suddenly from the window, muzzle a jackal's, eyes gleaming like green lava.

'That's it. Go and annoy someone else, why don't you.'

The window shut.

Markessa stumbled back down the garden, and one by one, appeased, the security lights went out.

4

'So you'd like to have a chat, Mr Hastings, after all. Very wise. Your bloke's swanned off to the Bahamas till the New Year, I shouldn't wonder. It makes you think, doesn't it, however do they accumulate so much money? Now, I've offered you our on-tap legal aid, haven't I? She can be here in – oh, 15 minutes I should say. Classy too. Double-barrelled name and all. No? You sure? How about Ms Cork?'

'I've told her to keep quiet until we can get a solicitor.'

'So you want to take the blame. Is that it?'

'I'm going to tell you where I was. I'll put you straight, where I can.'

'How generous.'

'I'd like a couple of answers, too.'

'Would you?' But Knox settled, composed himself to attend.

He looked, Jack thought, like a rotund good-fortune Buddha that had sat on the mantelpiece in his childhood. Before his father smashed it.

'You said he was poisoned. Steven.'

'In a manner of speaking.'

'You then asked me if I use white spirit. So far as I know, anyone in my business is likely to. And you asked Jula about pills.'

'So I did.'

'The sleeping pills aren't. You know that?'

'Antihistamines. Yes, sir. Not what we were looking for, frankly. But then I suppose you must have used all those up.'

'Steven said he was allergic to the cats and he couldn't sleep. So some doctor gave him something to cover both. The Inderal is for hypertension.'

'Yes, sir.'

'And one of the cats gets the others.'

'*Yes*, sir.'

Hastings fixed his eyes on Knox. 'If we killed him, why don't you tell me how?'

'Or why don't you tell *me*?'

'I don't know, Knox. Cos we didn't do it.'

Knox the Buddha cuddled up to his desk. He was happy.

'All right. This is how I see it, Jack. You don't mind *Jack*, do you, Jack? Well. You either arranged to see Mr Grace in Divers Lane, or more likely, you spotted his Porsche behind you when you were in the hold up, and took a notion. The other drivers would be only too glad to let you get out and go the other way – one less vehicle in front. Then you followed Grace into the lane and you, or your friend, used your car to push the Porsche off the road. Like that scene in *Ben-Hur*. Before your time, but you get my drift.'

The dark blue eyes watched him.

'*Then* you and your companion – this gent you say drove you back from Greenwich – nipped out and forced Grace into drinking a concoction. It was, by the way, Mogadon, with the brush-cleaner. Jog your memory?'

'We forced him. How did we do that? Don't you think he might have objected?'

'I'm sure he did. But there were two of you, you two strapping lads. I doubt he was in your league, Jack.'

'Then what?'

'You let him go.'

'Would we do that? I mean, we'd have wanted to see how it turned out, wouldn't we?'

'Maybe he got away. Maybe you didn't even really mean it. Just meant to scare the shit out of him, rough him up, give him a firm warning.'

'So it was me and him. Jula had no part in it.'

'Oh no. I think Jula asked you to do it, Jack. You planned it together. And she gave you the barbiturates. Maybe you'd been bombed up and ready to go for a long time, looking for an opportunity. And here it was. All the better in an unlikely spot. And keeping her in the dark so she wouldn't – er – feel too *involved.'*

'That's pathetic, Knox. How'd you get where you are?'

Knox's beady eyes bounced. 'Hard work, Jack. Staying up nights. Dedication.'

'All right,' Jack Hastings said. 'I'll tell you what I did and I'll tell you about the guy I was with. And a number where you might reach him, I'm not sure. Jula wasn't with us, and she didn't make any plan with me. She doesn't drive; you know that, don't you? If she went to Divers Lane, she'd have needed a cab, or she'd have had to walk there and back, which would have taken her hours. Check with Markessa what time she found Jula at the house. Before 7.30 was what I heard.'

'I haven't checked with Ms Philbin, just at the moment. That's a shame, isn't it?'

'Then call her up.'

'Suppose she's not there.'

'Why wouldn't she be?'

'And it's so late, Jack.'

'That hasn't stopped you so far.'

'You were going to tell me a story, Jack.'

'I was going to tell you the bloody *truth.'*

Rawthorn halted. Detective Chief Inspector Knox sat crouched over his desk, fingers dibbling on it, like a demented pianist from a horror film of the '50s.

'Yes sir?'

'Sit down. Let's think. I need a call made. Can't do that until 4.15, apparently.' He raised his brows. He was smiling, but was it from fury or elation? 'This is a first rate muddle, Ed.'

'It seems to be.'

'Father's too spontaneous, isn't he? That's the awkward bit. Head down and charge. And I've charged them. But it doesn't feel right, does it?'

'No, I don't think it does.'

'Hastings has disappointed me, too. He genuinely doesn't seem to know about Markessa going missing. I hoped he might. Thought he might be responsible. Haven't put it to him yet. Saving that one. Of course, he might be a top-class actor. He's gay. That's a turn up, wouldn't you say? I mean, I wouldn't have pegged Hastings for one of the boys.'

'Not every gay man goes camping, sir.'

'All right, all right. Call me old-fashioned. I'll just tell you what he told *me*. See what you think.'

He hadn't told Knox all of it. And there was plenty he hadn't told Knox about Dominic. Which meant he was still protecting Dominic, covering for him. It was hard to stop. Like giving up cigarettes, only he'd never smoked. Jack Hastings had seen his father smoking, smoking and boozing away every penny Jack's mother made, and that had tended to put him off.

The first time he saw Dominic, Jack had rated him fairly low. But that was Jack's mind. Jack's body had been less uninterested.

Meanwhile, Dominic was with Bash, and Jack hadn't ever been a poacher.

One of the earliest dislikes he'd had for Dominic was to do with Bash, in fact. Bash, grinning and bringing Jack coffee and cake, as Jack craned backwards, fixing the bar ceiling of the Iron Cherry, had introduced the name.

'Michelangelo Vincelli. Call me Vince, I prefer it.'

And Dominic had come through and said, sweetly, 'No. He's called Bash.'

Michelangelo Vincelli Vince made an open gesture of resignation.

'I say to him to call me Vince, but he won't. He calls me always Michelangelo. So I say if he don't stop, I bash him.'

'So I call him Bash,' repeated Dominic.

Dominic also had the ingrained habit (one Jack was rather allergic to) of referring to his male partner as *She*. ('She's out. Cleaning some friend's oven.' 'She made this pasta. If only she could look more like she cook.)

This was only once he thought he knew you. Before that, Bash was usually *He*. Although in moments of Dominic's emotion, Bash could slip in and out of *He* into *She*, and vice versa. 'He keeps threatening me. How he'll drop dead if I don't stop "upsetting" him.'

'Will he?'

'Well, he's got all these overweight diseases, blood-pressure, cholesterol. His father had a heart attack. He ought to lose some blubber and slow down. It's not my fault. I didn't *make* him. And I'm not a saint. I can't be lovely *all* the time.'

'Can't you?'

'I can with you.'

But Dominic's ideas of 'lovely', out of the sexual arena, weren't always Jack's.

'Oh, why make a fuss? I don't *drink*. You said you like that.'

'Okay.'

'So I have to have something.'

'Not that bloody awful muck.'

'It's nothing. The Incas used to use it, dear heart.'

'And where are they now?'

At first, Dominic had hidden his use of the drug, tipping it in his soft drinks ('See, I *never* use dangerous needles, dearest.') when Jack was out of the room. Then Dominic *let* Jack see. 'It's like farting in bed, darling. You can't keep up these façades forever, not once you're *intimates*.'

Jack Hastings didn't lecture Dominic. That was something he tried never to do with anyone. His father had been a lecturer, once on a rostrum, and later at home.

Dominic took Jack's non-comment for acquiescence. Never for approval. Dominic wasn't that stupid.

Jack hadn't touched Dominic while he worked on the bar, and when the bar was finished, he kept away from Dominic. It was Bash who had invited Jack over for dinner at the apartment in Docklands. And Jack had got out of it, although Bash's cooking was sensational. (Jack had also tried not to refer to Vince as Bash. But in the end he gave up. 'Who? Who?')

Eventually Dominic called Jack.

'Look, for God's sake, can you come to this dinner of her's? She's got four other people coming, absolute nerds, and some woman designer, a poncey tart. *She* keeps saying it will put work your way. She's getting upset. She says it must be my fault. I was rude to you or something inane. Please, Jack. She's making my life hell.'

He didn't feel sorry for Dominic, but for Bash. So he agreed to go over, and arrived about 7.00, in the surreal Docklands twilight, carrying a stony-clear bottle of wine from San Gimignano.

The apartment, all walls of glass and a view of the water, was empty apart from Dominic.

''Twas cancelled. I didn't have time to call you. She's gone off to see *Mama Mia*. Obviously, I don't get asked. Mama is still waiting for Bashy to have a traditional Catholic wedding and sire a host of *bambini*. But you've brought wine. The perfect guest. Let's drink some anyway. Or *you* must.'

Jack realised he had been incredibly naïve, and that he must have intended to be. The subconscious. It was five and a half years since Bristol and there hadn't been much in between. At first he hadn't even wanted there to be. Now Dominic, with his looks and charismatic youth and his eyes that burned, looking into Jack's, like leopards' out of shadow.

Naïve to come here. Naïve to stay. Jack stayed. He didn't have to do anything, just let Dominic seduce him. Which, sober Perrier put aside, Dominic did, soon enough.

Jack was angry afterwards, at himself mostly. They'd at least not done it in the poor sod's double bed, but in the guest bathroom shower. Christ, to class that as good manners –

In the following month, Jack made no move to contact Dominic. But Dominic always made the moves, first by phone, and then by arriving on the doorstop of the flats in Castlewest Road. 'Bashy has your address, dear. Isn't that fortuitous.'

He *fancied* Dominic. It was more than that. Nothing kind or friendly, nothing with any tenderness or even ordinary rapport. A type of excitement he hadn't experienced for years. Desire, like a street-car, rushing you away with it.

None of this, of course, was relayed to Detective Chief Inspector Knox.

'There were things about him that got on my nerves. He's a lunatic. I put a stop to it almost a year ago.'

'And he didn't accept that.'

Dominic hadn't. He'd called all day, half the night. When Jack wouldn't answer, Dominic filled up the answerphone with messages. Only once did he turn up. It was about 5.00 in the morning. Getting no response from the sleeping house, Dominic threw pebbles, gathered on the beach, up at Jack's balconied window. Being Dominic, and rather large pebbles, one cracked the glass.

The neighbours were then treated to the theatre of Jack in the pre-dawn street, wearing only a pair of jeans, holding Dominic by the throat. The film had no proper soundtrack. Jack had spoken softly.

Afterwards, he couldn't remember what he'd said. Dominic remembered. 'You told me you'd break my neck if I didn't leave you alone. I said I had to see you. I said I'd sit in the street. You said you'd kill me. When I started to cry, you slapped me across the face like some girl.'

In the end Jack had shut the door on Dominic, and Dominic went down to the esplanade, and to the nearest phone, and called him.

'You *are* killing me, Jack. I need you, Jack. If you treat me like this, it's murder. You're murdering me. I'm dying. I'm dead.'

'Then fucking stay dead.'

Dominic had used the very sentiments Bash had employed during Dominic's previous affair. 'You're murdering me. Do you want my heart to explode? Eh, you little queer? I give you everything, I look after you. And like dirt you treat me. You'll kill me, you murderer.'

But Jack had scared Dominic, less the threats than the icy rage inside the eyes, the terrible voice, the dead-phone silence after it.

Dominic went back to Bash, and for several months, Jack

hadn't heard from him.

'I thought he'd given up. Found somebody else.'

'When he seemed so attached to you?' Knox hadn't looked prurient, only genuinely curious.

'Dominic is attracted to Dominic. He likes an audience. But there'd always be plenty of those.'

Jack didn't mention to Knox, had no reason to, that once, before their parting, and only once, he had spoken to Dominic of Jula Cork.

'I don't want to be late for this woman I'm going to see.'

'Oh. A *woman*? Who's that? Some bint who wants her rooms revamped.'

'A friend.'

'A *friend*. And you'd rather dash over to see her, this *woman*, than stay here and play with me.'

'Not necessarily. About equal, I'd say.'

'You shit. What is this?'

'A joke, Dominic.'

'I don't believe you.'

'Fine. But I'm going for a shower. Alone. And then I'm going out.'

'To *this woman*.'

'It's a party. A pretty naff party.'

'She's no good at parties, *this woman*?'

'The guy she lives with – look, let go.'

'Tell me about *him*. Much more intriguing.'

So Jack, for a few seconds, described Steven Grace, and Dominic lost interest.

They had been in an easy-going phase, right then. Which was undoubtedly why Jack hadn't lied about driving over to Jula's. And Dominic hadn't pressed him any more at the time.

But Dominic must have brooded on it. Although *brood* was apparently what Bash did.

All their meetings thereafter had a little 'How's your *woman*? Have you seen your *woman* recently?' grated on them.

Jack would answer yes or no, or some other brevity. He never detailed Jula's appearance or nature, said nothing about where she lived or what she did. He never gave her name. These things that he would, he thought, tactfully and tentatively, have brought to the notice of a lover he valued, he kept under lock and key from Dominic. When he stopped seeing Dominic, he tried to forget everything to do with Dominic, which included Dominic's questions about *the woman*.

This September, when Dominic rang Jack, it was 9.30 on a Saturday morning, and Jack was just going out to an auction with a client.

'Hi, Jack. It's Dominic. How are you?'

'How am I? Wondering why you called.'

'Yes, I don't blame you. Sorry about all that last business. You were right about my sweeties. They do make one bloody irrational. I'm a lot better now. Off the stuff. On a programme. Bash arranged it. He's been a tower of strength.'

Jack had never heard Dominic sound so sane. He'd forgotten that Dominic had had training as an actor. Either that, or it was the naïvety taking over again. Jack had been celibate since Dominic, and even Dominic's voice now had a certain quality, a certain *galvanic*, which its air of abashed, slightly nervous apology, only increased.

'Look, the reason I called. Some big magnate friend of Bash's has bought a place at Greenwich. It's an absolute *mansion*. Twenty-foot high ceilings, a Victorian conservatory, a servants' kitchen, marble *everywhere*. It's just the kind of thing you like tackling, and he wants someone in to do it, sort of Napoleonic crossed with Edwardian. Could take your whole team – Barry, Surinder – and Jocelyn for curtains and covers. Better yet, he'll pay. Cash no object.'

'It sounds okay,' said Jack, still cautious.

'Don't be put off by me. I can send you the guy's number and fax, once I get them. Mind you, I think he'd rather go through someone he's met – he's the canny type. Perhaps Bash could make the first contact. Would that be better?' Jack didn't speak, and Dominic said, in a calm, adult way, 'If you'd like the work, I don't want you to miss it because I behaved like a twat. You don't have to see *me* at all. Honestly, Jack. It's fine.'

'Look, I have to be somewhere –' Instinctively, a hesitation, in which, previously, Dominic would have inserted, 'Off to see the *woman*?' Now there was only a polite lacuna. 'Can I give you a call tonight? About 7.00?'

'Sure. Bash will be at the Cherry, but I'll be around.'

All day, through other activities, Jack thought of Dominic. Not continuously, but off and on, now and then, like a lighted sign that didn't work properly, but still had life in it.

Dominic had come to his senses, hadn't he? People did. He was 21 – or a bit older now, 22, maybe. And Bash had stood by him.

The danger might now lie more in Jack's not being able to keep his hands off Dominic, rather than Dominic's wanting to resume their meetings.

And if Dominic really was pulling himself round, and was trying to make it up to Jack, turning the work offer down could be detrimental, at a crucial stage.

Naïvety.

Wanting to be naïve.

There were plenty of memories. Hot white memories on a background of dark gold.

Jack Hastings called Dominic up, and said he thought he'd like the job, and it sounded as if it would take him, and his team, up to Christmas. Which would be helpful money-wise, especially for Jocelyn and Barry.

'That's great. How do you want to play it? Actually there's a chance I could take you to meet the guy next week, maybe, see the house. If you can make it up to Greenwich – meet around 12.00, say?'

'Him, you and me,' said Jack.

'Well, not if you don't want. I can just give you his –'

'It's okay, Dominic. It's fine. The job sounds a winner. Thanks for thinking of me.'

Dominic said, without a trace of nostalgia, 'I think of you a lot, Jack.' And then, 'You helped me pull myself together.'

All this, in paraphrase. A matter of a couple of minutes in the telling. And Knox, keeping a straight face. In fact behaving perfectly well. He looked now like a fat, thick gnome, but someone must have drummed political correctness into him. Or else he didn't mess with aliens, even those charged with murder. Or else he wasn't a complete cretin.

Jack, with Barry, had been working on an empty flat in Seatree. That night they kept going until midnight, and slept in sleeping bags on the floor of the main room for an early start. The windows were open to dispel the reek of paint. Barry verbally missed his girlfriend, a thing that always made Jack ponder if Barry was making sure Jack knew nothing was doing, there … The paranoia of the gay? In any case, rather than thinking of Barry, of whom he never would have thought in that way, Jack had to admit he was remembering Dominic.

In the morning they finished off the paintwork and cleared up. Payment sorted out, Barry left. No-one was moving into the flat for two more days. Jack used the bathroom to shower and shave.

This was also the day of one of Jula's dinners, given suddenly as usual, to keep Steven Grace quiet. An evening of fantastic food and stinking company, Grace going on about Grace, and Markessa tweeting at him, and Jula sitting, to all appearances composed and virtually absent.

He met Steven as rarely as possible. Grace was one of those men who flirt with other men, just as they flirt with women – that is, until they think the flirtee is fairly hooked. Then the little snubs and digs begin. Jack gave nothing back. He acted the strong docile bod, speaking only when spoken to, and then amiably and not for long.

It was also unspoken, between himself and Jula, that he was there for her. Grace knew it and didn't know it. Jack suspected that Steven sensed he, Jack, had no sexual inclination toward her, without quite figuring out why. Mainly Grace was concerned only with himself, and therefore easy to deflect. Ignore. Normally in the end he would take Markessa aside to show her new clothing, or some crap he was writing, or *going* to write. And Jack and Jula, discarded menials, would serenely wash up, and go to sit out in the yard or garden with the cats.

Initially, Jack had needed to meet Grace. In a way, from the very first, he was watching him, trying to learn enough, one day to thrust him out of Jula's life forever. Not by killing him. To plan to kill him wasn't in Jack's physical vocabulary. Nor would Jula have borne with that. But such a leaky boat as Steven Grace could eventually be put in a dock of some sort. It was, Jack felt, a matter of time more than strategy.

Also, he was looking forward to seeing Jula. He always did. And this restful feeling, like homecoming, was so unlike the *restless* imminence of meeting Dominic again, that it half amused, half irritated him.

He took the train up about 10.00, missing the worst of the rush-hour inflow to London, and then the other train down. And met Dominic, as they'd arranged, in the Figurehead around 12.30. But not the guy with the mansion. He was represented solely by an empty space.

Dominic stood up as Jack came toward him. Not an old-world courtesy. It was as if Jack himself lifted Dominic to his feet.

And he did look, what Dominic himself would have called, 'Ravishing. Ravishing-ready-to-be-ravished.'

'Jack – so good to see you. My God. Sorry, I'm shaking.'

'You look well.'

'I am. You too.'

'And that's more than I can say for Mr Mansion.'

'Really sorry, Jack. He hasn't cried off, he *wants* to meet you. But some stock market thing came up – you know what they're like. And he was off like a ferret down a rabbit hole, mobile phone clamped to his face.'

'Will he be back?'

'He said he would. Or, if not, have some lunch and meet him there in an hour.'

Two things. Seeing Dominic, being with him, all trust was gone. But wasn't it sex that drove it out?

Surely, for Jack, Dominic's trustless quicksilver was half what the turn-on was – aside from the rest of it, which was turn-on enough. Better accept that.

So, give him the benefit of the doubt. Don't assume he's lying.

Don't get crotchety.

'Okay. Let's eat.'

But along with the urge to reach out and take, the urge not to. The urge not to be there at all.

Dominic said he'd get lunch. That meant, of course, Bash would get it.

Jack Hastings would have had steak, if the mansion-owner, or he himself, had been paying. Instead he chose the omelette.

Dominic ordered some sort of fish, and toyed with it spitefully, like a cat.

Neither of them had much to drink. A Budweiser for Jack, and a bottle of Perrier for Dominic.

He looked *too* well, didn't he? Although the modern drug programmes were excellent, could he look this 'Ravishing', so soon off the genuine article?

Don't ask him about it.

Jack didn't ask him.

And Dominic didn't say anything, either.

In some people that would be what you'd expect. Reticence, humiliation, even a wish to spare the other person. But Dominic would have said it all. The agony and the anguish. A Performance.

'It's nearly 2.00. Maybe we ought to get round there.'

'Yes, you're right. Another drink?'

'No, thanks, Dominic. I want a clear head when it's business.'

'Sure, Jack. I should recollect, shouldn't I?'

He paid. They left.

The wide room, green and russet, with the figureheads of its name ranged round the walls, scarlet and black and gold. Every one of them watching. 'All eyes on you,' as Dominic had said. What he liked.

They walked up from the river, and went toward the park. Slowly looking in shops, taking their time.

The heat was dense and the air smoky. Trees crisped and gilded by the sun and pollution, glittered on the mazarine sky. Blackheath, named for plague death, was the colour of dark limes, and starred by ice-cream vendors.

'We ought to go sun-bathing,' said Dominic. 'Or you should. I like you brown. Shall we?'

'What about Mr Mansion?'

'Well, I think he's probably forgotten us. I'm sorry, Jack. I really am.'

'And you're really sorry you lied to me, I bet.'

'I didn't. I didn't lie.'

'Then let's go to the house. See if he's there.'

'He won't be.'

'No, he won't be.'

'He's a tycoon – or a raccoon. You know. They rush about. Those black-ringed tails. It's all the friction.'

Dominic, being cute. Dominic looking like a young god of the Greeks. And the Greeks would have liked Dominic all right. Made allowances for Dominic.

'Okay, Dominic. Well, it was good to see you again. I hope you get what you need.'

'Jack – for Christ's sake – where are you going –?'

'To catch the train. I have to get back. Things to do.'

'People to see.' Dominic lowered his eyes. 'I've let you down. Honestly, Jack, it isn't my fault.'

'Let's just forget it.'

'I'll call him tonight, Jack, find out –'

'Right.'

'Let me buy you a drink. It doesn't count now, does it, since he's run off. To say I'm sorry.'

Naïvety. Or just straightforward lust.

It could have been the best, to go over the river, get to the apartment, empty of others, go in with him. Have him. (*Just to say sorry, Jack. It doesn't count now.*)

But it would count. It would be a score. A black mark.

'I don't want you to hate me,' said Dominic. 'I can't stand it. The last time – that hurt like hell, but it also *helped* me to see where I'd gone wrong. But now – they said I shouldn't get upset.'

'You mean the drug rehabilitation people?'

Humbly, 'Yes.'

Suppose it were true? Don't upset him. Don't knock him off the rails if he's really dragged himself back on them.

They went to a pub. It had connections with Lord Nelson, and Dominic went to the gents' and came out very bright and started making Nelson jokes. 'What do you *need* the other arm for?' 'Kiss me hard-ee, Hardy.' 'And *that's* how you went blind? Oh, really?'

Bright. From the gents'. Jack didn't go in with him. Obviously. And so, what else did he do in there? He took the can of Perrier he'd told the bar girl was fine, no need for a glass. His eyes were full of summer lights and fireworks.

'What are you taking, Dominic?'

'Excuse me?'

'I mean, instead of what you usually take.'

'Oh, some stuff. Stupid stuff.'

'What's it called?'

'I forget.'

'It's getting on for quarter to 4.00 now. I wanted to be back by 6.00, at the latest. I need to get going.'

'The Docklands Railway is amazing, isn't it, Jack? Robot trains.'

'Blackheath Station is better.'

Dominic looked thoughtful. 'It'll be a rush; I don't think there'll be a train till 5.00.'

'There will be.'

But, by some divine-malign intervention, when he'd got there (Dominic walking with him) the earlier train was cancelled.

'*Sod* it.'

And then Dominic seeming to change. Looking sad and

adult, like the voice on the phone.

'I've messed you around. I'm sorry. Didn't mean to. Why don't I drive you back? The car's not far from here.'

'No. Thanks.'

'It's simple. M25, A21. No strings.'

'No, there never are, are there?'

Dominic, standing in the London village, outside the station, his face pale and grave. Suddenly like another face, from so long before.

'I can't help it, Jack. I'm mad on you. Not planned. I know I don't mean a thing. Let me just do this, Jack. Get you where you need to be. And then – then no more.'

'Dominic – look,' thrown, not thinking, 'we'll talk about this another time. I have to get back. There's this – I don't want to let someone down.'

'Oh, would it be the *woman*? You're like Sherlock Holmes about this *woman*. Bash likes Sherlock Holmes. And Biggles. Biggles and Ginger. Just like a drink. Mix me up a Biggles and Ginger.'

'Fuck off, Dominic.'

Dominic slumped against the wall. It could have been an act. But his clear skin was green, as if the sea had come in behind it.

'Stand up. Do you want someone to hurry over and *help* you? Maybe a helpful policeman? With what you've got inside you?'

Dominic straightened.

Jack thought, *Come on, you bastard. You knew what he was up to. He's mental. And you probably helped.*

They went and had another drink, two Perriers. Both unadulterated. And in the end, he let Dominic drive him back; the M25, the A21 and off onto the Seatree Road.

'He wasn't happy. But in control.'

'He hadn't been drinking?'

'No, he doesn't drink.'

'And then what?'

'We hit the roadworks and the faulty bloody lights, and Dominic came off his trolley. Quite a few drivers did. He was yelling and jumping about, so I got out and pulled him back to the car. And then the lights cleared and we went on.'

'And that's all?'

'Sorry to disappoint you.'

('Sorry, Jack, sorry. It doesn't count now.')

5

Sat alliteratively in the Sierra, in Saxon Vale, Seatree, Dominic had no thought that anyone else was aware of him.

For, like lamps, they had all gone out. They had forgotten him, even the supernatural source that sometimes guided him. He was alone.

Even Bash was gone. Heart-exploded and dead?

And perhaps Jack, so like a fantasy anyway, had never existed.

The girl was a mistake. The *wrong* girl.

And Dominic.

'I'm real?'

He felt real. He was touchable and, speaking aloud, heard his own voice. But to anyone *else*?

Dominic looked at the dash of the cab, and took a chance.

He switched on the mike.

'Hallo? Your cab's here. Want it?'

There was a sound like someone clearing catarrh. And then a man said, 'Is that you, Bill? *Bill* your radio's rotten – all crackly. Don't sound like you – are you there?'

Like a séance.

Are you there?

Knock once for no, forever on and on for yes.

'Bill? … there, Bill?'

Dominic thought of his actor's training. Since he had lost his own soul and his own body and his own voice, now he had to be this other one. Bill. And Bill was what? Judging from the interlocutor, the very thing Dominic had tried to train himself out of. But then, acting taught you also to recapture it, the accent of the past.

''Ere, mate,' said Dominic in, not the accent of the past, but stage cockney, 'this radio's rotten, innit?'

'God – Bill. Am I glad you're back on. I haven't got a single driver. All down sick. I thought I'd have to do this one meself. Or get the dog to. Yeah?'

'Yeah, get the dog, lord love a duck.'

'Don't use that language on the radio, Bill, for God's sake. Anyone could be listening.'

Dominic laughing. In silence.

'You still there, Billy? Listen, it's the Gatwick run. You on for that? Decent money. You'll do it, won't you, mate?'

'Right, mate. Kiss me pearly-whirly, mate.'

'Eh? *Bill*? These radios – Bill, can you hear me?'

'Loud and clear, Ginger.'

'Nah, Ginger's off, mate. Listen. Divers Lane, 4.00 am. Can you make it? Divers Lane to Gatwick.'

'Let the dog see the rabbit, mate.'

'The dog? No, come on. 4.00 am. All right?'

Dominic stopped laughing 'Tell me where it is, this Divers Lane.'

'Yes, nobody knows. Used to be a private road. But I looked it up. I can give you directions. Hang on, mate.'

A dog barked.

Had it seen the rabbit?

Dominic waited, and then directions came. They scorched into his brain, which now, within the husk of Bill, was laser-toned and ginger tiger-burning bright.

'Tiger, tiger, burning bright, don't cross the road, look left and right. Although they may just see your light.'

'What mate? Sorry. The dog got hold of me sandwiches.'

'Chocks away,' said Dominic.

'No, he's had the chocs already.'

6

When Dominic lost it at the stalled lights, Jack faced the situation for what it was.

Until then, Dominic had been talking only a little and coherently enough, bitchily of course, but he normally was. Avoiding, evidently, any reference to Bash. And none to *amour fou.*

But after they'd sat blocked in the car, again, for ten minutes, and people were getting out and clustering round the lights like angry wasps, suddenly Dominic began to shout.

'I can't stand this! Why is this happening? Nothing works in this useless bog of a country!'

'Cool off.'

'Don't tell me to cool off. Look at them – morons – Christ, what do I do now?'

'Sit and wait.'

'Like a good little girl? Fuck you –' And the door was flung open and Dominic was out.

Jack left him to it, and then went and got him. Dominic struggled. Jack dragged him back to the Range Rover.

'Get in. Sit down. *Listen.* You're out of your skull. Don't play this for laughs.'

And Dominic deflated.

'You're right. Sorry. Yes. Oh God, Jack.' And as the crowd seethed aimlessly yet aggressively on, and the heat trickled down the windows, 'I've left Bash. Walked out. I didn't tell you.'

When Dominic started the car again, Jack Hastings thought, *He's liable to crash. Ripe for it.* Usually he could drive, whatever he'd had or done. But now he was all over the place. And the sun was going.

Self-preservation. Why stick a noble name on it? Jack reached over and put his hand on Dominic's shoulder, left it there a moment too long. 'Steady, Dom.'

And they steadied.

'I've got to talk to someone.'

'All right. When we get to the town.'

'Thank you, Jack. I need to. I appreciate this.'

They drove back to the flat Jack had finished decorating that morning, in King's Street North. Jack had always intended to go back there that evening, shower again, and change, then drive up to Jula's in the blue van marked Gothix, which was parked at the kerb.

Instead they got out of the Range Rover and walked up into King's Street East, to the Invasion pub.

They drank water, which Jack now felt was coming out of his ears. Dominic's voice ran insistently into them the other way.

He'd left Bash, he said, that morning. Run off when Bash had gone to the Cherry. He'd taken some clothes, and his car, which Bash anyway had told him was his, and a few bits and pieces. Nothing Bash would care about. Nothing important.

'And I left her a note. On the blackboard in the kitchen. I wrote it in pink chalk. Pink. Bad taste. But you can't write black, can you, on a blackboard?'

'Call him. Will he be home?'

'He might be. I don't know.'

'What did the note say?'

'Not much. There wasn't room for much. Just, *You were great, but time to move on.*'

He meant, to move on to me, Jack thought. *Next stop.*

'He won't want to believe it. Call him. Do it now. Leave a message on the answerphone.'

'She – he – I don't – I can't.'

'Why not?'

'I can't stand him, Jack. I tried to. But he gets on my tits.'

Jack tasted a sourness that had nothing to do with the water in his glass. That poor bloody guy, with his jowly, wanting-to-be-happy face, his black-wet eyes, his out-of-this-world cooking.

And Dominic. Prince of Darkness.

'You need him, mate. Call him. Tell him you were off your head. Pray he'll want you back.'

He'll want you.

I want you. And I'd like to fry you in Bash's biggest, hottest pan of bubbling oil.

'I love you,' said Dominic, softly. 'It's you I want.'

The pub wasn't crowded, but there were a few rough-looking geezers in there, the kind that were straight enough to rule a line by.

'Come on. I need some air,' Jack said.

Obedient, Dominic got up and followed him out.

King's Street North, near the Range Rover and the van, was now empty.

Jack's watch said 7.07, but the pub clock had said 7.35. It was dark, windows lit, the day was over.

'Right. Listen to me, Dominic. There's nothing for us. I mean you and I mean me. We packed it in last –'

'You did. *You.*'

' – Last year, and I only saw you today, as you know, because you lied to me about a job.' (*And I'm lying now. But so what?*)

'Don't Jack – I can't –'

'You can't what? Grow up, Dom. If you don't want Bash, leave Bash. Once he gets over you he'll find someone decent and a halfway all right life. You're doing him a favour.'

'He said it'd kill him – or he'd kill himself. That if I went I'd be murdering him.'

'It's not my problem, Dom. Not anymore. That's it. Get in your nice car, and go away.'

'Jack – Jack –'

'That's it.'

Dominic caught hold of him and Jack struck him off. It wasn't such a violent blow, but full of rage, full of pain. Five and a half years of it. And the rest.

And Dominic fell on the pavement in his suit so expensive it didn't have a designer label, and lay there. And Jack went into the building, and up to the flat.

He took a shower, remembered he'd left his spare clothes in the van, put the originals back on, the shirt with the tear in it where Dominic had resisted at the traffic lights. Got the special flowers for Jula out of the bucket where they'd been unfolding since that morning.

When he went down he felt almost okay. Until he saw the van door was open, and Dominic was sat there, inside it.

Dominic could undo car doors. Jack had known that. Forgotten it.

Or not?

It didn't matter, did it? Not now.

'What glamorous flowers. For me?'

'Get out.'

'Wanna make me, baby?'

He'd had some more of whatever he was taking that day. The mood swings always indicated this. Either more dramatic or more desolate or, as now, abruptly light-hearted, believing nothing at all could go wrong, or stay wrong, in a golden world whose centre was always Dominic.

Jack did a swift mental inventory of the van's contents. There was nothing too valuable. The essentials were on him, or locked upstairs in the flat, where he'd spend another night, since Steven was home.

Jack shrugged and turned to walk away.

'Come on, Jack. Take me to see your adorable *woman*. It is *the* woman? Afraid she can't stand the competition? You've tried to screw with her, haven't you, sweetness? Didn't work, did it? Or did you have to lie there and think of *me*?'

Jack walked back to the van. He spoke in an almost soundless voice so Dominic must strain to hear.

'If you damage this van, I will find you and beat you to a pulp.'

'Wow, Jack –'

'And if you come near me again, I will do the same.'

Dominic's feathery high was melting down to a quick persecution.

'Me – you'd do that to me?'

'I'll cut your face open, Dom,' said Jack. 'I'll make a mess of you, I warn you. It's a promise. You won't get me, and by the time I've finished, you won't get anyone.'

Leopard eyes, now the eyes of a deer that sees a leopard.

Dominic tried to speak. No words came.

'So long, Dom,' said Jack.

He looked back once, at the corner of the street. But it was a reflex.

The day had made him sick. What he had just said made him sick, and angry, at himself, and at the cause. He could hear the blood hissing in his ears.

He wanted now only to look forward, and so he did. At Seatree in the gathering of its lights. At the lit buses. At the hill up to the house in the fields. At Jula. Sanity. The independence of the solitary state.

Jack, who delivered the two- or three-minute paraphrase of all this to Chief Inspector Knox, told him nothing of how Dominic had followed him. Because he knew nothing of it to tell.

'All right. Thank you for your statement.' Knox wrinkling his brows, thinking. 'And you don't reckon the gentleman will vouch for you through any of this time period?'

'Do you?'

'How about the pub – anyone see you?'

'We kept a low profile.'

'What about your van – when you picked it up later, all right, was it?'

'He hadn't vandalised it, no. He'd just got out, shut the door of the van, gone to his own car – he must have, because the car wasn't there when I went back. He drove to London. To Bash, or some mate. He still has a couple, surprisingly.'

'Mmn. Of course, it could all be a colourful invention. Instead of your argument, you and he could have been unanimously duffing up Steven Grace.'

'We weren't.'

Knox sat back. He demonstrated the supergluing action, this

time with fingertips and chin.

'I just have this strong sensation, Jack, that you've had dealings with the police before.'

To his interest, Jack Hastings grinned, and the ornate face changed like rubber.

'Too right I have.'

'Perhaps you could elaborate.'

'Mostly when I was young. I spent quite a bit of time hanging around the local nick.'

'A young offender were you, Jack?

'No such luck. My mum was a WPC.'

'She was – a police officer?'

'There you go.'

'I suppose your dad wasn't a bloody Chief Superintendent?'

'No. A lecturer in history who gave it up to spend more time with a bottle. My mother earned the money and she looked a knock-out in her uniform. Still would, if she put it on. I've never been on the wrong side of the law, I'd never dare.'

'Another surprise,' said Rawthorn.

'And it's for real. We checked her under her own name. She's separated and lives in Chiswick. Early retired with a commendation seven years ago.'

'Do you credit the story, I mean about his lover and the argument and so on?'

'It's concocted-sounding enough to be true.'

'Yes.'

'There was something else he said about Jula Cork.'

Rawthorn waited.

Knox said, 'He told me he understood she'd explained to us about why Grace was blackmailing her.'

'You said it was because of a book, sir.'

'Yes, a book. And Hastings said to me, did I think a woman who was capable of such compunction over a bastard like Leonard Cork, was also capable of killing, or arranging the killing, of anyone in cold blood?'

7

Jula lay back on the mean little bunk, looking up at the ceiling. There was nothing there, or in the room, to see. It was, she assumed, a cell. She was in a cell. She had been charged with murder. Rather than fear, she felt only astonishment. As if she had fallen suddenly down a shaft into the earth. Where was she? How had it *happened*?

Plenty of people must feel this, the guilty or the innocent. For a writer, perhaps it was useful. That voice, always at such moments, objective. *For a writer, everything is of use, Jula.* Leonard's voice. Leonardo.

One heard the theory that, in old age, one could recapture entirely the memory of childhood, even those things that had been, consciously, totally mislaid.

Jula regarded this premise with horror.

It might mean she would come to recall the month after David and Vivien vanished from her life. So far, she never had. It was a blank.

In this void, however, vague floating images, phrases ... There had been a policeman in dark blue, who was very kind to her. His young face – he was younger then than she was now – hung in the emptiness. She hadn't responded to him, hadn't been able to. And Mrs White crying, and Harry White saying, 'Not in front of her, Mary.' And the two parts of her body, separate yet indivisible, though also, now, stripped of all meaning, the Rabbit and the Bear.

And a journey. Yes. There was the memory of that. A long taxi ride, and then a train. Or was this only the brain filling in from later knowledge, and subsequent occasions?

Certainly the journey had no features, no colourings. It had only labels – words – a word-memory, the kind of which she had heard, but which Jula, who usually stored all information in images, possessed for no other time, no other thing.

Had Leonardo travelled with her? Perhaps he had only sent the housekeeper, Mrs Finch. In the unseen memory, a being was there, but it had no name.

And names were soon important.

'Of course, I shall be changing your name.'

And the child, frightened, staring. 'Shan't I be Jula anymore?'

'Don't be a silly fool. Naturally, I mean your surname.'

And he changed her surname, which had been her unmarried mother's (Dunlass), to the family name of Cork.

And *he* was Leonardo. 'Don't call me uncle. It's pointless and suburban, and it makes me sound two hundred.'

Had she ever asked why not *Leonard*? But Jula had heard Vivien and David refer to him by both versions, and by another version too, *Leon*. To his face they never called him Leonard.

Years after, he had said to her, 'What a father, landing me with a lower-class name. God knows where he dug it up from.'

She sometimes thought, subsequently, it might in fact have come from the town four or five miles from the house at Seatree: St Leonards. Curiously perhaps, the sound of the town and the sound of the man never evoked each other – the visual memory of each – so different.

However, 'Leonard' was 'lower-class', but 'Leon' or 'Leonardo , with the flavour of classical Spain or the genius of Renaissance Italy, was acceptable.

Leonardo.

She'd decided, those times when she had seen him before, that he looked like David, but somehow soured, spoilt.

Either the interval had altered him, or her perceptions

had.

He was a thin, *hollow* man. He had a long, hollow face, and the black eyes, which in David had been large and vivid, in Leonardo were hard, non-reflective and filmed over. He was a man, as she later described him, who seemed to wear glasses, yet who didn't. (Peculiarly, when at last he had to, his gaze was softened. But the illness was very likely responsible for that.)

The house in Derbyshire, the first 'home' she had with (Uncle) Leonardo, her father's brother and now her guardian *in loco parentis*, was spectacular. And, to her mind, ugly.

It was, apparently, 'after Inigo Jones'. A flat-fronted building of light grey stone, with oblong, eyelidded windows and an eyelidded, oblong door. Four chimneys lifted from the sloping roof at the front, as if to hold the sky at a proper distance. Under the terrace the green lawn ran down and down, bare of anything, to a formal garden of statues, and blackish once-topiary, which Leonardo disliked and had let become shapeless.

There had been 'grounds', but most of the land was sold. Inside the new wall, matched grey to the stone of the house, were chestnut trees of great beauty. Sometimes foxes cried there in the autumn. Leonardo would call someone in, by stealth, to shoot them.

'I've no objection to hunting, Jula. But half the time the things get away. They're vermin. Oh, I don't care about all these griping chicken-keepers. But the *smell* of a fox. I can't stand it. And they dig everything up.'

For the same reason, grey squirrels were regularly shot, for snatching something or other, or because they knocked over expensive terracotta pots on the terrace.

By the time she might have gained enough courage – or desperation – to ask him for a pet of some kind, she knew not to. Cats and dogs dropped hairs, had fleas, also scratched things, were incontinent. Smelled. Hamsters, even, smelled. As did birds, which besides were noisy. Fish might have been all right, they were aesthetically pleasing. But not worth the effort, constantly dying. Rabbits – why would anyone want a rabbit? And foxes would get the rabbits, which couldn't be kept, of course, inside anywhere in the large house.

Would Leon have liked a snake? Jula had put this to him, idly, in her eighteenth year.

'God forbid,' he said. 'You aren't thinking you want a snake, are you? You have to feed them live mice, which would be a nuisance, and they would escape. I know it's some bloody fool fad with young girls at the moment. But no, Jula. I wouldn't like it.' He feared not the cruelty of life's system of prey and victim, but the 'unpleasant aspect'.

Leonardo disliked so much. Animals. People. Aspects. Even the house, which was 'adequate' but too 'big'. And the garden, which had to be 'looked after'.

He had disliked Jula, as a child. Always?

As memory began to reform beyond the gap, the nine-year-old child found Leonardo looking at her, and heard him say, 'I thought, you know, that you weren't David's daughter. Your mother was quite capable of hoodwinking him. I told the Old Man so. But when I saw you, in that repellent Eltham flatlet, I could see she hadn't lied.'

Did Jula fly at him, screaming that her mother wasn't a liar and her father not an idiot?

She sat still, and all the words soaked into her. ('After what he said about Vivien' was now explained.)

Coldness settled like snow. *Indoor* snow, unavoidable. And Leonardo told her that for this reason, because *he* had vetted her and seen that she was good, the Old Man, her grandfather, David Cork's father, had left her the house in Seatree and a 'Quite reasonable income. At 21, as well. I hope you'll be ready.'

Although he detested her, he would never admit, years after, that he had. 'Oh, Jula. Don't be so ridiculous. Not *like* you? You were a child. And you had great promise.'

'I always had the impression, Leon, that you didn't.'

'Now this is some fancy. You're coming up to your

period, aren't you?'

Fastidious to a rare extreme, Leonardo had never quibbled at using the female cycle against all women. 'Some silly pre-menstrual nonsense.' 'Some raving menopausal harridan.'

In her early teenage years, his abrupt sexual or lavatorial asides had degraded and made her jump. He *appalled* her. His dismissal of the pain and emotionality of such things also astounded her. 'Among our workers, two or three females who cry off every month. A *bad* period. What utter bunkum.' 'Love? Love is the product of the adult mind, if it even exists. Never confuse biology, Jula, with affection.' 'There's no need for anyone to be constipated. I have never been.'

Behind the grey house, Derbyshire rose into the Dark Hills.

How many afternoons had Jula sat at the window of her draughty bedroom, staring at them, like some benighted creature in a Brontë novel, somewhat geographically shifted?

It wasn't a child's room. Not even of a freakish and mature child such as Jula Cork née Dunlass.

Thick, thinly-striped regency paper, costing hundreds of pounds and not to be marked, pale watered lemons and whites, the narrow bed and the mahogany desk, not to be *scratched.*

In Leonardo's bedroom, too, the bed was narrow, although it had a tester. He slept alone, and the bed proclaimed it.

Two women came to clean the house, and there was a gardener and odd-job man named Riddles ('God, that man's name. To be so unaware.'), to whom she was forbidden to say more than hallo-goodbye.

Mrs Finch saw to the organisation of the house, and cooked meals. She was a bulky woman with faded hair, at whom Leonardo sneered in private, 'buttering her up' when she was present. In turn, he was convinced she doted on him. 'Eye on the main chance too, no doubt.' (The disclaimer was always added – no-one could be trusted, especially flatterers, however sincere they seemed. Leonardo impressed this on Jula. One noted he was more lenient, however, with those who made a 'fuss' of him. Secretly he knew himself worthy of admiration. Others of course were not.) The adult Jula doubted Mrs Finch culpable of any more than trying to do her job, quite well aware of what she was up against. If she flattered, it was in the line of duty.

To Jula she wasn't harsh, but never warm. Who could be warm there?

The first Christmas came. By then, Leon had engaged a couple of tutors for his niece. 'Those terrible run-down slummy schools, of course you've learnt nothing. I wonder you've even learned to read.' Leon told her she should 'con' a piece of Shakespeare to say to him on Christmas Eve.

Jula had mentally recorded bits of everything she liked from the beginning, simply for her own pleasure. She had acted out the death of Ophelia (with invented words) and the hand-washing of Lady Macbeth, for an enthralled, tickled, but essentially appreciative Vivien and David. Now she knew enough to know that Leonardo would be the worst of all audiences. Hadn't he even dismissed her awe for Laurence Olivier's filmed *Hamlet* – 'Too contrived' – and a wonderful TV (his TV) production of *Antony and Cleopatra* – 'Over-impassioned'?

Jula spoke for Leonardo, Portia's famous speech from *The Merchant of Venice*. She'd gambled he might approve of Portia, decorous and controlled, rich, intelligent, deceitful – the sort of woman Leonardo seemed to think admissible. (This child's detective work would come to be paramount as she grew older.)

But she stumbled twice in her rendition, seeing his glassed-over eyes. And he said, when she had stopped, 'Yes.' And then, 'Your S's are rather sibilant, aren't they, Jula? We'll have to watch that. "Upon the *plaissse* beneath." It isn't a good play, you know. He varied, Shakespeare. A giant, of course. But there are better vessels, and better parts. *Don't* bite your nails.'

'I'm sorry –'

'For God's sake, child. What's going to become of you?'

But it had *already* become of her.

On Christmas Day there was no tree – 'Commercial manoeuvring' – and the cards stood, the ones Leonardo considered reasonable, along the mantelpiece. Not many, and less once they had been pruned.

He gave Jula a book. It was an illustrated Omar Khayyám. A thing of wonder and joy – and she still had it. When she ran to thank him, he held up his arm to ward her off. 'I'm pleased you like it, Jula. Remember to wash your hands before you read it.'

Dinner was revolting. She would never forget it, even after all the other Christmas dinners just the same. A turkey, and beef. Potatoes not roast but boiled. Endless greens, a home-made stuffing with chestnuts that was sweet the wrong way. No talk, beyond Leonardo's comments.

There was no Christmas pudding, no mince pies. Leonardo ate cheese, and Jula had, as an afterthought, ice cream dredged up from the freezer.

A point was made of watching the Queen's speech, which in the past David and Vivien, although invited downstairs to do so, forgot or never bothered with.

Leonardo studied and then criticised the Queen. Presumably he had watched simply in order to do so.

Upstairs, alone, Jula, her hands washed, began to read Omar Khayyám's poetry, unstumbling, to the Rabbit and the Bear. And to show them the pictures. And in the midst of this she began to cry. All three of them wept their hearts out, flesh and toy-fibre, and the tear marks were there to this day, all over the exquisite art of Edmund Dulac.

Steven never believed any of what she told him about Leonardo. At least, not at first.

'It sounds like a Victorian melodrama.'

'Yes, it does.'

'The poor lorn infant sent to the cold wicked guardian. And the house – you make it sound like a stately home.'

'No, it wasn't. Only 26 rooms.'

'Oh, well. A rabbit hutch.'

'He didn't use all of them.'

'And he had a flat in London, too?'

'Yes.'

'It must have been cramped.'

In those days, she had always tried to treat Steven as if he were being gently frivolous, not confrontational or sarcastic. 'We were. That is, I got in his way.'

'That's you, Jula,' Steven said.

And she'd smiled. It was a funny joke, the put-down of friendly intimacy.

Aside from being 'in the country,' Leonardo worked three to five days a week at the Cork Building, in London, just off the Strand. But she had never been taken into the grey and glass block, ten storeys high. (The hub of the Old Man's paper empire.) She didn't know what Leonardo did there. Years later she dreamed of him, a dream transcribed afterwards into her writing, seated on a throne of glass – like God? – while *Metropolis*-like workers scurried to and fro, a great distance beneath.

Just after her thirteenth birthday, Jula was sent to the private school in Wimbledon. She used to stay in Leonardo's flat in SW5, except for the occasional long weekends and holidays, when she would go up to Derbyshire, alone, by train.

The London flat was capacious – Leonardo's term. And it was. An arena of a sitting-room that looked out to the private garden in the square, drawing and breakfast rooms, a small library, and Leonardo's study, which, in his absence, was always kept locked like his bedroom. There were in all five bedrooms, two with *en-suite* bathrooms, and a strange guest lavatory with a tiny window and no heating, done in dark brown. Jula had an irrational fear, as an adolescent, of being shut in there for misdemeanours.

In the London flat there was no housekeeper, only a 'man' with a 'foreign' name, Katz, who came and went, and must in all the years she knew him, have spoken only a dozen or so sentences to her, and these all the same: greetings and farewells, dinner arrangements, and messages from her uncle to be found on this notepad or that.

Jula was left even more alone in the flat. But she had her homework, and the TV, large and Technicolor as the two TVs at the house, the record and cassette player Leonardo had bought for her, and the books she was allowed to choose from the library, between lockings, once her hands had been washed.

She was also, when Leonardo was present, allowed to bring friends home for Tea.

The Tea was opulent, unpleasantly so. In winter, mounds of hot crumpets with butter, and jam sponges baked by Katz. In summer, pâté sandwiches, fruit ices, sliced fresh pineapple.

They embarrassed her, the Teas. And the girls who accompanied her into her uncle's flat, unprepared by Jula's agonised, tactful warning, tended to laugh nervously at him later. While later, Leonardo in turn, mocked *them*.

Caught in the middle, Jula. Trying to excuse both? Perhaps. There had been nothing to embarrass her in her early life, and loyalty had existed too. But against Leonardo there could be no defence.

'Good God, Jula, the ghastly thin gawky thing – why, she was almost as tall as I am!' 'Jula, that girl's *spots*. Surely only male teenagers have spots? And she ate three chocolate meringues. Greedy *and* unwholesome.' 'I think you must be, evidently on your mother's side, a descendent of Jesus Christ, befriending such peculiar young women.'

So the Teas soon stopped.

She disliked the school, anyway. Not the lessons, exactly, but their outriders. 'It's an expensive school, Jula. I understand you're expected to spend at least three hours, each night, and more at the weekends, on your homework. See that you do.' And timing her. Or, if she were alone, afterwards wanting to see the evidence, the pages of writing in her uneven lawless hand, leaning now forward and now back.

'Your handwriting worries me, Jula. Don't they ever reprimand you?'

'Yes, Leon.'

'Then do something about it.'

Years after, it occurred to her that part of the erraticism of her writing might have been caused, even in the most mundane essay, because her mind ran back and forth with every character and thought. As they swung and swayed, so did the letters.

But by then, most of this torment was over.

She never met her grandfather, the father of Leonardo and David, the Old Man. He died the year after Leonardo had adopted her. She wasn't taken to the funeral.

If Leonardo mourned she never knew. She thought not.

After she had left him, once in the flesh, and a second time in her soul, Jula realised that he had seen women now and then. In Manchester, she thought, and in London, too. Probably neatly one in each city. But he had never mentioned them, and they never entered the house or flat when Jula was there. Once she had seen a pencilled note to Katz, *Send ten long-stemmed RR to Number One.*

Red roses? And was *One* an address – or did he actually file his courtesans by number only? And again, was it rank – One, Two ...? Or merely their order of establishment?

And so she partly concluded that Leonardo had no deep feelings at all except, naturally, of fastidious disgust, contempt and despair for humankind.

He read, aside from a few classics – Hardy, Dickens, Shakespeare – mostly non-fiction, which was more suitable for the male taste. He was especially interested in post-Elizabethan England, the Regency, the Greeks. But was this only because these things confirmed his absolute conviction that the world was better then, and that by now human beings were worthless?

As an adult she came to see that no, this wasn't quite the case. Humanity fascinated him – at a very safe distance.

'From this dung-heap,' he said, quoting someone who had written it, 'spring the flowers of great drama and profound thought.'

He saw himself as a philosopher. Although he himself never wrote a line, never painted a picture or played an instrument, Leonardo, for Leonardo, came of a chosen race of men, an intellectual instigator. In his way, an artistic fascist.

His opinions of himself and the world extended also to women, and perhaps in a more awful manner.

He demanded everything from them – while expecting little or *nothing*. They must strive and always fail.

Vivien, for example, he had dismissed to Jula's ten year old face as 'A pretty little tramp. Oh, she hooked him easily enough. But what was she? She couldn't even spell the word pompous. Pom – P U S, that was how she had it.'

Of course, he had seen her mother's rather badly-typed manuscripts. Stories he could never have dreamed of, let alone written.

If Jula had been a boy – what in God's name would have happened to her – to *him?*

She had been saved something, because Leonardo knew she was an inferior.

Thank God at least she hadn't been fat or thin, had what, in her twenties, he came to call, almost stunning her, a 'lovely face'. And she had shown finally what he could accept as 'talent'.

'Understand this, Jula. There are no *great* women artists, in any walk of life. It's no-one's fault. Biology is against them.' (The very thing he derided and denied when they themselves 'made play' with it.) 'But there's no reason a woman shouldn't use her intelligence, if she has any. And you have a gift, Jula, very definitely. You say you wrote this novel during this year? What about your school work?'

'I did that too.'

'Yes, I think you have done. Very creditable. Now, let me go through your book with you. Some of the ideas are absurd. But I'd expect that. You're not yet 17. And you use far too many colours, Jula. Look at this. Ten different shades over only two pages.'

Why had she shown him the novel – her first, very slender, work, but the most until then she had ever written? Why? Because her life revolved around him. And she had no-one, no-one else.

Some would have held the outpouring to themselves, concealed it. But she was always too open. (He had told her so.) Always. Trust and frankness had been bred in her for nine years, even to some extent spontaneous display. Leonardo had gone a long way in damming (damning) her vocal ability to communicate. ('Be quiet child.' 'Stop chattering like a monkey.') But the pen – inadvertently perhaps, three hours a night – had encouraged her to speak.

He pulled the novel apart. He jeered at it and at her. At the same time saying she had talent, at the same time reminding her that, being female, her talent would always have grave limitations.

Somehow it didn't stop her. It only stopped her showing him another word, until at twenty, she found, to her own great surprise, that she had written *Under a Cloud*. Which, on re-reading it, seemed to her not to have been written by herself at all.

There had been more 'experience' by then.

A year at college, which she had resisted and left, a course Leonardo had sent her on unleavably, where she was taught to cook – for women should be instructed in these things, where it wasn't natural to them. The two or three boyfriends she had had, and Leonardo had somehow, and accidentally every time, met.

'He isn't good enough for you. Be careful. You're ignorant about these things.' And, 'This boy with the appalling accent.' The one from Glasgow – she had loved the way he spoke. And, 'You must value yourself more, Jula,' when he had caught her crying and she admitted, a perfect fool, that there had been a separation. 'Put yourself on a pedestal, or no-one will. I'm ashamed of you.'

But the novel – the novel he *liked*.

Most oddly (or not?) it reminded her of when she had been 13, and Mrs Finch and she were in Manchester, shopping in their tepid, uncompanionable way. And then Mrs Finch had seen the sanitary protection in Jula's bag, and flushed and said, 'Oh. And your uncle said I was to speak to you about it this year.'

'It's all right. My mother told me.'

'But you – were only nine –'

Jula said, in her normal unevasive way, 'I found some of her things once, and asked her what they were. She told me then.'

'I see.' And Mrs Finch was shocked.

Mrs Finch and Leonardo too, no doubt. This pair, who would have left Jula to terror and panic if Vivien – feckless lily of the field – hadn't told her, so charmingly and straightforwardly, what was to come, and why.

Leonardo and Mrs Finch would have had a worse shock if they had known that, at 18, Jula went to an NHS clinic in London, where she was sensibly advised on the Pill, and six weeks later, embarked on her first sexual liaison.

She had learned *some* deception.

Not enough.

'This is a remarkable piece of writing for a young woman of your age, Jula. I think I should show it to Piers. I was a little put off by the sexual antics, however. Were you trying to be commercial?'

'No, Leon.'

'Can I take it you write from experience?'

She had turned away. Not answered.

But she thought instantly of that weird moment, eight or nine years ago, when Leonardo had walked into her bedroom at the grey house.

She had been on the verge of stripping off her nightdress to put on her minuscule bra and pants, and stopped, just as he had stopped, there, in the doorway.

'Jula, hurry up. You're very late for breakfast and Mrs Finch wants to clear.'

And stood there, waiting. Both of them. She for him to go. And he – was he? – to see if she would remove her nightdress and put on her clothes in front of him like a little girl. But a little girl of 11, 12, already changing into a woman.

And she had had a nameless revulsion, never then analysed, and excusing herself, hurried back into the bathroom. When she re-emerged, he was gone. After that she dressed in the bathroom, until eventually she requested a lock for her door.

'Why ever do you want that?'

'To feel private, Leon. Like your study.'

'Oh, all right then. Have one.'

He never abused her with violence, or sexually. He seldom *touched* her at all. What had it been? A moment's recalcitrant male curiosity? Or simply his total selfish unawareness? Not, *not* the prelude to some other horror –

Never abused by him violently or sexually, she had nevertheless been abused by him. His voice, his words. His *philosophies.*

On her side was it precocious reticence that had made her scurry for cover, or only the alarm that he might now criticise her naked *body*? Why else had she been so afraid in the arms of her first lover, afraid not of physical love, but of failure, inadequacy –

Piers Barker read *Under a Cloud.* He wrote to her a very nice letter, saying she seemed to have inherited her mother's and father's talent and a distinct ability all her own. The few changes he requested were put to her so sensitively and sensibly, she felt in fact reassured by his diligence on her behalf.

The book was published ten months later, was well received by most critics who noticed it, and sold briskly. Leonardo: 'Don't try to write about men, Jula. I've never seen a single woman pull it off.'

'Do you mean a married woman might be able to?'

She had found a way to talk to him by then. After all those years. After five or six men of her own who, while not being

David, were decidedly not Leonardo.

'You know what I mean, Jula. Write about women. Your female characters have three-dimensionality.'

'How *should* I write the men?'

'I can't tell you. You couldn't grasp it.'

She came to see, testing him in these conversations, that since he was to be her yardstick, she must make men of whom he approved. Or, she must never try to explain them, to get inside their minds. Respect – was that the key?

For her written men *were* like him. Cold and remote. Shut up in dark towers that no woman could approach, or if she did, only find herself upbraided and the chamber-pot upset on her head. Where she *failed* was in giving these men the psychological trappings to explain their towers of stone.

She was trying to explain Leonardo.

And the women, the women too were Leonardo's women, chilly and self-sufficient, able to cook *cordon bleu* meals, and maintain a spotless house and skin. Coming undone only because they reverenced the male species and fell in love with the gods in the towers.

He liked her women.

They were the models of the proper female type. And they could never win.

She saw *this* only after. When finally, out of his domain, and out of his sight, she read her books again.

She saw that she had been playing Leonardo's game. And he had changed her.

Worse than all the mental sadism and denial, the crying child with her toys and her clean hands, was that day in London she heard a woman talking in a thick Irish brogue. And Jula thought, *I can't understand her. God what an awful accent –*

And it was *him.*

It was Leon. Speaking there in her brain. She had *become* Leonardo. In his own image.

Vivien had been half Irish.

And that woman was the voice of the Celtic poets, the harpers of the rain-green land.

But it was too late.

From now on, from that day on, it could only be a battle, between her true self and the possession of Leonardo, which had chained and claimed her mind.

After *Under a Cloud* there was *The Best Girl*, and then *Admonitions*.

And then she went to see the house at Seatree.

She'd thought it was irrelevant almost, to go. And Leonardo had said, offhand, 'Of course, you don't need to live in it.'

She had her own freedom, didn't she, under his two roofs. Three rooms all her own in Derbyshire, and an extra room for a workroom at the flat.

She was frightened, too.

Because of this house –

When she got up the hill, and witnessed it there, slightly dilapidated in a twilight winter afternoon, the white fence, the gazing windows, the dark fields, all apprehension died. Vivien and David hadn't even seen it, had they? They'd never got this far.

'Oh, Jula. How absurd you're being. Live there? It's miles from London. Who'll look after you? You're quite useless. You don't see this since everyone does everything for you. I don't fancy your chances out there, in fact. It will be a pig-sty, the way you used to have things in your bedrooms. And the allowance – there isn't that much money, either. You do realise that? The upkeep of a house – and I can't run around after you.'

'No, Leonardo.'

'So, that's settled.'

'I'd like to try.'

'Go then. Get on with it. You'll be back here whining in a couple of months.'

After she left him, they seemed to get on better – by post. He would be, by letter, and next briefly by phone, *affectionate*.

About this time he bought the property in Scotland. Perhaps to show her what she had forfeited, he pressed her to visit. The house was at Blaymore, just outside Edinburgh. Jula was very taken with the pale charcoal and parchment city, its huge central platform, the *European* quality of its streets and buildings. Leonardo inveighed against drunks in gutters.

The new house too was grey. It was a frigid spring and a frigid visit, Leonardo's smiles soon melting in the blazing glacier of disapproval.

'You look very untidy, Jula.' And, 'Your last book, well, it isn't your best. Dare I say, it could be your worst?'

However, once this ordeal was behind them, they continued to meet in London, every month or so. He would travel down from Scotland the day before and call in on the paper empire off the Strand.

At first she had failed to accept how she dreaded all these meetings. After the Scottish visit, she gave in to reality.

Leonardo insisted always on taking her out to dinner or lunch, as if to show her what she was missing. (Although he complained constantly about the quality of service, food and wine.) Sometimes they went to the theatre. She had learned by now that, even with actors and writers he condoned, he could never let go by anything until, along with any praise, he had added some barb.

He, who had once described a production of *Antony and Cleopatra* as *over-impassioned* – as if obsessive, world-tottering love is best served, like revenge, *cold*.

'Tennyson, I have reservations about Tennyson,' said Leonardo. 'Not always, of course … *The Perfect Tragedy* … Well. I'll trust you, Jula.' (Her taste, now formed by his.) 'I look forward to seeing you. That most of all.'

There she had been at 31, still trying to 'sell' him favourite writers of her own. Never a woman, admittedly. Never anyone too modern.

And still kidding herself that he might like Churchman. And that, as he now, only now, but always, told her, he liked her. *Loved* her.

Later, she would have to accede that he had convinced himself. That her suggestion of his un-love had wounded and perhaps frightened him. She had thought he had no deep feeling, but all living thinking creatures do, in whatever twisted and confused form. He had no understanding of himself. His self-esteem was the most vulnerable part, amply displayed by his disavowals of flattery, which flattery he relished. Any whiff he might catch that he was in some way incomplete, let alone monstrous – of course. Who could bear that?

She never found out what he would have said of the play. That was the night he didn't meet her at the National Theatre, the onset of his illness. When she thought he had … gone missing, as had two others in the past … And also the night she met Steven Grace, and believed she had found once more, in lover's form, her magical father, and been so wrong, so wrong, so wrong.

She wrote the book when she was 25, long before that night. She had been living in her house a few months – and hadn't gone whining back to Leonardo.

In all other respects, it was as he had foretold.

At first she was tired from the move, and the slight renovation she'd needed done.

She lay in bed, playing music on the machine or listening to the radio. She slept a great deal. Then passing down to make cheese on toast, pick up an apple, drink tea. She left dishes and cups in the sink. She didn't make the bed or even change the bed for six weeks.

She didn't wash her hair, and bathed for sheer animal pleasure, not cleanliness.

Before the move, she'd begun on her fourth novel, *Columbine.*

But *Columbine* was broken like a string of beads; she had to gather them up and re-thread them. She didn't.

Instead she began to think of Leonardo. She began to cry, her tears hot as blood.

And then, in the third month, she got up, went like a zombie to her new workroom, and sitting there, crying and swearing and sometimes laughing very loudly, she wrote *The Prince.*

The title she chose at once, Machiavelli's title for his study of a Renaissance tyrant, Cesare Borgia. A man of power and evil, an abuser.

Jula's book was a study of Leonardo. She spared him nothing, and herself not much. The story though was lean. The niece of the Prince suffered his oppression until the last twenty pages, during which she murdered him.

As a rule, writing long-hand, and then typing, a novel took Jula a year to 18 months – only *Admonitions* had been shorter, eight months in all.

Jula wrote *The Prince*, a work of approximately 70,000 words, in three weeks.

When it was finished, and roughly typed, she cleaned the house throughout, reverted to a more orderly regime, and took two young cats into her life.

She assumed she had exorcised her demon, and could now be magnanimous. There was no need for publication.

Indeed, publication was out of the question.

Despite what he had done to her – and what she had seen with new, painful clarity as she wrote – she didn't want to punish Leonardo. She felt she had transcended him. And in a way, despite her later lapses in his company, still fawning, arguing, she had. Revenge, served hot. Cooling now, as she thought, in a deep drawer.

She finished *Columbine*, typed it, and sent it to Piers.

'This is a very good book, Jula. I enjoyed it a lot. And it ought to do quite well.' This was how her books did, quite well, no less, no more. 'Just one thing. There's another piece in with it. Rough typed, about 15 pages. It's – Jula, it's extraordinary. What is it? A short story? I'd love to read the rest.'

She felt icy. (Revenge, cooling.) 'That wasn't meant to be in there, Piers. I don't know how it was. It's a private thing.'

'But it's wonderful stuff, Jula.'

The subconscious, the motivator Leonardo always denied had any hold over a thinking person. By which he meant a thinking *man*.

But a woman, a drunk bacchante, an idiot – and yes, it could be PMT that made her so careless. Or gave her the excuse to be.

Piers nagged her. She'd never known him to nag before. He wasn't Leonardo's friend, merely an acquaintance. He had never spoken particularly highly and never badly of Leonardo. Although Leonardo had sometimes been scathing about Piers. 'Fiction for silly women and pseudo-intellectuals, like himself.' This, naturally, after Piers had accepted Jula's first novel.

'Piers, I'm sorry, but it *is* private –'

'But you've written it. Don't you know, Jula, of course you do, that some of the best literature ever penned comes out of cauldrons like this one? Oh I can see it is, my dear. It *bubbles*.'

Women had no stamina. No principles. They could always be talked round. Yes, Leon.

She gave Piers the manuscript, begging him for utter secrecy. In the past she'd always trusted him. Or was she trying, then, to break in the glass?

He phoned her. 'I'm speechless. No I'm not. I can see why you don't want – *someone* to know. And I promise you, he never will from or because of me. But Jula, this is a masterpiece. It's the best thing you've done. You have to let me publish it.'

'No, Piers.'

Three months later she signed the contract, and in due course, the book appeared. For a pseudonym (pseuds and pseudonyms, Leon) she chose a name Leonardo would mock and avoid – Cora. Cora Julian. He had never learned, despite his interest in ancient Greece, the origin of the name Cora, which he associated 'with charladies' – the Greek Kore, the maiden, whose other title was Persephone, Queen of the Dead.

The novel was an enormous success. And for a time she was afraid. But Leonardo, pursuing his tomes of history and his men-only classics, must have walked past the book that was their doom a hundred times. He never saw it.

It was Steven who did that.

All those years after, when he found it on her bookshelves, not even hidden from him, since he never read her books.

Later he told her, 'I was looking for some cash, some miser's stash, since you keep me so short of it. I could just picture you concealing money in your study. And then the name struck me. Rather obvious. Cork-Cora, Jula-Julian. And no author photo. And then I read the blurb. It's *Uncle*, isn't it? I can tell. From all those lurid tales you told me, on and on, boring me senseless, when we first met. I've read it, your book. Not my sort of thing. But it's not bad. I suppose *he* wouldn't like it.'

Jula, standing before him. Naked: no lock on the door of the mind.

'What *would* he say if someone gave it to him?'

'He's ill, Steven. He has multiple sclerosis.'

'MS. Just like the abbreviation for manuscript. How apt. He liked me, didn't he?'

'Yes.'

'Think he'd trust me if I told him this was *his* book?'

'Please Steven. I'm not proud of it. I couldn't help it. It was like being sick.'

'And then print the sick? I'd have thought you would be proud; I mean, stabbing him in the back and he doesn't even know. I think you ought to own up. I think I should help you *confess*.'

Leonardo had met Steven in London. It was Steven who had pushed Jula for the meeting, discarding her trepidation. And he was right. Leonardo had been – impressed.

Where Leonardo demanded and despised homage from a woman, from a man, when cleverly applied, it not only flattered, it convinced him.

Steven, well-spoken, elegantly and quietly dressed, triumphed. True, a few barbs were stuck into him. He laughed at them with seeming appreciation. He asked Leonardo's opinion. Attended. Appeared enlightened. Though always dismissing Jula's record of the man, Steven had learned from it thoroughly. He didn't put a foot wrong. And Steven's lies, which at the time had also convinced Jula, were seamless.

'I'm most surprised. He's quite all right, this young man of yours. He *listens*. Not very sensible' (the disclaimer) 'the way he puts me on a pedestal. There you are. He said he lost his father early on.'

His *son*? Leonardo's – *David's* – son?

And the pedestal on which one must be put. On which, even old and ill, one must be put.

'I twisted him round my little finger.' Steven, almost feminine. Leonardo's version of feminine, in victory.

But now, 'Don't, Steven. It would hurt him so much.'

'You should have thought of that, shouldn't you? Anyway, you hate him.'

'No. I – did. Or I didn't. Not now.'

'Now he's ill. Stiff as a board and going blind. But I could read it aloud to him, couldn't I? He thinks I have an educated voice.'

'Steven, please leave this alone.'

And he patted her arm, kissed her cheek.

'Could you let me have a hundred? I really need to get up to town.'

She let him have the hundred.

And the rest of her life, that too she let him have.

Strangely, sometimes it occurred to her, the writer's mind always digging, dissecting, that perhaps Steven had even kidded himself, as time went by and the matter seldom alluded to, that the deal was not what, obviously, it was.

That, in fact, he had been joking with her, and she knew quite well that he was joking. That he would never do such a thing – amusing though it might be. And well-deserved by both niece and uncle.

That, if she ever believed it at all, his threat, it was only in order to have an excuse to hang on to him. To grapple him to her.

He always had the air that it was she who held fast, he who wished to break free. And if he ever betrayed her, he would have had a sane reason for that, too.

He had squared it cleverly with himself. As he always did, with everything. People who do that may be – invincible.

Until tonight. Until the moment in the mortuary chapel, seeing Steven there, lying open and white like a book. Steven dead and speechless. A blank page. And the chains let her go. Did Lucifer faint and weep with joy as he fell?

8

The white cab drove up into Divers Lane at a modest, law-abiding 30 mph. It parked just down from the house. If the driver noted the police car on the opposite verge, he gave no sign. But then, there were a couple more such cars further down, still stationed outside the Hamiltons' residence.

'He's early.'

'They always are, aren't they, if you're not ready,' said Sharon Kenton. 'Or late if you're in a hurry.'

Tony Kenton spoke to the phone. 'He's here, sir. The cabby. Ten minutes ahead of time. Arrow Cars.'

The house stilled gemmed the darkness with its full panoply of lights. And now the cab driver decided to add to the volume. He blasted his horn.

Sharon tutted. 'I've a good mind –'

'He might wake up some foxes, you mean.'

'All right. Maybe it doesn't matter here.'

Neither of them had seen the Alliats, but, going by the house, might have assumed George at least wouldn't jump to a driver's horn.

However, he was off on his hols, wasn't he? And here he came, the wooden door opening and the lights flooding out, and George standing in silhouette, big, powerful, brawny old George, with two cases and a holdall hanging effortlessly from his meaty hands.

'He's all ready.'

'He can't wait. Where's he supposed to be off to?'

'Brazil or something.'

'Perhaps we could stow away.'

There was no view of the woman, Mrs Alliat. But then as the

man descended through the front garden, past the lamppost and the arch of jasmine, the front door mysteriously closed.

He didn't glance back.

The lazy driver had got out now. He was practically bowing and scraping, opening the boot for the cases, undoing the rear passenger door.

'Cor. He's dishy.'

'Looks like a yuppie to me,' said Tony. 'One of those sunbed faces.'

'He's only a kid. And he can't be a yuppie, can he, driving a taxi at 4.00 am.'

Alliat was stood by the car, not yet getting in. And now he stared at the house.

'Heck,' said Sharon.

'What?'

'*His* face.'

They were silent.

She said, 'What's that all about?'

'It looks like anger. Unless he's in pain.'

The almost-old face, with its bright pallid eyes. The iron moustache, and marble teeth shining too white. A grin of something that had nothing to do with humour.

Then the driver was there again.

'Off to sunny Gatwick, mate?'

The accent – weird. Sharon flicked a look at Tony, but he was watching.

'Gatwick, yes. I take it you know the way? The last time the fellow didn't.'

'Found me map, mate. Got it all worked out. Head for East Grinstead, take no notice of East Grinstead. On to the M23 all pearly.'

'I beg your pardon?'

'Trust me, squire. You won't go far wrong.'

Alliat, turning powerfully and ponderously, like a bull, swinging into the back seat. And the driver in his beautiful, creased suit, swimming back around the wheel.

One door slammed. The other slammed.

'Something wacko there.'

'And no seat-belts done up.'

The cab thrummed and came cruising up and past them, heading away smooth as silk for the Seatree Road.

Tony started the car.

Sharon spoke to the phone.

'Alliat's off. We're right behind them. But can someone check with Arrow Cars? Find out who the driver is. He looked odd … too classy. And doing an *EastEnders* accent, only not very well.'

DC Poecock presented himself to Detective Chief Inspector Knox at precisely 4.20.

'Get through?'

'Yes, sir. And got a mouthful an' all.'

'Well, he's reckoned a brilliant cook. Something nice, was it?'

DC Poecock frowned, and recited.

'He said, sir, before I could say a word, "Stop ringing me, you bleeding little rat. I bin asleep one hour all night. I get up now cos I always get up now. You leave me, fine. Now you stay out. Never I see you again. Your clothes I buy you in box on pavement. Ring again, I get police.'

Knox stood awestruck at Poecock's possibly embellished performance.

Rawthorn said, 'I take it you didn't resist the cue.'

'I said, I *am* the police, sir. We're trying to contact a Mr Dominic for whom we don't have a second name. I understand – at which he was off again. 'He don't live here. He lived here once. Never no more. And you, you leave me alone. I done nothing.'

'You reassured him.'

'I said we were simply making routine inquiries. Then I got another mouthful in Italian. And the receiver went down and nearly bust my eardrum.'

'He could be lying,' mused Knox, 'this Bash – Vincelli – whoever. But, according to Hastings, Dominic said he'd left

Vincelli, which could account for Vincelli's annoyance, and the emotional outburst. *Plus*, Hastings was right about the time. Vincelli always wakes up, it transpires, at 4.15, because he used to have to, to get the 5.30 breakfasts in some café years ago.'

Knox paced, peering into imagination. 'Poor bloody devil. Years of graft and then he gets his sea-legs, and then he meets Dominic. No, I reckon our Dom's just done a flit, like Hastings thinks he might have. Which saddens me, as I could have done with seeing him. Even if he was going to lie. After all, Hastings could be lying about everything, and I'm glad I can see *him*.'

Poecock said, grimly, 'Shall I call the gentleman back, sir?'

'No, Edgar Allen. Can't have you getting another nasty shock. You won't make old bones at this rate.'

Rawthorn stepped back as Knox reared from a relaxed to an erectile posture, and slammed his hands together with a noisy crack.

'Got it. Got it by the yak's turnips.'

Poecock and Rawthorn stood there.

'What's been driving me mad all night – the salient thing I couldn't remember about the Alliats.'

'Yes, sir?'

'*Bones*, Rawthorn. *Bones*.'

'Look, they've given me biccies. There're good to the old man.' Knox drank some tea, and dipped in a walnut-knotted slab as large as a playing card.

Rawthorn, as usual, attended. He had learnt a lot from Knox as time went by, and part of the harvest of this information was never to try to speed a denouement.

Not until the whole of the walnut card and half the cup of tea were gone did he begin to be told.

'Nine, ten years ago. The renowned hurricane of '87. We had it bad up here, though it was worse on the coast.

'In the morning, when most of Seatree was out gathering up the broken walls and window panes, and having fallen trees extracted from the roofs, the council sent a couple of work-gangs and a tree specialist up Divers Lane. Protected woodland up there. Some oaks and cedars going back four hundred years, all with preservation orders. But storms don't bother with those.

'The Alliats' mansion must have been one of the older houses in the lane. Most of the others down this end were built in the '70s and '80s. But the Alliats' place went up between the wars.'

He glanced at Rawthorn. 'It's all coming back to me. George Alliat owned the house and some land at the back, where there was one colossal tree, an oak, I believe. Not in fact one of the sacred band, less than a century old. Anyway, it was down. And they went to take a look at it.'

The roots of the tree, Knox said, had mostly come right out of the earth, as had happened a lot. Then the trunk split. Half the oak was left almost upside down. One of the main causes for the destruction, coupled to the storm itself, was the wetness of the ground everywhere.

And up with the roots had been torn something else.

'A royal grave, my son. No. Tell no lies. Not royal – some of the bodyguard of King Harold II. The last English King. It was quite a find. Bones and shields and gold bits, and so on.'

The nearest house, in fact the house directly overlooking the uprooted oak and opened grave, was the Alliats'.

'When they knocked them up, George Alliat came out and talked to the council chaps. The wife wasn't about, your Miranda, she'd fallen down the stairs or something in the night, and nearly broken her ankle.'

'Or he'd pushed her down the stairs.'

'Or he had. Whatever, Alliat didn't seem very interested or particularly cooperative. I remember all this, you see, from the local rag – this wasn't my patch then, but I kept in touch. The paper got stroppy and called him *bullish*. Or was it *mulish*? They described a bit of stump left in the ground as looking like a split tooth. Journalists knew how not to write in the '80s. Anyway, it didn't matter. The historical societies and the British Museum got on to it, and in the end they had the lot out and took it off for analysis.'

Knox raised another biscuit, looked at it sadly. 'No, darling. Knoxy mustn't, must he?' And put it back on the plate.

'The thing was, these bones, when they carbon whatsited them – they found three skeletons that probably pre-dated the 13ᵗʰ Century and could have been older. And one skeleton that didn't. It was only twenty or so years of age.'

'Really?'

'Oh, show some fascination, Rawthorn.'

'*Really*, sir?'

'Forget it.'

'Whose skeleton was it?'

'They didn't find out, Ed. That's the conundrum. A very young man, I recall that, and he'd been in a fire. And he hadn't a single tooth. I recall some dentist or other having a field day there, on about the state of the teeth of the modern English young. Harold's knights, you see, had almost every tooth still in their skulls.'

'And was Alliat suspected of anything?'

'He must have been. But he had a blameless record, as I remember. So for that matter did she. Additionally, they'd lived in London, and only moved to Seatree and into the house around 19 years before the hurricane. The bones, I mean the recent ones, were in the ground for nearer 21. Then, no-one came forward claiming anyone had gone missing at the right time, either here, or down in Rother.'

Knox picked up the biscuit, snapped it in two. 'Just half then. Anything strike you?'

Apart from crumbs? 'This. The Alliats didn't move.'

'I'm thinking that.'

'A lot of people wouldn't like that, would they, a fairly recent corpse, or the remains of one, pulled up adjacent to the garden?'

'Then again, if word got round, maybe they tried to sell up and no-one would buy. So they sat tight and got used to it.'

'You can see the place from their kitchen.'

'*Can* you?'

'She's domesticated, cleans and undoubtedly cooks. She'd be

constantly looking out on it.'

'Maybe she's not nervy.'

'I'd say she was incredibly nervy.'

'Then he isn't and doesn't trouble. You said he bullies her, knocks her about. What she thinks won't matter. Anything else?'

'He wasn't interested, rather obstructive, mulish, the paper said.'

'Or bullish or doggish. He just didn't want people rummaging about on his land?'

'Who had the house before the Alliats?'

'Now – there's a point. Wait. No-one had it. It'd stood empty for several years – ten or so at least. It was in a bad way. Tramps used to use it.'

'But the Alliats presumably had it repaired and done up. Unless tramps build book galleries and lay white carpet.'

'So you're saying?'

'Maybe they didn't live there for a couple of years, but they could have been *around* there for longer. Waiting for the house to be fixed. Still living in London, but coming down from time to time?'

'Must have been checked, Ed. Couldn't have led anywhere.'

'The biggest proof of innocence isn't simply that they'd moved in and lived precisely where they did for ten to 12 years?'

'Could have been seen that way. Do you want a biscuit?'

'No, thank you, sir.'

'Love, eh, taken your appetite. Ah.'

'I'm not that keen on biscuits, sir.'

'You see, Edward. There's no motive, is there? There's this young boy – under 21, I think it was – and he's snuffed it. Unidentifiable. No connection to either of the Alliats, or someone would have found it. And they arrive around two years after, and live happily in the house that backs onto the grave.'

'*Happily.* Should we redefine the word? Dr Terry told me Miranda's self-inflicted psychosomatic injuries were ongoing at their arrival here.'

Knox now superglued the last half of the biscuit to his closed lips. 'Hmm.'

'And how do we apply all this to Steven Grace?' asked Rawthorn.

Through the clamped biscuit, Knox said, 'Mnn.'

'If he killed before, Alliat may have the credentials for killing Grace,' said Rawthorn. 'But we don't know why he killed before, if he did. And the same now.'

Knox removed the biscuit. 'Better eat it, hadn't I? I've contaminated it now. Give me a poss scenario.'

'Grace's car goes off the road. Maybe Hastings and his lover shouldered it off. Or not. Whatever, they've either split or weren't ever there. Grace isn't seriously hurt, leaves the car and the mobile phone, which doesn't work, and walks down the lane. When he reaches the Alliats' house, he goes in the door.'

'As you would.'

'As you would. George Alliat, rather than being late home, is already there. He doesn't want to offer Grace a lift in his own no doubt costly vehicle. He does offer him use of a phone. There isn't one in the lounge. Perhaps it's another mobile, and he has to get it from somewhere else. While he's out of the room, Grace, who Jula Cork told you thieves things, pockets one of the snuffboxes. When Alliat comes back, he doesn't notice.'

'Grace didn't call anyone. Home, AA, Road Rescue – no cab company we've traced. Nobody. Not even little old us.'

'Perhaps he thought, once he'd got the snuffbox, he'd better get going.'

'So,' said Knox, 'he leaves. Alliat realises he's lost one of his objects of art, and pounds after him. Having first mixed a quick dose of poisonous booze.'

'And having caught Grace, and poured it down his throat, he pushes him into the Hamiltons' garden, then leaves, forgetting to pick up the snuffbox that had caused it all.'

They looked at each other.

'Duff,' said Knox.

'Yes. About as duff as it could get. This doesn't make sense.

And frankly, unless the snuffboxes were regularly closely checked by the Alliats, I don't think even they would notice at a casual glance that one was missing.'

'But,' said Knox, 'you fancy Alliat for this, don't you?'

'In a way, sir, because the other crime – I mean the bones – couldn't be connected to him, and now this can't – it seems too much of a coincidence. Two deaths. Two clean sheets. He's a big strong aging unbalanced man, with a filthy streak in him a mile wide.'

'So it would be nice if it was him. Satisfying, like a morality play.'

Rawthorn shrugged. 'I concede that.'

Knox said, 'At least Mr and Mrs Kenton-to-be are following Alliat to Gatwick. And the boys there have been alerted. What we need right now is a god from the machinery to lean out, and point us the way.'

There was a knock.

'Enter, *Deux ex Machina*!'

Poecock put his human head round the door.

'Sir, Mrs Knox called.'

'Not the god then,' remarked Knox, 'just the machine. What did she want?'

'It was a bad line. I couldn't hear what she said. But she sounded in a bit of a state. Upset.'

'I'll give her a call in a minute.' Knox, unabashed. Or pretending to be.

'And there's a Ms Dover here, asking for Inspector Rawthorn.'

Rawthorn got to his feet. So did Knox, eyes gleaming.

'So I get to meet the inimitable She.'

9

It was good – it was so good – to have a drink. A real drink. One of her treats always, when he went away. There was never time during a day, and never at weekends, because he checked the decanters, and the bottles in the kitchen cupboard, and any other likely place of concealment. Although she hadn't tried to trick him again after the evening when she thought he had broken her nose, he still did those checks every couple of days. The last had been this morning.

But when he went away, she could drink the house dry, if she wanted, and then buy some more. He never checked the *bills*, only paid them, and anyway, there was enough cash left for groceries – several hundred pounds – which again he never checked, only added to.

Had that been his one indulgence of her? That during those weeks when he escaped her, she too might be allowed again her little escape into alcoholism?

And then she could admit all the truth.

She lay back, deep in the large ivory bath, the water filling it up and up. The intoxicating scent of the essences she had poured into it, going to her head like the almost clear drink in the glass. Vodka and tonic, done tonight in an extra-special way. The lemon slice *and* the cherry. A woman's drink. A silly wretched inferior trustless woman's drink.

Tears came. The drink released them. It was such a relief, to cry.

She spoke aloud, to the ivory bathroom, voice rather slurred now, sleepy.

'I still love you, George. You stopped thinking I did. But I do. How wouldn't I? After what you did for me. Oh George. My darling. My lovely darling love –'

Then a wave of drifting honey rolled in like a comber from the outer sea, the sea of night and sleep. Rosebalm and lavender, cinnamon and myrrh.

How wonderful to cry. And to stop crying. To let go.

The bath, with its healing salts, stinging a little in the bruises and the wounds. But the sting fading.

A marvellous throbbing. The sense of the soul detaching itself. Levitation.

'I couldn't love thee, George, so much, loved I not vodka more –'

Miranda Alliat giggled softly.

She drained her glass.

A top-up?

No, she didn't need any more. (*You're drunk, Miranda.* Well, she'd been drinking since he left.) And it was three bottles to manage ... or four, or six ... which she'd find difficult to manage now. She laughed again and rested back her head.

No more fear. Don't think of what might lie ahead. This was *her* holiday.

What a beautiful amber-pink colour the bath was going as the water mixed all the essences she'd put into it.

So simple. Like so many things. All that struggle earlier. And really there wasn't any need.

Just ... let ... go ...

Leigh had put on eye make-up. Rawthorn noted this as she sat talking seriously to them in Knox's office. A mask? Or just a flirtatious Venetian domino –?

'She said to come tomorrow morning. Any time. And to bring someone. When I said, "Who should I bring?" she said, "Perhaps a man friend or someone from the hotel."'

'Which made you concerned?' said Knox.

'I didn't know what it made me. The whole thing seemed bizarre in the extreme.'

She had been sat in the bar. If she were honest, sat there in a trance.

When Edward Rawthorn had let her go, she had folded herself back onto the chair, and sat there. She felt something she hadn't felt for years, had never really ever felt. *Divided.* Divided unwillingly from another. From *him.*

'Should I apologise?' he had said.

'No.'

'Are you sure?'

'I wanted you to. To take hold of me and kiss me. That's funny, isn't it? What they say about a raped woman. She asked for it. But I did. I asked you to do exactly what you did.'

'And now?'

'And now – I need to think. I *think* I need to think.'

'Yes. I didn't mean to go as fast as that, Leigh. I *am* sorry. You don't need that kind of treatment.'

She smiled. 'Or do I? Depends who it's from.'

He too looked thoughtful. 'I'll get out. May I call you in the morning?'

'In the line of duty? I won't have a choice, will I?'

'As a friend.'

'No. Call me as the first man who's kissed me like that for almost two years.' She paused in wonder. 'My God, I'm blushing.'

'And *I* should be. Get some rest, Leigh.'

'It's inappropriate to wish you the same?'

'Probably. But I'm used to all-nights.'

When he was gone, the room seemed enormously empty. She sat at the centre of it, the focus of a new world.

What astounded her, much more than her excitement, was that the spectre had – abruptly, totally – shrunk to nothing. She had been repeatedly told she was not HIV positive, and that she had very little to fear. Not believed this. Now, suddenly, because this man believed it and trusted it, she found herself able to credit the facts. It seemed a decade since she'd been able to walk upright, not bowed down under the weight of terror and bitterness. If truly that was over – what, then?

She tried, in her head, to reason with herself. Sort out her psychology, her sincere wants. Couldn't. And she tingled. Which made her smile again.

He was a bloody policeman, for heaven's sake.

And still – confound the man – she *still* didn't know what colour his eyes were. She who dealt in colour, and form.

Tomorrow, when she met him tomorrow – and she would – that must be the first thing she took note of.

And then, a sort of dream state, sat there quietly, as if she were again 14, and had just received her first adult embrace. Which in reality had been very unrewarding, awkward and non-thrilling.

Ed Rawthorn – was the exact opposite. Almost frightening, that power and electricity. Perhaps he was always doing this. A practised seducer straight out of a paperback women's romance. Who bloody cared?

She heard the phone ring in the reception area, distantly, and a murmur from the receptionist. Forgot it, didn't listen.

And then the auburn-haired girl came walking in, treading as soft as a cat.

'Ms Dover?'

'…Yes?'

'I'm sorry. Had you dropped off? I didn't know. There's a woman on the phone for you.'

Softness fell from Leigh with a clank of alarm.

'I'll come.'

It must be an emergency – she hadn't given a name – it was almost twenty to 5.00.

'Hallo. This is Leigh Dover.'

'Miss Dover – oh, how strange. I thought you would be asleep.'

'Who is this, please?'

'Miranda Alliat. Do you remember? We met much earlier tonight, here at the house.'

Leigh, feeling cold now, straightening, *listening*.

'Mrs Alliat. Yes. I recall.'

'I'm sorry to intrude on you. I remembered you told us where you were staying. I meant simply to leave a message.'

'About what, Mrs Alliat?'

'I'm wondering if you could do me a great favour?' The voice, pretty, faded petals, and now also slightly slurred, as if from great tiredness, or conceivably, alcohol.

'What do you want me to do?'

'There's no-one I can ask, you see. My doctor's unreachable until 8.00 or 9.00 in the morning. That's – I don't really want to wait that long. And I don't have any friends here.' A statement, not even self-conscious, not asking for sympathy, *uninterested*. 'Would you just come to the house, tomorrow morning?'

Leigh opened her mouth to ask *Why?* Instead she answered, 'I don't know what time I can make it, Mrs Alliat.'

'Oh, any time will do. Once it gets light. Or lunchtime. Perhaps bring someone with you.'

'Who?' Leigh's tone was sharp.

Miranda Alliat had no reaction to it. She sounded encouraging, helpful, someone trying to persuade a child.

'A man friend would be best. Or a man from the hotel.'

'Mrs Alliat –'

The receiver clicked gently. And the line was dead.

As she went upstairs, Leigh knew that here was an excuse to see him again, and so swiftly, and that almost made her, instead of putting on eyeshadow, mascara and a light coat, take off her clothes and get back into bed. Wait for the morning, as the fluttery slurry lady had said.

'But I knew I couldn't sleep, and I didn't want to wait for morning, Inspector,' Leigh said to Rawthorn now. And to Knox, 'It rattled me, that call.'

'A very rattling call,' Knox agreed. 'Rawthorn, get Poecock and go over there now. I'd come with you, but I'd better ET BT and phone home. The wife,' he added to Leigh, 'tugging the leash. Probably nothing. But it's been one of those nights.'

Outside, Leigh said, 'Is it illegal for me to go with you?'

They were very business-like. ('Inspector.' 'Ms Dover.')

'No. Are you sure you want to?'

'I'm not sure I want to. That's why I want to.'

Outside, the silent streets. The Martian-invader glare of street lamps. The chill, vast deep of night. The darkest hour before dawn.

She sat in the back. She looked at him, his broadish shoulders and ordinary hair. She wanted to touch him, but not only now from sexual attraction. Now she was scared.

10

Darkness.

The house had no lights.

He almost drove past it.

'Will you wait in the car, Leigh?'

'I'd rather not.'

'I don't need to tell you, stay back, out of the way.'

Beyond the car, a black void, in which floated vague amorphous shapes. Although, above, the stars were hard and bright. The always-indifferent stars.

The open gates creaked. Poecock and Rawthorn walked up the drive between the hedges, which now were carvings from the void.

The garden sloping. Ghosts of flowers. The somehow awful ornamental lamp that had never been lit. Whispers of leaves. Of men.

'Hell – the door's already open, sir.'

The hall gaped, and in the throat of the void, the white carpet, like a sea of ice, glowed and flowed between the universe of the real and some other dire and dreadful place.

And – a smell of roses.

'What's that noise?'

As she came up, Leigh heard it too. She froze, seized by pure primitive terror, out of which Rawthorn's voice spoke reasonably.

'The water pipes. I've heard it before. So there's someone in. Find the light-switch, can you? I can't.'

'Neither can I, guv.'

'It's here,' Leigh said, a frightened but clever child, dutifully keeping behind them.

The void was flooded by a golden-rosy sunrise, a false dawn that lied, saying here was light and all was well.

The house rocked to the asthmatic screaming Rawthorn had explained as water pipes. The noise pierced through and through the head. And, working on and on inside it, a persistent *racketing*, like – like a horse galloping on tin cans –

And – a waterfall.

In fantasies and dreams only, does Niagara plash down the indoor terraces of a house? Niagara that is the colour of watered Burgundy –

'Christ, guv, the *stairs* –'

The carpet. The white carpet. No longer white. Pink carpet. Flushed deeper in small pools. Red carpet.

Rawthorn spun to her. '*Don't come up.*'

She shook her head.

She watched the two men spring forward through the slashing pouring red-dyed water, up the stairs, away from her.

Where she had left the front door open to welcome them, she had locked the bathroom. But the trail was easy enough to follow. It was where the water came from, pushing through the elegant bedroom, from under the white and gold-trimmed door. And this door was nothing either. It took four seconds to kick in.

Rawthorn's gorge came up and hit the base of his throat. But this had happened before, been dealt with before. He shoved his response aside, and went forward to turn off the taps.

He was stone-calm again as he looked into the bath.

The water smelled sweet of aromatic oils, faintly metallic and foul with blood. The blood was still quite red there, and at first he couldn't be sure that anyone was in the water.

Then he saw Miranda lying at the bottom of the bath and the water, the oils and the blood. The tub was a rich-man's, and easily big enough to hold a small woman's naked full-length body.

She had cut her left wrist only, but quite deeply. Deep

enough.

Five bottles were on the side of the bath. Two were bath products. One, vodka, nearly empty. One, tonic, half full. And a chemist's bottle with a label, which had fallen over.

He reached past them and pulled her out, like a mermaid from the sea. The third woman he'd held that night.

She was whiter than the carpet. And more dead than any corpse he had ever seen.

BOOK THREE

Constant Light

'Love is a growing, or full constant light,
'And his first minute, after noon, is night.'

John Dunne ('A Lecture Upon the Shadow')

4.00 am to Dawn

1

The Print-Out

*He has never known that I can use the computer. His computer. Well,
I never have used it, until recently.*

*But he tried to teach me, or he said that he was trying. Just as he
'tried' to teach me to drive a car.*

*In both cases I learned. After all, I had the knowledge beaten into
me. Just the way my father used to claim, so proudly, that he was
trained at his first school. He was always keen to pass the knack I on.
'A good hiding.' Of course, he only hit the boys. He wouldn't hit his
daughter. It was his disapproval he struck me with. When I was a
child this used to terrify. By the time I was 19, it looked different.
Petty. I left home. But I suppose modern psychologists would tell me
the damage was already done.*

*Don't people tell you such a lot of things? In books. On the radio.
And now on television, too. And somehow, all the things they tell you
come too late to be of any use.*

*However, I can use George's computer, and here I am typing this
up on it very efficiently. I used to be able to type almost a hundred
words a minute on the old manual machines in the office, where
George first saw me. I'm rather slower now. But that doesn't matter.
As long as I'm quite finished by five o'clock, or a quarter to, to be
absolutely certain. George never arrives home before that. Usually
much later, between quarter to 6.00 and 6.30 pm.*

*Once I stop typing on the keyboard, I – let me put down the
computer jargon correctly – go to 'File' , and then save the file onto a*

floppy disc, and then eject the disc. Then I drag the original file to the computer 'Recycle Bin' and delete.

Then I hide the disc in one of the places George never looks for bottles, because it's too small – my make-up box. Also I shut off the machine. It has plenty of time to cool down.

Then I get ready, and go downstairs. Before starting dinner, I prepare the house the way he expects it to be. The front door pushed to, but open to welcome him, and, if it's getting dark, the lights on low so he can turn them up to full.

I've done that for years. I've also kept the house, as they used to say, 'spotless' – whatever that means. In my case, dust free, polished and hoovered, every day. There are also things I do on a rota through the week, washing items and ironing them, cleaning the bathrooms – I clean George's bathroom every day too. Shopping is mostly delivered. If I walk down to Seatree, I take a cab back. The drivers don't like me, because I never talk to them. I also attend to the garden, which takes up a lot of time.

In fact, I have very little time. And yet, somehow, I make time now, for this.

The first drafts on the computer I destroyed.

I don't think I knew then what I was doing, what it was leading up to.

If I seem calm now, that's because of the drafts, the practice *in being calm.*

Why I need to write it all down I'm still not sure. But my mother was a great believer in lists. She always had a notebook full of them, lists and procedures, mostly formats for how to please my father.

And I've kept lists for twenty or so years with a similar purpose of pleasing George.

If I don't please George, I suffer.

But then, I suffer even if I do.

What shall I say? I hate and am afraid of George – that's far too simple.

I love and adore George, then. The way I always say I do, even in my head.

Also too simple.

But it's already time to stop, and I have a lot to write, I think. My speed isn't as impressive as it used to be, only about 75 words a minute, now.

They would never have hired me at this speed, and then George wouldn't ever have seen me.

I wonder what would have become of me, then?

George and I met when I was 23 and he was almost 28. That was in 1956 – or thereabouts. The funny thing is, I have to add to that, because I always get muddled on the year. It may have been 1955 or 1957. I could work it out, but why waste the time? I remember our ages. That's more to the point.

He was very old for 28. I thought he was over thirty. But by 'old' I mean mature. He was the handsomest man I'd ever set eyes on who wasn't on the cinema screen. Tall and broad-shouldered and long-legged, with large, beautifully-shaped hands, and wonderful teeth – which was quite rare in England then. He boasted to me later on that he had only ever had to have one filling in his whole life. I was most envious, having had several. He could crack nuts with his teeth – a trick that always frightened me. I was afraid he'd break part of the perfect dentition. He never did.

He used to laugh at all my fears. 'Darling girl, I'm tough enough for the both of us.' He used to say that to me, and he'd pick me up and hold me up high, like a doll. He was very strong, it was true, and I was very small and light. I weighed only seven stone then, I don't weigh any more now. Sometimes, less.

I was what they call **dependent.** *I didn't mind it. One didn't then. It was 'feminine', and I rather liked being looked after, protected, doors opened for me and flowers bought me, and holding a man's arm in the street, although very lightly, of course, not to 'hang on' to him.*

We made love before we got married. We went away for a weekend to Richmond, which was charming, then. Booked in, naturally, as Mr and Mrs Alliat. I wore my diamond, and my wedding ring, which he'd already bought for me. That's supposed to be extremely unlucky.

I didn't enjoy the sexual part of the weekend. Or rather, I didn't feel any passion. Only nervous – and then triumphant. I was glad George had possessed me. And I trusted him. It was only some months after we were married (in a registry office in London) that I began to relish the physical side of our marriage. I surprised myself. I thought women only behaved like that in rather absurd novels that were sold to men under counters. But apparently not.

Over the years, once or twice, George's friends compared me to Marilyn Monroe, the film star. I was always flattered. But George told me that he thought I was the lovelier. (Why do I put that down? To indicate, I think, that once he did love me and value me, and I him.)

We didn't try for children. I didn't want them and I don't think George did. He said he didn't. I had one scare when I thought I'd fallen pregnant. But it wasn't anything.

I was too much a child myself, even in my thirties, to hunger for children of my own. And George – aside from his accountancy, which brought in a great deal of money – had only one true obsession, Oh, not me. His painting.

It was a tragedy, in its way. He never put it like this, and I only understood long after. (Educated by people talking on the TV, I forget about which thwarted artist.) Young men like George went into solid jobs, then. The matter had been decided for him. I remember he once said to me that everything had been like that. Even the War, during which he grew up from childhood, had been someone else's decision; and when he was evacuated to some place in the North, that too. (Even I'd been luckier, sent to my aunt in Derbyshire.)

In those days, the young weren't allowed to decide for themselves very often. Now they seem to. Perhaps their contempt for previous generations has enabled them to break free.

I don't think we were contemptuous enough. I don't think we knew what we were doing, our generation, or most of it. We lost our youth, or let it be taken from us. I think that's why so many of us regret it. Or – why I do.

George should have been an artist. Although he was an artist – that is, I suppose, the difference between what one does and what one is.

And so, whenever he could, he painted. Very wonderfully. Very.

At first I was in awe of his talent. And then, after we became engaged, he painted a portrait of me.

I found the sittings uncomfortable – sometimes he'd get so impatient if I moved – but his impatience then was never threatening. The finished picture was incredibly lovely. I could see myself in it – and yet, not. I was almost – shy of it. But I would sneak up and look at it, **peeping.** *It used to hang in our bedroom then, in the house in London. Of course, that was before George destroyed the painting.*

(I didn't see him do it. I only heard the sounds. I knew what it was. I didn't go near him. Later, he came and told me flatly there was dirt on the carpet in the bedroom. That was the flecks of paint, bits of the canvas and the frame. On the wall, a gap. After I cleaned the mess up, he said the room was still dirty, and that was the first time he hit me. Only a light slap across the face. Inevitable, in a way, since he'd just torn the replica of my face to pieces with his bare hands.)

In a normal year, George would take two longish holidays. And for each of these we would go abroad. To Italy, to France, once to Ireland. At first I looked forward to these trips so much. I thought we'd spend time seeing the sights and famous places, lazing over long lunches with wine, making love in hot, high-ceilinged hotel bedrooms, and in fields of poppies.

We didn't. We would go out very early, find somewhere, and then George would paint.

He would paint and I would sit. Looking at the view, at first, maybe taking a little walk, but not too far on my own in a foreign place – I'm hopeless at languages; I needed George to translate. Finally sitting, reading. Falling asleep. He wouldn't even stop to eat the picnics, let alone to stroll into the wonderful little towns and villages. He'd drink a gulp of wine, have a bite out of some cheese, and then he was gone again, back into his work.

At night, usually we missed dinner, coming back too late. We'd have something in our room, and he'd fall asleep, exhausted.

Once there was a theatre – it was an open air theatre, a reproduction of the Greek theatre at Delphi – is it Delphi? And I wanted to go. And George said, yes, we must. But then we didn't go. And he said, 'Oh, you wouldn't have liked it, darling. You know you couldn't follow the French.'

I sound extremely selfish, don't I? George worked all the year at a job he didn't dislike exactly, but which wasn't the true work he should have been doing, and I grudged it to him, greedily wanting his attention, and to 'do things' like a spoilt child.

But oh, those golden villages, with cats lying on walls in sunlight, and tables out under fig trees, and the churches baked like bread, and George saying, 'No, look there on the hill, that's better for what I want.

A glass of wine? But we've brought some.'

Things were for painting, not – experiencing. Even me, perhaps.

I'm not saying he wasn't attentive. I mean, physically. But not so frequently by then, I have to admit, as I would have liked.

Even I realised that was unreasonable of me. He had to work hard, he was tired. No, it wasn't the lack of love-making. It was – that he forgot *me.*

Yes, he forgot me.

He'd made love to me, and married me. More importantly, for George, he'd captured me on canvas. Now he – went elsewhere.

I recall a woman friend in London – a sort of friend, I've never had a close woman friend. 'Oh you should be thankful, Miranda. At least he leaves you for paints and brushes, not some floozy.'

And I was *grateful.*

What rubbish. I resented it. I tried very hard not to. But I did, I did.

Even at home, after the first couple of years. He would come in and go up, almost straightaway, to the attic room he'd converted to a studio. In the evenings, most of the weekends.

'Darling, look, this dinner with those people – all this dressing up and – chat. Can I back out? You needn't. You go, darling.'

'I'll be the only woman there without a husband.'

'Then think of the fun you'll have, making all the other husbands fall for you, and all the other women insanely jealous.'

And then, the weekend breaks, as they now call them, in some country hotel in acres of ground. And I'd spend the day in the beauty parlour, and meet George for dinner, George with his eyes glazed over, full of the view he'd been painting, so full I could see it on the irises, between myself and him.

Some other woman said to me, 'You should have had children, Miranda. That would give you something to do.'

Is that what they have children for? To stop them being bored?

And I was bored. A stupid, useless woman.

At that time, everything was done for me. The cleaner and the woman who cooked. Shopping delivered then as now. The only shopping I did was for myself, make-up and clothes, and costume jewellery, and lunches alone, and the pictures, alone. All paid for by my hard-working husband. And now we made love only once or twice a month. And one day, as I was buying silky stuff, trying to 'interest' him, alone as ever, it came to me. I was almost forty years old.

That means nothing now. It shouldn't mean anything. And you see some women now, of forty, or fifty, who look quite wonderful. But my generation of women – to most of us, forty was a landmark. No, a shipwreck. Through that gate, the road ran steeply downhill, down and down into the lands of loss. And on that road one ceased to be a woman, and one grew old.

I walked out of the shop, an expensive shop, where they would just shrug their shoulders at the mannerless bitch who had turned and gone without a word, leaving lingerie strewn on the counter.

I went to a pub and sat in a corner and drank gin and tonics.

Even that then, in the early '70s, wasn't done much by decent lone women – especially women of my age.

I felt old, and thought they'd class me, the men seen through a veil of smoke, as some old slag. Probably I even wondered if someone would take me for a prostitute and try to pick me up. And the fact that no-one did made me even more certain that no-one could want me. I, pretty Miranda, once compared to Marilyn Monroe.

Which brings me to Seatree.

About that time, the same time that I rushed out of a shop into the arms of a double gin, I read something in a newspaper, something very odd that stuck in my mind – haunted me, as they say – and that involved a place called Seatree.

I'd never heard of it, but the name, as well as the story, struck me.

I think I even looked it up on a map, and couldn't find it. Then later, some years later, I did see it on a large-scale map of the area, the Sussex Weald.

After I started to drink a little heavily, if I can put it like that, I didn't always feel that I minded so much about George, about being neglected. Then again, sometimes I'd be angry. But I hid it all from him. I was in the wrong. Women were supportive of their husbands, or else naggers.

I passed forty, and thought, well, it wasn't so bad. I started to lie about my age. But in a peculiar way. I used to find myself saying, to shop assistants, cab drivers – 'Oh, I'm at that awful age, 38 – not long before the big 4-0!' Hoping they'd argue, I think now, that of course I didn't look 38! Sometimes they did argue, too. From pity, no doubt.

What did they care?

For myself I didn't really think I looked forty, and it's possible I didn't. A huge red brand-mark doesn't suddenly appear on a woman's forehead.

When I was 41, however, I still announced periodically that I was 38. (Once I even did it at a dinner party, one of the rare ones to which George accompanied me. He didn't bat an eyelid. I thought he was being tactful. Actually, I think he just forgot my age, although never birthdays. On every one he gave me some exquisite piece of real jewellery. Until he stopped giving me anything at all, except, as the ladies in the rough streets of my childhood used to say, the back of his hand.)

I stayed 38 a few years. I stayed 38 until I too ceased to care.

Miranda Rosalind Alliat was a cliché, wasn't she? A vapid and insecure woman. And a cliché does what clichés do.

That year (The Year), George was arranging a holiday for us to Venice. Venice! This is what he said: 'The apartment we'll rent has a most wonderful view, 18ᵗʰ Century palaces and the Ordolpho Canal. I can sit on the balcony all day, just painting. Even at night. Undisturbed. Something I've always wanted, Miranda, to do ten or so studies of the same image, at different times of the day and night.' And he named some painter who had done this. I can't remember who it was. Someone unmarried?

Did I cry, 'But George, I want to see Venice!'? No. And why not? Because he would have said, 'Of course you must, my darling. We'll sort it all out so that you can.' Which would mean I would see it alone.

I recollect that morning. It was about 8.30. I was sat in my dressing-gown over cold coffee. The sunlight was pouring in from the little walled garden, hard, piercing March sunlight, sparkling on my wedding ring and the engagement diamond, blinding me.

Then I got up and poured myself a gin. I didn't usually start that until lunchtime.

Well, *I thought.* It seems everything you do now, Mrs Alliat, is to be done alone. Even in the bedroom department. So.

And I decided to catch a train and go down to the seaside for the day. I knew George wouldn't be back until 9.00 that evening, there was some meeting or other he had to attend. He'd hate that, missing his studio.

I got dressed, and made up. And then I stood by the mirror, admiring myself. Preening, as George said – says. Although now he says it in a different voice.

I can recall what I wore. A green and cream dress and a necklace of green shells, and a cream coat – the style they called a swing coat. I think they did. Narrow-shouldered, an A-line, widening to mid-calf. And boots of beige leather. And my hair in a sort of page-boy style, shoulder-length, swept from left to right across the brow like a wave. And sublimely bleached, of course. No hint of grey.

Did I look good? I thought so. Not a day over 38? Surely only one day over.

The shells of the necklace made me want the sea, That and perhaps the brittle glassy light. And I remembered the name of the strange place, a few miles inland, which seemed to cause odd things to occur. Seatree.

Let me go to Seatree and be lost for a day. My one day over 38.

It was like those feelings one has in youth. I hadn't had them for years. Decades.

At the station I didn't think they would find Seatree among their routes, but there it was. The Hastings train. A journey of about one and a half hours.

Easy as pie.

What did I believe was going to happen to me? Nothing, I expect. Those extraordinary excitements have no real basis in life. You go to a dance, feeling like Cinderella on the verge of a fantasy ball, and it's dull, and the men are dull and ugly, or no-one notices you.

Don't analyse, then. Simply follow the feeling through. On the train I felt radiant and happy. I felt independent.

It seems trivial now, and foolish. It was.

I could have had lunch at the Savoy, gone to a play, or something. Instead I ran off to an obscure little place between South London and the sea. And dolled up to the nines to do it.

People did look at me. I mean, men.

I was used to it, or I had been. And then recently it had seemed not to be happening.

But on the train even younger men gave me a glance, here and there.

And I didn't think they were thinking, Overdressed rich bitch, *as perhaps they were.*

London drew back and the countryside came in about the train.

There was more of it then, wasn't there? Witches' brooms of bare trees glittering with birds and sunlight, flocks of sheep and clusters of cows, and flashing cuts of water.

After an hour, I started watching for the station.

We were a little late, I think.

I even had a plan. I would look round the town, perhaps have lunch. Then I might go back to the station and continue on to the ocean. If Seatree bored me, I'd do that anyway.

Once or twice on the train, I'd thought, George doesn't know where I am, and that I'm doing this.

As I walked out of the station, I thought it again. There was a clock that said quarter past 12.00. I can see it now. A quaint clock with red and black curlicues around it. And it was slow, too.

In those days, aeons since, the '70s, you came out of Seatree station into a country lane, and had to walk for ten minutes between trees and hedges, to reach the High Street. There was a tractor in a field. And a squirrel ran over the lane. A grey squirrel, but I hadn't seen one except now and then in a park.

When I got into the High Street, I confess though I was disappointed. It looked parochial rather than rustic, and there were women shaped like pouter pigeons in awful macs, strutting up and down, and some little, unexciting shops – and nothing much else. Also, it felt very cold. Deflation.

What did Miranda do? Guess. She walked along the road until she came to what she took to be a pub, and went in for a stiff drink.

They had a fire in the big room. Real logs. And marvellous old bottles and barrels and things. The beams looked genuine. And on the wall, this notice about being able to offer brandy that was two hundred years old.

There were a few people there; I didn't notice them – except that I didn't see anyone who interested me.

I sat down in a wide leather seat toward the back. It was in a booth, quite private. I'd ordered a double, cursing myself as always for not having the guts to order a triple, or better, two doubles. I'd never been sure they'd serve me if I did.

Well, mysterious Seatree was a wash-out. And although this pub was pleasant enough, there was nothing here for me.

What had I been anticipating?

I hadn't truly admitted it, until then. A man, of course. A man. What else?

The drink was gone. And then, what with the other drinks I'd had before I came out, in the icy sea-ish air, I felt light-headed. Perhaps they had a dining-room; I thought I'd noticed one. This was a hotel, wasn't it, more than just a pub? And with a strange name. The Fighting Man.

I'd better have lunch there. Then I could find a cab, if they had such things, and go and look at the sea. The purpose of my journey.

'Hallo.'

That was all he said. How I heard it. Miles away in irked replanning. Having given up.

'Can I sit here? If you'd rather not, I won't.'

He was about five feet ten, very slim. He had brown hair long to his shoulders, as they wore it then – and some still do. Silvery eyes. Yes, it sounds fanciful. But they were. And so clear. The clarity of youth. He was about twenty. Younger …

I said, stuffily (startled), 'Yes, all right.'

'You're kind,' he said. And sat down facing me. He had a glass of beer, mostly full. Articulate, long-fingered hands. But the nails were bitten. Neurasthenic. 'You looked,' he said, 'so nice. I just wanted to get closer.'

I stared at him.

He said, 'I don't know anyone here. You look as if you don't belong here either.'

I heard myself say, 'I've come down from London.'

'Yes. You look like that. Glamorous. You look like a film star.'

He gazed right at me as he said it. With those silver eyes.

'How flattering,' I said. Archly. Harshly.

And he smiled, and said, 'Sorry. I say what I think. I don't mean to be rude. Can I buy you a drink?'

He looked poor. Not the way people do now, or did for that matter when I was young. Poor the way they did in the '70s. Clean though. He smelled appealingly of shampoo and soap. A student, perhaps?

'I'm drinking gin. I'll get it.' And then I said, 'And for you, would you like a drink?' As if I'd been practised in this sort of thing, buying

drinks for men. But surely I was still under the impression I was being gracious, benign, Lady Bountiful. Motherly?

'I'd love a rum,' he said. 'It's freezing today, and it warms me up. But I can't afford it. And I've got the beer.'

So I went and bought myself a double gin and a double rum for him. Even before he told me his name.

I start earlier now, so I can type all this. I neglect the house, then hurry to attend to it, slapdash and scared. But George hasn't noticed, or if he has, doesn't need my 'sluttishness' as an excuse anymore to hurt me.

To me it seems almost uncanny now, thinking back from George-now to George-then. But George-then hatched the George of now. George and I, and Nicky. That was his name. Nicholas Ingram. He told me over the next couple of drinks.

My appetite had gone, and I didn't think he might be hungry. He reproached me for that later. At the time he didn't mention it.

We sat talking.

Was I telling myself that at least I'd met an interesting person, and so the day wouldn't be entirely wasted? I can't recall. I felt fascinated by him, tremulous and electric and girlish. And I kept a tight rein on that, being very careful to maintain my dignity. After all I was 38, wasn't I, and although he hadn't told me, he couldn't be more than 21 at the most. And he was behaving as if he couldn't get enough of me. He had the look in his eyes, which kept fastening on mine whenever I allowed it, the look I'd known from all men in my life until the last two or three years.

He even did buy me a drink. It was a single and he didn't provide tonic, but at least he'd done his best.

I say we talked, but really he did the talking. Men always do – do they, still? The thing I'd missed so much was George's talking to me.

Nicky – he said he preferred the shortened version of his name – told me he had run away from a foster home where his foster father treated him very badly. At the time I was moved and horrified by the things he outlined – being locked in a cupboard, even once locked out in the garden on a winter night. Now, I wonder if all the tales were true. They could have been.

He said he'd been living 'off his wits' since the age of 15. He did various jobs in various places, to earn a little 'bread'. Mostly he wandered Britain, sometimes hitching, sometimes with enough money to board a train or a coach. Sometimes he simply walked. They used to do that in mediaeval times, didn't they? They had to. I like it. Walking, you see more.

He spoke well. I mean his accent was educated. (I wondered afterwards, because the sort of background he described didn't seem conducive to that.) His actual voice wasn't all that attractive. I didn't really think about this at the time. Rather rough, though, and toneless. He had perfect teeth when he smiled. Like George? I never considered it.

Nicky let me in on his secret when I asked if he was staying at the hotel. 'You're joking. I couldn't afford that. But I'll tell you what I do. I sneak in and use their guest bathrooms now and then. They're always nicer in this sort of place. No-one's caught me. If they do, you just apologise, explain you mistook it for the gents' downstairs. I only once had one woman say, "But you've had a **bath***!" And I said, "Full marks, ma'am. Before I left home."'*

I was rather admiring. His carefree, venturesome life.

More so as he told me things he'd seen and done, in Scotland, Wales, the North of England. And Devon. Devon was especially good, where he'd worked on some sort of Roman excavation. 'About a penny a day, but great. I found something, too. A legionary's ring. Worth a packet, although of course I didn't steal it. You do get a reward, though. A share of the booty.'

In the end the bar was emptying. The licensing laws were different then, and there was no more drink on offer.

I wondered what would happen now, and I was going to suggest we have a coffee somewhere. But then I thought he would probably want to be off.

On the pavement outside the Fighting Man, I noticed for the first time how thin his jacket was, a sort of threadbare velvet thing, and he had no coat. Seatree was so cold that day. So cold.

Then he said, 'Miranda –' I'd allowed him to call me that – 'there's a place I'd really like to show you.'

I was all lit up from the gin. It used to have a glorious effect on me. And I thought, He doesn't want to say goodbye.

'All right. Why not? I did come here to look at Seatree.'

'You're special,' he said, 'a woman like you, and you're ready for anything.'

'Not anything,' I said severely. I would keep gently reprimanding him like this. He only laughed.

'It's a bit of a walk. Is that all right?'

'Oh yes.'

My God, he didn't lie. Of course I did walk, in London, through St James's and Regent's Park, along the better streets.

At first, it was just streets. Uphill, but not too taxing, just a slope, and a rather beautiful terrace of old houses with enormous trees in their front gardens.

Then there was open land again, or land closed only by trees. We picked our way along a rather muddy track. My boots weren't the right sort for a full-blown country walk, but I ignored that, and when a bramble in a hedge tore the hem of my new coat, I didn't take much notice.

Under some trees, the grass was very green, acidulously bright. And there were little drifts of yellow and purple crocuses. I pointed these out to him artlessly. He didn't answer. Conceivably, after the wild heathers and mountains, rural England was quite tame.

There was a closed gate across the end of the track, beyond it, a wider, muddier track, all pebbles and puddles.

'Is it much farther?'

'No. Not much.'

'What is it, exactly?'

I'd stopped, wanting a rest, and to rest my feet, which were beginning to hurt. I didn't feel the cold – the gin, the walk – but more – how shall I put it? – vulnerable to the open air.

'Oh, don't get fed up, Miranda. It's something I found.' I must have looked blank, although I'd been all interest and enthusiasm until then. He said, 'There's a house up here. It looks quite impressive, but it's falling apart inside. It's where I've been shacking up.'

A spangled rush went through me, my heart to my head, even from my feet to my head.

Did he mean – was he inviting me –? His face was wild with cold, and – yes, desire, the intensity of wanting. And he reached over and took my hand. The right, unmarried one.

'There's a space I've cleared. I can make a fire. It won't be too bad.'

On my back in a ruin, gazing up at the sky through the broken roof – bricks under my spine.

My **mind** *spun. I was horrified – and, as the young say,* **turned on.** *Yes, aroused. I wanted to.*

And all round the core of molten feeling, ideas of getting filthy, ruining my clothes, being miles from anywhere, by which I meant out of my depth – all these ideas meant nothing. Or making my need more **vital.**

I heard myself say, 'Nicky – you know I'm old enough –'

'No you're not. Come on. You're amazing.'

And he pushed the gate open and we walked up that private muddy track that now I know as Divers Lane.

When I think of it now I burn with shame and panic. I can still remember so well what I felt. I've never been surprised at what happened. I have a dreadful suspicion that I would do it again in that situation.

Do just the same. That's reprehensible, I suppose. Even Jesus Christ, having forgiven the transgressor, added the proviso, **Sin no more.** *But I have to be honest and say that I believe I would. However, also, I have never been forgiven.*

He led me off the track, presently, and up through a wood, a towering wood of ancient trees. There are less of them now, and mostly trapped in gardens.

I saw the house first from the back. It didn't intrigue me at all, just a big, long building, with some windows boarded up and others smashed out. (I didn't know, naturally, that I would come to live in it almost two years later.) Those huge terrible weeds were growing in the ground around it – mare's tails I think they call them – and thistles with spikes.

The wood curved round, leaving a space behind the house. There were massive cedars, and a great oak. In summer, I thought vaguely, in the margin of my consciousness, it must look pretty. The weedy garden and then this meadow, spreading down to the trees. Perhaps wild flowers as well as weeds.

In that I was correct. Or didn't I even think of it, then? Memory plays tricks. Those blue mists of flowers spilling to the oaks and cedars, greenness.

'It's this way,' he said.

'Oh, but I thought we were going to the house –'

'I want to show you what I found, first. Then we'll go in. I've got a kettle, and some tea. And some apples. I'll cut them up for you – look,

I've got this.' And he drew a short, thin knife out of his pocket. I stared at the knife, and then dismissed it. It really was the sort you did slice apples with, incongruous but reasonable.

'I'm getting cold, Nicky.'

'No, you must see this. It's important. After all, I'm waiting, and I'm bloody starving. You don't eat, do you, just drink?'

'I wasn't – hungry –'

'Well I was. You never thought of that, did you, Miranda?'

I'd recoiled. Now I recoiled again.

Suddenly he tossed the knife up in the air, and I thought he'd thrown it at me. He hadn't, he caught it. But in that second, I became rather frightened. I thought, I don't know anything about him. He's been ill-treated. He hasn't got a job or any family. He roams about. He could be dangerous – or mad – or both.

'Come on,' he said, impatient now. 'You're not the lady I took you for. You're letting me down.'

And I thought, Does he want to have me out here, under the trees? He might even have something wrong with him. Some sexual thing – *I'm* the mad one –

And yet, I was still ready to lie down with him. In those days, there were straightforward cures for sexual diseases, and one was treated in confidence.

'All right,' I said, more playful than I felt.

And we went through the long grass, and over to the further trees, and up to one tree, the oak.

At once he knelt on the ground, and scrabbled there. (I thought of that film about St Bernadette, at Lourdes, trying to dig up the holy spring as the Virgin Mary had instructed her.)

There was a sort of hole.

'It's down here. A fox was at it in the night. I checked, you see, because sometimes foxes unearth things. Look, maybe you can help me a bit. Use the knife, I'm not asking you to spoil your manicured hands.'

Speechless, I stood there.

Then he got up and held the knife at me, the bad-mannered unlucky way, the point directed toward me. And I took the knife, mainly because I preferred to have hold of it myself.

'Please can you explain, Nicky? I don't know what you're talking about.'

'Okay. Listen. It was clearer this morning, but there was some rain about 7.00. And the soil's dropped back in. I could see bones in there.'

'Bones –?'

'Human. And they looked **old.** *I mean* **really** *old. Like the dig at Devon. And then there was something that looked like a sword –'*

'Nicky –'

'Archaeology, Miranda. Heard of it? God, you really are a dumb blonde. We could make a lot of money. Only I don't want anyone else in on it, and you'd need to advance me a bit. I'll sort things out. Get on to the proper people. By the way, I don't mean museums. Let me have, oh, say a hundred pounds. That should see me through. Well – say a hundred and fifty.'

'You want me to give you a hundred and fifty pounds?'

Everything seemed draining out of me. Not only lust and drink and body-warmth and sanity – but some primeval precious thing that had no name.

'Look, you'll make a bomb if this is what I think it is. Have you heard of Harold?'

'What?'

'1066. Oh, woman, for Christ's sake. The Norman invasion of England.'

Then he told me something about King Harold, who died at Senlac, apparently, just a couple of miles away from here, and the legend of three of his crack fighting men, who escaped the battlefield and then killed themselves and were buried in the vicinity.

More than just a history lesson, I learned from his demeanour and his voice what he thought of me. The intensity and desire in his face had been for this (presumably illegal) excavation, the money.

So it was silly of me, wasn't it, to say, lamely, 'I thought you wanted me to come here with you for something else.'

'What? To show you my snazzy pad?' Then he laughed. 'All right. We'll leave it. I'll sort something out. Bye bye.'

And he turned and walked off toward the derelict house. Leaving me standing there.

I've said I'd been frightened of him, and now I had been insulted by him, and dismissed. Why I did what I did I don't know. By which I mean, I know which instincts drove me, but not why my intelligence, since I'm not entirely a fool, didn't check me.

In fact, my brain furnished quick clever reasons for what I did. Swashbuckling reasons.

So then I walked after him, and followed him into the house.

There was a hole in the wall for an entrance, and then the lower room, which later became part of the big room with the book gallery, once the upper room was knocked out. There was still a bathroom above, almost where my bathroom is now. And water had run through from it, across the next-door upper room, and so down into the area below.

The space was full of rubble, and the remains of a fire. Quite a big one, too big to be quite safe. And a sort of – how can I describe it? – black light.

He was stood there eating an apple.

'Oh, Nicky,' I said, frivolously, 'of course I'll help you. I just didn't catch on. But honestly, I'm not much use digging things up. Let's talk it over, shall we? Make a plan.'

And I went up to him, and looked up into his face. Striving after the look I'd seen there, in the hotel, even though I understood it was for money, and not for me.

*I think I must have believed that if I paid for him, I could still have him. I **wanted** him. Or someone.*

And another man, less young, more canny, he would have helped me out, wouldn't he? I could have found someone like that quite easily in London.

But not there. Not in the ruin. Not Nicky Ingram.

*'Oh, I **get** it,' he said. (Could he truly have been so naïve – worse than I was – or was it simply an unbalanced malice?) 'I **see**.'*

'Let's be friends, Nicky.'

'Christ, you thought I was going to fuck you. Bloody hell, Miranda. What do you think I am? You're older than my fucking mother.'

I stepped back, and trod unevenly, and my foot turned.

He watched.

I righted myself.

'You're an old girl, Miranda. God, what are you – 45 – 50? Done up like a dog's dinner, and old. Sorry, dear, I couldn't stomach it. If

that's the deal, I'll just have to bow out.' And he bit into the apple, which in some fables represents death.

If I say I don't know what happened, that wouldn't be true. And yet, also, I don't know.

My balance went again, and this time, I floundered forward, instead of to the side. And my hand went up, and I could say I meant to slap his face. But I had the fruit knife in my hand.

Maybe I forgot I did.

His flawless cheek undid in a thin long line, finer than a hair it looked, and then the blood sprang out, and half his face was crimson, and I staggered away.

Age also scars. That's what the lines and wrinkles look like, to me. Bad scarring that no-one has bothered to mend.

His mouth opened.

And then he made a noise, and started jumping incongruously – jumping, until he fell over, and not staying still then, but bucking and rolling, in and out of the black place of the dead fire.

I recall that quite clearly. And I thought he was writhing in pain or rage. I don't mean I thought it in words. I suppose one would say, it was an assumption.

The noises he made were awful. And then they stopped and he rolled some more and then stopped rolling and was still. He lay face down.

Now I 'assumed' he'd fainted.

But the mindless state I'd been in seemed to be washing off me. I was going very cold, and I'd dropped the knife. I was standing shivering, repeating idiotically, 'How could you say that to me? Why did you say that?' Blaming him, showing him he had made me do what I had.

And then, somehow I realised, and I stood absorbing what I'd realised. And then I went nearer and looked down at him.

He didn't move. I couldn't bring myself to touch him.

I stood there for about forty minutes. Waiting. He never moved. I never touched him.

The part-eaten apple had flown out of his hand and lay by a rucksack in the corner.

I thought about my mother saying to me fiercely, 'Never **run** *with a sweet in your mouth like that. You could choke.'*

That's what happened. He'd had a piece of apple in his mouth and when I sliced his face open with the knife, he'd choked on the fruit.

I couldn't have saved him. I didn't know anything useful. Had anyone heard of that thing, a something *manoeuvre, that stops someone choking? I wouldn't have known how to administer it even if I'd heard of it.*

Anyway, I hadn't grasped what was wrong.

He would have been scarred for life. Or had I only meant to slap him?

In the end I went outside. It was an isolated country place. Birds were singing, and for the first time I noticed some daffodils growing across the meadow, near the oak tree with the grave under it.

There was a bloodstain on my coat, up near the right shoulder. Not very big. It didn't really look like blood, only nasty on the smooth cream surface.

I had no idea what to do. I'd never had to think for myself, not really.

I walked back through the wood to the track, and went down and through the gate, and then on to Seatree. The light was going. Somehow I didn't think it was nightfall, only an overcast. I don't think there was a sunset, as such.

Outside the lighted chemist's in the High Street, two women glanced at me.

Maybe they were thinking, Why does that bitch have blood on her coat?

The stain was exactly where I might have pinned flowers, earlier in my life. Just there. A red rose.

But it was almost dark by then.

There was no-one in the station, but the London train was announced. I got on the train, and went home.

2

'I'd say she meant business, wouldn't you? She imbibes alcohol and barbiturate, cuts her wrist, and lies down in a nice hot bath.'

'Yes. But we got there before she intended. There was a chance of saving her life.'

'You did your best, Edward.'

'The point is, sir, she drowned.'

'I just sense she may have thought of that, too.' Knox stroked his nose, like a man calming a restive dog. He looked gloomy. The solution was coming clear, the long night running to an end. As the windows also promised.

But Rawthorn *crackled.*

He stood there, angry, cheated of the life of Miranda Alliat. And then, slowly, he let go of that life.

'She'd have been in for a lot of trouble. And she'd had enough.'

'A merciful release, Eddy. But you don't find it easy. With women, I mean. Puts me, in a contrary way, in mind of Hesketh, our famous multiple killer. The Saxon Vale murders in the '50s. Said the only woman he feared was a live one. And you're that in reverse. Dead women churn you up.'

'Yes.'

'You'll never get seasoned. I don't. Even that drunk bastard in the Hamiltons' garden, the aptly named Mr Grace. One minute prancing about, and then down the sink. Arrows of Artemis, Rawthorn. Or is it Apollo?'

But Rawthorn had long ago ceased to react to Knox's displays of the classical, if he ever had. As for Knox's sensitivity to corpses, he hid it very well.

It was true, however, that Rawthorn hated coping with a

woman's cadaver.

He had worked on her for a year – 12 minutes maybe – before Poecock eased him away.

'Give up, guv. She's out of it.'

Judging by the bloody water that manual resuscitation techniques had ejected from her lungs, it was already hopeless by the time he had got her out of the bath. And he had known that, hadn't he?

The blood-loss was considerable, too, the alcohol and hot water keeping her veins flowing strongly. And she hadn't mucked about with the cut. She'd used, not the razor blade he had expected, but a large meat knife from the kitchen. And when he had trodden on it, turning from her body, his eyes blackened. Only for a second. (She drowned also in her own blood.) ('I could drink your bathwater.') But a second could last a long while.

And Poecock again, a steadying hand. And unfairly wanting to smack Poecock in the mouth.

Let it go now.

She was a murderess. Double sin upon her brow. Manslaughter probably, technically …

Leigh had found the telephone and called the station.

She'd also identified, as *he* should have done, the rattling noise that went on, after the pipes had ceased their banshee shrieking.

'A computer. The printer's working.'

So they went into what was evidently Alliat's study and office, a surprisingly pleasing room, with prints of Turner and Cezanne on the walls. The floor here was dry. As well it was, because the manuscript was piling up all over it.

Miranda had left the machine on continuous print, and stocked it with five hundred sheets of paper. Though the confession – if that was what you could term it – didn't require more than a tenth of that amount. Luckily she had numbered her pages.

The symbolism of the printing of these words, over and over, on and on, hung heavily in the air as the aroma of bath essence and death.

'Don't go through,' he said to Leigh.

'No, I won't. She's dead?'

'Yes.'

His shirt would have been enough to upset people. Wringing wet, and bloody.

Leigh said only, 'I'm sorry. I thought she would be.'

'Yes.'

Downstairs, in the two-storey iceberg of a room, hung with its gleaming jade and gold, its antique books, and stapled by its pillars – and caricatured by the dire trophies he had yet to learn about:

'Ed – the ceiling.'

Bathwater, pink and red, had run through Miranda's bathroom, adjacently above, somehow soaked up into the walls and joists, channelled over, and now was sprinkling, like a gentle rain of mercy, out of the painted ceiling.

He thought of the line, *The sky is falling*. And even as he thought it, some of the blue daylit ether, a sunny cloud, a single swallow, broke from the plaster and scattered down.

Then the vehicles began to arrive outside, the aquamarine and red lights, like a party strobe, on a darkness already changing.

Sterne the SOCO marched into the house stone-faced, a party-pooper.

'*Grace's* fingerprints are what you want, right?'

'Yes. From in there.'

In there. The room of a dying day.

3

The Print-Out

That night it rained again, at least in London. I came home in the rain, and when I got indoors I went straight up and had a very hot bath. My feet were blistered. When I looked, my stockings were torn and my boots had blood on then. I threw them away. And strangely, my underclothes. I don't know why.

George got back about nine.

When he saw me, he said, 'My little love. Have you caught cold?'

I hadn't meant to say anything. In a way, I almost felt there was nothing to say.

But when I looked at him and he spoke to me, something gave way in me. I was so used to relying on George. His strength, my feminine fragility, they underpinned our life together.

I ran into his embrace and began to cry. He led me into the sitting room and held me. No hurrying up to his studio tonight.

It gushed out. I can't remember what I said. I know I told him everything. If he answered or prompted I have no notion. I think he stayed very silent until the end.

I know I held nothing back.

I told him about Nicky. Not only that I'd killed Nicky, but how I'd gone with him. And why.

Probably I blurted out that I'd been lonely, and – ghastly words, I doubt I put it so crudely – that I was sex-starved. And old.

The killing, that was the least of it.

He held me all the way through.

When I finished, he put me away a little, and asked several questions. I don't know what, or what I said. I must have said something about it being an accident, that Nicky had choked. Did I ask if that would make a difference? But then, I'd run away, hadn't I? And

I'd caused it all. The terrible thing I did to his face. I don't know if George gave an opinion.

At last he poured us both a drink, brandies. And I broke down again and started on about the two-hundred-year-old brandy at the hotel.

Of course, I'd already said I'd been there, met Nicky there. Was among the last to leave. And how, coming back, the women had stared at me in the street. The blood on my coat, which, peculiar as it now seems, I hadn't thrown away with the boots and underthings.

I can recollect saying several times that I'd been seen. That, when they found him, they'd know what I had done.

And George said, 'Yes. I'm aware of that. You in your glad rags looking like a million dollars. Yes, they'd have seen you. They won't forget.'

Then he gave me some hot milk, as if I were a child, and supported me up to bed. It must have been after 10.00 by then.

'Take these aspirin. Yes, three. They'll do you good. I have to go out now. It's all right. But I probably won't be back until tomorrow. When Mrs Bevis comes, just say you've got 'flu. Stay in bed. Don't talk to anybody. Don't worry. Trust me, Miranda. It's all right. I'll see to it.'

He went out and I took the aspirin and the milk, and I don't remember anything else much until I woke about 6.00 in the morning, and he wasn't there. But then I fell asleep again.

He left a note for Mrs Bevis. She brought me tea and some toast at 8.30.

'You do look poorly, Mrs Alliat.'

And then I slept again.

And when I woke up he'd come back.

'We won't talk about it,' he said. 'Try and get some more sleep.'

A week later I can see Mrs Bevis saying to me, 'Poor Mr Alliat. He still went into his office. And he had the 'flu worse than you, I reckon. Oh he did look rotten that day. I said to him, "You should see your GP, Mr Alliat." But he laughed and said he was all right.'

And he said to me that first evening the same thing. 'It's all right, Miranda.' And when I stared at him he turned away and said, 'Let's forget it now.'

I remonstrated, but not then. A month after, or two months. And then he lost his temper. He shouted at me. 'No. I don't want to discuss

it. Forget it. It's done.'
  It was done.

*Have you ever had something that you feared very much, probably in a
dream, and then you wake up and you think,* **Thank God, it wasn't
real, I can put it out of my mind?**

*But then gradually you remember, and no, it truly is real. It truly
has happened, or is about to.*

We went to Venice that summer, as planned.

*It was the very holiday I'd wanted, and that we hadn't ever had. We
did everything together. I can't think what, now. I'd have to look it up in
the guidebooks we bought. The churches, the gondolas, the lunches, the
dinners. We even went out to Verona. I think, somewhere there, is a
building supposed to be Juliet's house. Did we look at it? Or did we
avoid it?*

*One thing we didn't do. We didn't make love. In fact the huge room
had only twin beds. When I mentioned this, he told me it was the only
one of the 'good' rooms available.*

*Before Venice, gradually I'd tried to get emotionally close to George
again. The strange thing was that previously, all those years when I'd
felt forgotten and neglected, we had been also incredibly close. And now,
when he spent so much more time with me, we were not.*

*Of course, sometimes he went up to his studio. I would hear him
walking about there. Or sometimes nothing, and on a couple of occasions
I found an excuse to go up, he was sat there on the couch. Sat there. 'Just
thinking,' he said.*

*He didn't paint a thing. And he didn't paint in Venice. There wasn't
such a wonderful view from the window of our room. In the end, I
realised he'd changed the reserved apartment for a hotel room without a
view, but having twin beds.*

*I tried so hard. Everything I was, as a woman, supposed to do and be.
Sweet and gentle, tender and attentive. And he must have tried even
harder than I. We were so courteous to each other. We made little jokes
and laughed uproariously. We kissed each other politely goodnight, and,
at home, moved apart in the wide bed.*

*I drank, partly 'in secret', just as I had already been doing. But where
he'd sometimes referred in concern to the way the gin went down, trying*

to make light of it, saying Mrs Bevis was tucking in – now he said nothing. And he also drank more. I noticed properly on holiday. Two bottles of wine at lunch and at dinner. Several whiskies through the day. And a nightcap, a large one. He said a tooth was bothering him, and the whisky helped.

Soon after he got back, he began to look ill. One evening he came home early, and went straight past me without a greeting. In the sitting-room he was pouring himself a tall glass of whisky.

'Darling – what is it?'

'Something stupid,' he said. His face was like a rock, and then I saw his eyes were puffy, and his jaw looked odd, lopsided.

'Have you been in an accident?'

He laughed shortly. 'Could say that. Bloody dentist.'

The awful thing was, as I fluttered around, all sympathy, I was thinking that here might be the bridge to bring us near to one another again – his pain, my care.

Presently he said, 'Stop fussing, Miranda.' And then, 'For God's sake get away from me.'

He'd never spoken like that. Not to me. I don't think to anyone.

I backed away, and he said, 'He reckons I'm going to lose the lot. And the pain I'm in, I can well believe it.'

'George – your beautiful teeth –'

'Yes, my beautiful teeth.' And he threw the glass and it smashed to pieces on the wall.

He didn't tell me until over four months later, by which time every one of his teeth had been extracted, and the expensive yet unwieldy dentures were in his mouth. This altered the shape of his face. He looked like a stranger. There was also a dreadful recurrent infection. For weeks he was stuffed with antibiotics. His skin was nearly green and his breath smelled. He knew and he could do very little about it. He began graphically to explain how the basin was full of blood, about the taste of pus and mouthwash. He made me feel ill, but I knew it was worse for him.

I hoped so much he would be better for Christmas. In the past, we had enjoyed our Christmases. I even liked the shopping. I'd dress a tree, and I'd cook the dinner, and it was always a success. He gave me beautiful presents. He didn't go up to paint. Sometimes we'd go for a walk late at night – the city sparkling with frost, even once, snow, the local streets with the old-style lamps, and soft lit, long windows, some with coloured lights.

In the days leading up to Christmas, he said he felt better. I tried so hard then, harder even than before. But now he didn't meet me halfway. He ate the special breakfast I brought him in bed. He opened my gifts, glanced at them. 'Thank you, Miranda.' (To me he gave a bracelet of dark sapphires. It was exquisite but I made even more of it than I would usually have done. He coldly said, 'All right. You've made me understand you like it.' This was the last gift he ever gave me. Oh, the last but one.)

We ate Christmas dinner at the traditional time – or is it the Victorian time? – about 3.30.

He made no comment on it, although I'd tried to make it the best meal I had ever created.

When I tried to ply him with more, he filled his glass with the last of a third bottle of Hock, and he said, 'Miranda, be quiet. No, I don't want any more of this muck. I can't taste it. It could be bloody pigswill for all I'd know.'

It seemed the gum infection had impaired his sense of taste. The dentist and the doctors hoped 'temporarily'. 'But I doubt it. I think that's it, now. Thank God for booze, eh? Tastes like crap, but that doesn't stop it having an effect.'

'But darling – you must see a specialist.'

And then he got up, he rose from the table. He seemed gigantic, terrifying. And his eyes were full of hatred. They had been for some while, of course. It's just that, in him, I hadn't known it for what it was.

'No specialist can help me, Miranda. Because it's a punishment. Obviously, it couldn't fall on you, dear little dainty and delicate Miranda, no not on her. But on me. I'm strong. I can bear it.'

And then he flung his napkin down and let the glass drop and it broke like the other one, and he said, 'Leave all this rubbish. Come into the other room. I'm going to tell you. It's bloody time you knew. Christ almighty. Maybe you've even forgotten.'

'Forgotten –?'

'That you killed someone last March.'

'How could I forget?'

'Oh, I'm sure you've found a way.'

As I followed him into the other room, the room we called the television room, I knew that in a manner of speaking he was right. He'd told me to forget what I'd done. And I had blocked it away from myself. When I thought of it, I pushed the thought out of my mind.

In later years he would tell me that. 'You're such a wonderful ostrich. Head firmly in the sand.'

But what else could I do? It had happened. I couldn't undo it. I was too much of a coward to stare memory in the face.

It would have needed George to say to me that night in March, Miranda, we must go to the police at once. Don't be afraid, I'll phone the solicitor, and we'll go with you. You ran away because you were shocked. They will understand that. And any decent coroner will see what really happened to him. What you did was appalling. But you were frightened and besides, you never meant to kill.

And George said none of that. Was he only protecting me then, or was he also protecting himself? Not only afraid I couldn't stand the repercussions of my act, but that he too couldn't stand them. Wouldn't stand them.

I sat on the sofa, and he stood by the fire. It was burning brightly, cosily. We'd been going to watch something I thought, on TV, in an hour.

Instead, like a magician, he took me back.

The night after Nicholas Ingram died, George drove straight down to Seatree. He was always good with maps, clever at finding places. And he used the map and found the place. The way up from the High Street was simple, of course, and didn't take long by car. He parked somewhere below the track. I think he must have driven in among the trees. No-one saw the car, or if they did, it was never remembered.

When he got into the derelict house, George stripped, and put on some old clothes. Then he went to work on the body.

He called it that – him that – the body. Never by name. Just as, after that night, he's never used my name, except when he really wants to hurt me.

I won't try to reproduce the way in which he told me, graphic and detailed, precisely as he described the infection in his mouth. Just the facts.

George. Clever, thinking of everything. He knew that the police could identify through dental records. And so he pulled out every one of

Nicky's teeth with a pair of pliers, put them in a plastic bag, and smashed them with a hammer. Then he made up a fire on the same patch of rubble Nicky had used, and burned the body down to bones.

He made sure, he said, that only bones were left. And then he carried them out in another plastic sack, and dug out a part of the ancient grave under the oak, and shovelled them in with the other bones already there.

Then he resealed the grave. (He did it very thoroughly. Subsequently, he used to make me go out and inspect it. It stayed undisturbed and undisclosed for over a decade, until the night of the storm.) After that he burned the rucksack and its contents.

When he'd finished what he called his 'rescue mission', he washed in the house in the dirty water coming down from the pipes above. Then he changed back into his ordinary clothes. The old clothes he then burned in the remains of the fire. Then he doused the fire, and went back to the car.

He drove down to the coast and threw Nicky's knife and some pieces of partly burned metal, and the fragments of Nicky's teeth, off a cliff at Fairlight. The tide was in.

Then he drove back to London.

'I can't say back home. Not home. Would you call it home?'

Imploringly I thanked him, tried to; he shut me up abusively.

We were silent.

Then he said, 'I have an idea about that.'

I couldn't of course say anything.

He said, 'I mean about a home. The perfect home for us, you and I.'

Then he went out of the room and I heard him upstairs, and presently understood that he was destroying the picture he had painted of me.

Later, after he hit me, I thought – hoped – now it had come to a head, burst like the abscesses, possibly we could repair our marriage and go on.

That night he slept in the guest-room. We have never slept together since, in the true meaning of those words.

I'm taking too long over this. And I don't have much time, do I, now? Only until tomorrow. The day he goes to Gatwick for the plane. George.

Can I précis? I must try. But I can't help it, somehow, all this is rushing out of me. This jumbled patchwork of the past.

He came down here, to Seatree, in the New Year. He told the various estate agents he was looking for a property in the area – handy for London, but near to the sea. If nothing had turned up on the house, he was going to say he had heard of a place in a bad way, but of the size and type he was looking for.

However he never had to do that. One of them, going on George's stipulations, and that cost wasn't really a problem, that he'd quite like to start virtually from scratch, presented him with the details of the wreck in Divers Lane. It was a good plot. A field went with a large garden, right down to the woods. And the road was private.

They did warn him that the house was in 'quite a state'. Also, unusually, that some of the woodland was due to be felled for farming purposes. All but one big tree, an oak, they thought, centuries old, just inside the perimeter of the land that went with the house.

George went to look at the house. Rather than jump at it, he made a business of sudden doubts. He beat the owners – some estate elsewhere – down to an 'acceptable' price.

Before the builders even began, George had a low wall built around the field and the garden, almost invisible, but enclosing, as a matter of course, the oak tree.

Later, when the work on the house was well in progress, he again went down. It was early summer. I was in hospital then. He hadn't visited me before, but he came into the private room that evening, and put something on the bed, wrapped up in a patterned paper. I expect the nurse thought it was flowers.

'The garden's going to be cleared in a few days. I thought you'd like a memento.'

I didn't say anything. I was dizzy, and numb from painkillers anyway. I undid the paper, and there on the bed, on the lilac counterpane that matched the curtains, sprawled a bunch of weeds from the house garden – mare's tails, thistles, tangled, spiky, horrible things, all clung with dirt and dead insects.

'You look shocked. I suppose you can't help that with that black eye. I think you should keep these. Dry them and spray them, perhaps. Don't throw them away, will you? I'd be upset.'

The other thing he did, before the farming people cut down the trees over the wall, was to paint the view.

He hadn't painted, as I said, since that night the previous March.

Now he sat there day after day, with the builders racketing about behind him, cursing him no doubt for being there, snooping on them. Although sometimes they came down and were taken aback by his talent. One of them I met in Seatree years after said to me, humbly, 'A real artist, your husband. I asked him, like, if he ever done portraits. My little girl – she was a lovely little thing. But he said he don't paint people. I think he thought I had a bit of a cheek.'

The picture. Yes, it was beautiful. The sweep of the pale arching field, with its froth of milky blue flowers – I don't know their names, sometimes they still come up, although they die in August. And the cedars twining through the oaks, and the great oak, all held in a still dance of shades and shadows and green thrill of light.

His best picture. I think it was. Is. The last one.

He never showed it to me, as he did the weed monstrosities, there in the private clinic where his money and his fists had put me for a suspected skull fracture. (And the lies, my fall, all accepted.)

I saw the picture first when he took me to the house, and ushered me inside.

I went like a lamb. No more resistance. It had been when I had wept and screamed I couldn't live here – wouldn't – never would – that he had first beaten me.

So many firsts. So many lasts.

'White carpets, you see. Spotless. Blameless, like the virgin's white for marriage. But then, although you won't know, traditional marriage white isn't for that. Do you know what it's for? To frighten off demons and ghosts.'

The ceiling of the high room with the gallery had been painted by a professional from London.

'The sky's the limit, isn't it? The only direction for people like us, is up.'

I wondered, long after, often, if he'd been trying to be found out. Trying to get me found out. The way perhaps I am, putting this on to disk.

Not just buying the house, but the builders and the wall – someone stumbling on the grave. They didn't, though. No-one did.

Even the painting, put up there on the wall of the room. George said he had deliberately shown it to people – people coming to do things to the house. But they seemed to think, he said, that it was some view in France. Not a grave. Nothing to do with us.

No-one ever had thought that. Not even in the weeks after the hurricane. That is, they saw what was there after the tree came up, and learned it wasn't just those old bones Nicky Ingram had been so keen to unearth. But they never discovered who had died, and never connected it to us. No-one remembered me. Why should they? Just one more aging, well-off woman. As for Nicky, he was an itinerant. They hadn't even caught him in the bathroom of the Fighting Man.

We moved into the house. We have lived here ever since. We did as man and wife do. He worked, and I kept the home. On my own now. Dusting and polishing and hoovering. All the proper wifely things. The washing in the machine, the ironing, ordering the shopping. The cooking. I washed the windows. I made the garden grow.

I thought I'd die of exhaustion at first, but one becomes quicker, more efficient. I had to. He would come home at night, pour himself or have me pour him the drinks I was no longer allowed, and then inspect the house from top to bottom. If anything wasn't as it should be, I would receive a slap, or perhaps he would bang my head against the wall, twice, never more than twice. Or, when he still smoked, crush out a cigarette on my neck or on the inside of my thigh. If I'd been very remiss, of course, it was worse.

In fact, that night of the storm when the grave came up, when we saw the tree tug out like a great-sailed ship and split and crash away, George seemed to think that had been my bad housekeeping. By then, he would beat me almost every week, and inflict some slight injury almost every night without 'provocation' . But when the tree fell he rounded on me. I fled out into the upper hall. I don't know why. Normally it was better to let him do what he must.

He caught me anyway.

'You've let things go. Not looked after it, have you? That grave – that bloody grave. I told you to keep it in repair –'

Then he shook me, and as he did, he shook me away and I tumbled down the stairs, and heard myself far off, squeaking like a mouse. I thought I'd die. Was I glad? God knows.

When he saw I'd only been bruised and had hurt my ankle, he carried me up and dropped me on my bed. Where I passed out from the pain.

In the morning, they found the grave. We knew they would.

I can only assume he never thought it worthwhile, trying to move anything from it.

I remember being at the hospital in Seatree, on the Brow, for the X-ray the doctor wanted, and I was thinking, Any moment someone will come and say I'm being arrested.

But nobody did.

They spoke to George. Discounted me. What could I do, feeble little old thing with her foot up on a stool?

Why didn't he tell them? Blame it all on me. I could have done it. Oh yes, George, what you did, I could have. I'm stronger than you think. I've lived through all the years of this. Oh God, George. Yes.

But then, I didn't run away, did I? Why is that? I don't have any money of my own, but I could steal some from the housekeeping. And surely I could have found some job or other – typing, or if that was no use, stacking shelves.

Or would he follow me and find me? He's never threatened that. I don't know if he would.

I haven't gone. Haven't tried.

Something keeps me here.

And I've borne so much.

And now –

Now.

Often at first I used to ask myself if he was driven mad only by what he had to do, or felt he had to do, that night, when he pulled out a boy's teeth and burnt his flesh.

The psychologists would say that was it. Why else did George's perfect teeth become infected? And his need to live here.

But sometimes too I've thought it was his rage at me. That I'd been willing to commit adultery

Or worse – that I'd been willing, and no other man had wanted me.

Really, I have to finish now. And I wonder if I'm finally afraid to put it down. The thing I have been working toward.

Until now, the eve of this holiday, George has worked every day, except *at the weekends, in London. This means that I have had those days, or part of those days. A few hours, from about 8.00 in the morning until about 6.00 or 6.30. The hours when I am not in his shadow. Fawning on him, trying to avert his wrath, **suffering** his wrath.*

If I meant to pay the price for what I did, I've paid it. By now, surely I have.

Last week he told me. He's at last going to retire. He will work from home. He need only visit London once a month, if that. Apart from his holidays away from me, he will be constantly in the house.

With me.

He opened a bottle of champagne. None for me, of course.

'Can't let you have it, can I, turn you back into a drunken whore.' And then, playful, 'Will you be glad to see more of me?'

I kissed his hand, a supplicant. The Pope's ring. All that night, lying in my bed, the toe he broke by stamping on it, throbbing, and feelings of red hot pins, and crying, crying in terror.

How did I hold out for so long? I can't now.

And he's changed me. He's remade me in his image.

Oh, yes, George, you have. Just like God.

The dried weeds stand in the jade bowl. The picture of the grave is on the wall and there, the ugly stone apple. Your very last present, which you bought for me from a gift shop in the town.

Another memento. An apple. What Nicky Ingram choked on. The apple of death.

It's simple, George. You can't taste anything, can you?

Upstairs, the tubes of paint you still buy, and the bottles of white spirit.

And in my possession, the thing Dr Terry prescribed to help me. 'Yes, Mrs Alliat, I do agree about tranquillisers. But you're very run down and you need to sleep.' Mogadon Elixir. I've tried it. Like the white spirit, it doesn't show, poured into whisky. Not cloudy, as I feared. And tasteless. And you won't taste the white spirit, not you. Even to me – it's just like a very inferior brand.

So I'll fill your decanter as I always do, my best darling. One third of whisky to one of Mogadon and one of white spirit. Or perhaps just a little more whisky, in case.

And you'll drink it, gallons of it, as you always do. And then you'll be sleepy and you'll go out like a light, and I'll tip your head forward, as the doctor carefully explained all those years ago, warning me to be careful, closing the trachea, cutting off your air. While the white spirit burns out your insides.

You'll be dead in an hour or less. Although I will be cautious. I'll wait.

By then I'll have cancelled your cab to the airport. 'My husband has decided to drive himself. He says the driver got lost last time, and he almost missed the plane. I'm sorry.'

Later I'll drag you outside. Oh yes, I'm strong now – all that gardening and housework. It's September, and I've often had bonfires before, from the garden. Early leaves, fallen boughs. No-one overlooks the house, not even now.

I'll burn you, George, the way you burned Nicky. Just the same. But I'm luckier than you. I won't have to pull out any teeth. Your dentist did that all those years ago.

Later still, I'll get your car that I can't drive, and drive it out into the lanes leading toward Gatwick. I've studied the map this time, and I've worked it out. Even I, idiotic Miranda. And somewhere out there I'll run your car off the road, into a tree, or let it go over into a ditch, and leave it there with your luggage for the plane, and maybe a door open, as if you got out to wander away.

And then I'll walk back. With my bad foot. I'm used to walking on it now, used to being in agony. It will take all night. I don't mind. I'll have the rest of my life to get over it.

And your bones? Oh those. I'll put them in the old grave and cover it up. Lightning doesn't strike twice. I'll grow something there. Roses perhaps.

After you don't come back from your holiday, I'll report you missing. Or if they find the car, they'll tell me that you're missing.

And I'll be very sad. And bravely optimistic. And frightened. Of losing you.

But the car may not be found. If I can, I'll run it off into some wild part that will be overlooked, or not investigated for a long while.

And people do disappear without trace. People who try to live in Seatree.

That was how I read the name of this place, George. In that newspaper, all those years ago, 21, 22, 23, 24, however many.

A couple travelling down to Seatree never arrived. They just vanished. I forget their names. They left a little girl, it said. It was an awful story. Almost supernatural. Unnerving. Desperately sad. Just how yours will be, my best and only darling love.

4

Turning, he looked at the windows.

'Shouldn't the sun be up?'

DC Poecock said, 'It's overcast, sir.'

'You've read this?'

'No, sir. DI Rawthorn did.'

Knox grunted. 'It's a meal in a biscuit, I tell you that.'

Rawthorn said, 'Where are you up to? Oh, right.'

'Yes,' said Knox. He put the manuscript down and stretched, joints cracking loudly. 'And it looks like it's just what you say. Sterne's fingerprinting confirms that too. Grace was in that room.'

'Miranda Alliat killed Steven Grace.'

'Yes, Edward. And without intending to. Murder by mistake, like her first little escapade.'

Poecock looked at them, offended.

'Tell him, Inspector,' said Knox, 'or he'll bite.'

Rawthorn said, 'When I saw the Mogadon bottle by the bath, that was when I wanted Sterne in for Grace's fingerprints. Which were all over the place, as it happens. The mantelpiece, the table with the snuffboxes, on the knick-knacks – everywhere. Very tactile, Mr Grace. Incidentally, there were bottles of white spirit in Alliat's study cabinet, three of them, all only partly full. As Miranda says, she poisoned the whisky with Mogadon elixir and white spirit. She knew Alliat couldn't taste it. I told you about Alliat's teeth earlier.'

'Yes, guv. I've had toothache ever since.'

'And I've seen the proof too,' said Rawthorn, 'from the strength she made his coffee and the sugar she put in it. Sometimes sweet and salt tastes can still be experienced, even if the rest's gone.'

Poecock opened his mouth.

'Go on,' encouraged Knox. The last threads were still before him. He spun them out.

'Well,' said Poecock, 'I take it you're saying Steven Grace ditched his car and went to the house, as you would, and got in through the door she says – you say she says – she always leaves open for George Alliat's return.'

'And?'

'He couldn't find anyone, Grace, I mean, though I don't see why not, and Alliat wasn't back, held up at the roadworks out of London. So Grace, who was a tyke, stole a snuffbox and drank some of the poisoned whisky, left, and ended up dead at the Hamiltons' down the road. But he *could* taste, guv – so why didn't he –?'

'I'll come to that,' said Knox, 'because *that* one I have the answer to. What I don't get is how Alliat waltzed in later and poured himself full of whisky, as our DI Rawthorn here himself witnessed, and was still charging about hours later after – and is now alive, awake and on the way to Gatwick.'

'Even *I* was offered the whisky,' said Rawthorn, 'by a more-or-less composed Miranda.'

'Off her trolley? Ready to slay any mere male in a radius of twenty miles?'

Knox pip-pipped for silence. Then gave up.

Rawthorn said, 'You'd better finish her print-out, sir.'

The Print-Out

This won't take long. I've been too self-indulgent, and now I know that what I've written will be seen, I feel – well, rather embarrassed. I could type it all again, I suppose. I won't. I've had enough, you see.

But –

But.

Didn't someone say that a piece of writing was like a spell? You have to finish it. Beginning, middle, end.

George left at 4.00. Eight minutes to 4.00 am to be exact. Off to your holiday, George. What do you do there? I think you even try to paint. And can't. Destroy the canvases. But God knows, perhaps you do now what I had to do then. You just sit somewhere and drink. You might as well be here. Thank God you're not here. Oh God – George. I wish you were here. I wish you were with me. I want you back, I want you so much. I always have.

That was stupid. Any tears falling wet on this electrical thing might be dangerous. Which would be very funny.

Well, you see, George, I didn't kill you.

Evidently.

I meant to. I thought I could. I was drunk on the idea of it. That's what it felt like, being tight.

And I was like that all this morning, and I did everything. Made the house pristine for you, and then mixed up the concoction and put it in the whisky decanter. And I went over and over what I had to do. Let you die, and then drag you out, burn you, carry the bones to the grave. The car. The return. Over. Peace. Peace and alcohol for as long as I'd got left. Bliss.

The only detail I was still debating was when to cancel the cab to Gatwick. You see, I thought if I did it before you came home, you might ring them in the evening, to check with them, and so discover. It was better to call once you were unconscious, but that might be late – how long would this stuff take to affect you? They always seem so belligerent, cab drivers.

This confused me. A ridiculous woman.

I kept asking myself which was best, and not being able to decide. And then suddenly, it all became real.

That's the only way I can put it. Before, it had been like a sort of dream – a daydream, killing you, George. And now I saw that it was there in front of me, and I was going to do it.

All this was at 4.30, 4.40 in the afternoon. (I'd already undone the front door, as always, in case you were early.) And you might be early, home in less than half an hour, because you wanted extra time before the flight.

I wanted a drink so badly then. Knew I didn't dare. There are always four bottles of vodka kept in the kitchen, and the full decanter upstairs. The theory is that they are for guests. The vodka is to tempt me to disobedience.

Years ago I'd have done it, and topped the decanter or bottle up with water. But you always knew. Obviously, I was different after a drink. Of course, I've said, I drink when you go on holidays. But I replace the bottles then. One curious thing. Sometimes the manufacturers alter the shape of the bottle, or the label. Yet you've never queried this.

As I said, I think you know it happens at these times. And you allow it. Allowed it.

Whatever, I couldn't drink when you were there to guess.

If I'd had a drink, I believe I could have done it. Truly, I think I could have.

But not sober, as it transpired.

As I thought about it, my stomach began to churn. Then that awful sensation – I barely made it to my bathroom.

I remember some man in the bus queue once saying, boastfully, 'I didn't know whether to sit on the lavvy or lean over it.' My own problem. Luckily the bathroom is quite small and the tub close   to the lavatory, I ran a lot of water. The pipes made a nightmare noise. I think I fainted once. I'm not sure.

Then I seemed over it,   and I came out and stood wretchedly in the bedroom, looking out at the fields behind the garden, where the wood had been, long ago. The sun was going down.

I wrestled with myself. I tried to gain control.

But the moment I thought of it – your dead body, and hauling it, cold as a slab of meat, and the fire – and the stench you described to me at such length that Christmas afternoon, the rich roasting smell of burning human flesh –

I stumbled back into the bathroom again.

I know I fainted that time. The water was still running and the pipes made the most awful sound, and perhaps that brought me to. And then I sat there on the white carpet to scare off ghosts, and I said, 'I can't then. All right. I can't.'

After that, gradually, I came out of it. Everything lifted away. I felt rather dizzy, but no worse than I do sometimes after you've beaten me, and I'm used to continuing at those times where possible, in case you lash out at me again for my 'laziness'.

Even after the taps were turned off, the noise of the pipes took a long while to subside.

Then I saw the bedroom clock – it was getting on for 7.00.

One whirling minute of terror and panic – you would have been home long ago – I hadn't heard you in my illness, or over the pipe noise. You would have drunk the whisky – you would be dead or dying – and everything to do – and then I knew, George, that you hadn't yet come home. Because if you had, you would have come up here. You would have kicked in the bathroom door.

It didn't matter what state I was in. I must always be there to welcome you, murmuring softly, as you stalked by without one word.

When I got downstairs, it was true. You'd been delayed. You told me later, talking to the air as you normally do now in my company, that there were roadworks, and faulty lights.

At that time it only seemed to me the hand of Providence, or an act of God.

I ran quickly to the whisky decanter and carried it out, and all the glasses, because somehow one or two of them looked dirty and that would mean a blow. (So soon were you alive again for me.)

In the kitchen I washed and dried everything thoroughly. Refilled the decanter, and brought it back and set it in place.

The strangest thing in that moment. Some psychological foible, I expect. Refilled by wholesome alcohol, the decanter looked more full. I can't explain this. Probably I'd short-changed you with the poison, not filling the decanter as full as I habitually did, not noticing it until now.

It didn't matter.

I went back upstairs and changed my dress and repaired my make-up. There was time for all that – I'm very quick, now – before I heard you – easily, in a quietened house – and hurried down.

Just a little pause to refill my glass. I had to get used to vodka. My drink used to be gin. Another test you set me. I am used to vodka now. I passed.

Oh, that glass you made me give that young woman who came here – Miss Leigh Dover. She didn't want it. I did. And when she left, you watched me as I poured it away.

She's going to need it tomorrow, a triple vodka. I should feel awful about that. I hope she brings someone with her, as I'll suggest, when I leave the message.

Do you remember, George, when you punched me so hard I fell back against the clock, that time in London, and the glass face smashed and the hands came off? Time stopped. I kept thinking that in the hospital afterwards. You always took me to a hospital or a doctor, if it was so bad I couldn't go on my own. And I used to say, 'Thank you, darling. Oh, how kind you are, when you're so busy. Thank you, thank you.'

Why couldn't I? Why couldn't I kill you?

Tonight, I watched you drink the harmless whisky. Gallons of it. I watched.

And we had guests. So many visitors, tonight. And all the police cars up and down. What did that policeman say? Some man killed along the lane. Was it a car crash? I can't recall. A shame, I suppose.

Whoever it was said that suffering ennobles was mad. It doesn't. It makes you bloody selfish. I don't care about him, the man who died. Or about that young woman who hated George so much, and who is going to find me in the morning.

I don't give a damn.

Nearly over now. One more drink, then mix the special drink. Nicer than the one for George.

Then call the hotel. Leave the message, get the knife, the large one, I think, for steaks – you see, pissed out of my head, I can consider it without a qualm. Then run the bath and get in and all shall be well, all manner of things shall be well.

In a funny way, I think it was all the police cars. Probably I'd have gone on with George. Until he killed me, or he had a stroke from over-exertion, slamming me into something, or raping me, saying as he does so, 'This is want you want, isn't it, Miranda? This is what you can't do without?' Like tonight.

Oh, I might have thought of this. I must have done, before. Can't recall, actualllly. Look how I've spelt that – drunk. Drunken whore. Shan't correct it.

But the police. The cars. The uniformed men in the lane, and the plain clothes man, if he was, who came here. I can't remember what he looked like. Yet attractive. I'd have liked his attention, if I'd been younger. But I'm not younger. And I'm not due to be any older, either.

I kept thinking, This would have been what should have happened, then.

After Nicky, I mean. The cars in the lane and the police.

It was like going back in time again. As if I had to be made to. And I think, if I'd had to own up, and go to prison, I think I'd have done this then.

So I'll go up now. To the warm, scented bath. I'll go up now. Good night, George. Good night, darling, sweet dreams, my love. Sleep well.

5

Mrs Knox burst up the station steps as Jula Cork and Jack Hastings were descending them.

They stood, arrested by near collision, in the greyness that might have been occluded dawn, or benighted day.

'Oops, I'm sorry, luv.'

A middle-aged woman in a pink mac, and pink curlers under a red silk scarf. A younger woman and a man, dark and sombre-eyed, silent.

Passing each other, gone from each other.

PC Welch ran after the red and pink.

'What? What?'

'Hang on a minute, Mrs Knox, please. He's up to his eyes –'

'I can't. I've waited since 3.00 am. I told you, I couldn't sleep properly. And the TV'd been out all night. It'd play his video, oh yes, that recording I did for him of *NY Whatsit*. But nothing *I* wanted. And then he –'

'Yes, Mrs Knox. You have told –'

'Then he goes off. But you see – I said, didn't I, but it bears repeating, doesn't it, really? – I put the TV on, on the off-chance, and there it was.'

'Yes. Mrs Knox –'

'This is important.'

'I know it is – It's –'

'And he couldn't even get up and come round. Couldn't get our phone to work, couldn't get through, I could've been – and no-one heard what I said. So he sent you.'

'Yes, Mrs Knox.'

'I've a good mind not to tell him. I could just up sticks, you know. It was mine, you know. Not his.'

'No, Mrs Knox.'

In the station, the few early occupants stared with interest.

'Go and tell him,' she said. 'I mean, just tell him to come out. He hides in that office. He hides here. Tell him *I* want him.'

PC Welch nodded and moved away. When he reached Knox's door, he heard, faintly, behind him and below, a rough hilarious cheer go up, catcalls, whistles. Even so, he hesitated before he knocked.

'Steven Grace walked into the house and drank the poisoned whisky meant for Alliat. Then left. She didn't hear him because she was throwing up in the bathroom and had the water running, which causes the pipes to make a row.'

'We've heard it. That would happen.'

'Okay. Then she gives in to her *crises* of conscience and rushes down and throws the poison out, cleans the decanter and the glasses, and incidentally the glass Grace used, and replaces everything sparkling clean and non-poisonous. Luckily she doesn't re-dust the whole room. Then Alliat gets home and everything is hunky-dory.'

'Except for Steven Grace.'

'Who pegs out down the lane.' Knox sat back.

Poecock said, sullenly, 'Guv, I get the bit about her thinking the decanter wasn't quite full – and she doesn't know what she's seen –'

'True of so many witnesses,' lamented Knox.

'But if he only knocked back a glass or less, obviously because he could taste the muck in it and didn't like the taste – even a double – I mean, it wasn't cyanide. Would it have been enough? White spirit, anyway, he'd have thrown it up, wouldn't he?'

'Boy Wonder, Edgar Allen Poecock. Mr Holmes would have been proud of you. Yes, he didn't drink much, and no, that much wouldn't have been fatal. To someone fit.'

Rawthorn said, 'DS Wren's called in with the pathologist's further findings. Grace did die of a heart attack. He'd been through the mill already, but it was Miranda's whisky that killed him. As you say, made him ill and more than violently sick, and that undoubtedly triggered the coronary.'

'Could have happened anytime,' said Knox, 'the way he was going on. But it mightn't. If he'd taken care, had his pills and come off the sauce, and the fags, he might have been good for years. Didn't get the chance.'

'Bloody hell –' said Poecock, 'sir. You weren't kidding. She killed two men, two *strangers* – both by accident?'

And *this* man,' said Knox, 'she didn't even know about. She says, a shame, but I don't give a damn. She doesn't even wonder what he died of. She doesn't connect it up.'

'Blimey,' said Poecock.

'Women,' said Knox.

'You let Hastings and Ms Cork go, sir,' said Poecock after a moment.

'Yes, and I wouldn't put it past *him* to come up with something, wrongful arrest and so on. His mum'll egg him on.'

'But couldn't he still have run Grace's car off the road? Done that and then left him stranded there?'

Rawthorn said, 'I had someone check the butterfly on the internet.'

'Pardon, sir?'

'It was smashed on Grace's windscreen. Leigh Dover saw it. I took a look later. Diesoptera. It's quite a large species, not native to this country. But Esham Park's not far away. I think it flew straight at him. His reflexes were lousy from the booze he'd had. God knows what he thought it was – the wingspan, according to the info, can be over six inches. Grace lost control of the car and went into the ditch.'

'Blimey,' said Poecock again, very quietly. 'Butterflies.'

'Drunken drivers,' Knox amended severely. 'Which reminds me. Have they got hold of our Kentons yet?'

'No, sir. Their mobile's playing up. Still trying.'

'How,' said Knox, 'can sunspots work at night? The sun's not *there*.'

'Another car's gone after them.'

'All right. But the Gatwick routes are variable from here, back roads, lanes, right up to the M23,' Knox scowled. 'He's an accessory, George Alliat, to the Ingram business first, besides he caused the rest of it, with his bullying. I don't want him catching that plane.'

Less than a knock, there was a commotion outside. The three men looked up.

The door came open suddenly.

PC Welch and WPC Fellows appeared – and disappeared behind a springing woman in bright pink plastic curlers.

Knox rose.

'*Daphne!*'

'Ceefax,' responded Mrs Knox.

Welch was there. 'I'm sorry, sir –'

And then WPC Fellows, a firm young woman, coming between Knox and his wife in a trained movement.

'Excuse me, madam. *Sir.*'

'Yes?' asked Knox.

'We finally got an answer from Arrow Cars. A man there who says he's called Norman, and either has a bad cough or a dog –'

'*Yes?*'

'He says he was out on a call, that's why no-one picked up the phone. However, he now agrees the description of Alliat's driver doesn't tally with Bill Mills.'

'Bill *what?*'

'Plus we've traced Ms Philbin.'

Knox, puzzled.

'Markessa,' said Rawthorn.

'She's turned up at a farm just outside Battle. Ms Philbin claims she was abducted by a man called Dominic in an Arrow cab, who threatened her with a gun and then threw her out barefoot. The woman at the farm confirms Ms Philbin's feet are in a terrible state, and they've called an ambulance. From the description –'

'The driver of Alliat's cab is Dominic. Yes?'

Daphne Knox pushed WPC Fellows aside. Taken off guard,

WPC Fellows gave way. Something she would have to watch in future. 'Charles, *listen.*'

'Daphne, not now.'

'Charles – it was on Ceefax.'

'Daphne …'

'There were only two winners, Charles. And it was ten million tonight.'

Knox opened his mouth and left it open. Open-mouthed he stared at his wild pink and red wife. They all stared at her, and for the third time Poecock softly murmured, '*Blimey.*'

'Charles Knox,' said Daphne in the steely voice of a sentencing judge, 'we've won the lottery.'

Leigh was stood under a tall chestnut tree, wan, beautiful and smoky-eyed, a morning wind combing back her hair.

Rawthorn took all this in as he walked toward her.

'He's given me an hour off to see you to your hotel. With what's going on, he shouldn't have, but that's him.'

He had changed his shirt, shaved. He looked tired, she thought, and hardened over the tiredness. A clean and tidy little boy who had stayed up much too late. *And your eyes are what? Let me see. Grey, is it, like Dad's? Or – are they more tawny –?*

'The car's just there.'

'Could we walk?' she asked. 'It isn't far, is it. Do you have time?'

'Yes. After this, though, we're going to have our hands full for quite a bit.'

'Especially in the circumstances. One of the policewomen told me. They were rather elated.'

'I can't see Knox as a millionaire, somehow,' Rawthorn mused. 'It's a big responsibility, being suddenly rich.'

The sky was grey, heavy and low. They walked at an even pace, not touching.

'Is it dawn?'

'It must be.'

'This reminds me,' she said, 'of being very young, after an

all-night party.'

'Rather a grim one.'

'Sorry. That was tactless of me.'

'No, it's nice you see it like that – I mean, you see us like that.'

'Do I? Is that what I said?'

'Yes, Leigh. It is.'

They stopped. There was another tree, crowned in green drooping late summer flags. With here and there an edge of crisping copper, that seemed to have begun only in the night.

'These trees are so lush. They've left them to grow. I can remember them from twenty years back. Do you know the legend of the Sea Tree, Ed?'

'I don't.'

'The tree so tall that even in the deep valley, from the top of it you could see the sea. And witches climbed it to call storms inland. One particular witch – what was her name? – Atti, that was it. Atti Luff.'

He laughed and she looked at him, and in the empty, grey-ceilinged street, they moved easily and hungrily into each other's arms.

'I love your kisses,' she said.

'That's just as well.'

When they walked on, turning out into the High Street, where now a milk float was cruising, and a fed-up man and dog jogged past, Rawthorn spoke about Miranda Alliat. And stopped seeming like a boy.

'The ironic thing – two things, in fact: if she'd done it, killed him and heaved his bones into the grave under the oak stump – once we knew the history, that would've been the first place we'd have looked.'

'She'd lost her mind,' Leigh said. 'All those years of his abuse. Poor, poor woman. She couldn't even do it. She tried to put it right and thought she had. Surely no-one could convict her of Grace's murder?'

'They might. God knows, it was premeditated, even though she got the wrong guy. Manslaughter. Which can be a weird one.'

'What was the other thing?'

'You know you're hearing this in confidence? Yes, of course you do.'

'Yes, Ed, of course.'

'Something's already turned up on this young man who died in the '70s, this Nicholas Ingram. He came from a well-to-do family, but he'd been picked up twice in his teens for threatening behaviour – both times toward older women. If she'd owned up, lied a little – said he'd attacked her for her money and she cut him with his own knife in the struggle – It wasn't the actual cause of death. And a good solicitor. She'd almost certainly have got away with it.'

Leigh sighed. She shook her head.

'Now *I've* been *bloody* tactless,' he said.

'Oh – no, *no*. I've had to get over that. Men with knives. I'm glad you told me. I'm – what shall I say, flattered by the confidence.'

'Don't be flattered. I think I needed to talk to you.'

'Whatever happens,' she said, 'please don't let's lose that.'

The milk float stopped.

Rawthorn turned abruptly and strode over to it.

The milkman, startled, confronted him. Then relaxed. Coins jingled. When Rawthorn returned with the milk bottle, shaking it up, Leigh was grinning.

'What was that?'

'He knows I'm the Law – and of course expected the worst. It's an occupational hazard. Do you want some?'

'Milk. Pure cholesterol, and terribly fattening, and unsuitable, they say, for adults. Yes, please.' She too drank from the bottle of milk. 'Oh lord. This takes me back too, to the green days of youth when milk was still good for you.'

'It still is in moderation, Calcium, A and D.'

When they reached Boots, the milk was finished. She could see now many changes in the High Street. While above the nearer roofs, the shopping centre raised its huge and inappropriate fairy-tale towers. As if to warn, all seeming romance ends in something like a shopping bag.

Leigh said, 'Miranda's confession – what was she doing? Implicating George, but also telling him the invisible power she had over him, however briefly.'

The hotel was in sight.

'Maybe. She was so soft, so malleable. She killed twice, and never really noticed. Things happen to people,' he said, bleakly.

'Bad things. And good.'

'Why did you come here?' he asked abruptly.

'Just to think, to look around. The places of my childhood. A whim.'

'And you met me.'

'I met you.'

He held her arms, gently, looking at her, she thought, the way you study your subject for a painting.

'Ed, listen a moment.'

'I am.'

'How can I put this – you've helped me more than any counsellor or doctor – or policeperson, come to that. When you made me speak that out – what happened to me, what went on happening – I think I can get better now. Because of you.'

'I'm glad. But you know that.'

'Yes. Oh, Ed. This is going too fast.'

'I know.'

'Part of me keeps saying, *Don't refuse this – this gift, this luck.* Part of me would like to lead you straight up to my room.'

'If only,' he said. He smiled gravely.

'And I won't,' she said. 'I don't think I can. Or if I could, it might be a disaster. Something that's going to damage both of us, wreck what perhaps we *can* have. If – we wait. Or am I blowing this up into a great romance? Is it meant to be a casual couple of nights?'

'No.'

'But I know nothing about you. You could be married with 17 children.'

'I was, once. Not the children. No children, just the marriage, except we weren't married.'

'I'm sorry. I shouldn't have –'

'Yes. You should. It's all right. It's long over. Amicably over.'

'Then … this has to be taken seriously, doesn't it?'

'Yes, Leigh. Very seriously.'

'If I say – if I say I mean to drive back to London tonight, or early tomorrow – that I need time –?'

'Whatever you want, Leigh. Yes, I wish you wouldn't. But I can see you probably must. Will you leave me a number?'

'Of course.' Her face flooded with something, a sort of loosening, sadness – hope. She said, 'And will you have dinner with me at the hotel tonight – or breakfast tomorrow – or is that impossible right now?'

'I do get meal breaks. I may not be able to stay that long. Perhaps a good thing.'

She put out her hand and touched his lips. Her touch was so light he scarcely felt it, yet he knew he would be aware of it for hours. Had that cool finger marked a full stop, or a comma?

They both smiled then, tiredly.

She said, 'I can't imagine where you live. Is it a flat? A house? A *caravan*? Ruined castle maybe? Or do you just materialise?'

'You'll have to find out, won't you?'

'How will I do that? *You're* the detective.'

'One day, when I take you there.'

The leaves were noticeably yellowing on the apple trees. From the pears, already, some were flittering down, thin brown slips, like shed wings. Jula reached out and caught one. She examined it, amazed by it. The outside world. Her garden. Freedom. Peace.

Others too had thoughts of freedom. Jula had fetched the cardboard box, in which she had left the mouse for Lavender-recuperation, and placed the vessel, open, on the ground. As she stepped away, the mouse scrabbled urgently, and burst forth. Some of them were more cautious, even needed coaxing. Not this one. It took off like a clockwork toy wound to fullest capacity, vanishing in three seconds into the temporarily cat-free, overgrown garden. One more prisoner released unharmed.

'Are you okay?'

'Yes, Jack. Are you?'

'No.' He assumed a parody version of Knox's voice. 'There you go, son. Out you come. Balls-up, I'm sorry to say. Abject apology.'

'He said that?'

'Something like that; he doesn't play by the rules. And I'd like to drop the bastard right in it up to his thatch.'

'Mine was a woman officer, with tired eyes. She offered me a proper loo and some tea. Shall we forget this, and go on with things?'

'If we're bloody Buddhists, maybe.'

She shrugged. She let the pear leaf flutter on to the earth, its destiny. The grey thin sky was coming away from something brighter beyond it. Impossible to say if the sun was up, but it must be.

'You're exhausted,' he said.

'No. I don't know what I am. Heartlessly happy, perhaps I'm not sure.'

He put his arm around her, and she leaned against him.

'It feels like New Year,' she said, 'time for resolutions. I'll find someone to sort this garden out.'

'I can find you that, if you want. Surinder's brilliant.'

'Yes, I'd like that. Not too much of a clearance. And replanting. It's restful, here. And the old trees. The cats climb them and fall asleep. But I never collect the fruit. Or just one or two. I'm wasting it. I thought I was letting it be quiet, but I expect it would rather be acknowledged.'

They stood, looking out to the fields, folds of ash under the sky.

Jack said, 'Sure you don't want me to go?'

'Not until you want.'

'Later then. Oh God, Jula. I don't know what I want, do I?'

'Dominic.'

'Yes.'

'You speak about him a lot. You remember a lot. Do you think –?'

'No. Goddamn it, no. No. Everything he does is shit. A little drug-taking moron with the constancy of a cuckoo.'

'He's been constant to *you.*'

'Christ. Just what I wanted.'

She turned in his arm, and looked up at him, 'Jack, you and I. We know we can't have any more than this. What we have is special, but there's always been that fact. The fact of other relationships, that could give us everything. Love and sex can be separate. But you don't *have* to separate them.'

'Right.'

'Don't be angry.'

'I'm not. But I don't think Dominic is what I had in mind.'

'Jack, everything he does that offends you so much – is it conceivable that, if you gave him what you never have – your concern, your support – even some constructive fury – he could change?'

'You can't change people, Jula.'

'Yes you can. You can change them for the worse. So why not for the better?'

He pulled away, so she left him. His moods of rage or acrimony never offended or disturbed her. People must have room, particularly the ones you care for.

In the kitchen, she wrote, *Phone Katherine Churchman at FM,* and propped the note in front of the stopped clock.

She had that treat to look forward to as well. And her new book started four weeks ago. Oddly titled, now she considered it, *Still Lives.* A still life. A life free of Steven.

How terrible to think that. How wonderful to be able to.

Perhaps she would feel sorrow for him one day. Not yet. Love rarely fades to nothing. There are always dulled embers left behind, seeming virtually dead. But blow gently on them, and see.

Love stays love, or turns to hatred. Hate back to love.

In the garden, Jack was standing glaring at the fields. Presumably Dominic had acquaintances who knew where he had gone to, even if Bash was out of the picture. Meanwhile, breakfast, maybe. Eggs and toast and grilled tomatoes and fried mushrooms. The big brown pot filled with tea.

Birds were flying and singing. A break of light, after all, was actually carving off the premature grey of coming winter. The sky was yellow there now, like the daffodils of premature spring.

Nero shot suddenly from the yard, with Lavender close behind.

'You heard a pan rattle, didn't you?'

If they could bark, they would. Instead two strident choruses of meowing, Nero's hoarse and Lavender's reedy.

She fed them lavishly. They had had a lot, but times had been strange. They could have a little of the egg and mushrooms, too. Straightening from their purring snorting heads, she saw Jack in the doorway.

'We're having fried cat food.'

'Yeah, I'm starving. Didn't know until –'

'You heard the frying pan rattle. I guessed.'

He sat at the table, buttering bread.

'What you said to me – is it – would it be a problem? I mean, he's – I mean he and you – he'd behave stinkingly. He's crap.'

'Then I'd ignore him. Until he starts not to be.'

'Yes, you could. You'd put him in his place. Teach him a lesson he needs.'

'Does he? Hasn't he had enough?'

'All right. If I gave it a try –'

'It won't break us up, Jack. Not unless you want it to.'

'*He* might very well want that.'

'Then he might have to be disappointed.'

Jack laughed, stopped laughing. 'It's a piss-awful idea, isn't it? He'll find some other mug.'

'Jack, did I ever tell you what Leonardo did about my toys?'

'No. Something foul.'

'He told me, when I was 12, to throw them in the dustbin. My rabbit and my bear. And by then, and this is the awful, awful part, he'd got to me, Jack. And I knew he was right. I was too old for toys. It haunts me still. Maybe that's absurd and pathetic, but it does. Oh, I didn't actually throw them away. I donated them to a children's hospital. They were in good condition, I'd always taken care of them. I hope they were loved, and helpful. Maybe they were just pulled in pieces. It breaks my heart even now. Yes, they were toys. But I loved them. For *me* they were real. And they were the only friends I had. And that's what I did.'

'Poor little kid. I hope he –'

'He *is*, Jack. That's not it. I lost. You will, if you're not careful. Don't let censure tell you who your friends can be. And don't throw them in dustbins. Don't donate them to somebody else you don't even know.'

'Dominic – the rabbit or the bear?'

'I'm not saying he's a toy. It's what *I* did, because I thought I must. Dominic is your lover. Don't let go, Jack, unless you're absolutely sure. It's a long drop. Grab him before he hits the ground.'

He got up. His eyes, dark blue, catching from the rift now lifting up the sky, flamed yellow. Embers.

'All right, girl. Okay. After breakfast. I may have to phone around.'

'Or now? I'll cook slowly.'

He caught her hand and clasped it. His hand was burning from the fire that had passed across his eyes. He went out.

She smiled as she tossed the mushrooms, glad for him, thoughtful. And the cats gobbled and growled on, devouring what others had snared for them and others had served.

6

'What's wrong with your eyes?' George Alliat asked.

'Lord love a duck, squire, you don't miss much.'

In the still-night-black back seat of the cab, Alliat shifted slightly, staring into the driver's mirror, at the driver.

'They're running with water.'

The driver said, in another voice, 'I'm crying. Ever heard of it?'

'Pull over,' said Alliat.

'*A votre service.*'

The car glided down through lessening speed, onto the verge, under the trees. Headlights drilled blazing green from darkness.

'Wipe your face.'

'You're very authoritarian, aren't you? It doesn't do any good, you see. Wipe and wipe again. But they come back. The tears, I mean.'

'What the hell's the matter with you?'

'I'm in despair,' Dominic answered softly. 'I don't expect you've heard of that, either.'

(Up the narrow road, the other car, pulling in quietly. 'They've stopped, Tony.' 'I can *see*.' 'What's up – should we –?' 'No. Stay put. He said follow, not apprehend.' 'The mobile's conked out and the radio's useless. He could be saying something else, and we wouldn't hear it.' 'Look, Sharon, we'll just sit tight.')

Dominic, sat in the driver's seat, patted his coat pockets. Then he said, 'No more on me. That's a shame.'

'Who are you?'

'Who am I? A lost traveller on the seas of night.'

'You're not a cab driver, are you? What is this, some proposed mugging? Well, go on. You can have the cash. Struck lucky, there's quite a bit. And the luggage, have that, if you like. Take the ticket, too. Go to bloody America. That's if you can make it to the airport, which I doubt.'

'You're very generous, offering me all that, with a police car tailing us, and now squatting just up the road.'

'Oh, the car. Some blighter got killed earlier. They've been chasing around all night.'

'Why are they following you, though, dear?' said Dominic. 'Think you dun it, do they? Or is it just we didn't do up our seaty-belts?'

'Maybe. I've got no faith in British justice. It makes a lot of mistakes.'

'You speak as one wot knows?'

Dominic switched off the engine as he had formerly switched off the radio. He angled round and looked George Alliat over.

'My,' said Dominic. 'What a big strong gentleman.'

But Alliat sat, impervious, only looking at him from his pale soulless eyes.

Dominic dropped campness from his style. He said, 'We're on the road to nowhere.'

'That can be said of anyone.'

Dominic sat round again, his back to the passenger.

'This is almost like a confessional, isn't it? In the Catholic church. Not facing each other. Is that why people tell taxi drivers so much? Why taxi drivers talk so much?'

Alliat said, 'If you're just doing this for kicks, let's get on to Gatwick.'

'You didn't seem enthusiastic.'

'I'm not. Somewhere to go.'

'Running away.'

'That's right,' said Alliat.

They sat.

Somewhere in the hedges, the woods, a bird, woken by the static lights of the car, called for the dawn.

'Or you could get out,' said Alliat. 'I'll drive the damn thing.'

Dominic said, 'Look, I've got this.'

'A gun. Did you remember to load it?'

And Dominic laughed. 'You got me, baby. No. Clean forgot.' He discarded the weapon, which fell down on the floor of the cab.

'Come on, stop this nonsense. Get out.'

'Or you'll make me?' Dominic glanced over his shoulder. 'It might be fun.'

The sky was lightening after all. It wasn't the headlamps that had aroused the bird. Alliat's face, coming from the night, was like the mask of a crocodile, plated, crinkled, without any capability for expression. And then it moved and the smiling headstones of the teeth shone out.

'He was about your age.'

'Oh, who?'

'Nicky. I've never forgotten. His face wasn't much to go on, all swollen from choking. But young. I'd suspect the Eumenides, if they hadn't failed me all these years. The way she did, too. My God, she killed him for only saying no. And what I've done to her – I thought she'd try. Spineless little bitch. Poor little bitch. What time is it?'

'I don't know.'

'Look at the ghastly golden watch thing you're wearing.'

'My ghastly watch thing says 5.05.'

'Do you know, I've had this conversation with one or two, now and then? Told them. Here and there. Even said it out in French, in the Auverne, and in German once. Bloody tourist in the Louvre. Thought I was a crank but went and got a gendarme, and the gendarme just came and wagged his finger and winked. They loathe the British, the French, but they hate and despise the Germans. Nobody forgets a thing.'

'You're confessing something then. Is that it? A murder?'

'Your eyes are like his, too. Not from what I saw, bulging, and the veins broken. From her poignant description.'

'My best feature.'

'Let's get to the airport. The sky's grey.'

Dominic started the car.

'I'm going to be late,' said Alliat. 'You've fannied around, lost yourself, haven't you? It's going to take another hour or more. No. I won't make it. No, I won't.' Alliat pulled a hip flask from the holdall on the seat and drank deeply. 'Want any?'

'I don't drink alcohol.'

'No. Very wise.'

They had driven back smoothly onto the slender road. Cats' eyes sparkled like gems. (Behind them, the ghostly police car now woke and began once more to dog them. Sharon and Tony, tense and silent, no longer on a date.)

'I wonder what it's like to be dead?' said Dominic. 'I know someone who might be. I took away his gun so he couldn't use that. He gets hysterical … but anyway, he might not have needed the gun, if he got hysterical enough. Got ill enough. Then there's someone else I know, someone wonderful, be happy to kill me. Put me out of my misery. Lots of options. So I wonder. Is dead a good choice?'

Alliat. Face quite shut, all but the drinking, speaking mouth.

'We *are* dead. How do you find it?'

'That's very clever, but if this is death, then dying's going to be what?'

'*Burst your sheath, my heart, and come forth!*'

'Excuse me?'

'A poet said that. I used to read poetry sometimes. It helped me see things better. Can't read now.'

The trees, furling and closing, in the headlamps, in the grey formlessness, furling and closing. Bursting forth. Fading away into the past.

Alliat drank: 'Go faster.'

'We have the pigs behind us.'

'Sod the pigs. Go faster.'

('Hell's bells – what are they up to now –?' 'I'm trying this phone again, Tony.' 'What speed are they doing – fifty – sixty –?')

'What they call the silver hour,' said Alliat. 'Fascinating, and difficult to paint. The dark twilight. Like the blue hour in the evening. Hour of the wolf. Shapes that you mistake for other shapes. Those trees, merging and becoming walls, or ceasing to be anything at all.'

'As if you could drive straight through them,' Dominic whispered.

Alliat gripped the seat in front, Dominic's seat.

'Do it.'

'What? Do what?'

'Drive straight through.'

'Can't. We'd hit them.'

'Hit them.'

'Hit them,' murmured Dominic, dreamily. He smiled. The guide, the psychic guide, now in human form? The old man of legend –

Alliat, gripping the seat with his old liver-spotted hands, his painter's hands that had gone blind, showed all the white stones of his teeth. 'Do it.'

'Tony –'

The police car screamed as it scrawled to a halt, turning, skidding a little on the dew-slicked roadway.

It seemed to Sharon Kenton that she saw the impact twice. In her mind's eye as they sprang from the car, and again three seconds later.

Truly an arrow now, the white cab, fired from the bow of the road, up across the savage verge, where thick dew sprayed like smashing glass, and headlong against the palisade of trees.

The noise was vast and leaden, deep as a bomb, shaking the floor of the world. But over it came a coda of breaking things, which flew up and away, shimmering, glittering, as the dew had done in the moments before. And then the thud, which pushed Tony and Sharon back, almost tumbling them, the fist of explosion.

Fire, palest, whitest yellow. A ball of light. So sudden, final.

The mobile came alive in Sharon's hand. She gabbled into it even as she ran forward, knowing that they were too late, seeing, through the shattered shell of the cab, what lay twice, and twice unmoving, as it was consumed.

'Bloody *fools*,' said Tony. There was soot on his angry upset face. The air quivered, dancing at the heat like highest summer.

And over beyond the trees, in a patch of half-veiled sky, the sun was rising, surely no brighter than the burning car.

OTHER TELOS TITLES

CRIME

<u>PRISCILLA MASTERS</u>
WINDING UP THE SERPENT
CATCH THE FALLEN SPARROW
A WREATH FOR MY SISTER
AND NONE SHALL SLEEP
SCARING CROWS
EMBROIDERING SHROUDS

<u>MIKE RIPLEY</u>
JUST ANOTHER ANGEL
ANGEL TOUCH
ANGEL HUNT
ANGEL ON THE INSIDE
ANGEL CONFIDENTIAL
ANGEL CITY
ANGELS IN ARMS
FAMILY OF ANGELS
BOOTLEGGED ANGEL
THAT ANGEL LOOK
LIGHTS, CAMERA, ANGEL
ANGEL UNDERGROUND

<u>ANDREW PUCKETT</u>
BLOODHOUND
DESOLATION POINT
SHADOWS BEHIND A SCREEN

<u>ANDREW HOOK</u>
THE IMMORTALISTS
CHURCH OF WIRE

<u>TONY RICHARDS</u>
THE DESERT KEEPS ITS DEAD

<u>SAM STONE</u>

<u>THE JINX CHRONICLES</u>
1: JINX TOWN
2: JINX MAGIC (Autumn 2015)
3: JINX BOUND (Autumn 2016)

<u>KAT LIGHTFOOT MYSTERIES</u>
1: ZOMBIES AT TIFFANY'S
2: KAT ON A HOT TIN AIRSHIP
3: WHAT'S DEAD PUSSYKAT
4: KAT OF GREEN TENTACLES (Autumn 2015)

.

THE DARKNESS WITHIN: FINAL CUT
ZOMBIES IN NEW YORK AND OTHER BLOODY JOTTINGS

<u>RAVEN DANE</u>
ABSINTHE & ARSENIC
DEATH'S DARK WINGS

TELOS PUBLISHING
Email: orders@telos.co.uk
Web: www.telos.co.uk

To order copies of any Telos books, please visit our website where there are full details of all titles and facilities for worldwide credit card online ordering, as well as occasional special offers.

9 781845 839116